Mind Binder

The Halls of Abaddon
Book 1

Susan Nadathur

Azahar Books
Puerto Rico

Azahar Books
72 Calle 65 de Infanteria
Lajas, PR 00667

Author Website: SusanNadathur.com

Publisher's Note: This is a work of fiction. Names, characters, places, and incidents are a product of the author's imagination. Locales and public names are sometimes used for atmospheric purposes. Any resemblance to actual people, living or dead, or to businesses, events, institutions, or locales is completely coincidental. Unless otherwise noted, Scripture quotations are from the King James Version of the *Holy Bible*, whose text is in the Public Domain.

Interior Book Layout © 2013 BookDesignTemplates.com
Cover Design © 2020 PrimeDesigns

Ordering Information: Special discounts are available on quantity purchases by corporations, associations, schools, and others. For details, contact: SpecialSalesDepartment@SusanNadathur.com

Mind Binder / Susan Nadathur -- 1st ed.
ISBN-13: 978-0615535227

*Dedicated to every young person
struggling to find the light.*

"I left the light in my heart on in case you ever wanted to come back home."
Lennon Hodson

1. JADIEL

The White Robe Penitentiary

I have a blessed life, I'm told. It's 4:00 am and I'm allowed to be awake. How many orphaned juvenile delinquents can say that?

I brace my ankles under the bottom bar of the cell door. I've already done fifty sit ups, but I think I'll do fifty more. Why? Because I can. They haven't taken all my rights away. And because compulsive exercise is the only way I can have control over my blessed life.

I continue to crunch my aching abs. The sun is not yet out and I'm awake doing sit ups. Nobody in their right mind would find a blessing in that. I'm only up because I can't sleep. I've been running laps inside my head since lock-down last night. Despite all the pacing and mental thrashing, though, I could not stop this day from coming.

Today is my seventeenth birthday. No big deal. No one cares. The day is only significant to me because six years ago today, my father was murdered, and my mother taken hostage.

How does anyone ever stop stressing from that?

I unhook my ankles and switch to push-ups. The exercise feels manic now. But *I can't stop.*

Keys clink in the distance. I sit up. It's the morning guard, making his rounds.

A beam from the guard's flashlight hits me in the face. "Up early today, Jadiel?" Michael stops in front of my cell.

"Yeah, couldn't sleep." I grimace. There's a pain in my side from breathing too hard.

"You all right there?" Michael saunters closer.

"Yeah, I'm fine." My standard response.

"Hmm." Michael taps his night stick twice on my cell door. "You take care now."

If Michael knows what day today is for me, he will never say. He is not allowed to. The past is the past. All that matters is today. Trauma processing is not a high priority at the Maion Correctional Facility for the Rehabilitation of Spiritually Delinquent Juvenile Angels.

I drape my arms over the bars and watch Michael make his way down the corridor. And then, as I have been trained to do, I focus on today. Michael is on guard duty.

That's a positive in all the negative of this morning.

My forehead hits the bars and I let out a long sigh. I have spent six years monitoring the guards. I have studied their movements. Every minute of every hour of every day. Michael is the only guard who is not annoyingly dedicated to his job.

"Hey, Gabriel." Michael raps on the rails one cell down. "Wake up, buddy. You're dreaming bad again."

Gabriel mutters a sleepy, "Thanks, Michael, I'm okay."

For the first two hours and forty minutes of his shift, Michael is a model employee. He patrols the boys' cell block, waking Gabriel out of bad dreams, offering a friendly word to those of us who happen to be awake. But from exactly 6:40 to 7:00 a.m., he abandons his post at the garden gate. I don't know where he goes or what he does, and I don't care. Whenever Michael is on duty, I have twenty minutes to be alone with my best friend, Kiriela.

Like me, Kiriela is a student at the ultra-rigid, ultra-conservative Maion Correctional Facility. But unlike me, she did not do anything to merit being here. Not really. Except for the one time — maybe two times — she mouthed off to her father, she was a model citizen. One infraction. That was all it took for the courts to send her here.

The Maion Correctional Facility is God's celestial "re-training" center — a gray stone school erected on the outskirts of Heaven to accommodate all the young offenders in need of spiritual discipline. Imagine living under the "Protectorate" of the most conservative, most up-tight bunch of holier-than-thou guardians *ever* and you will start to understand why I hate living here. My wings are clipped. I'm not allowed to leave the property. I can't cut my hair. And worst of all, I'm forbidden from being with the girl I love, my best friend, Kiriela.

Those being polite call this place "The White Robe Penitentiary." I call it Heaven's Hell. Ruled by the Holy Warden and governed by the Corrections Council, it is the equivalent to a holy city in perpetual lock down. The only thing that keeps me sane here is every minute I steal so that I can be alone with Kiriela.

I move back from the bars, twist my hair into a knot, and throw on my school uniform. White pants, white shirt, white work boots (no sandals allowed at school). With so many colors to choose from, why are we stuck wearing white?

The cot creaks when I sit down. I glance out the window. By the position of the moon, I figure I have approximately one hour before Michael comes back to escort us to breakfast.

I grab my sketchpad and a pack of colored pencils. For the next one hour, I can draw color into my life.

"One of humanity's greatest weaknesses is …" Daniel — sitting on his cot in the cell across from me — is studying out loud for today's exam in Human Behavior.

Impulse control. I supply the answer in my head while Daniel hesitates.

"Humans are most vulnerable when …"

They are in love. I think about that one as I sketch. The professors here present concepts such as love and weakness in sterile, academic terms. As if love should only be studied and not experienced. I've never understood that. Some of the best art, music, and literature is inspired by the greatest love stories of all time.

Throughout history, couples in love have caused wars, incited controversy, and inspired masterpieces. Helen of Troy was another man's wife, but when Paris, "the handsome, woman-mad Prince of Troy" saw Helen, he had to have her. Helen and Paris ran off together, setting in motion the decade-long Trojan War. My story is not like that. Lust is not love.

Love is bigger than oneself. It comes of its own will, in its own time, subject to no human planning. And while passion is part of love, true love is an intense longing for someone — knowing that your world would be empty if she were not in it.

"Line up!" At precisely 5:15 a.m., Michael returns and opens the cell doors.

"Too early." Gabriel shuffles into line in front of me, rubbing the sleep from his eyes.

It is insanely early. But I'm used to it, I guess.

Michael waits for the last student to get into line, and then escorts us to the dining hall, where we greet the Holy Warden.

Marius is *the best* Holy Warden Maion has ever had, according to our teachers. He greets each and every one of us individually, each and every day. First the boys, and then the girls.

"Good morning, Jadiel." Marius touches my forehead with his fingertips. "You are blessed."

"So I am," I say. The required response.

Marius looks at me longer than he usually does. His grey eyes search me. He knows. He knows what today means to me.

I look away. Marius once fought for permission to counsel me. Permission was denied. The spiritually delinquent don't need therapy, the Council said. Prayer is all that is needed to be fully functional after any life-altering tragedy.

I sit down in my assigned chair and search the girl's line. Kiriela isn't there. She's late. Again. That'll cost her a detention.

Which isn't always a bad thing. Kiriela and I met in detention. It's where our friendship was formed. Despite the hyper vigilance of the teachers assigned to sit with us, we managed to communicate. Sometimes, we slipped written messages to each other. Other times, our communication was simpler: eye pointing, eye rolling. A stifled laugh. After six years and countless hours of detention, we know each other well.

I hear rustling in the hallway. And then I see her, run walking to the end of the girl's line. Snarls knot her hastily combed hair. Her choir robe is unzipped over her uniform. Agatha — the guard from the girl's cell block — strides sternly behind her.

While Marius continues with the morning blessings, Kiriela stuffs a music notebook into her school bag. She's probably been up all night, working on her latest composition. Music is her passion and her official position. She's one of the few angels of music in Maion.

"Good morning, Kiriela." The Holy Warden's gaze shifts from her disheveled hair to her open robe to the composition book sticking out of her satchel. He touches her forehead. "You are blessed," he says.

"So I am." She takes a deep breath. She's breathing evenly now, but her cheeks are red and her fingers restless. She's trying — unsuccessfully — to zip up her robe.

Marius stares at her, crunches his brows together, and then goes for the music notebook. "My office. Three p.m. today." Without another word, he tucks the composition book into the folds of his gown and moves over to the podium.

Kiriela looks down at the ground, and then up to meet my gaze. I touch the tips of my index and middle fingers to my heart — our sign. Her face transforms from embarrassment to joy. She understands what I'm communicating. Michael is on duty and she should meet me in the garden. A smile brightens her face as she returns the sign.

"Good morning." The Holy Warden climbs up to his winged podium. He holds up his white beard so that he won't trip on it when he walks. He looks out over the room. "Let us bow our heads in prayer and ask for the blessing of our breakfast." He lowers his head.

Gabriel yawns. He's lucky Marius didn't see that. Marius has little tolerance for sleep deprivation. It shows a lack of discipline. I cover my mouth when I yawn. At least I'm not as obvious. I wait until Marius closes his eyes before revealing my early-morning fatigue.

"Thank you, Father God, for the bounty of your table." Marius recites the Morning Prayer. "Keep our hearts pure and our minds clean. For we are blessed."

"For we are blessed," I repeat, along with all the others. And then all two hundred of us eat our fig and almond yogurt. As we do every day (unless it's Sunday when we fast).

"Bowl aside." Malakiy, the Correction Council's number one angel, points at my half-eaten breakfast.

I look up at him, spoon still in my mouth. "I'm not done yet." The spoon bounces in my mouth when I speak.

"You're done." Malakiy pushes my bowl away and plunks a scroll in front of me. My hand tightens on the spoon. Malakiy is one of the few angels I don't get along with.

Malakiy is Kiriela's childhood "best friend." They grew up together. He's three years older than her, which makes him nineteen. He's probably in love with her, except his righteousness won't allow him to act on it. He's Captain of the Young Guardians, an esteemed title that requires noble thoughts and actions (rudeness at the dining table notwithstanding) and the Council's shining star. He gets all the choice assignments. All the most prestigious humans to guard and watch over. He is also Kiriela's father-approved protector. His entire life's mission is to keep her away from bad boys like me.

"Wait." Daniel turns his bowl away from Malakiy and continues eating. Malakiy nods, and then waits for him to finish.

I glance over at Kiriela, jerk my head at Malakiy, and mouth, *what the —?*

She shakes her head *no*, meaning, don't do anything stupid. That's hard for me. I struggle to control my emotions. Sometimes, I can do so successfully. Other times, I fail.

Today cannot be one of those "other times."

The clock on the wall strikes 5:45. Breakfast is officially over. Now it's time for the Daily Reflection. That's the worst part of the day. It's led by Malakiy.

"Kick me if I nod off," Gabriel whispers.

"You know I always do."

Malakiy finishes distributing all two hundred scrolls to all two hundred students, and then man-poses behind the podium.

"Please open your scrolls to today's verse." Malakiy unrolls his scroll and waits for us, the open parchment held out in front of him.

When all the rest of us incompetents have finally unrolled our scrolls, Malakiy announces today's verse: Romans 13:12. And then in that annoyingly angelic, booming voice of his he reads, *"The night is far spent: the day is at hand. Let us therefore cast off the works of darkness and let us put on the armor of light."*

I shake my head. Time to tune out.

A shadow passes over my desk.

"Jadiel." Marius is behind me. "Come with me, please."

This can't be good. Marius only calls students out of the Daily Reflection when there is something urgent on his mind. Like a student infraction.

I release the scroll. It rolls back up. I leave it on the table and follow Marius into his office.

"What do you think he did this time?" Daniel whispers to Gabriel.

"Same thing he always does," says Gabriel. "Forget that he doesn't make the rules."

If I didn't know Gabriel better, I might think he was bad-mouthing me. But he's joking. He and I are tight.

"Have a seat." Marius motions for me to sit in the white leather chair in front of his desk. He sits in a more elaborate chair on the other side. The back is carved into two gigantic wings.

My stomach twists. Marius is staring at a piece of paper on his desk. He's worried about something. Whenever he can't look me directly in the eye, it means he has to tell me something he doesn't want to.

"Tell me," I say. "I can take it."

Marius blinks, and then looks up at me. "You have been commissioned to paint a … special piece of art." He hesitates on the word *special*.

Not what I was expecting to hear. I'm an angel of art. I paint portraits and murals all the time, on commission — which in Maion means basically for free. In exchange for my upkeep and education, I paint portraits of the Council members. Biblical scenes, too. On the walls and ceilings of the Courthouse, the Cathedral, and wherever else I am assigned. But one thing I don't do, I don't go to Marius's office to receive my commissions.

"Um …" I'm not sure what to say. "Another portrait?"

"A mural." Marius looks back down at the paper. "For Adriel's office." He slides the paper across the desk. "Here's a sketch of what he wants."

I don't look at it. Adriel is Kiriela's father. Lieutenant General of the Warrior Angels. Supreme Leader of God's strongest fighting force. He's all about service, discipline, and following rules. My knee starts bouncing. "Why me?" I push down the panic in my voice. Adriel is not only Kiriela's father. He is the angel who charged me with attempted murder the day my father died.

"It's a logical choice." Marius speaks like he's stating the obvious. "No other artist comes close to your talent. Why would Adriel not want the best painter for his commission?"

My heart kicks. I can barely breathe. Adriel is a perfectionist. He'll watch my every brush stroke, which will make me borderline crazy.

"I can't do it." The words come out before I can stop them.

Marius crooks his finger over his mouth and stares at me. I allow myself five seconds of panic, and then pull myself together. No matter how much I don't want to, no matter how anxious I feel right now, I have to take this commission. Just like I have to get up for breakfast. and suffer through the Daily Reflection. Just like I have to go to work in the morning and attend classes in the afternoon. I have no choice. I push down my knee and force it to stop bouncing. Strength — not nerves — is what I need to feel powerful.

I shift my focus to the paper. There's a simple sketch of a warrior angel, sword drawn, foot on the head of his defeated enemy: the fallen angel, Lucius.

My heart starts beating overtime. Delete what I said. *I can't do it.*

Buried memories surface. Some of the details of that night six years ago have faded, but my memory of *him* — my father's murderer — is branded inside my head.

I suppress the memory. And then I say, "Lucius has not been defeated. That painting would be a lie."

Marius looks down at his desk. His brows draw together. Slowly, methodically, he taps his finger on the desk. "The painting will represent what has been written, and what will come to pass." His voice is stern, but not harsh. He speaks with authority. But I don't believe what he is saying. Lucius is untouchable.

I stare at the portrait on the wall behind Marius's desk. The Supreme Being in that portrait could have prevented the carnage that night. He could have stopped Lucius from infiltrating the city, from attacking my family. I stare harder at the portrait. God stares back at me. His face is severe, uncompromising. Cold. Silently, I repeat the same vow I made when I was eleven. *I will have my revenge.* I will finish what I was not able to complete that night.

9

I will kill Lucius for what he did to my family.

"I understand how this assignment may be difficult for you." Marius drags me out of my head and back to the present, where he insists that I live. He speaks softly, like a father talking to an angry child. "On the other hand, painting this mural may be a way for you to … heal."

"Heal?" I push back the chair. Buried anger surfaces. "I will heal only when *he* is dead." I snatch the sketch and stab my finger on Lucius's half-drawn head.

The shadow of something unidentifiable passes over Marius's eyes. Anger? Compassion? Concern? I'm not sure. And I don't want to figure it out. I want to leave. Now. Before everything I've suppressed for the last six years explodes inside of me.

"You may leave." Marius's lips are drawn tight. "This conversation is over." Revenge is never a topic Marius will allow to feed. "Work will start on this commission tomorrow."

Whether I like it or not.

My stomach churns as I head back to the dining hall. Marius is the closest thing I've had to a father since Lucius stabbed my own father to death in front of me. I owe Marius my allegiance. He fought for me when other members of the Council argued for my relocation to Correctional Building 3. Tighter discipline for more troubled inmates. *The boy is only eleven*, Marius had argued. *He just lost his parents. Let some time pass. I'll take responsibility for him.* I yank open the dining room door. I feel like I might have let him down.

I slide back into my seat. All eyes are on me, but I see only Kiriela.

"Are you okay?" she mouths at me.

I shake my head *no*.

"Five more minutes." She makes our sign.

I nod, control my breathing, and return the sign.

"No way." Gabriel leans in and speaks to me in a controlled whisper. "You're not" — he shifts his eyes from me to Kiriela — "Adriel's daughter. Are you insane?"

My stomach feels like someone kicked it.

"You get caught and you're going down. You know, to" — Gabriel lowers his voice, and then whispers the dreaded place — "Abaddon."

"It's not what you think." I stonewall my face. Internally, though, my insides are churning. For the first time in six years, someone has caught on.

2. JADIEL

Family Legacy

The bells chime in the Cathedral's tower. It's the end of Daily Reflection and the beginning of the workday. I fall in line at the door. My racing heart wants out of the dining hall. There's a knot digging a hole in the pit of my stomach. Relationships that aren't Council-approved are against the law here. I have twenty minutes to convince Kiriela that we need to talk to Marius about our up-until-now-secret relationship. Before someone else does.

As calmly as I can, I walk with the rest of the students out of the dining hall and toward the Courthouse — where I'm working on my current commission. The Courthouse is next to the Cathedral, where Kiriela works. Her job is to sing in the choir.

Most of the half and three-quarter breeds — like Kiriela and me — end up being either art or music angels. My mother was half human. My father, pure angel. I was born nine months after they hooked up. Kiriela's story is similar to mine. The only difference is that Adriel is her father and Castiel was mine. Adriel is a high-ranking political appointee. My father was a city guard. And so, according to the politicians, *my* father was a sinner. Adriel was only weak. For one forgivable moment in his otherwise stellar life. And where I was the product of supernatural sin, Kiriela was the discreetly but fully accepted "gift" of a-once-in-a-lifetime indiscretion.

Regardless, we are both three-quarter angels with "human tendencies." That's why The Council has assigned us to their "creative placements" in music and art. A not-so-subtle attempt to channel what they call our "genetically unavoidable but controllable natural passion."

Discreetly, I search for Michael. He's gone. And I have twenty minutes. I pull back from the others. Gabriel looks over his shoulder. I walk forward, pretending I don't see him. When Gabriel turns into the library, I head back to the unguarded gate at the entrance to the garden.

Finding the familiar opening in the stone wall behind the garden's gate, I slide sideways through a six-foot stretch that the maintenance staff has neglected to repair. Once clear of the crumbled stones, I break into a run. I can feel the muscles in my face relaxing, my pace quickening as I sprint to our spot, a reflecting pool hidden among a grove of weeping willows.

When I reach the pool, she's there, staring into the water. She has her wings out. Flecks of sunlight highlight her golden hair. Her fingers — long and delicate — pencil music notes into the composition book spread out on her lap. The sight of her — lost in her music, her wings unfurled — stirs things up inside of me. She's not supposed to free her wings. None of us are; unless it is to defend, protect, or comfort hurting humans.

But sometimes, we release them to protect and comfort ourselves.

I sit down beside her. "Another composition?" My heart pounds.

"Yes, and it really wants to be freed from my head." She smiles and closes the composition book. "But it's going to have to wait." She brushes a strand of hair from my eye. "Because right now, nothing is more important than you."

Her touch unnerves me. I shiver. She folds her wings around me.

"I've missed you." The warmth of her wings envelops me. "So much." I lean forward to kiss her. A twig snaps. I look up. A peacock scurries out from behind a rose bush.

I scan the area. A sense of impending dread crawls over me. *Something's not right.*

"Kiriela ..." *I have to tell her about Gabriel.* "I —" My racing heart robs me of the breath I need to continue.

"Are you okay?" She takes my hand.

I close my eyes. The touch of her hand on mine feels so good. So right.

"Jadiel?" She squeezes my hand. "What happened with Marius?"

I shake my head. "Nothing." My knee starts bouncing. Now is not the time to tell her about Adriel's commission.

"What's going on?" She squeezes my knee. "You seem stressed. Do you want to talk about? You know —"

"No." I stand. Kiriela is the only one I have ever talked to about the night of my eleventh birthday. But I don't want to talk about that now. "I want to talk about us."

"Us?" Her voice falters. "There's nothing to talk about, Jadiel."

I take in a deep breath. And then blow it out. "There's a lot to talk about, and we don't have much time, so ..."

Her eyes widen. So blue. So scared. "No, don't, Jadiel. Don't say any more." Her plea is nearly breathless. "It will only make things harder for us."

I know what she's thinking. For the last three years, we swore our love to secrecy. Silenced our affection. Promised each other we would be discreet.

We can't afford to do that anymore.

Gently, very gently, I touch her wings. Like me, she has an uneven patch of feathers where her wings have been clipped. The cut is not large; it doesn't need to be. Even a small clip can impair flight. I run my fingers down the edge of her feathers. They're soft. So soft. My body tightens. I hard-focus on her wings. The missing feathers will grow back when we are no longer a flight risk. The tightness presses into tension. I draw back my hand and take a deep breath. As tempting as it is to stay here, in this moment, I'm only postponing the inevitable. I need to tell her about Gabriel. Before our time runs out.

"Gabriel knows about us." My voice breaks. "We have to talk to Marius."

"What?" She folds back her wings. "Are you serious?"

I squeeze the bridge of my nose and study the ground. "He figured it out, this morning, when he saw us talking."

"No." She shakes her head. "Tell me it isn't true."

I open my mouth to speak but no words come out. "I wish I could," is all I manage to say.

"All right, let's take two steps back." Kiriela flips into her characteristic "fixer" mode. "Does Gabriel *know* about us, or does he just suspect something?"

"He suspects. I did not confirm, or deny, anything."

"Okay, fine. No matter what Gabriel thinks he knows, he has no proof. But we can*not* go to Marius. Our relationship was not pre-approved. Revealing it will compromise us."

Part of me agrees. Talking to Marius may compromise us. But the other part knows that we can't go on like this. It's getting harder and harder to hide what we feel.

"Our secret is on the verge of being exposed." I sit down beside her. "We can't risk getting caught. It's better if we come forward, before someone else does."

"Gabriel won't say anything." She takes my hands in hers. "He likes you. You're kind to him." Kiriela's faith in others is both her greatest strength, and her biggest vulnerability.

"Kindness only goes so far." My faith in others is not quite as strong. "Have you forgotten about group accountability?" According to the student rule book, we are required to report any observed sins. The Council's way of keeping us from wrongly influencing each other.

"Nobody takes that seriously. Have you ever seen any student betray another? There's an unspoken code. We're all in this together."

"Until we're not. I trust Gabriel, but ..."

Gabriel wants to be Adriel's apprentice. Reporting me would make that happen.

"We can't keep hiding like this. Gabriel is only part of the problem." I finally say what I've wanted to for a long time now. "We're in love with each other. There's no crime in that. Love is meant to be experienced, to be lived. Not to be pre-approved or contained. Love is passion, and poetry. Music. The very essence of God. So why aren't we allowed to experience it? Freely and without constraint?"

She looks at me as if I should know the answer. "Because we live in Maion, where love is limited."

That's the propaganda we've been given. Love is limited — restricted to the parameters outlined in Maion's ancient Book of Laws. Relational "pairings" are determined by the Council — for one purpose only: the advancement of God's Kingdom.

"Why does love have to be limited?" I revert to argument, as I always do when I feel trapped. "That doesn't make any sense. Maybe if we're honest about how we feel, someone, maybe Marius, will help us."

"I know you want that to be true." She sighs and rests her forehead on mine. "But remember who we are. Marius will never allow you and me to be together."

"It shouldn't be up to Marius." Tension bubbles inside of me.

"But it is." Her response leaves no room for argument. Marius is part of the Council, bound by its rules. Art and music angels are traditionally paired with the guardians of science and technology. Warrior angels are paired with protectors — to balance powers and complement training. And any "offspring born of lust," like Kiriela and me, would *never* be paired together. Too much sin in the DNA.

"I know the patterns," I say. "But why can't we be the exception?"

"Maybe we could be, if traditional pairings were our only obstacle. You know how my father feels about you. Without his consent, Marius would never recommend our relationship to the Council."

"Your father. Your FATHER." I punch my forehead. "Why does it always have to be about him?"

"Jadiel" — Kiriela removes my fist from my forehead — "you need to calm down."

"What I need is to be free."

"Breathe." She lifts my chin so that our eyes meet. "Just breathe." As she has done so many times before, Kiriela guides me through several deep breaths.

"Sorry." While she gives me a moment to step down my emotion, I think about what I will never say to her. Adriel hates me. Or maybe, he fears me. He was the first to find me that night, with a dagger dripping blood. It was his charge of attempted murder that sentenced me to Maion. His word holds weight, with both Marius and the administration. I resent that he has so much control over my life. That everyone except me has a say in how my life will be shaped and who will be in it. "There is no freedom here, Kiriela. Only unjust laws."

"I know." She puffs out a breath of air. A blonde curl gets caught in the airflow and bounces on her forehead. "But who are we to challenge laws we cannot change?"

"We are thinking, feeling beings with the ability to make our own choices."

"And we will make those choices, but not right now." Her tone urges caution. "We need a plan in place, not just an emotion."

I had a plan when I walked into the garden. A plan I believed in. "We will go to Marius" — my voice grows firmer — "and seek his council. He's strict, Kiriela, but he's also fair."

"Yes, he is, but what about my father?"

"If we can convince Marius that we're committed to each other, he might agree to talk to your father. Adriel respects Marius. And Marius is wise. He'll know what to say to your father."

"And what is Marius supposed to say to him? That we love each other, and we know that because we've been meeting secretly behind his back for the last three years?"

"No, well, maybe, I don't know. It's complicated with your father, but with Marius, we can be honest." Marius may not always agree with me, but he always listens. "He'll help us with your father."

"You're kidding, right? My father is a tyrant. Mediation won't work with him. And in case you've forgotten, we're not human. We're not supposed to feel romantic love." She's quoting the latest lecture from our Human Behavior class. *Romantic love is necessary for humans, so that they will be attracted to each other, and then later, procreate.*

"That is what we've been taught." I agree. "But while it may be true that holy angels do not experience romantic love, you and I are different. Our *parents* were different. We feel things other angels don't."

"Stop it, Jadiel." She clutches the bottom of her sleeves. "We can't think like this."

"Why? What are you so afraid of?"

"Losing you. Losing what little time we have together. Seeing you hurt, or exiled, or punished because of me. My father will destroy you if he finds out how you feel about me."

"Not if we have Marius's support."

"*If* we have his support. If we don't, not only will our secret be exposed, but we'll be arrested for breaking the law." Kiriela has always been the sobering, practical voice in our relationship. "We have only one more year left at Maion. Then the rules will lighten up. We'll be allowed to petition for our partners. And then maybe, with Marius's support, we can be together. But if we go off and do something stupid, like announce to the world that we're in love, in defiance of the law, you know what will happen."

"Yeah, I know. We'll be kicked out of Heaven."

"Or worse. We could be sent to Abaddon."

"Abaddon isn't the death sentence Marius wants us to believe it is. That's just his way of scaring us into submission."

"Really? You really believe that?" She shakes her head. "Abaddon is a school in Hell. Lucius is the Superintendent. What part of that does not sound like a death sentence to you?"

"All right. *Fine.* But how long are we going to let some stupid law control our lives?" I'm trying hard not to be side swiped by the mere mention of his name. "We're in love, Kiriela. It's normal to have feelings for each other. Desires."

"Normal for humans, not for us."

"Why do you keep denying the part of you that is human? The part that is *real.*" I keep my gaze steady on hers. "You are one-quarter human, Kiriela, and that's a good thing. Being human is a blessing, not a curse." I press my palms to her face, and for a second, I falter. A sudden rush of heat to her face has warmed my hands.

I stare at her. She stares back at me. And then suddenly, all the arguments, all the tension vanishes. My gaze shifts to her lips. She looks up. I lean down. My mouth hovers over hers. Her lips part. And then suddenly, she freezes.

"What is it?"

Before she can respond, Malakiy rips her from me. "Get away from her!"

"Let go, Malakiy." She struggles free of him. "I don't need your protection."

"Actually, you do." Malakiy is staring — alpha angel like — at me. "Your father has returned. He and the other warriors are at the front gate."

"But he wasn't supposed to be back until —"

"The mission was aborted." Malakiy's nostrils flare. "The Battalion was called back."

My eyes shoot from Malakiy to the city gate, just over the garden wall. The sentry is raising the drawbridge. Gabriel, gesturing wildly, is drawing Adriel's attention to the crumbled wall which gave me access to the garden.

My mind flashes back to the snapped twig. Gabriel followed me into the garden. My chest heaves. He betrayed me.

"Go. *Now!*" Malakiy pushes me onto the pebbled pathway leading out of the garden. "If Adriel catches you —"

"What is the meaning of this?" Adriel swoops down on us. In one sharp move, he folds back his wings and unsheathes his sword.

"Father, please!" Kiriela runs in front of me. "Don't hurt him!"

"Don't hurt him?" The point of Adriel's sword is aimed at me. "I will destroy him."

"Take it easy, Adriel." Malakiy pushes Kiriela away, standing between me and the sword. "Nothing happened."

Malakiy will do anything to protect Kiriela, even if it means defending me.

Adriel lowers his weapon. We could have walked away, then. Adriel respects Malakiy. Kiriela's friend and father-approved guardian is one of the Battalion's favored protectors. The incident would have ended there. But Adriel's sword, raised against me, makes me go half crazy. Six years ago today, Lucius's sword was at my throat. Dripping with my father's blood.

"Destroy me and you destroy your own daughter." I shove Malakiy aside and stand before Adriel. "Is that what you want for her?"

"Jadiel, stop!" Kiriela fights herself free of Malakiy.

"Seventeen years old and you think you know it all." Adriel's eyes blaze.

Like a cornered lion, I claw back. "You don't know anything about me or what I think. How could you? You don't even know your own daughter." *Idiot.* As soon as the words spew from my mouth, I know the consequences my stupidity will bring.

"You arrogant, ignorant boy." Adriel points his huge, ringed finger at me. "If you ever speak to me that way again, I will smite you."

"Smite me? You've been reading too much Scripture."

Adriel tenses, but does not move. His gaze fixes firmly over the garden wall. I follow his gaze. The Holy Warden, flanked by the Council, is heading toward us.

"Maybe if you and your father had read more Scripture," Adriel says, his gaze glued on the approaching Council, "you wouldn't be the rebellious delinquent that you are."

"Father, that's cruel!" Kiriela moves toward me, but Malakiy holds her back.

"Silence, Kiriela," Malakiy hisses. "Do *not* make things worse than they already are."

Adriel's attack has its intended effect. I cringe, as I always do when I hear a slurred reference to my father. I am my father's son. Product of rebellion. Bloodline of deceit. Sin and darkness follow me, will always follow me, until there is no longer any purity, any light left.

In a circle of white robes, the seven council members surround us. It's over. Before I even have a chance to change my legacy.

3. JADIEL

To Live Among the Fallen

I look out the window of the cell that has been my home for the last six years. Adriel's accusation haunts my head. *Maybe if you and your father had read more Scripture, you wouldn't be the rebellious delinquent that you are.* I will always live with the stigma of my father's tragic decision. Six months before he was murdered, my father stopped reading Scripture and started following Lucius. At first, that meant reading clandestine tracts dropped off at our back door. Meeting with friends in secret places to engage in philosophical discussions. But then, Lucius showed up in person. That's when our life started to unravel. The authorities did not believe that Lucius infiltrated the city on his own skill and cunning. They alleged that he was let into Heaven by my father. Or so I have been told, by those who don't want to talk about the past.

Marius is heading for the Courthouse. He's wearing his gold robe. He only wears his gold robe when he presides over a trial. My throat tightens. The morning light is just beginning to paint the horizon. The sky is a palette of color. Red blends into orange. Yellow into white. Even while I am drowning in grief, the sky remains beautiful. I soak in the colors. Soon, black will be the only color I see.

"Hey, Jadiel." Michael raps on my cell door with his night stick. "You okay?"

Surprisingly, Michael was never investigated. As far as the Council was concerned, Michael never left his post.

I turn away from the window and sit on my cot. My head pounds with so many unanswered questions. Will Kiriela stand trial with me? Or has Adriel already had her re-assigned to some undisclosed location? He was *furious*. And not only because of me. Kiriela called him out, in front of his number-one admirer. Adriel will *never* forgive her for that. Calling him cruel is one thing, but doing so in front of Malakiy? Unpardonable. And it's all my fault. I allowed my rage to be stronger than my love. I couldn't control the flashback. *I've destroyed you, Kiriela.*

"You scared?" Michael is still standing at the door.

"Nah." I twist the gold ring on my middle finger. "How bad can it be, right?" I'm petrified. But Michael doesn't need to know that.

"You'll be all right. You're strong." He says it like I'll have to be. Which I will. I know where I am going.

Michael starts to move on when I stop him. "Hey, Michael?"

"Yeah?"

"Have you heard anything from the other guards? You know, about Kiriela?"

Michael hikes up his belt. "You know we're not allowed to—"

"Please, I need to know." I hate compromising him, but I'm desperate.

I get up and stand in front of Michael. "Please, tell me what you know."

Michael looks over his shoulder, and then back at me. "Her trial is tomorrow." He lowers his voice. "But she'll be all right, you know, what with her father and all."

If that is supposed to make me feel better, it doesn't work. My stomach cramps. "Can you get a message to her?" I match Michael's tone. He's risking his job, talking to me.

Michael looks around, scratches his neck. "I don't know, it's —"

Normally I wouldn't push him, but nothing in my life is normal now. "Tell her I'm sorry." I talk fast. "I was stupid, and impulsive. Tell her I'll find her, whatever it takes."

Michael coughs. "I don't think —"

"I'll find her."

Sandaled feet shuffle in the distance. Someone's coming for me.

"Here, take this." I tug the ring off my finger and shove it between the bars. "Keep it for me. It belonged to my father."

"But don't you want to take it —"

"No. It won't make it past Abaddon's gate." After all Marius went through to persuade the Council to allow me to keep my father's ring, I can't let Abaddon's guards steal it from me now.

"Who says you're going ..." Michael lowers his gaze. "Yeah, okay. I'll keep it safe." He takes the ring. "Until you ... come back."

I smile. Knock Michael's fist. As confident as we sound, we both know. I will not be coming back.

Michael sniffs, and then composes himself. Malakiy is now standing in front of my cell.

"Open the door." Malakiy issues his command and Michael unlocks the door. "By order of the Corrections Council, presided over by the honorable Holy Warden, you are hereby summoned to trial for the sin of willful disobedience and the act of treason against God." His face unreadable, Malakiy produces a pair of cuffs and restrains my hands. I don't fight him. Cuffed and shackled, I go with him to the Courthouse.

The Council is already there, sitting on their designated benches. From the defendant's chair, I study the painting I never got to complete. *The Judgment of Solomon*. The composition is transparent and geometrically obvious: two groups, consisting of two different women and their families, frame a central scene: a wailing baby. Both groups are lower than the king, who looks down upon them. I had intended this compositional effect to create a sense of fairness. To echo the judicial process.

At precisely 7:00 a.m., Marius strides across the room and takes his place behind the judgment bench. Brows crunched, he opens the scroll in front of him. He scans it. Then he bangs his gavel and raises his hand.

"Bring forth the accused."

Fists clenched, I look straight ahead as Malakiy leads me to the bench.

"State your name and the crime for which you stand accused."

Marius doesn't look at me. And I stare at my painting behind him. Solomon's face is divided by a shadow into two profiles, representing the twofold consequence of his verdict—sad for one of the women, happy for the other. I wonder if Marius feels like Solomon did: tormented by inner doubts, wondering if he will make the right decision.

"My name is Jadiel." I start out strong, but then weaken against the gravity of what the Council already knows but is forcing me to say, "I am accused of the sin of willful disobedience and the act of treason against God."

"Go on." Marius looks up at me. A candle on the bench casts shadows on his face. His eyes look tired. Sad. He extends his hand, encouraging me to continue with my statement.

"I disobeyed the laws of Heaven." My voice does not waver. But my resolve does. I look at Adriel, which I swore I wouldn't do. He is sitting off to the right, next to Malakiy. His face is stone cold. Emotionless. Like me, his hands are shackled. Once, I would have felt smugly justified by that. Now, I just feel numb. I look away. I can't bear to see Adriel's face when I say, "I fell in love with a girl I was not authorized to be with."

Nervous movement ripples across the room.

"Proceed." Marius's voice is stern but not unkind.

Looking directly at him, and only him, I speak the truth that will condemn me. "I am guilty of the sin of human passion." I take in a deep breath. I'm not leaving it there. With my last words, I will protect her. "I take full responsibility for my actions. I, and only I, am guilty of this crime. I forced my will upon Kiriela. She should not be punished for my disobedience."

"Is that your full and complete statement?"

"It is."

Marius stands. "Then so be it." He hits his gavel on the bench. "For the sin of willful disobedience and the act of treason against God, you are hereby expelled from Maion."

A low murmur rumbles over the Council seated behind him.

"That is not the judgment agreed upon by the Corrections Council." One of the jurors — Ramiel — stands and addresses Marius. "You do not have the authority to overrule our verdict."

"He's young." Marius's voice catches. "Foolish, even. But he is not —"

Hope surges. Maybe the Council will be swayed.

"He is a sinner." A second Council member — Dina — rises to her feet. "As it is written in the Book of Laws, rebellion of the disobedient shall be punished." Dina is the Council's most respected scholar. No one — not even Marius — will challenge her knowledge of the Law.

"And he will be punished." A flicker of pain passes over Marius's aging eyes. "He will be expelled. Cut off from his education and his official position."

I swallow. My insides feel gutted out.

"That's not the punishment for treason." Adriel takes two steps forward. "The punishment for treason is exile to Abaddon."

"Adriel, please." Marius speaks with a voice drained of all its energy. "I know you have been personally offended by Jadiel's actions. Your anger is justified. He has dishonored you. But I cannot send him to Abaddon. He is —"

"He is too much like his father." Ramiel stands beside Adriel, in clear support of his position.

"His father was corrupted by evil." Marius paces his words carefully. "Enemy infiltration into an angel's mind is not inherited. It is a weakness and a choice."

Enemy infiltration. That sounds so sinister. Marius must be manipulating the rhetoric for the Council's sake. My father may have been many things: a radical, a non-conformist, a freethinker. But one thing he was not; he was never weak.

"Enough, Marius." Dina approaches the bench. "You cannot continue to protect this boy." The other Council members follow behind her, until all six members stand in front of the bench. "The majority rules." Dina's voice is strong. "Jadiel is sentenced to Abaddon. You must honor the verdict." She holds out a feather pen.

Marius sits frozen on the bench. His eyes turn a cold, steely grey. He stands. And then he staggers against the bench.

I rush forward. My movement is restricted by the handcuffs, but I manage to help him up. Malakiy goes for me, but before he can stop me, I snatch the scroll from the bench and spread it out in front of Marius. "Sign it," I say. "You will not lose your honor because of me."

Marius takes in a deep breath, shuts his eyes, and says, "I can't."

"You will." I grab the pen from Dina and shove it in his hand. "It is no longer in your power to defend me."

Marius lets out a long, painful sigh. "I will always defend you, Jadiel, even if I cannot save you." His hand trembles as he positions the pen over the parchment. The room falls into silence as he scratches out his signature. When the ink is dry, he rolls up the scroll. Then he walks over to a writing desk close to where Adriel is standing. From a box on the desk, he takes out a small spoon and two pieces of wax. And then, holding the wax-filled spoon over the flame of a candle, he waits for the wax to melt. Each second that passes tightens the lines around his mouth and draws out the fury in his face.

My eyes moisten, and then blur from staring too long at the flame. I blink, and then look up. My eyes lock on Adriel's. His gaze is hard. Unforgiving. For all that my father may have done wrong, he did one thing Adriel is incapable of. He loved, and forgave, unconditionally.

I stare at the spoon in Marius's hand. When the wax finally melts, Marius pours a red circle onto the edge of the scroll, embosses it with his seal, and then turns toward me.

"Your document of transfer." Marius's hand trembles as he gives me the scroll. "To the Halls of Abaddon." He nods at Malakiy. "Unlock the cuffs."

Malakiy frees my hands.

The burden of responsibility weighs heavily on Marius. The creases in his brow deepen and his eyes grow weary. He puts his hand on my shoulder. And then he looks me in the eye and says, "Love is perfected not when it is easy, but when it is long-suffering. Remember that, Jadiel, and you will know what it really means to love another person more than you love yourself."

And then with nothing more than an outstretched hand, Marius blasts me out of Heaven.

To live among the fallen.

4. JADIEL

The Island of Death

I spiral downward, spinning and flipping and twirling until I crash into an immense body of water. Churning waves propel me to the shore. I can't move. Waves splash over my body, and then recede. Somewhere in the distance, a boat knocks against its mooring. I force myself up to a half-sitting position. I lift my head, and then survey my surroundings.

I'm on a desolate beach. For miles there is nothing but sand and sea. In the distance, there's the outline of a city. That's it. No hell fire. No oppressive heat. Which can only lead to one conclusion: I'm not in Abaddon.

A small glimmer of hope emerges. Maybe Marius managed one final act of mercy.

I stagger to a stand and look out over the horizon. The sun is setting over the sea. Hopeful now, I stand in awe. The sky is streaked with brushes of yellow, orange, and red. The clouds are cotton-candy pink. Silhouettes of birds fly across the magenta sky. As the sun slides lower over the water, it changes from canary yellow to tangerine. I wish I had a canvas and a palette of paints. I have never seen anything as magnificent as this sunset over the sea.

A soft shiver on my shoulders grows into a large shudder. And then, just as the sun sinks into the sea, my wings unfold behind me. For one glorious moment, I feel fully alive.

The wind kicks up and ruffles my feathers. I smile. But then, I watch in horror as black stains seep into the tips of my white wings. My smile fades. I fold back my wings. The process of evil has begun. And there is nothing I can do to stop it.

Something scurries over my foot. I look down. It's a black rat.

My leg jerks and I shake it off. But then there are two more. And then a whole army of them, circling around me. I jump to my feet. One of the rats bites me. I smack it away and it lands against a sign: *Caja de Muertos*. My skin crawls. The word *muertos* means death. This God-forsaken, rat-infested island must be the entrance to Abaddon.

I stumble back. One of the rats gets plastered under my boot. The rest of them fall into formation behind me. And then like an army of synchronized soldiers, they start to move forward, pushing me ahead of them. The rats force me to the edge of a dark forest. Smoke and mist hang over the trees. The rats stop moving, forming a hairy black barricade between the forest and the beach. They don't go any further and I can't get around them. With an increasing sense of dread, I leave the rats behind and set out along the path that leads into the forest.

The trail is rocky and uneven. Snakeskin litters the forest floor. Animal skeletons block the path. Attempting to avoid one, I trip on a briar and stumble forward. Thorns pierce my hands as I fall on top of them. Blood drips from my palms and a trail of sweat trickles down my face. I look up. And for one brief second, I panic. I can no longer see the path in front of me.

And then, subtle changes take place in the environment. The trees begin to sway, as if shaken by a strong wind — yet there is no wind. It's like watching a video clip with the sound turned off. Even the familiar sounds of the forests — the eerie rustling of rodents — has suddenly vanished.

I stand up, wipe the blood and dirt from my hands, and continue down the path. Trees have become shadows and it's almost completely dark. I force my eyes to adjust, but this is no ordinary lack of light. This darkness is palpable, as if it has power. A power that can consume me. Destroy me. Condemn me. My throat tightens. This darkness is not simply the absence of light. It has a distinctively evil presence. A penetrating, nauseating foulness.

Despite my best effort not to, I hyperventilate. The smoke and the gloom rob me of my breath. I collapse against a burnt tree. Desolation and despair bear down on me — emotions I have felt before, but never with such intensity.

For the first time in my life, I know what it feels like to be completely lost.

Forcing myself to stand straight, I walk deeper into the woods. The smell of sulfur and smoke clings to my clothes. A filthy, decaying odor hangs in the air, poisoning the atmosphere. The smell comes from the carcasses of dozens of dead animals scattered along the path. Sheep. Rabbits. Chickens. Goats. I push back the bile crawling up my throat. So many animals lie rotting in their own blood.

The heavy flapping of wings draws my attention upward. Black vultures with red heads circle overhead. The hair on my arms rises. I can feel something evil, lurking in the shadows.

And then from out of nowhere, a grey green creature with curled horns crashes into my path. It has a goat clamped in its claws. Around its head it wears a strap-on lamp. The beast glares at me with pure, unrestrained hatred. Like a hungry predator staring down its prey.

"It's okay, Chupa. He's on his way to Abaddon. Let him be." Somewhere in the distance, an ancient voice speaks softly to the beast.

Chupa? Where am I? Chupa must be short for *Chupacabra*, the legendary goat sucker found in Latin American countries like Mexico and Puerto Rico. According to local lore, the goat sucker attacks farm animals, drains their blood, and leaves them for dead. *Am I in Mexico?*

Chupa hisses, and then shifts his gaze from me to the distant voice. The beam from his headlamp cuts through the darkness. Faintly, I see an old man, standing on a wooden bridge. The man wears a hooded robe. A leather satchel circles his chest. Under his gnarled hands, he holds a wooden walking stick.

Is he for real? The old man's skin is like cured leather, harsh and cracked. He has oversized ears and sunken eyes. His mouth is a soft crater, collapsed into his face. Slowly, I move forward. *Is he still living? Breathing?* He looks like he should have died decades ago.

Under his hood, the old man is balding. The few white hairs he has stick up. His presence does not feel evil, but it is disturbing. He does not look over as I approach. He just stares out over the water that gurgles underneath the bridge.

"Hello?" I call out. The old man's filmy eyes do not move or change position. "Hello!" I speak louder. Maybe the man is deaf. "Can you hear me?" The old man continues to look out over the water.

"Hello, Jadiel." A deep, guttural voice speaks to me from behind.

I turn to see a gigantic horse-like man wearing nothing more than a tattered pair of pants and black boots. The man stares at me. I stare back. He has a mane of flowing black hair and the body of a pumped-up iron man. He's over seven feet tall, his bare upper body a cluster of interconnected tumor-like muscles with massive veins.

"I am Equus Centurion," he says. "Keeper of the Keys."

"What keys?" I have to ask. I'm not in the mood for the slow reveal.

Chupacabra snarls.

"That's enough, Chupa." Equus Centurion pats down the beast. "No need to be hostile." He speaks to the creature as if it is a child. "Come, join me." He motions for the beast to come forward. And then, like a kangaroo, Chupacabra hops forward with the goat. The odor of rotting flesh trails behind him.

Equus Centurion turns his attention back to me. "Follow me," he says. And then he heads toward the bridge. A huge ring of keys hangs from his massive hand.

Enough of the bizarre. l need answers. "Where am I?"

"You will find out soon enough."

"Hey!" I shout at the man's back. "I asked you a question! Where am I?"

The Key Keeper looks back. His elongated face, square chin, and oversized teeth really do make him look like a horse. He snarls. "Unless you come with me, you will never know."

I pick up a stone and hurl it into the water. The old man turns and looks at me. His corneas are the color of cooked egg whites, filmy and seemingly sightless. "Come," he says. And then he turns and follows the Key Keeper across the bridge.

I trail after him, overcome with an inexplicable instinct to trust the old man.

As we continue through the forest, I observe the goatsucker, who unsettles me. Unlike the old man, who is a peaceful presence, and the horse man, who is neutral, this unholy being is entirely evil. The creature is short, not more than five feet. His skin is thick. The scales and long tail make him look like an iguana. But he has the face and head of a kangaroo.

And I thought I had mutant DNA.

After a while, the beast drops the goat and pads off into the forest.

"Don't go too far, Chupa," Equus Centurion says. "Meet us at the gate within the hour."

"Where's he going?" I ask the old man.

"Hunting," he says.

I brave another question. "Can you please tell me where we are?" Maybe asking politely will favor a response.

The old man shuffles on in silence. After a while he says, "You're on an island in the Caribbean called Puerto Rico."

"But I thought I was sent to Abaddon."

"You were. Every country, every island, every place on Earth has an entrance to the Underworld."

If the entrance looks like this, I wonder, what horrors yet await me in Abaddon?

After some time, we finally stop in front of a large iron gate that guards the entrance to a cave.

"Document of Transfer." Equus Centurion holds out his hand.

My heart stops for a second. This is no longer a dark trek through a spooky forest. It's Abaddon. My hand trembles when I give him the scroll. He nods at the old man, who reaches into his sack. The old man pulls out a burnt piece of parchment and something forged out of iron.

Equus Centurion takes the iron manacle and turns to me. "Hold out your arm."

"Why?"

The Key Keeper squints his almond-shaped eyes at me. "Because I said so."

I glare at him, and then shoot a glance at the iron. It looks like a slave bracelet. The wrist band is attached to a chain, which is fastened to a silver ring. Forming the ring's band are two wings. The purpose of this shackle is clear: it chains me to Abaddon.

I take two steps back, seriously thinking of bolting. But then Equus Centurion grabs my wrist. A struggle ensues. I've almost freed my wrist when the old man shuffles forward.

"Equus, let go," he says.

The horse man growls but unclenches my wrist.

The old man turns to me. "I am Professor Epicurus Mendax," he says. "Would you please hold out your arm?"

I look at the old man, whose eyes focus on me for a moment, and then immediately cloud over. "Don't fight it," he whispers under his breath. "Not here. Not now."

The soft, grandfatherly way he speaks, and his whispered message, have a strange effect on me. I stop struggling. It might work to my benefit to trust the old man. If he is anything like Marius, he may become an ally. Professor Mendax clamps the iron manacle on my wrist and pushes the ring onto my finger. I fist my chained hand. Then

I take the parchment the professor gives me — my document of entry into Abaddon, Lucius's Institute of Reeducation for the Fallen.

"Chupa! Where are you?" Equus cups his hands and calls for his pet.

A loud rustling of leaves and a bobbing beam of light signals Chupa's approach. He bounds out of the forest and skids to a stop. In his claws he holds a lamb. The creature looks injured. Its body is flaccid, but its eyes are open. It bleats, but only barely. There's a wound in the animal's neck. Blood trails from it, staining the lamb's white wool red.

"Drop it." Equus nods at the dangling animal suspended by the neck.

Chupa's eyes grow wide. He drops the lamb.

I stare at the limp animal. And then look up at Equus Centurion. "You're just going to leave it here, half dead?"

Equus stares at me. "What do you propose I do with it?"

"I'm taking it with me." I pick up the lamb and hold it in my arms.

"Its death will be on you, then." Equus turns from me. "Follow me."

I follow him to the gate. Nailed to the iron bars is a sign that reads, *Abandon all hope, ye who enter here.*

5. JADIEL
The Hall of Lost Wings

I stare at the sign, written in jagged lettering. Lucius always had a flare for the dramatic. As I stare at Lucius's handiwork, it occurs to me. The Council's punishment has given me an unexpected opportunity. I finally have access to the one person I need to see dead.

The thought gives me strength. I stand taller, bracing myself for the horrors ahead.

Equus sifts through his keys. Finding the one that opens the gate, he turns to me and says, "Step inside."

I step forward, mentally ready. But then a surge of sudden dread sweeps over me. My eyes shoot to the right. And then to the left. I swear I saw a black shadow, hovering around me. My fear betrays me. I let go of the lamb and sprint back down the path. *I can hide in the woods.* Whatever bravery I thought I had was stripped from me by the mere presence of a shadow.

My wrist burns under the manacle. Two seconds later, I'm tackled to the ground. A bolt of pain shoots through my back, but I can't scream. Chupa has pinned me down, one paw on my throat, another on my chest. His claws dig into my neck. He's salivating on top of me. In a matter of seconds, I'll be ripped apart.

"No, Chupa!" Equus's boots pound the ground as he makes his way toward me. "Stand down."

Chupa snorts. Snot falls from his nose and onto my forehead. He snorts again, and then backs off. The gut-wrenching foulness of his breathe makes me want to puke.

Equus moves forward, and then stands over me. "Get up."

I battle my churning stomach, wipe the snot and spit off my face, and stagger to a stand. The pain under the bracelet has intensified. I grip my wrist and exert counter pressure. The bracelet is not only a mark of ownership, it's a flight deterrent. I shift my gaze to Professor Mendax. "You deceived me, old man, for the first and last time."

"That's not how we talk to Lord Lucius's anointed." Equus smacks my face. And then he pushes me toward the gate. "Start walking."

Stunned, I start to walk. The force behind that blow was crippling.

When we reach the gate, I snatch up the lamb. Equus shoves me through the open bars and waits for Professor Mendax and Chupa to follow.

A chain scrapes over the bars and Equus secures the padlock. He grabs a torch off the wall, and we descend deeper into the cave.

As we go down, it grows darker. Hotter. Around me, I hear anguished screams. I clutch onto the lamb. The creature's head droops. Its tongue hangs out. It's so hot I can barely breathe. I drop the lamb and rip off my shirt. The heat is stealing every ounce of my strength from me. Exhausted, I collapse to the ground.

A knotted hand finds my shoulder. "You'll get used to the heat," Professor Mendax says. "We all do. After a while."

"Good to know," I gasp.

"Get up." A voice that sounds like grinding stone snarls at me.

I look up. A disfigured man with a coiled leather whip stands above me.

"Water, please. I need water." I stumble to my feet.

"There is no water here." The man limps closer. "Sorry." His *sorry* sounds like what a mass murderer would say when he is about to mutilate his prey.

"Oh God." I slump back against the wall. "I'm thirsty." My mouth is so dry that it hurts to even swallow.

"No God here either." The psycho demon holds out his arms and then points at his legs. "See?" His limbs are unequal in length, out of proportion — without symmetry. I have never seen a more gruesome deformity. The sight of it is enough to convince me that no written description, no matter how poetic or creative, can ever compare to what is really down here.

"This is Portiel," Equus says. "He will take over from here."

The Key Keeper disappears into a connecting passageway. Professor Mendax and Chupacabra follow behind him.

Portiel glares at me. "I don't care what you need or what you are suffering." He draws closer. "So, don't ask me for anything." His foul breath spews petrification and waste. "Read my lips." He's almost in my face now. "I am not your friend."

I feel a violent, evil presence such as I have never felt before and greater than I could ever possibly imagine. Portiel hates me in a way that surpasses any hatred I have ever known. I want to run, to find a way out. But I have absolutely no strength in my body. I can barely move. A once forgotten Bible verse comes to mind. *I am counted with them that go down into the pit. I am as a man that hath no strength.*

I reach for the lamb. When I crouch down to pick it up, I hear a soft, almost indistinguishable bleat. The lamb struggles but manages to raise its head. If that weak, wounded creature still has the strength to raise its head, how much more should I have to do the same? Gently, I scoop up the lamb and walk taller toward the guard.

Portiel is not impressed. "Follow me," he says. "Do not stop. Do not fall behind. And DO NOT talk to me." He circles around on one leg and starts to move forward. "It will not go well for you if you do." And then like a crippled hunchback, he steps forward on his longer leg, swings the shorter one around, and limps down a narrow corridor illuminated by fire light.

After tremendous exertion, I force my legs to work. Unable to fight back — for now — I follow behind Portiel.

The deeper we go inside the corridor, the heavier the air becomes. Smoke clings to the walls and a foul, decaying odor hangs in the oxygen-depleted atmosphere. I struggle to breathe.

"Can we stop for a minute?" My lungs are suffocating.

"No." Portiel snaps his whip. "Keep up."

I fall back against the wall. The rough-hewn stone is hot. I take in a scalding breath of air. Surprisingly, it seems enough. Partially recovered, I continue behind Portiel.

After a slow, agonizing descent, we finally stop at the edge of an open hallway. Portiel lights a long row of torches and a huge hall is illuminated. "Welcome to the Hall of Lost Wings," Portiel says, flatly.

Before us is a long room lined with hundreds of glass cases. In each case there is a pair of wings. Some are small, others big. Some are tattered, others whole. Some are black, some are white. It is the most glorious, most chilling sight I have ever seen.

As I limp down the corridor, a grim reality emerges. The wings are in various states of decay. The newer ones, closest to the entrance, are mostly white and completely intact. Some have black tips. A lump forms in my throat. I swallow against it, and then read the names of the angels whose wings have been encased in glass. Azael. Samael. Gadreel. I wonder how long their wings have been here. A few days? A couple of weeks? How long does it take for an angel's wings to turn completely black? According to Marius, the process is slow but steady. Each lie, each small act of rebellion or defiance, adds to the deterioration.

I continue down the hallway. As I do, the wings grow darker. Cases are more tarnished, the wings inside more severely damaged and increasingly black. Skeletal frames remain. Clumps of feathers line the cases. Further down, only black ash and feathers are left, piled up on the bottom of the glass cabinets.

I stop short. I can't move. All I can do is stare at the name on the case in front of me. *Sariel.* My heart strangles my lungs, and my legs weaken. Inside this case are my mother's wings.

A sharp pain lashes across my back. "I told you not to STOP!"

An oppressive feeling takes hold of me. It has been six years since I lost my mother. Since Lucius lusted after, and then stole her from me.

My chest constricts. The last memory I have of her is a scream.

I collapse to the floor. I can't bear to think about what I've seen. My mother's wings are completely black. Decimated. All but a few of the feathers are on the floor. But, as deteriorated as they are, they're still here. What does that mean? Is my mother alive? Is she here?

"Get UP!" Portiel's lash bites into my back. "On your feet. NOW!"

I bear the first lash. And the second. But on the third strike, I set down the lamb. Then I rise to my feet, catch the whip, and twist it around Portiel's neck. I may not have been trained to fight, like Marius's warrior angels, but six years of taking out my frustrations in the gym have made me strong. "Try that again," I say, with cold, calculated, seething fury, "and I will choke the life right out of you."

"Jadiel!" Equus strides into the hall. Chupa is behind him. "Release him!"

I tighten the whip. "Don't mess with me," I say. And then I purposely repeat the guard's own words, "It will not go well for you if you do." I release the whip.

Portiel falls back, hands clutching his throat. "You're going to regret that." His eyes burn with an angry fire. "I'll make sure of it."

"You will not live long enough to try."

Chupa glances at Equus with a look that asks, *Can I tear him apart?*

"No, Chupa." Equus motions with his hand. "Stay." A smile hides in the corners of his mouth. Chupa growls but stays where he is.

Equus turns to me. "Go. Change into your new clothes. Everything but the shirt." He speaks calmly but his voice is lethal. "There is a wardrobe adjustment room at the end of the hall. Your clothes are in a locker with your name on it."

I move to go, but then turn back for the lamb.

"Leave it." Equus stops me. "Epicurus." He snaps at Professor Mendax.

The professor shuffles forward and picks up the lamb.

"When you are finished changing," Equus tells me, "meet us over there." He nods toward a separate area at the end of the hall. A rough wooden stake stands in the middle of the alcove.

My heart hammers a blow to my chest. There is blood on the stake. I hear a soft bleat. I glance back at the lamb. It's squirming in the old man's arms, trying to escape.

I take a deep breath, shoulder past Portiel, and head down the hallway.

I have already blocked out the memory of my mother and am now trying not to think about what I know is ahead. Repression is my go-to form of defense. I strip off my clothes and exchange my white pants, shirt, and boots for black ones. *Place old clothes here.* A sign attached to what looks like a trash shoot gives me my instruction. I dump my old clothes into the shoot. In a swirl of hot white flames, the clothes combust.

Dressed in my new attire, minus the shirt, I walk out into the hallway. There's another guard now, who looks exactly like Portiel. The two clones grab me and pull me toward the stake. Equus nods and Portiel ties me to it. The hemp rope burns my skin. Portiel has made sure to tie the rope especially tight.

"As decreed by Marius, the Holy Warden of Maion, you are no longer worthy of your wings." Equus's voice booms off the stone walls. "I hereby decree that they shall be removed from you." His voice strengthens when he says, "Unfold your wings, Jadiel."

I hear Equus's command, but I can't move. The terrifying reality of what is about to happen has finally sunk in.

"NOW."

I can't. I can't release them. My wings are part of my identity. Part of *me*. Without them I am nothing. Without them, I am powerless.

"Do it now or I will do it for you." The tip of a knife is at my shoulder blade. With one precise turn of the knife, Equus can externally stimulate the release of my wings.

I close my eyes. That's not going to happen. I focus all my energy on my back. There's a soft flutter, and then a loud swoosh as I release my wings. I am not now, nor ever will be, powerless.

"Portiel, you may proceed." Equus removes his dagger.

"Strong wings." Portiel slides two curved knives into my field of vision. "It's going to be fun to cut through all that muscle."

I deafen my ears and control my mind. Power comes from within.

Portiel withdraws the knives and there's a pulling sensation on both shoulders. It feels like nothing for a second. Shock and adrenaline are doing a wonderful job of masking the pain. But the grace period doesn't last. The second set of cuts go deeper. My brain fights to deny that much hurt. But I'm losing the fight. Portiel's blades slice down my flesh. My shoulders feel like they're on fire. Pain radiates down my arms. I take in a sharp breath, numb my mind, and hold my scream inside.

"So strong, so brave." Portiel lets out an evil laugh. "They all are." He hisses in my ear as he makes the next cut. "Until my blades hit them here." He plunges in the knives. They hit a pair of nerves. Pain sears through the wound. Blood spatters to the floor. My head spins. But I do not cry out. I will not give him the pleasure of my pain. My body sags against the stake. Pain comes in waves. Travels down my spine. But still, I do not cry out.

"No need to drag it out, Portiel." Professor Mendax speaks in a voice weakened by age. "Two quick cuts will do."

"Don't tell me how to do my job, old man." Portiel continues to slice off my wings. Inch by inch instead of in one compassionate tear. With each cut, he removes a part of me. Wings that once protected, once comforted, once loved. My heart rips open. I will never hold Kiriela in the same way again.

"Get on with it," Equus says. "We have to get him to the assembly. Preferably on time."

"All right. Have it your way." Portiel's tone is only agreeable on the surface.

My scream echoes through the hall when he finally severs my wings.

6. JADIEL

The Halls of Abaddon

I fade in and out of consciousness. Someone cuts the rope binding my hands to the stake. My body crumples to the ground.

"Put on your shirt." Portiel throws a black shirt at me. I manage to wear one sleeve, but then I have to stop. I feel like I'm going to faint.

"What are you waiting for?" Portiel shoves the other sleeve at me. I force my arm into it. Before I can fasten the buttons, he yanks me to my feet. With my shirt half open, he drags me out of the Hall of Lost Wings and down a dark corridor. "Button up your shirt." He hits the back of my head. "Show some respect. You're entering the Great Hall of Abaddon."

Still in shock, I button my shirt. My eyes blur, but I stare straight ahead. The Great Hall of Abaddon is a massive auditorium cut from the inside of the cave. Rows of red chairs incline upward, from the floor to a smoldering black ceiling. Around the ceiling, lost souls float and flail. Their screams silence the newly fallen, who sit in the chairs as if chained in place.

"Sit." Portiel pushes me into the nearest chair. Hard. So that my back hits the chair. It feels like someone jabbed a hot iron rod into the two bleeding wounds on my shoulders. I go for Portiel, fully intending to attack him. But my legs give out. I collapse back onto the chair. Portiel grins, and then limps away.

I stare at the ring of fire in the center of the auditorium. Inside the fire is the school's symbol, a capital "A" with a ruby in its center.

Framing the symbol is a banner with the school motto: *Learning today for a destructive tomorrow.*

I don't blink. Nothing I see here will affect me. Nothing. I steel my mind and shift my gaze to the pool of black water circling the ring of fire. Around that pool sits what looks like "the administration." Equus Centurion and his pet are with them. He — like all the others — is wearing a black robe.

"Rise all." Equus Centurion moves forward and gestures for us to stand.

I stagger to my feet, and then fall back against the chair. There's a weight on my shoulders that shouldn't be there. The phantom feel of my severed wings is as real as the excruciating pain of their removal.

I steady myself, staring at the initiates in front of me. On the backs of their shirts are two wet marks just below the shoulder blades. Blood does not show up on black, but it does leave a stain. On some shirts, the stains are large. On others, barely noticeable.

My shirt is wet from my shoulders to my lower back. Portiel will pay for his cruelty. But for now, I wait for the true enemy to appear. After six agonizing years, I will finally have access to the crazed assassin who abducted my mother and took my father's life.

A cloud of thick black smoke forms in front of us. Flames of fire frame an open doorway. Lucius's grand entrance, I suppose. I wonder, just for a moment, if my mother will be by his side. And then through the smoky haze an image emerges. One strong, formidable being.

"Please welcome the honorable Headmaster of Abaddon," Equus says, "Alastor Principium."

The initiation of new recruits must be beneath the Superintendent of Abaddon.

The Headmaster take his place behind the podium. He looks like he's been carved out of stone. A gray gargoyle of contrasting cut marks. He has two wings of unequal proportion. The larger one is chiseled to look like bones, the smaller one like feathers. On the right side of his body, he wears the armor of a Roman soldier. On the left side, the toga of a Greek scholar. His face seems stolen from an ancient graveyard. His cheeks are sunken. His eyes yellow, set deep within hollow black sockets. Above those eyes there are cracks, as if the man has sat too long among Hell's harsh elements.

"Applaud now," Equus says. As if he is talking to morons.

While the rest of the fifty-plus students applaud, I scan the auditorium, wondering if Lucius is hiding in the shadows. I sense his presence. But I don't see him. I touch the scar on my chest. This mark, sliced into my flesh by Lucius's sword, will forever connect me to my enemy.

"You may sit." Alastor Principium motions for us to be seated. "Welcome to Abaddon, Lord Lucius's Esteemed Institute of Reeducation for the Fallen." His yellow eyes bore into us. "Originality. Strength. Individuality. Free thinking. You must have demonstrated one or more of these admirable qualities or you would not be here. I congratulate you. In Abaddon, we embrace independent thinking. The power of choice."

Apathy greets the Headmaster's welcome speech. Most of God's former angels are staring at the ground. Everybody's on autopilot. Silent and scared.

"At this time," Alastor Principium continues, I would like to invite Abaddon's head administrator, Madam Magna Tractatori, to the podium."

Madam Magna Tractatori glitters as she steps forward. Her wings are made from smoldering tree branches. With an inflated sense of importance, she stands behind the lectern.

"Thank you, Headmaster Principium." Magna Tractatori's voice is smoky and crackles as she speaks. She turns to us and says, "Consider yourselves in the presence of greatness." With exaggerated reverence, she extends a hand to the Headmaster. "Students under Alastor Principium's tutelage have learned more of the Black and Subtle Art of

Human Manipulation than under any other headmaster in the history of Abaddon." She shakes her shoulders, as if what she is saying is so spine-shudderingly amazing. "It is through his ceaseless efforts, and those of countless other highly accomplished instructors, that humans remain in our hands. Our Headmaster's utter defiance of God — or as we call Him here, *The Adversary*, and his steadfast refusal to consider Our Enemy's ridiculous gibberish about Redemption and Grace will, I trust, be an inspiration to you all." She glances over at Portiel, nods, and then says, "Screen please."

Portiel presses a button on the wall and a gigantic scroll-like screen rolls down in front of us. The screen stays black as menacing music in a minor key crawls out and over the audience.

"Now that you are part of our Esteemed Institute," Magna Tractatori says, "you are going to need to learn new ways of thinking and behaving." Her orange eyes glow with the reflection of a slow burning fire. "I know this may seem ... intimidating, but don't worry, you are not alone. We are all here with you" — she brushes her hand over to the group sitting around the podium — "your mentors and your guides. And through this beautiful, cosmic connection, we will teach you everything you need to know. But first, the rules."

My stomach contracts. I have learned to hate that word.

Words grow into view on the massive screen as Magna Tractatori reads what she should have memorized — centuries ago.

"Rule number 1: From this day forward, you must give up all claims to the status of Holy Angel, and all powers associated with said status. You will no longer be allowed to guard, protect, go into battle, or engage in any other activity associated with your former status. That includes painting or singing, for those of you who were formerly angels of music or art."

"I don't think too many of us care about our former status." The brawny angel beside me speaks to me but keeps his eyes focused forward. His arms are crossed, as if to prove that the small spots of blood on his shoulders mean nothing to him. "A change in status is why most of us are here," he says.

I say nothing. My brain is frozen, iced into the last thing I heard. I will never paint again.

"Rule number 2: You are to submit to a spiritual trainer, known as your S.T., who will instruct you in the ways and norms of our Esteemed Institute. Most of you have already met your trainers, in the woods before entering Abaddon."

So, is my S.T. Equus Centurion or Professor Mendax? I hope for the latter.

"If you were greeted by two of our faculty in Abaddon's Dark Woods, the one who held the keys is your S.T."

Of course. My brain thaws out of freeze frame. My mentor is Equus Centurion. Who else would it have been? Rule number two fades out and rule number three bleeds onto the screen.

"Rule number 3: You will live and study here, in Abaddon, but your work will be among the humans on Earth, for that is where the fallen are truly most effective. On Earth, you will operate out of your S.T.'s command center, his home and your bunker whenever you are on assignment outside of Abaddon."

"Bunker. Now we're talking." Someone behind me likes the army vocabulary. Slowly, the student body is waking up from its stupor.

"Rule number 4: You will pledge your allegiance to Lord Lucius by signing a contract. This contract must be signed no later than six months from the day of your fall, but only after you have spiritually secured six unsuspecting humans. Meaning, you will have successfully engaged in the Great Commission of undermining faith and upending morality." Magna Tractatori looks bored, like she's repeated these rules one too many times. "You may ensnare any human who has opened a door to you, but all major assignments will be given to you via text message. If you do not know what a text message is, consult with your S.T."

I'm pretty sure not one of us knows what a text message is.

"For those of you who are extra motivated and choose to secure more than the required six souls, there will be super special rewards." Magna Tractatori snaps back to life. She glows as she announces the bonus round. "The more souls you secure, the quicker you go up in the ranks. The quicker you go up in the ranks, the faster you will be granted favor. And the more favor you earn" — her fire eyes burn into mine — "the greater is the chance that you will meet Lord Lucius." She's still staring at me. "So deliciously simple, don't you think?"

Unlike in Maion, no one here seems obligated to reply.

"Once you have signed the contract, it is binding and irrevocable and will cut you off for all eternity from our enemy — God — and all those who worship Him. If by six months you fail to sign, you will be chained to the dungeons of Abaddon and tortured until your weakened spirit is made compliant. Once acquiescent — I love that word — you will be brought back here for re-training." Her eyes sparkle. "Let me show you what happens when you come back to Abaddon under those circumstances." She turns to Portiel. "The curtain, please."

Portiel opens a heavy velvet curtain. Behind it there is a two-way mirror. A group of what looks like students sit passively in their chairs.

"Those are our candidates for the Shadow Game," Magna Tractatori says. "A special little game Lord Lucius has designed to break down human recruits and reprogram failed demons. Those students are in the initiation phase. Watch what happens to the weak."

We all watch in morbid fascination as a man who looks like Portiel binds the hands of a boy no older than fifteen. Then the Portiel clone drags the boy to the edge of the water, where two other teenagers already stand. The water is an extension of the same pool found in this room, with the exception that the water on the other side is a bright, fluorescent green.

The clone shouts an order, and the three teenagers kneel. And then, as if they are nothing more than three sacks of garbage, the clone pushes them into the water.

Horrified, I watch the teenagers thrash in the water, slowly morphing into younger versions of Portiel. All three are deformed now, one leg longer than the other, one arm stretched down below the knee. Eventually, they are pulled from the water. As they are, their souls ascend, wailing, joining the other lost souls circling the ceiling.

A shocked silence falls over the room. The alpha angel beside me unfolds his arms.

"Oh my." Magna Tractatori shakes her shoulders. Again. Must be her signature move. "There is no music to compare to the final wretched screams of a failed soul." And then, with the sole purpose of adding to the drama, she points a charred finger at us. "But no worries. What happened to those losers will not happen to you. Follow the rules. Win and convert humans, reap souls, and you'll be fine." She drags out the word *fine.*

"I assume by now you are getting the picture." Magna Tractatori smiles insincerely. "Rebellion in Abaddon is different than turmoil in Heaven. But no need to worry about that." She cackles unconvincingly. "You are all God's rebels. That's why you are here. You are going to be Lord Lucius's strong, loyal soldiers." She pats her heart with a twig-thin hand. "I can see it already." She sighs. "But enough of that. Are there any questions?"

"Yes." Pain shoots through my shoulders as I sit forward. "Where is *Lord* Lucius?"

"Oh dear." Magna Tractatori flutters her long lashes. "Well ... *ha ha ha.*" Fake laugh. "Lord Lucius is a *very busy* administrator. Only a few of The Chosen are graced with his presence." She looks around nervously. "Any other questions?"

I am silent. For now. Soon, I will be one of "The Chosen."

"Thank you, Madam Tractatori." Alastor Principium returns to the podium. "As always, an excellent introduction."

"Did she just blush?" The female on my other side whispers to me.

"Hard to tell," I say. "Slow burn seems to be her constant."

"All rise." Alastor Principium extends his hands. "You will now be escorted to your dormitories." He nods at Portiel. "Comrade, you may proceed."

"*Comrade?*" I repeat.

"A fellow soldier," the brawny angel says. Because I didn't know that. Stupid me.

"Thanks for the clarification," I say, "Comrade ..." *Brawn.*

Comrade Brawn. I manage a half smile. Someone just got himself a nickname.

I line up with the others and follow Portiel to a communal dorm room. "All the way to the end." He pushes the first student in line. "Last bunk on the right." We file in after the girl and claim our cement slabs, according to our position in line. "You, above her." The next in line follows the first and climbs up to the top bunk. All the comrades are quiet.

Until Comrade Brawn says, "Co-ed. Nice."

Comrade Brawn sits on his assigned slab next to mine. He glances at the female on the bunk above me and says, "If this is what we gave up Heaven for, I'm all in."

I lay silently on my slab, in a forced fetal position. Unlike Comrade Brawn, I don't have an ounce of energy left in me. I can barely move, let alone speak. Purposefully occupied by the misery of our initiation, I'd almost forgotten the pain of my slaughtered back. Now that I have nothing to distract me, the pain is once again front and center. It feels like the knife is still hacking at my flesh, burning, ripping through me.

I force my thoughts away from my back. I'm no stranger to pain. I can handle it. I survived Lucius's sword and I'll survive this. Soldiers can't afford to be weak.

A muted groan comes from the bunk above me. The boy on the next slab over clamps his hands over his ears. I'm not sure if he's drowning out our moaning comrade or blocking out the cries of the damned. Wails and shrieks pierce the silence of our shell-shocked group. Some of the students mimic the moans. Others start to shriek. It's all I can do to keep it together.

"I'm thirsty. Please. I need water." A student in a far-away bunk pleads for what we all need. Water.

And now that the word is out there, the image is strong. I force spit to accumulate in the back of my throat and swallow that. My throat clicks. I work to get more spit, but there's nothing left to work with. Mentally drained and physically exhausted, I curl tighter into myself. Tomorrow there'll be water. There has to be.

Against an agonizing soundtrack of dry coughs and moans, I finally fall asleep. Tomorrow will be a new and even more horrible day.

7. KIRIELA

What's Become of Him?

Are you okay, Jadiel? My heart aches all over again. *Are you suffering?* For the last seven days, I've been glued to my father's communication device, but there's no news of him. I got Michael's message. Jadiel said he would find me. I believe him. He will find me. If he can.

As quickly as the thought comes, I banish it. Of course he can. He's Jadiel. No one can hurt him. He's strong. I cling to my faith in him. He's an angel. He's light. Abaddon can't contain him. I flop backwards on my bed. Seven days ago, I was in Maion, negotiating a future with Jadiel. Now I live in exile, without him. The Council banished me from the realm. They wanted to send me to Greece, but Marius insisted on Puerto Rico — for reasons only he understands. The Council granted his request and made me my father's prisoner.

Well, that last part was not actually The Council's decree. My father took it upon himself to never let another "Jadiel" happen in my life.

I stare out my bedroom window. There are no bars to obstruct my view of the green parrot nesting in a palm tree. There is no lock on my door. But I feel more imprisoned now than I ever was in Maion. The mental agony I'm in is worse than any penitentiary.

That same Jadiel my father demonizes lied to protect me. I will never stop feeling guilty about that. We were in this together.

When the details of our relationship leaked out after we got caught, the Corrections Council decided that Jadiel's disobedience was severe enough to merit him joining the rest of the fallen — although I don't know where exactly that took him. The Council said he "manipulated my young mind into acts against God and my honorable parents." My father sticks with that conclusion. It was all Jadiel. It had to be. Adriel's daughter would *never* have deceived him —unless she had been manipulated.

How little my father knows me. Jadiel did not need to manipulate for me to fall in love with him. It happened naturally, built on small moments of connection and optimism. Jadiel's positivity conquered me completely. I fell in love with the way he saw the world, more innocently than I do. I fell in love with his passion. It exploded into his art and colored everything he did, including loving me.

I push away my binder of sheet music. I've spent hours with this binder, staring at the music notes, singing the lyrics. Music brings me comfort, but it doesn't lessen my guilt. From what Michael told me, Jadiel convinced the Council that he, and only he, was guilty of our crime. He said he forced his will upon me. That is so far from the truth. When I tried to explain that to my father, he wouldn't hear it. He chose to stick to the narrative that I should not be punished for Jadiel's disobedience. At least not by the court. My father's punishment is his own brand of judgment.

Because of Jadiel's false statement, I was judged less harshly. Unlawful gathering in a public place outside of specified hours was the crime I was charged with. A minor crime. My father was also given a margin of leniency, mostly because The Council decided he had acted under "righteous anger." But he did engage in a violent confrontation and was therefore found guilty of breaking the law requiring peaceful co-existence among the inhabitants of Heaven. He, like me, was sentenced to live in exile on Earth. Our angel status was not altered, but we are no longer allowed the privilege of living one step away from Heaven's Gate.

"Alexa!" My father's voice booms down the hallway. "I need to talk to you!"

Alexa is my mother. She chose to leave Heaven, and her position as a guardian angel, to join her husband and daughter in their forced exile. The new family dynamic has been challenging, to say the least.

"Yes, Adriel, what is it?" My mother speaks with that calm, cautious voice she always uses when my father is either angry or irrational.

"I do not want Kiriela attending public school. It's undisciplined. I will not allow any more wild behavior from that girl. She needs a structured environment. A home tutor is the only option." The debate between public school and home tutoring has been going on for days.

"Home schooling will not work, and you know it." My mother speaks in that clipped voice she uses when she's trying not to scream. "What will you have her do? Stay here all day and learn about life from history books and home tutors?"

"Yes! If that's what it takes to keep her safe and away from boys like Jadiel."

"So that's what this argument is really about," my mother says. "Keeping her isolated."

"Keeping her *safe*, Alexa. That's what I said. Don't twist my words against me."

"She would be safe if you were here to protect her."

"Oh, so this is about me now?" My father's voice rises with his frustration. "I'm a Warrior, Alexa. You knew what that meant when you decided to be with me."

"Yes, Adriel, I did. But I did not know what it would mean for my child."

"*Our* child, Alexa. She's *our* child."

"Then be a father to her."

I let out a huge sigh. August 5th — the official start of school — is only one day away. Maybe then the arguing will stop.

I crush a pillow over my face and press it against my ears. But because my father's voice is powerful, I still hear every word he shouts at my smaller, weaker, half angel half mortal mom.

"What's that supposed to mean?" My father's voice rumbles around me like a tidal wave. "I have always been part of Kiriela's life."

"She needs a father, Adri, not a warden." I can hear the cautious restraint in my mother's voice. "Sometimes, I think you are too strict with her."

"I just need her to obey the rules."

"Which she does." My mother's voice wavers, then firms as she says, "Most of the time. She's young, Adri, be patient with her."

"*Patience* is not what she needs right now." My father's voice accelerates. "Patience is not going to prevent another Jadiel from ruining her life."

I squeeze the pillow tighter. Why can't he at least *try* to understand? Have sixteen years conveniently erased his memory? Or have those sixteen years turned into a harsh reminder of the consequences of his own forbidden relationship? This is not the first time I have felt my father's resentment. Life would have been a lot easier for him if I had never been born.

"Adriel, please." My mother speaks softly. "It's done. We need to move forward."

"Your daughter is incorrigible!" my father fumes. "How many times did I tell her to stay away from that boy? You think she would have listened. Now we are all paying the price for her disobedience. That boy has destroyed our family."

"You're looping, Ari," my mother says. "Jadiel is no longer a part of Kiriela's life."

"You know better than that, Alexa. Jadiel is a fallen angel now. He could be anywhere. Kiriela must be vigilant."

"I'll make sure she's careful," my mother says.

"The only way that will happen is by keeping her locked up."

"Or by giving her the tools she needs to survive."

"We're not going back there, Alexa. My decision is final. We will find her a tutor."

"I know you mean well," my mother says, purposefully softening her tone to take back the control he took from her. "But keeping her locked up here is only going to make her more vulnerable. We're not in Heaven anymore. She needs to learn how to survive in the real world."

"I'm going out." The walls rattle when my father slams the door behind him.

Which means, *I need time to think.* Ten years of living under the same roof once taught me how to read the dynamics between my parents.

Two hours later, he's back. With Malakiy.

I jump off my bed and run toward the front door.

"Malakiy, what're you doing here?" I speak in bursts while trying to catch my breath.

"He's on assignment." My father answers for him. As if that should be answer enough.

Of course it's not, so I ask another question. "What assignment?"

"Marius sent me to protect a boy Lucius has targeted." Malakiy spits out the truth before my father can stop him.

"Lucius? You mean" — my voice catches — "the same Lucius who killed Jadiel's —"

"Yes." Malakiy cuts in, saving me from my own stuttering.

"I've consulted with Malakiy." My father re-asserts his control over the conversation. "Kiriela will be going to public school." He avoids looking at my mother, who is smiling.

I hold in a huge sigh while sending a silent *thank you* to Malakiy. And then to Marius, who I'm sure sent Malakiy here not only for a boy's protection, but also to keep an eye on me and my family.

"Here, these are for you." My father hands me a silk bag with lace ties.

"What is it?" I open the bag.

"A pair of sandals I had commissioned for you."

My heart skips a beat. This is the first gift my father has ever given me.

I run the tips of my fingers over the sandals. They're soft. Smooth. Supple. I smile as I think of a conversation I once had with Jadiel. *"I love how you feel things so intensely,"* he said. *"Where I see colors, you feel texture."* I finger the tiny white pearls along the edges of the sandals. They're smooth and cold to the touch. My fingers travel to the heel, where there is a small button. I press it. A tiny white wing unfolds from the heel.

"They're beautiful," I whisper. "Thank you."

"They're designed to protect you." My father's tone softens. "The wings will give you speed in case you fall into danger." Finally, after sixteen years, he sounds like a father to me.

I nod. That's the best I can do. My words are cut off. I'm swallowing too hard to speak.

"Wear them whenever you are away from my — or your mother's — protection. And do not ... look at me, Kiriela." I look up and meet his gaze. "Unless you are in your school shoes, do not, for whatever reason, remove these sandals when you are outside our home. Is that clear?" I nod, still speechless. "Remember, Kiriela, you're not in Heaven anymore." With that, my father turns and heads down the hallway.

I turn to Malakiy and say, "What just happened? How did he?" — I'm struggling my way out of speechlessness — "how did he get these?" I clutch the sandals to my chest.

"He ordered them from one of Maion's cobblers, the son of one of his Warriors. He placed the order soon after Jadiel's trial, knowing what was likely to happen at yours."

The lump is back in my throat. "How did they get here?"

"With me."

I breathe out hundreds of breathes of pent-up emotion.

"I'm so glad to see you," I say.

I turn toward my mother. "Did you know about these?" I show her the sandals.

She nods *yes*. "It was the first thing your father saw to before standing trial."

My heart skips a beat. I take a deep breath, turn to Malakiy, and refocus the conversation. "What did you say to convince my father? About me attending public school?"

"Exactly the same thing your mother did." Malakiy smiles apologetically to my mother.

She smiles back at him. "It takes a while," she says, "but he usually comes around." She turns to leave. "I'll be in my room, if you need me."

I step outside with Malakiy. There's so much I want to ask him. But the first thing I say is, "Have you heard anything about Jadiel?"

"No more than you." Malakiy sits on the front steps with me. "Marius no longer has jurisdiction over him. There's been no contact since he left."

"Since he was condemned, you mean." I keep my gaze fixed firmly on the ground. "We have to find him. I can't live another day not knowing if he's all right."

"I'll find him, don't worry."

I look up. "Can I ask you a question?"

"Sure, what is it?"

"Why do you keep helping me with Jadiel, knowing how much my father dislikes him?"

Malakiy looks off into the distance. "I don't do it for Jadiel."

I nod. Somehow, I knew that. "Tell me about the boy you're protecting."

"His name is Dante Vega. He's a senior at the local high school."

"I'll be studying at the local high school." A thought is forming. "I can help you watch out for him."

"No, you need to stay out of it." Malakiy's eyes turn an intense shade of blue. "Adriel is right about one thing. You cannot give into your desire to be like your mother. Alexa is a trained guardian. You are not. Promise me you will stick to music."

I think about that for a minute. And then I say, "I promise I will do what I think is right."

Malakiy sighs. "As will I."

He reaches for a stick and writes a phone number in the sand. "Call me whenever you need to." He throws down the stick. "Be careful, Kiriela. Lucius is lurking in the shadows, waiting for you to make the wrong choice."

8. JADIEL

Boot Camp

"Get up, you swine." A bucket of hot water lands in my face. *Water.* I awake with a start. And then, frantically, I push what few drops I can gather off my face and into my mouth. I'm so thirsty I could rip out my throat. I scrabble for more drops, but they've already evaporated. I look up, desperately searching for another splash of water. What I see are all the other new recruits, as desperate and as dry as me.

"Eat." Portiel shoves a bowl of something foul at me. "You've got five minutes." I swear the room gets darker and drops ten degrees when he approaches.

With sustained disinterest, Portiel distributes twenty bowls from a rusted serving cart to the twenty new recruits in our dorm room. We're all starving, but no one eats.

"What is this?" one of the recruits finally asks.

"Looks like oatmeal," someone else says.

"Oatmeal is brown," another offers.

He has a point. Whatever is in our bowls is charcoal gray.

"Just shut up and eat." Portiel snarls at us.

While we try not to gag, Portiel limps slowly around the room, making sure we see his coiled whip. I can feel his presence as he gets near me. Like a heavy shadow in a tomb. He stops in front of the boy next to me. Like the rest of us, the boy hasn't touched his food.

Without warning, Portiel bats the bowl away from the boy. Grey gruel slops to the floor. A maggot crawls out from under the mess.

"Any comrade who doesn't eat, doesn't eat again for another forty-eight hours." He jerks into his lop-sided walk and continues his reign of terror.

I'm just about to hurl my food in his face when a flash of white catches my attention. I look down. Half-hidden under my bed is the white lamb, nibbling at the toppled mush. I glance over my shoulder. No one's looking. With my foot, I push half of the gruel closer to the creature and further under the bed. Hopefully, the lamb will stay safely out of sight.

Then, learning from the lamb, I eat my food. Calories are calories. If I'm going to survive this hell hole, I need to eat. And eat fast. Right hand scooping at a rapid-fire rate, I shovel the slop into my mouth, a survival skill that didn't take me long to learn. Eat fast so you don't taste anything. Don't think about what you're eating. It's calories and you need them. Do what you need to do to survive.

"Dump it." Portiel stops before the boy a few slabs down and points his coiled whip at the floor. The boy stops eating. "You're pussy eating. Dump it. NOW!" He uncoils his whip.

The boy flinches, and then like a robot on auto pilot, he dumps the entire contents of today's sustenance onto the floor.

I move my foot and block the lamb from going after the spilled food.

Portiel grins, snaps his whip, and then continues to circulate the room.

I turn my back because I don't want to see him. But then, I feel him. He's right behind me. Breathing. Waiting. Watching. Hoping.

Refusing to become his next victim, I dump the remaining gruel down my throat, holding it down with an immense amount of effort. We're not given any water, but I can't think about that. It only makes me more desperate. I clutch my revolting stomach, repress my thirst, and eventually stagger with the others to The War Room — the location of our first class.

An acrid, metallic odor that smells like burnt charcoal hits us as we arrive.

"It smells like burnt ash that someone pissed on before they died." The recruit in front of me blocks his nose with his hand.

"Spent gunpowder," Comrade Brawn says. "Look at all the barrels."

I scan the room. Dozens of wooden barrels line the walls. They're round, with bulging centers, bound by metal hoops. Drifting over the air is a heavy layer of smoke that tastes like steam and sulfur. I cough. My eyes water. I try to stifle the next cough but doing so only makes me gag. I choke it out on a blast of hot air.

Choking and gagging along with me, the new recruits and I stumble further into the room — a round, exaggerated space with maps nailed to the walls. The maps are marked with red dots and black lines. Strategies of war are being planned in this room.

As if the maps are not menacing enough, a wretched parade of soldiers dressed in bloodied army fatigues circles the room. Like zombies they shuffle, around and around and around the perimeter of the room. Relentlessly. Continuously. Without stopping. To avoid getting sucked into the hypnotic anxiety of the circling soldiers, I look up. The ceiling fresco is an enormous chess board. On one side of the board are the black pieces. Horned. Misshapen. The demon army. A clawed hand hovers over them, about to make its first move. On the other side are the white pieces, with halos instead of horns. What looks like God's hand from Da Vinci's *Creation of Adam* holds a pawn between two fingers. Like the black pieces, the white ones are misshapen. They've melted into sad, shapeless figures under the oppressive heat.

Through a seriously dry, hacking cough, the recruit behind me says, "Water, please." He chokes on his next words, "I'm dying here."

I work saliva into my parched throat harder than I have ever worked anything in my life. The tingling in my throat tells me that another cough is coming on. I keep working up spit as my eyes troll down and focus on a disturbing collection of portraits on the wall. Covering every inch of available wall space are framed portraits of infamous military men: Adolf Hitler, Joseph Stalin, Benito Mussolini. And scattered amongst the infamous are hundreds of mini portraits, all of them images of unknown soldiers.

"Please find your seats." The age-weakened voice of Professor Epicurus Mendax scratches across the room.

With their fists to their mouths, coughing as if dying from lung cancer, the students pull out chairs and take their seats around the one massive, circular table in the center of the room.

"Welcome to Military Intelligence 101." Professor Mendax's egg white eyes stare at us without seeing. "Today's lesson —"

Several uncontrolled coughs interrupt his lecture.

"Today's lesson," the professor repeats, "will serve as an introduction to the war that is ahead of you." More coughing from the student body. The professor's eyes squint into slits. His mouth drops into a sigh. "Comrade Bellator, where are you?" He shouts, as well as an old man can shout. His voice sounds like gravel mixed with sand.

A wall parts and a man in uniform marches through it. He looks like Hitler, but more grotesque. The mustache Hitler wore so proudly on this man is a tangled nest of fire ants. The swollen bumps on his inflamed face are, horribly but undoubtably, ant bites.

"How can I be of service, Sir?" Comrade Bellator flicks off an ant, and then salutes.

"These recruits need water." The crater in Professor Mendax's face sinks deeper. "How am I supposed to teach with all this infernal coughing?"

"Yes, Sir." Commander Bellator swipes out his salute. "Right away, Sir."

Water. I sit up. The promise of hydration has me fully focused on what I've been trying to repress. The need for ice-cold, refreshing water.

When a shot glass of murky brown liquid is placed in front of me, I almost scream. But my thirst is stronger than my disappointment. I down the dirty water in one long swallow.

Surprisingly, it's enough. I'm not coughing anymore. No one is.

"That's better." Professor Mendax looks less irritated now. "This is Comrade Malum Bellator, my assistant." He turns to his assistant and says, "Comrade Bellator, the first image, please."

Comrade Bellator pushes a button, and a massive screen rolls down before us. He clicks on a hand-held gadget that looks ultra-tech. A beam of light comes through the device, and then three words appear in the space in front of us: *Abaddon's Army: Objective.*

"Every military operation is directed towards a clearly defined, decisive, and attainable objective," Professor Mendax says. "The objective is the most important of all the principles of war. Without the objective, all other principles are pointless." His eyes turn yellow in the projected light. "Our objective is precise and clear." New words bleed onto the screen. "To steal souls, kill faith, and destroy what is left of the Adversary's army." The professor pauses for a moment, and then adds, "The Adversary, to be clear, being the Supreme Autocrat who discarded you from Heaven and dumped you down here."

It wasn't exactly like that, I think. God did not send me here. The Council did. I may not be a fan of God right now, but what's true is true. My expulsion was not His fault.

"Once the objective is identified," Professor Mendax continues, "patience is required. It is never strategic to initiate a full-blown attack against the enemy. Much more efficient is to plan minor but strategic attacks until one day, the enemy wakes up and realizes that he has been defeated. Let me illustrate the point this way." He nods at Comrade Bellator, who wheels over a metal cart. On top of the cart are two water-filled cauldrons placed on grates over two separate fire pits. One pit is stacked higher and burns stronger than the other. Beside the two cauldrons is a tank of water, containing two live lobsters. "Please, gather around the demonstration cart."

No one moves. Because no one cares about the lesson or the lobster. The water those lobsters are floating in, however, *yeah*, that has definitely caught our attention. In less than a second, there's a mad dash for the tank. There's pushing and shoving, each one of us intent on being the first to get that water. "Enough!" A gunshot paralyzes us. "You were told to stand around the cart." Comrade Bellator holsters his smoking gun.

A stunned silence falls over the room.

"We can overtake those two ancient instructors and grab that tank." Comrade Brawn's voice is low, controlled. Like me, he still wants that water.

"We could," I say. "But is that strategic? The first rule of warfare is to know the enemy. We don't know ours, yet."

Comrade Brawn nods. "I agree. Wait for my sign."

Two beats later I respond, "I'll wait, and when the time is right, I'll give you mine."

Comrade Brawn stares straight ahead. But slightly, barely noticeable, his eyes flicker.

"Observe." Professor Mendax draws our attention to the two pots. "The water in this cauldron is boiling hot." He points to the pot over the more densely stacked fire. "In this one" — he extends his hand over the second pot — "the water is lukewarm." With a rubber-gloved hand, he reaches for one of the lobsters. It snaps at him, fighting to be freed. The professor dumps the battling lobster into the boiling water. It scrambles against the pot and claws its way out. The professor lets it go. Then he takes the second lobster and plops it into the cauldron with the luke-warm water. Unlike the first lobster, this one doesn't struggle.

Its brown shell turns pink, but it doesn't resist. Instead, it floats in the warm water, comfortable, lethargic.

"This is exactly how we want our enemies to be," Professor Mendax says, "comfortable, content, and completely unaware that soon, their death is imminent."

"That's sick," one of the students says.

"But the strategy is flawless," Comrade Brawn says.

Comrade Bellator adds more wood to the slow-burning fire until, finally, the water in the second cauldron is boiling hot. By now, it's too late for that poor lobster. Its skin is red. It's not moving. And now, it's sinking, dead in the water.

"Just as this creature understood what was happening to him," Professor Mendax says, "it was already too late. Subtle, steady, and relentless. That is how you will defeat the enemy."

Suddenly, portraits which once hung straight flip upside down. Painted mouths begin to move. Groans and strangled cries let loose over the room.

I hear something over my head. I look up. The melted chess pieces have mobilized. Heads down, shoulders drooping, they're marching down the wall.

"What the ..." I fall away from the cart.

"What's going on?" The boy beside me shoots a terrified glance at the now living, breathing, moaning art gallery.

"I have no idea." My voice doesn't come out as steady as I'd hoped it would.

"Trapped within these walls," Professor Mendax says, "within the portraits, the maps and the mural, are the souls of our deserters." His cloudy eyes scan, and then focus on the stunned students. "You do not want to be one of these tormented souls who decided to desert before they even entered into battle."

From inside one of the portraits, a boy with a soldier's cap squeezes his head. Strangled moans crawl over the room as he methodically beats his head against the frame. A chain reaction follows until the room becomes a head squeezing, frame banging loop of torture.

"That's it. I'm out." One of the students bolts for the door. Two others follow him. Frantically, one of them tries to open the door. He can't. It's locked from the outside.

"Comrades Afriel, Jophiel, Zadkiel, would you please return to the classroom." Professor Mendax directs his filmy eyes at the door. "You were not granted permission to leave."

The way the professor speaks — politely, with respect — and the way he knew which three students were at the door is unsettling. How could he have known that if he can't see?

Afriel, Jophiel, and Zadkiel return to the classroom, more shocked than subdued.

As for me and Comrade Brawn, we've forgotten all about the water we were sure we'd be able to steal. And by the time I refocus, the water is gone. I'm getting to know my enemy. Surprise attacks will stop being surprises from now on.

"That will be all for now." Professor Mendax reacts no further to the terror of his students. "Your next lesson will be a field-op given by your respective trainers." He dismisses us. "Go now and learn. Today is only as good as the destructive tomorrow it brings."

9. JADIEL

Know Your Enemy

"He manipulated us." I follow my S.T. down a dark passageway. We're heading for my first field-op training. Streams of bubbling lava flow on both sides of us. I'll be glad to be out of here. Field-op means going up. To work in the towns and villages where humans live.

"What did you expect?" Equus steps over a fallen rock. It's smoldering, black burning into red. "You're in Abaddon."

I step over the sizzling rock. I want to look back, sure that a melted chess piece is creeping behind me, but I don't dare take my eyes off the narrow path. One missed step and I'll be melted, too.

Equus and I exit Abaddon in a different place from where we entered it. Dawn is breaking. After an undefinable amount of time spent in darkness, the growing light ignites my thoughts to beauty. As the sky changes from charcoal to plum, I already cherish the blue that is to come. I stop and scan the horizon. Streetlights twinkle in the distance. A lone object travels across the sky, red lights blinking, marking its downward path.

"Move." Equus pushes me forward. "This is a mission, not a pleasure tour."

A soft breeze blows loose strands of hair into my face. It's cool. Refreshing. Not even Equus Centurion can rob me of this one moment of peace.

We walk a short stretch of road until my trainer stops at an iron gate. The school's emblem is carved into the center. He points a gadget at the gate and pushes a button. The gate opens automatically. Remote control, I guess.

"Wait here." Equus disappears down a lighted path leading deeper into the property.

I look around while he's gone. Palm trees line a circular driveway. Orange flowers that look like birds in flight are planted in between the palms. In the distance, a grey stone mansion catches the morning light. I soak in the light, the colors. If I were to paint this scene, I'd start with the palm trees. Usually, I'd start with the focal point. With the mansion. But my spirit doesn't go there. It gravitates to the trees — reminding me how much I miss the Maion gardens.

How much I miss Kiriela.

My thoughts turn to her. What must she be suffering? Did Michael deliver my message? Does she have hope, or are her days filled with despair? Is she angry with me? Will I ever see her again? My mind stumbles and my heart aches over all the unanswered questions.

A low rumbling invades my thoughts. I follow the sound over my shoulder. Three beams of light, two smaller ones with a larger one in the middle, cut a path down the driveway. And then I see it. A shiny black motorcycle with polished chrome wheels purrs to a stop in front of me. Written on the side of the bike are the words *Harley-Davidson*, with the word *Ultra* etched above the wheel.

"Get on." Equus lowers his legs, straddling the bike.

He's wearing a leather jacket, a muscle shirt, and a black helmet. His boots have a buckle over the laces. The same words, *Harley-Davidson*, are silver plated on the side of the boot. He shoves a helmet at me. I snap out of my awe-inspired stupor, grab the helmet, and climb up onto the seat behind him.

As Equus eases the bike into a smooth transition from the driveway to the road, I settle into the soft leather seat. Equus twists the throttle. A red needle swings up to sixty. Trees sweep by. Houses blur. The wind rushes against my face. For the first time in days, I feel alive.

Equus turns the handlebar and the bike glides into a lower-class residential area. A few feet later, he slows down, stopping in front of a one-level cement house in need of re-painting. He turns the handlebars to the left, switches the ignition to the locked position, and removes his helmet. He gets off the bike and opens a storage compartment over the back wheel. I swing off the seat and stand beside him. He pulls out a bottle of water.

"Here." He offers me the water.

I don't take it. *Is this a joke?* He's taunting me.

"Sometimes, Mendax's boot camp techniques are more self-serving than productive. If you're not hydrated, you're not useful. "So, drink." He shoves the water at me.

I screw off the top and gulp down half the bottle.

Half the water comes back up and drenches my shirt.

"Lesson number one." Equus grabs the bottle from me. "Slow and measured. Did you learn nothing from Professor Mendax?" He returns the water to the storage compartment.

"Lesson number two, know your enemy." He sounds like he'd rather be doing anything else than teaching me a lesson. "And right now, your enemy — or should I say, your assignment, is Dante Vega — an irksome seventeen-year-old currently on Lucius's hit list."

He moves around the bike and opens another compartment on the opposite side. "The first assignment of any operative is to understand his target, to analyze the enemy's beliefs, values, culture, and family." He glances at his watch. "It's six-thirty a.m. The boy should be awake." He reaches into the storage box and takes out a pair of antique binoculars. "Your first assignment is to watch and learn."

"You got any food in there?" I'm not listening to what Equus is saying. I'm hungry.

"Focus." Equus heads for a tree in front of the house. I follow him. He stands behind the tree and holds out the binoculars. "Look through these and tell me what you see."

I don't take them. They look like something out of a steam-punk sci-fi movie.

Equus shoves the binoculars at my chest. "Observe your victim." His almond eyes narrow as he stares at me. "What you see will help you decide how to act."

I snatch the binoculars from him and raise them to my eyes. "I see a teenage boy, sitting on his bed, with a laptop and a guitar. I lower the binoculars and stare at my spiritual trainer. "A teenage boy glued to his laptop is all I see." And then because I'm bored, and tired, and hungry, I add, "Now you tell me, what is it that *you* see through that window?"

Equus's nostrils flare. "I see what I need to. That's why I have the position I do, and you are nothing but a low-level trainee." His voice bites when he says, "Look again."

I shake my head and reposition the binoculars. Low-level trainees do not make it to the Inner Circle. I won't be low for long.

The bedroom door opens, and a young girl — maybe seven years old — enters the room. She's holding a stuffed toy, a monkey, maybe. "There's a young girl, entering his room."

"That is Dante's little sister, Elena." Equus turns on what looks like a scanner. Static crackles over the receiver. He fine-tunes the frequency and then says, "Listen, and then tell me what you hear."

"Dante?" The girl calls out softly to her brother. "I had a bad dream."

Dante sets his computer on top of a bunch of empty wrappers on the bed — protein bars, cookies, a half-finished pack of orange-colored crackers — and then holds out his hands. "Come here," he says.

My stomach growls. I want that pack of half-finished, orange-colored crackers.

Elena takes his hands, climbs up onto the bed, and curls up beside him.

"What did you learn from that interaction?" Equus stares straight ahead.

"Nothing. I didn't learn anything." I try to hand back the binoculars, but Equus won't take them. "All I saw was a teenage boy, who eats a lot of protein bars, and his little sister, who's looking for comfort."

"And where is that comfort-seeking little sister?" Equus mocks me. "In her mommy's room? Or in her big brother's?"

Am I supposed to state the obvious?

Before he makes me, Equus says, "She went to her brother instead of her mother. What does that tell you about their relationship?"

"She trusts him." *Which I will never do with you.*

"Precisely. And where do you think this boy will be most vulnerable?"

To move the process along, I answer, "Around his little sister."

"Very good." Equus's tone is sarcastic. "Continue watching and see what else you learn."

I put the binoculars back up to my eyes. Everything about this reconnaissance feels wrong to me. Preying on a family, a family that seems to care about each other, is *so* messed up. I lower the binoculars. "Can people see us?" If they can, we should be arrested. Stalking is creepy. No matter what the motivation.

Equus glares at me. "Of course not. We are covered in shadow."

I have no idea what that means.

Through the binoculars, I see that the girl has fallen back to sleep, snuggled up against her brother. Leaning away so that he is free to type, Dante alternates between writing on his laptop, fingering chords on his guitar, and scribbling in a music composition book.

"Another bad dream?" A woman, probably their mother, enters the room.

"Yup." Dante continues typing while his mother scoops up the girl.

"Have you been on the computer all night?" She frowns.

"No." Dante keeps typing. "Not really."

His mother sighs and walks with the girl toward the door. "Get dressed. It's getting late."

"I will, Ma." Dante grabs his guitar and strums a few chords. He writes in his composition book, and then types out a message on the computer.

"What's he doing?" Whatever it is, he's intensely involved. Reminds me of myself when I'm obsessing over a painting.

"He's networking." Equus makes it sound like something important. "Sharing music with thousands of others who think music is as inspiring as he does."

"And?" There's more to it than that.

"His reach is greater than even he understands. He has a natural connection with people. He chats with teens around the world. With the proper training, that kind of influence can be useful to us."

I don't want to hear anymore. The motivation is clear. Secure Dante's allegiance and through him, lock in thousands more.

Dante drags himself out of bed and pulls on a pair of black jeans, a black T-shirt, and a pair of black Converse high tops. Equus switches channels on the scanner when Dante leaves his bedroom and walks into the kitchen.

"Good morning, *hijo,* did you sleep well?" His mother turns from the stove and kisses his cheek. He mumbles a vague, non-committal answer, and then goes directly for the box of Corn Flakes on the table.

I feel an unexpected twinge of jealousy. My mother was never there to ask me how I slept. Her breakfast was always taken away from home, with Lucius and the rest of the Resistance. Before the communal breakfasts at Maion, I ate alone in my room.

I look back at Dante's mother. She's dressed in what looks like work clothes: blue jeans and a white button-down shirt with the words *Mercado Bakery* embroidered on the front pocket.

"Is that where she works?" I ask.

"Yes. Her job at the bakery provides for the family."

"What, no husband?"

"She's a single mother." A slow grin snakes up Equus's mouth.

"And?" I search for what he left out of his clarification of her social status.

"With no man in the house —"

"— Dante inherits a role he never wanted." *Yeah, I get it.* Provider. Protector. Consoler. I don't need Equus Centurion to explain what it means to be the substitute support when a parent is absent from the house. But I do need him to explain why that is important — to him. "So?"

"*So*" — Equus highlights my idiocy by emphasizing the word — "let me spell it out to you." He makes me feel small with nothing more than the tone of his voice. "Dante takes his man-of-the-house role seriously. Any threat against his mother or sister — whether financial or physical — will make him putty in our hands."

I don't buy it. That boy does not seem like potter's clay.

"*Hola*, Elena." Dante kisses his sister on the cheek. Elena is sitting at the table, playing with the hot oatmeal in front of her. "Where's my hug?"

She drops the spoon and springs from her chair. Leaping at Dante, she crushes him into a bear hug, then looks up at him and smiles.

"Look at my new shoes," she says, sticking out her feet.

"Those are beautiful shoes," Dante says. "Just like what a princess would wear on her first day of school."

The girl's eyes get huge. "Really?"

"Really." Smiling, Dante pours Corn Flakes into his open mouth.

"Dante, *por favor*." His mother sighs. "Sit down and eat, like a normal human being."

Elena giggles at the table.

Dante sets down the box. "Oh, you think that's funny?" He sweeps Elena off the chair and into his arms. He tickles her. She drops her head back in a fit of laughter.

"Spin me around," she says, gripping her legs around his waist.

Dante spins her in circles. She screams in delight.

"Not so rough, Dante," his mother says.

"All right. All right." Dante kisses Elena's cheek and sits her back down. "I'll see you after school. And then we'll play *Briscas*, like I promised." He raises his hand, and she slaps him a high five. "I'll be home late, Ma. Gia and I are going to hang out." He says it casually, but he seems super charged. Gia must be his girlfriend.

"Gia was a plant," Equus says. "By a former comrade. She serves us. The girl doesn't love him. She loves the pleasure of their relationship."

"I'm sure your former operative had something to do with that."

He smiles. "You're catching on."

What Equus says sickens me. The calculated, studied observation of a clueless target is unsettling. But even worse, my Spiritual Trainer manipulates love — which Dante seems to have an abundance of. A mother who cares for him, a sister who adores him. I'd trade my life for his in a heartbeat. Even though, I'm told, I'm the one with all the power.

Dante snatches his backpack off the floor, kisses his mother on the cheek, and heads for the door. "Bye, Ma. Love you."

"Where're you going?" His mother holds a ladle of oatmeal in one hand, a bowl in the other.

"School?" Dante says, as if trying to convince himself.

"You haven't had breakfast." She pours the oatmeal into the bowl. "Sit down."

"I'm not hungry."

Dante's mother frowns but does not force the oatmeal on him. "Why aren't you wearing your uniform?" she says instead.

"Nobody wears their uniform the first week of classes." His hand is on the doorknob.

"Dante —"

He opens the door. "Love you, Ma." With a smile, he cuts off his mother's protests. Then he jumps into a primer-patched Cavalier and drives away.

"Tell me three things you learned about our victim today." Equus looks out over the street, waiting for my answer.

Our victim? Is this what my life has become? Preying on innocent victims?

"Well, what have you learned?"

"That I hate being your trainee." I turn to leave, but Equus clamps my arm before I have a chance to get one foot forward.

"Never walk away from me. You are nothing. Remember that. NO ONE." He releases his grip. Authority re-asserted. "Even that human boy" — he points at Dante's car in the distance — "is more important than you."

My chest constricts. I absorb the blow. Humiliation is not going to work on me.

"What is so special about Dante Vega?" Deflection is a learned form of defense. It's also smart. The answer I receive will help me understand how Lucius thinks, and what he fears. "There must be hundreds of other teens equally as connected as he is."

"He's not special." The veins in Equus's temple bulge with excess blood.

"Then why are you hyper-focused on him?"

"Because he is a threat."

"A threat to what?"

"To Lucius."

"He's a boy. A human. How can a seventeen-year-high-school-student threaten the superintendent of Abaddon?"

"By having something you do not."

"Which is?"

"Untapped power."

10. DANTE

Gothic Nightmare

For the last two months, life was good. I hung out with Gia. Chilled with my family. But in about five more minutes, my life is gonna suck. I shift my car into second gear. While my mind transfers to the horrors ahead, I can't stop wondering what's going on with Elena. This morning was the third time this week she's come to me early in the morning, scared out of a bad dream.

I've been having bad dreams, too. Or more accurately, one recurring Gothic nightmare. It's always the same sequence of events. I'm chained to a wet stone wall, struggling to break free. A hooded jailer tears the flesh from my body with a blacksnake whip. The tormentor is insanely powerful. I'm half dead. And then I wake up. At exactly six a.m.

It's like there's some kind of dark force, hovering around our house.

I arrive at the school parking lot, cut the engine, and push open the car door. A black Corvette pulls up beside me. Within seconds, a swarm of beautiful girls buzz around the car. The Corvette, that is. Not my beat-up Cavalier.

"Oh, my God!" One of the girls lets out a high-pitched scream. "What an *awesome* car."

I hate when girls scream like that. I glance at the car they're drooling over. A riced-out beauty with chrome spinners and a modified exhaust for extra loudness. Neon lights flash around the rim. Reggaetón thumps from expensive, double bass speakers.

"Whose is it?" another girl asks.

That's a no brainer. The Corvette can only belong to one person. Armando Ayala.

As if on cue, the car door opens, and Armando emerges. He pushes his Ray Ban aviator sunglasses up over his cropped hair. A triumphant smile edges up the corners of his mouth.

There's a lot of pushing and shoving. Girls clawing to get to the front of the pack. There's a prize to be had. Armando Ayala is the leader of Los Conejos, a bunch of clones that idolize whatever Reggaetón star is the latest fad, blast rap over amped-up speakers, and think they rule the school.

"Take me for a ride," a girl says, finally emerging the clear winner. She wraps her arms around Armando's neck. "I'll do anything. Pleassssse."

"I bet you will." Armando takes a long kiss from her. And then coolly, he removes her arms. There's a faint, predatory smile on his face as he jerks the collar of his jacket over his white Jordan Jumpman polo. Casually, he strides toward the school, arm stretched out behind him, beeper in his hand. Still walking, he activates the alarm. The door locks click and with two short beeps, his Corvette is electronically armed. A chorus of sighs and whispers flares up the moment he's out of earshot.

No one notices that my car was left unlocked.

11. KIRIELA

La Colina High

At exactly 7:30 a.m., my father stops his Heaven-assigned white Impala in front of La Colina High. The gates are open, and students are walking freely on and off the school property. Some are eating fried turnovers wrapped in napkins. Others are talking with their friends. Many are glued to their phones, thumbs tapping out text messages. I have a phone, too. But I don't know how to text. My phone is "only to be used in case of emergency." To call home. Not text.

A slight wave of panic washes over me. I'm not sure I want to enter this strange, unknown world. What if I don't fit in? What if I say or do something stupid?

What if Malakiy talked my father into making the wrong choice?

I glance over at my father. He's about to say something when his eyes lock on a good-looking boy with a harem of girls sighing around him.

"Take me for a ride," one of the girls says. "I'll do anything. Pleassssse."

"I bet you will." The boy smiles like a road-side swindler who has tricked his victim into handing over her money. Still smiling, he presses his lips over the girl's mouth. With his tongue, he parts her lips. My skin tingles. The kiss is passionate but not sensual. Currents of electricity buzz through me. I'm no longer looking at the boy. I'm visualizing Jadiel. His kisses left me breathless.

"What is this?" My father's outrage snaps me out of my thoughts. He sounds like he's about to change his mind and bump me back to home schooling.

"Goodbye, Father." I grab my backpack and scurry to get out. Stay-at-home schooling with my father hovering in the background is ten times worse than my fears. "Thanks for the ride," I say, before he can change his mind about me attending public school.

No reaction. My father continues to stare out the window. While glaring at the boy, he says to me, "Make sure you're here at exactly three o'clock."

I promise I will be and then bolt to the front office. When I reach the secretary's desk, I take in a deep breath, and then announce myself as a new student by the name of Kiriela Cordero. The adoption of a last name was my mother's idea, to help me fit in.

"Hello, Kiriela." Mrs. Concepción, the secretary, is a chirpy woman. "Welcome to La Colina High." She shuffles through a stack of large manila envelopes on her desk. "Let me find your paperwork."

A girl with a short skirt bounces into the office. She sashays behind me and sticks a pencil into a machine on the secretary's desk. The machine whirs. When the girl pulls out her pencil, it has a sharp end. I make a mental note. *Pencil sharpener.*

"Here we are." Mrs. Concepción pulls a printed paper from the envelope. "Let's take a look at your schedule." She scans the paper. "Ah, yes." She nods. "Your first class is The History of Puerto Rico, with Mr. Pérez."

"Lucky you." The girl with the short skirt blows shaved dust off the tip of her pencil. She shifts her weight to one side, which lifts the skirt a few inches higher over her thigh.

I glance down at my own grey and white pleated skirt, stitched to the regulation one inch below the knee. My father measured my uniform with a ruler before I could leave the house.

The panic comes back. *I'm going to be one of those girls all the other ones make fun of.*

"You're going to *love* Mr. Pérez." The girl with the short skirt is talking to me, I think. She's not looking at me, so I'm not sure.

But by the way she stretches out the word *love,* her message is clear.

I'm going to dislike Mr. Pérez as well as his class.

12. DANTE

Rocker in a Rapper Controlled World

I drag myself into my first period classroom. La Colina High is the last place I want to be. History of Puerto Rico the last subject I want to be studying. As I move down the aisle toward my seat, I have only two things on my mind: meeting up with Gia and staying away from Armando Ayala. Armando used to be my best friend. But then two things happened: 1) He got rich; 2) He got popular. Poverty — mine — made him uncomfortable. Or maybe he was uncomfortable because his ex-girlfriend — Gia — became more comfortable with me.

I stop short. My seat is taken. Last row left corner. That has been my desk ever since the first day of tenth grade. Since Armando was no longer my friend and Carlos, C.J. and I started hanging out together in the back of the room. *That's my seat,* I almost say. But I'm glad I don't. There's a new girl sitting there. A pretty girl with a sweet face and sapphire eyes. She looks up at me. I stare back. I know I shouldn't (girlfriend), but I can't stop looking at her. She's like a picture from an ancient history textbook. Blonde curls fall halfway down her back.

I feel like a jackass, standing here with my mouth wide open. I'm not the only one gawking, of that I'm pretty sure. I am the only one, however, who is still standing.

"Sit down, dude." Carlos throws a crumpled piece of paper at me. "You're blocking my view."

I look back at the girl. She's staring at me. Major mental mess up. But even more mind blowing, she has broken rule number one of the

La Colina High female teen code: ignore every other living, breathing human male whenever Armando Ayala is in the room.

I shoot a glance at my former friend. He's sprawled behind his desk, one foot in the aisle. My stomach clenches. That position would normally not be significant. But limping up that same aisle is my friend C.J., unaware that he is about to be victimized.

I shrug off my backpack. Armando has purposely placed his red and white Air Jordan basketball shoe further into the aisle, closer to the base of C.J.'s cane. Tripping someone is always moronic, but trying to knock down a crippled kid, that's just frickin' insane.

"Don't even think about it." In two long strides, I'm standing behind C.J., blocking Armando's foot with mine. "Touch that cane, *cabrón*, and I'll break your face."

The room grows quiet.

Armando's foot stops moving. A muscle jumps in his jaw. "Threaten me again," he says, in a voice so cool and calm I want to punch the composure right out of him, "and it will be the last thing you ever do."

"Oh yeah?" I take one step forward. My fist clenches. I am just about to make good on my threat when the teacher marches into the room.

"Sit down, Dante." Mr. Pérez unloads a stack of books onto his desk.

I stand still, eyes locked on Armando's.

"Loser." I hear a few scattered words from Armando's minions. "Sit down, freak."

"Dante!" Mr. Pérez's voice is a sharp, authoritative bark. "Find your seat. Now!"

A muscle tightens in my jaw.

August 5th. Senior year. La Colina High. The nightmare begins all over again.

I slouch into the nearest chair. School sucks. But it can be survived. All I need to do is get through the year, graduate, and then get the hell out. After graduation, I'll work full time at my uncle's body shop. Mami can't keep paying all the bills.

I yank my music composition book from my backpack and continue working on the piece I started last night. I can barely stay awake. Gia and I were on the phone until two in the morning. At six, I was connecting with other music geeks on the internet. They're my lifeline. If it weren't for them, I'd be isolated — confined to the limits of my small town.

My head starts to droop. I push my notebook to the corner, lay my head on the desk, and close my eyes. If I can just get through the boredom, the intimidation, and the humiliation, I'll have my diploma and be out of hell in exactly 263 days. Look at it this way, I tell myself half-heartedly. Tomorrow, there'll be one less day.

"Mr. Vega."

I groan. Mr. Pérez is rapping on my desk. I lift my head.

"Would you please tell me what, in your erudite opinion, is one of the lessons we can learn from the Taino Indians?"

I stare at the man the students call Baboso, waiting to see how long it will take for the little bubbles of spit to appear at the corners of his mouth.

Baboso slaps my desk.

I sit back. The nickname "Baboso" was not chosen randomly. Mr. Pérez spits when he talks.

"I don't think Mr. *Ve.*Gah knows how to answer that question." Armando exaggerates my name so that I appear the fool, instead of him. "He's not too proud of his Puerto Rican ancestry."

I look over my shoulder at Armando. Our eyes lock. Being popular at La Colina High means loving everything Puerto Rican. Especially the music. National pride is everything.

"What do you know, moron?" C.J. hikes himself to a stand. He's ready to defend me, and by extension, himself. C.J., Carlos and I share one thing in common: our choice of music. We prefer Rock to Reggaetón. "You think liking a certain genre of music has anything to do with—"

"C.J., no." I hold C.J. back with my hand. This is my fight. I don't break eye contact with Armando when I say, "I am as proud to be a Puerto Rican as you or anyone else in this room." I shift my gaze from Armando to his Court of Fools. Not one of them meets my gaze. "But if being Puerto Rican means dressing like a drug dealer, disrespecting women, and humping like a dog to one-beat rap, there's something wrong with the definition."

I'm stereotyping the champions of Reggaetón, Puerto Rico's gift to music. Armando — the current guardian of the genre — is the same dude who used to listen to AC/DC with me.

"What's wrong here is *you*." Pedro Irizarry, Armando's very loyal, very obedient right-hand man, stands up from his chair. "Being Puerto Rican does *not* mean getting strung out on weed, worshipping Satan, and listening to rock music in English. You freakin' fag."

Nothing I haven't heard a thousand times before. All wrong labels. Except for one.

I am a rocker in a rapper-controlled world.

"Have you ever seen anyone actually worshipping Satan?" Infuriated, I shoot back. "I know I never have. But I have seen *you* stuffing weed into mutilated cigarettes." I'm just about to ask Pedro if the grass he smokes has killed off half his brain when the teacher cuts me off.

"All right, Dante, that's enough." Baboso glares first at me, and then at Pedro. "You two are the classic example of what is wrong with young people today." He frowns, crosses his hands behind his back, and strides to the front of the classroom. "When I was your age, we respected our teachers. We respected the flag." He turns sharply and moves back down the aisle, stopping abruptly in front of Pablito — a nervous kid who stutters when he speaks. Baboso rips the baseball cap, with its Puerto Rican flag, off Pablito's head. After tossing the cap onto Pablito's desk, he then continues down the aisle toward me. "We were proud to be Puerto Rican." Baboso halts in front of my desk. And then suddenly, he snatches at my earring. "What is this?"

"Owhh!" I jerk back my head. "My ear's attached to that."

Baboso backs off. But he continues with the monologue. "We knew that the lessons of our past were what formed our future." A dribble of spit lands on the desk after the word *formed*. Another follows right behind it after *future*. "We revered our past and honored those whose valor and determination made us the people we are today."

I sigh and search the room, welcoming any distraction. My eyes land on the new girl. Her eyes are already on me. It's like she's checking me out, but not really. More like studying me. Total mindblower. I'm really glad Gia is in another classroom.

I'm about to brave another look when Baboso raps his knuckles on my desk.

"And we *never* put our heads down in class or used our chairs as musical instruments." Baboso snatches my composition book off the desk. "Or scribbled in notebooks when we were supposed to be paying attention to the lesson. You can collect *this*" — he waves the notebook in my face — "from Principal Martínez."

The '*tí*' slings spit onto my right arm. I tighten my lips and shake my head. When Baboso turns his back, I wipe my arm across my shirt and remind myself, again, why I hate high school.

13. KIRIELA

The Cup of Knowledge

I feel sorry for that boy. The teacher *spit* on him. That's a whole new level of strange for me. Our teachers in Maion would never have gotten close enough — physically — to allow that to happen.

I let my eyes wander back to the boy who caused chaos in the classroom. He looks like the clothed version of Michelangelo's David. He has the same thick hair, the same strong facial features. But unlike the white marble statue, the boy's skin is the color of Father Abraham's people.

I try to concentrate on the class, but I'm distracted by the thought that I have never looked at a boy the way I looked at this human David. In Maion, we were taught that focusing on physical attributes was vain. So, we never did. I don't remember ever studying Jadiel physically. Although if I were to do it now, I would see the tender beauty of his face. The strength of his arms. The suppressed power of his wings. I can't think of a more stirring sight than that of Jadiel with his wings unfurled. Wings that once protected me. Comforted me. Healed me. Heat rushes to my cheeks. My stomach flip flops. Is this what it feels like to be a human teen?

I miss you, Jadiel. My heart skips a beat. *Where are you? I pray you are safe.*

I'm lost in thought when the girl I met in the office leans forward and whispers to me, "See that guy dressed in black?" She's staring at the same boy I was. "That's Dante Vega."

"So?" I whisper back. And then my heart jolts as the connection kicks in. Dante Vega. That's the boy Malakiy was sent to protect.

"Armando's going to KILL him," the girl says. "He's so freaking mad."

My stomach cramps. God, or Marius, or whoever is influencing this girl, is sending me a message. Dante is in danger. I sit up straighter and continue to listen.

"I'm Salena," the girl says. "Come join us for lunch. My friend Susana is making welcome-back-to-school drinks."

I have no idea what a "welcome back to school drink" is, but I accept the invitation. I need to find out more about Dante Vega. Salena seems interested enough in the boy to provide the information I need.

The next fifty minutes are lost to history as Mr. Pérez spits out his pent-up frustrations.

Three more hours just as frustrating as the first and it's finally lunch time, which means the students are free. That takes a little getting used to. Freedom isn't something I have much experience with. I follow Salena and her friend, Susana, to a mango tree behind the school. Here is where we will have what Salena calls our "liquid lunch."

"So, what did Dante do to make that boy, Armando, so angry?" I help Salena spread out a blanket she pulled from her backpack. I waste no time getting to the point. From what I've observed, there's a lot of interest in Dante Vega. But it's a cautious interest. As if nobody feels free to express their true feelings.

"Did you not see what he did?" Susana hands me a plastic cup half-filled with Coca Cola. *America's favorite drink.* I remember the slogan from a video in my Human Studies class.

"He defended his friend," I say. "What's so bad about that?"

Susana rolls her eyes. "What planet are you from?" She hesitates, as if wondering if I am still worthy of her welcome-back-to-school drink. I guess I am. She takes my cup and places it on the ground next to her backpack. After looking over her shoulder, she unscrews a bottle wrapped in a paper bag. "No one challenges Armando." She pours a clear liquid into my cup, stirs it, and then hands me the drink.

I stare at the drink. I'm guessing what Susana poured into the cup is alcohol. "There's more to it than that," I say, thinking about what Susana said. Her explanation seems too simple.

"You're overthinking it," Salena says. "Like Susana said, no one challenges Armando."

I catalogue that information and drop the discussion. I'm more interested in the drink. Marius once said that it is impossible to protect humans without first understanding them. I glance at the red plastic cup. Drinking from this cup may be my first step to true understanding.

"Come on, drink." Susana pushes the cup up to my mouth. "What're you waiting for?"

I push back her hand. If I am going to experience humanity, I'll do it on my own terms. I tip the cup and touch it to my lips. The drink smells sweet and harsh at the same time. It burns going down my throat. I gag. And then I spit the drink back out. "What is this?" I gasp.

Susana laughs, seeming almost too pleased with herself. "Rum and Coke," she says.

I put down the cup. Tears sting my eyes, but at least I'm breathing again.

"You don't have to drink it." Salena avoids looking at Susana when she speaks to me.

Susana snatches the cup and shoves it back at me. "You want to hang with us, or not?"

I consider her question. The "us" Susana's talking about is the girl group attached to Armando's gang. One thing I learned on our short walk from the classroom to the mango tree is that the girls who hang with Armando are faithful followers. They don't make a move, or have any kind of opinion, unless Armando allows it.

Power like that has to be watched carefully.

I raise the cup to my mouth and swallow. Fitting in may be the only way to see what's going on with Armando. Something about him does not seem … right.

By the time I finish my drink, I feel like I am floating. Susana and Salena must feel the same way because they start acting all light and happy. They giggle a lot. And then, still laughing, they start talking about Dante.

"You know what?" Salena is trying to keep her voice low, but the rum in her drink amplifies it twenty decibels higher. "If Dante wasn't with Gia, I'd hook up with him."

"What?" Susana looks horrified.

"I'm just saying." Salena looks away. "He seems kind of nice."

"Nice?" Susana explodes. "Since when do you think Dante is *nice?*"

"Who's Gia?" I interject. My voice sounds funny, like I can't get my tongue around the words.

"Nobody," Susana says.

"Dante's girlfriend," Salena clarifies.

"Why, exactly, are we talking about him again?" Susana glares at her friend.

"Why not?" Salena glares back. "He's actually interesting. Unlike ninety-nine percent of the boys in this school, he's not afraid to defend what he believes in."

"Careful, Salena." There's a touch of fear in Susana's warning. "Don't let Armando hear you say that."

"Why, again, are we giving Armando so much importance?" The words slur over my tongue. I'm completely lost. What they are saying makes no sense to me.

Susana eyeballs me. I think I might have made her angry. "Are you for real? Armando is our *king*. And Dante, for the record, is a total and absolute LOSER."

Salena shakes her head, but the move is slight, almost imperceptible — as if she doesn't want Susana to see her disagree.

I press further. "Does being a loser, in Armando's kingdom, mean listening to rock music?" Because that's all I got from the accusations thrown against Dante and his friends.

"Oh. My. God. What is *wrong* with you?" Susana is aggressive now. "Dante is a loser, that's all you need to know. Nobody cares what music he listens to. He's a loser because Armando says he is."

"Okay, sure, whatever." My voice sounds small and weak. I don't feel like arguing.

"Hey, are you all right?" Salena moves closer to me.

"No, not really." I don't know what's happening to me. I've never felt like this before. My head hurts and my stomach flip flops. I no longer feel like I can float.

"No more for you." Salena grabs the cup from my hand and pulls me up. "Let's go." She positions me toward the cafeteria. "You need to eat."

"No, what she needs is to start all over again, with a different set of friends." Dante is standing in front of me, looking concerned.

I sway slightly.

Dante steadies me. "Are you all right?" He grabs hold of my arm.

Shivers flutter down my spine. His hand feels strong and steady on my arm.

"I'm fine," I manage to say. I want to say something more, but before I can coordinate my thoughts with my mouth, Susana pulls me away from him.

"Don't touch her," Susana says.

Dante takes two steps back and holds up his hands. "Sorry. I was only trying to help." He turns to me. "Here, drink this." He moves closer and shoves a bottle of water in my hand. It's still cold from the vending machine. "You're probably dehydrated."

He's about to leave when he turns back and says, "Oh, and by the way, Susana. Along with being a loser, I also kill cats, practice voodoo, and torture my invalid grandmother."

Susana's eyes get huge. "You do?" Her voice is nearly breathless.

Dante shakes his head. "Seriously, Susana?" He looks at me. "My advice" — he turns to leave — "find a new set of friends."

"Shut up, Dante." Susana grabs my hand. "Come on, Armando's waiting for us."

Feeling slightly nauseous, I follow Susana and Salena into the cafeteria. I thought I could handle mixing a little rum with "America's favorite drink." Rum and Coke sounded like sugar heaven. But instead of a romp through Candy Land, I'm wading through murky waters. I want to lie down and go to sleep. But I force myself to stay awake.

I sense danger in the air.

"Where've you been?" Armando stands from a table in the center of the room. His eyes shift from Susana to Salena, and then stay fixed on me.

"Bathroom," Susana says. Her voice shakes slightly.

"Sit down," he says to her, still staring at me.

Susana pulls out a chair, quickly followed by Salena. I want to sit too but find I can't move. Horrified, I realize I'm still staring at him.

The hair on my arms stands up. There's something evil inside that boy.

"Would you like to join us?" His voice is smooth now. Seductive.

"No, I think I'll ..." I move away, putting the end of the table between us. He stands unmoving, watching me. He's smiling faintly, as if he's amused by me.

And then in one smooth step, he moves toward me so that we are separated only by the corner of the table.

I can't breathe. He's standing so close. I smell a faint hint of cologne, the metallic odor of the gold chain he wears around his neck. His eyes seem to hold some kind of power over me. They are black as midnight and dangerously unsettling. They fill my vision as he leans toward me, his body almost touching mine. I feel myself losing focus. The room begins to spin. But then I squeeze my eyes shut and break his power over me.

"Get away from me." I rebuke whatever force is behind Armando's hold. Something I learned to do in our Spiritual Defense class.

"Shut up." A skinny boy points a finger gun at me. And then, his mouth drops open.

I recoil. His breath smells like a dead rat. I cover my nose, trying hard not to breathe.

"Check her out man." The boy with the bad breath sounds a little slow. "She's like ... glowing or something." He tilts his head and stares at me, his mouth open again. "That's freaking weird."

Oh no! The rebuke triggered my angel spirit. The back-to-school drink was supposed to help me blend in. Which, apparently, it did. Until I rebuked whatever evil is inside Armando.

My wings strain to be released. My body is getting hot. We were told this would happen. If I'm not careful, the heat will make me sparkle. I think cold thoughts to bring my temperature down. Icebergs. Snow. Cold water from the vending machine.

"Armando, dude, did you see that? Her skin was —"

"Silence." Armando holds up his hand.

Rat Breath immediately closes his mouth.

And then slowly, Armando turns his gaze back to me. "Keep your eyes off my girl," he says to the skinny boy, staring at me in a way that makes me cringe.

Your girl? If I weren't feeling sluggish, and slightly out of control, I would clearly spell out how that is never going to happen.

"There's a party tonight at the mansion," Armando says. "I want you to be there."

"People don't always get what they want." My body is cooling and my mind heating up. "And for the record," I say, "I am not your girl."

"You will be." Armando's mouth tightens into a thin, straight line. "The king always gets what he wants."

14. JADIEL

Soul Reaper

"One of the most important lessons you will learn here on Earth is that humans are a self-serving, greedy lot." Equus talks as he walks down the path leading from his mansion to the beach. "Taking advantage of that fact, Lord Lucius has devised a strategy to use those imperfections to our advantage."

"Which is?"

"We make sure humans understand that the more they own, the more power they can hold over other humans because of those possessions. Money is power, and one of our most effective bait and traps."

Bait and trap? How have I gone from creating art to hunting prey? I could never paint a picture of my new life. It's too disparate from who I am. Who I still want to be.

"Get out your phone." Equus snaps me from my thoughts. "A strategy is only as good as its victim is weak."

I dig out the cell phone Equus gave me. My mobile command center.

"Go to Facebook." He waits impatiently as I open the app. "Search for Armando Ayala."

"How do I ...?" The screen goes black because I've taken too long.

Equus snatches the phone from me. He taps to revive the screen, thumbs an icon that looks like a magnifying glass, and then shoves the phone in my face. "What does that say?" He's pointing at the word *search*.

"Back off. I get it." I grab the phone and tap on the search bar. A screen pops up with letters and numbers. The keyboard. I know that screen. Because now I know how to text. What I don't know is ... "How do you spell his name?"

"A." Equus stares at me with a look meant to humiliate me. "R." He continues spelling out the name, like a pre-school teacher who hates his job. When my clumsy finger finds all the right letters, a boy's face pops up. He's wearing sunglasses, inside what looks like a classroom.

"That's our boy," Equus says. "Armando Ayala is eighteen years old. He's a student at La Colina High. He should have graduated a year ago, but the boy doesn't want to give up his throne. At La Colina High, a poor school in an even poorer town, this sniveling boy is King. He rules the school. Why? Because I have taken control of him and given him certain *powers*."

"What kind of powers?" A hunter must know his prey's defenses. So I've learned.

"Human powers are limited. Minor mind control. Elementary compulsion. Useful tools to implement our strategies, but Armando is nothing more than a pawn. A piece to be moved in a game he has no control over. With a little mind manipulation, a lot of guided persuasion, and most importantly, monetary incentives, Armando was easily corrupted.

"How, exactly, did you make that happen?" The unspoken question really being, is evil created? Or does it grow out of our messy, screwed-up lives?

"It was rather easy, really." Equus continues past Chupa's kennel at the edge of the property. The beast bolts to the chain-link fence and growls at me. "Puerto Rico's government coffers are seventy billion dollars in debt. There are few jobs. Few honest ways for a young person to make some cash to buy what he desires. I offered Armando what the government could not: the means to a better life."

"At what cost?"

"The cost, well, the boy will soon find out. As he focuses his attention on power and wealth, this obsessive desire will soon rob him of joy. In his frantic effort to acquire more riches, his passion for power will make it impossible for him to be at peace."

"Are you done?" I'm not in the mood for a speech. So much effort just to make people miserable.

"Are you an imbecile?" Equus stops in front of me. "I can make things go really well for you or" — his eyes narrow — "really badly. So, I'd think about what I'm saying, if I were you." He flicks his hand at me. "Put away your phone, before you drop or lose it."

I shake my head and pocket the phone. I refuse to let him get to me. "So, what now? What's the plan for Armando Ayala?"

"A simple task." Equus stares out over the water. The sea is rough this morning. Spray launches into the air when the waves crash onto the shore. "We need to get his signature. He hasn't officially signed our contract yet."

"Why not? You've already hooked him."

Equus turns and stares at me. "Because I was saving him for you."

His answer doesn't convince me. But I need six signatures. Looks like Armando Ayala will be signature number one.

"The mansion is hosting a party tonight," Equus says. "Armando and his friends will be there. All you need to do is challenge him to a game of billiards, toast each shot with a chaser of rum, give him his money when he wins — which you will make sure he does —"

"— I don't play billiards." A fact I hope will free me from this assignment.

"You didn't play billiards," Equus answers. "But I understand you are a fast learner." He snaps his fingers. "Follow me. You have ten hours to learn the art of the hustle."

***

Ten hours later, I'm trolling the mansion, passing out beer and staying sober. Losing the game tonight will not be a problem. I'm no expert at billiards. But I have to be on top of my game. *"Let the boy think he has what he desires,"* Equus says. *"Money and dominance. It's what Armando wants. It's what will make him sign the contract."*

And once he signs that contract, I become dominant. The trainee becomes the trainer. A "reward" Equus offers for putting my head — and my soul — in the game.

When I step out onto the terrace, I'm assaulted by a steady barrage of one beat thumps pounding out of amped-up speakers. *Boom. Boom. Boom. Boom.* I walk through the sweating, gyrating, inebriated teenagers partying in the mansion. I *despise* this music. It's mechanically synthesized. But the pulsing, hypnotic rhythm of Reggaetón pumps up the crowd. Necessary, Equus says, to *"get those hormones racing."*

"Can you see it?" Equus comes up beside me. "They're losing their inhibitions." A half smile snakes up his mouth.

"Dance with me." A random girl reaches out for me. I hold up my hand. She backs away.

"So strong. So resistant." My trainer's tone is mocking. "For now."

"You don't know me." I have no interest in other girls. Mine lives in my heart.

"I don't need to know you. I know the power of this music." Equus surveys the dance floor. "The repetitive beat, the subliminal message hidden in the lyrics. It all works together to inspire the kind of thoughts that lead to lust."

My jaw tightens. He's manipulating me. I feel the throbbing, pulsing beat of the music.

"I'm going for Armando." I turn and walk away. The sooner I can get Armando to sign the contract, the sooner I can be free of my Spiritual Trainer. For a few hours, anyway.

I stride past all the potential recruits I have no interest in and head for the library.

When I walk into the room, Armando is setting up his shot. There are two balls left on the table. The eight ball and the five. He sinks both with a perfectly executed angled shot.

"Impressive." I flip my voice from dominated to dominant.

"And you are?" Armando leans on his pool cue.

"Your next challenger."

"You any good?" Armando studies me.

I saunter over to the bar and pour a shot of Don Q. "Winner takes $500." I offer the rum.

"A hustler." Armando kicks back the shot. "Rack 'em up." He slams the empty glass on the bar. I pour him another shot.

I nod at the other kid. He racks the balls in their starting position. I take a pool cue off the rack. "Leave." I nod at the door. The boy scampers away.

"Call it." I dig a quarter from my pocket.

"Heads," Armando says.

I flip the coin and slap it on the table. Heads. "Your break."

Armando chalks his cue and removes the triangle. With a powerful break stroke, he pots a striped ball in the side pocket. The cue ball spins backward off the hit.

He then goes for the nine ball and sinks it into a corner pocket.

I take the table and sight my shot. The five ball shoots straight into a side pocket.

We match each other shot for shot. On the billiards table. Not at the bar. He's now pouring his own drinks. I wish that made me feel better. It doesn't. I'm hurting a human. How am I any better than those who hurt me?

Armando makes a skilled spin shot, and then goes for the rum. I reach the bottle before he does and snatch it from the bar. "Save some for the celebration." I squeeze his shoulder, aiming for a concerned drinking-buddy-tone to my voice. He's finished half the bottle.

"Give me that." Armando's eyes snap black. "He grabs the bottle and pushes me back. The strength of that push heightens my senses. He's drawn out his dark powers.

I clamp my hand on his wrist. "Get back to the table and finish the game." I don't need dark power to dominate this boy. He's going to kill himself if he keeps drinking. That conviction gives me strength. "Remember what we're playing for." I loosen my grip and dig into my pocket for the $500 Equus fronted me. I hold the wad up in front of me.

Armando eyes the money, sets down the bottle, and staggers back to the table.

He has the final shot. "Eight ball in the side pocket." He calls it, bridges his hand, and executes a perfect shot. The eight ball spins into a side pocket. Game over.

I breathe a sigh of relief. "Good game." I hand over the $500.

"Rematch?" He pockets the money.

"No, I'm done." My stomach twists. "But I'd like to make you an offer."

"What offer?" Armando stumbles against the table.

I reach out to help him, but then decide against it. He'll take it as a threat. I hold out a tattered parchment and a black ink pen.

"The promise of even bigger wins." I move the pen closer to his hand. "If you sign here."

"Is this some kind of crossroad demon thing?"

"Something like that."

"Cool." Armando signs the contract without reading it. "I'm in."

A knot forms in the pit of my stomach. Bile creeps up my throat. "To be clear about what you signed" — I toss the contract on Equus Centurion's desk — "you'll be answering to me now." I stare at a brown leather journal on top of the desk. "I will give you instructions.

You will obey them." I focus harder on the journal. I'm drawn to it. And I'm not sure why.

"Dude, no one tells *me* what to do." Armando leans back against the pool table, arms and ankles crossed.

I look up sharply and stare at him. "Then the deal's off."

Armando uncrosses his arms. "No, the deal is on. I signed a contract."

"You did." I return my focus to the journal. "But you didn't read the terms."

"*Knowledge is power,*" Marius always said. Armando lost his. Maybe I will gain mine. By reading Equus Centurion's journal.

"Whatever." Armando flops into the nearest chair.

It doesn't take much to unlock the journal. The click of a dial opens a pair of crossed wings and the journal folds out to the latest entry. *Recruitment Strategy #2: Signing on the Sick.* My throat burns. This entry is my next assignment.

As I read, my stomach aches. What Equus writes about so scientifically — ensnaring a terminally-ill human — leaves me feeling nauseous.

"I'm thirsty." Armando's statement triggers some level of anxiety in me.

I close the journal and turn toward him. He's slouched in the chair, shaking the empty rum bottle over his open mouth.

"That's enough." I snatch the bottle from him. "It's finished."

It's bad enough to see the destruction I've caused. I don't need a blatant reminder of my cruelty. Nor do I need the message that I may control Armando now, but when the night is over, I'll be thirsty, too.

"Here." I pour Armando a glass of water from a pitcher on the bar. "Stay here until you sober up." I head for the door. Then I climb the stairs and enter the nearest bedroom.

A hormonally hyped-up boy and a giggling girl occupy the bed. "Get out." I snatch a phone off the bed, shove it at the boy, and push him out the door. The girl finds her shoes and scurries after him. I slam the door, and then lock it behind them.

I flop down on the bed and close my eyes. I'm physically and emotionally exhausted. It's been eight days since the beginning of the end of my former life. Eight days since I last saw Kiriela. Eight days since I was punished for "the treachery of rebellion against God." All because I fell in love with my best friend. Where is the treachery in that?

I put my arm over my eyes to block out the light. Ironic that love has surrounded me with hatred. Equus Centurion and all the maggots of Abaddon despise the humans. They laugh at their destruction. I will never be able to forgive myself for what I did to Armando — which I would not have done if the Council had not exiled me to Abaddon. Maybe Lucius is right. The God-fearing are a bunch of self-righteous hypocrites. Boring and completely predictable.

My thoughts grow dark. The Lucius I once met as a boy was neither boring nor predictable. He was exciting. Creative and bold. A dark romantic rebel. One day when I was ten, my parents introduced me to him. From the moment I met him, I idolized him. I wanted to be like him. He was the ultimate poetic anti-hero. Stirring up rebellion. Planting new ideas into tired minds. It was all so insanely intellectual.

Until he became obsessed with my mother.

The walls start closing in on me. Instead of thinking about what brought me joy for a mere two seconds after locking myself in this room — Kiriela — I'm thinking about Lucius. He's *tormenting* me. Showing me the luxury of this mansion, the freedom humans have to love and be loved, only to later send me back to Abaddon.

I absorb the comfort of this huge bed in this enormous room. Then I think about the bed I slept on last night. The only thing good about my slab in Abaddon is that my lamb found its way there. I smile when I think of her. She has the whitest wool I have ever seen. It reminds me of the clouds I used to paint.

Clouds. I think for a moment. Cloud is *nubes* in Latin. That's what I'll name her. Nubes. Or maybe just Nube, without the "s."

I sink deeper into the bed. I have never slept in a bed so soft. I would do almost anything to stay here and not be sent back to Abaddon. Is Equus implanting desire in me the same way he did in Armando? What does desire start with? Comfort? Luxury? That first drink?

My eyes land on an un-opened beer bottle left behind on the bedside table. I snatch it, twist off the lid, and take a long swallow. I slam down the bottle. My trainer's bait does nothing for me. I sit up, push back my hair, and leave the room. What I desire is not found in a bottle.

I want peace. The guilt of what I did to Armando is gnawing a hole in my heart.

I go back downstairs. Loud music thumps in the background. Strobe lights distort the visual field, making people and their movements seem strangely unreal. Flashing in and out of the strobes, I see Armando. The water must have revived him. He's thrusting and grinding between two girls. Armando's minions, Pedro and Julián, are on the dance floor with him.

A text comes in. I glance at the sender. Alastor Principium. Cautiously, I read what the Headmaster has written. *Congratulations on your first conquest, Jadiel. I am pleased with both you and your trainer. I have already informed Equus but will tell you directly. Your next assignment is Dante Vega. He and your first recruit are sworn enemies, which means, happily for us, a built-in target for our treachery.*

I watch the moving dots and wait for Alastor Principium's next message. Now I get the easy sign. My success makes Equus look good.

Unlike Armando, the Headmaster continues, *Dante may prove ... challenging. He is naturally rebellious, a quality ideally suited to our purposes but tricky at the same time. The dear boy likes to challenge everyone and everything, which will also include us. He is intelligent, by human standards, but stubborn. Even more delightful, he is impulsive and easily provoked. So, here's how I want him handled. Subtly. Unlike with Armando, Lord Lucius does not want an easy sign. Is that clear?*

Painfully clear. The boy has a target on his back. I text back a message less biting than my thoughts. *It will be as you wish.* And then the affected add-on, *Sir.* What a good soldier I am.

"A message from the Headmaster?" Equus stands beside me.

"I'm sure you already know that."

Equus stares straight ahead. "Lord Lucius has a particular interest in Dante Vega. To be given this assignment is significant."

"Not to me." My stomach churns. "I don't want any part of this." Equus either doesn't hear me or doesn't care. He's too busy scanning the room. A predator on the prowl.

"Dante Vega never comes to the mansion," he says, "so your next assignment is on hold. But that doesn't mean you can't get busy." His eyes stop moving. "Choose your next recruit." He points at Pedro and Julián. "One of those two."

"No." I've had enough of soul snatching for one night. "No more."

Equus sneers. "Which one of those two is more vulnerable?"

On an intellectual level, I will analyze the boys and I will give him my answer. That's all.

I look for any projected weaknesses in the two boys. Julián is the less interesting of the two. A skinny guy with drooping pants and fake diamond earrings. His red and white "Air Jordan" basketball shoes would have been identical to Armando's, had they been originals and not knock-off cheap imitations.

While I'm studying him, Julián staggers closer to Pedro and says, "Check her out, man." He points at a girl with the tip of his beer bottle. "Ouch, she's hot!"

Pedro's mouth drops open. "Oh yeah." He says no more. He doesn't need to. It's clear what's on his mind.

"Sex is one of Lord Lucius's favored lures," Equus says. "And it all starts here, on the dance floor."

I hear a lecture coming on. I brace myself. With all the noise around me, maybe I can tune him out.

"Lord Lucius uses many tools to weaken and destroy young people." Equus skillfully manages to make his voice heard. "Music is one of his most powerful tools. The chainsaw of his destruction. Listen as I explain how it works."

No please, please don't. I get it. Really, I do.

"Music is rhythm," Equus says. "And rhythm is a physical element. As you can see, a mind dulled by drugs or alcohol can still respond to the beat."

I am *so* not interested in this lesson. But I do see some truth to it. Pedro is moving to the music around a girl who seems uninterested.

"Loudness adds to muddling the mind," Equus continues. "And then there is the repetition. An extremely primitive, but effective device."

I look back at Pedro. He's panting around his partner. She's staring at her nails. His face is flushed. Hers, distracted. Every five seconds, she looks up from her nails and smiles at me.

"And then there are the strobe lights." Equus draws my attention back. "Strobe lights split the darkness and reduce resistance, like the lights of an interrogator's third degree or the swinging pendulum of the hypnotist who controls behavior. So" — he turns to me — "what have you deduced? Which one is our next recruit?"

"Pedro," I say.

"And the reason why you chose him?"

"He has what you want. Desire."

"Exactly." A slow smile lifts the corner of Equus's mouth. "Good call." With his eyes fixed on Pedro he says to me, "Maybe you do want a part of this after all."

A definite *no* to that.

"Watch and learn." Equus leaves me standing. "The next sign is on you." He goes for Pedro.

"No, wait, what're you doing?" I try to stop him, but it's too late.

"Having fun?" Equus approaches Pedro. "Have you gotten what you wanted yet?"

Pedro tilts his head, and his mouth drops open. "I don't know, dude. What do I want?"

Equus inhales sharply. He pulls Pedro aside. "Do you want to hook up with that girl?" He nods at the girl Pedro was drooling over.

"*Uh*, yeah, dude. Wouldn't you?"

Equus stares at him, expressionless. "How much do you want that to happen?"

"*Uh* —"

Equus holds up his hand, stopping whatever idiocy is about to come out of the boy's mouth. "You can have her tonight, in exchange for one small thing."

No. "No!" A signature in exchange for alcohol or a wad of cash is one thing. It's the signer's choice. In this deal, the girl's choice has been taken away. Memories of my mother, abducted for Lucius's pleasure, spur me into action. She didn't have a choice, either.

Equus has already taken Pedro to a corner and rolled out the parchment. I snatch the pen from him. "Come with me." I drag Pedro out of the corner. Then I look him in the eye and say, "Leave the mansion. *Now*." Two seconds later, Pedro's walking out the front door and I'm feeling sick. I compelled Pedro to leave. I have no idea how I did it. All I know is that compulsion is a dark skill I did not learn in Maion.

I stride off the dance floor and toward the front door. My stomach is churning. I'm supposed to be hardened. A soldier of Abaddon. I'm supposed to feel strong. Powerful. But all I feel right now is an overwhelming sense of darkness and despair.

15. JADIEL

Uncertain Sanctuary

My manacled wrist throbs as I get closer to the front door. I inhale
sharply and hold my breath. That helps lesson the pain. At least for a
little while. I snatch the key to the Harley from its holder in the
hallway, shove on a helmet, and head for the bike. I take a deep breath,
straddle the bike, and then recall what I observed.

Put the key in the ignition. I do what Equus did. *Turn the engine on.* I
twist the key, set the run switch to its "on" position, and then press the
button with the incomplete circle. The fuel pump primes. Now all I
need to do is press the "on" button, and the bike should start.

I breathe out. The Harley turns on. Feeling more confident now, I
find the gear shift on the left handlebar. I twist the throttle. The bike
glides into motion. *My right hand controls the front brake, my right foot the
back one.* That's all I need to know as the needle on the speed dial
swings up to thirty mpg, forty, and then I'm on the open road, soaring
up to sixty.

I have no idea where I'm going. Or even what I want. All I know is
that I need to get away from the mansion. From the pointless party and
the shallow conversation. I need to be free of Equus and his lessons. I
twist the throttle into a higher gear. My wrist feels like it's on fire but
there is no pain strong enough to stop me now. I'm emotionally and
intellectually drained. I need someone to talk to — about something
other than deals made in exchange for the promise of sex, alcohol, or
money.

A half an hour later, I'm parked outside a small church. This is the last place I should be and the only place I am drawn to. It's 8 p.m. and the church is open. Aluminum slatted windows have been cranked outward. A spotlight focuses on a worn wooden cross on top of the angled roof. The cement walls need paint, and the front sidewalk has grass growing up from the cracks.

I take off my helmet and walk up to the church. My wrist is red hot now. Staring straight ahead, I grip my wrist, and then step across the portal.

The air inside is heavy with incense and recently extinguished candles. The odor of Catholicism. Scattered people sit with heads bowed or eyes glued to the Bible. An old woman dressed in black prays before the altar. I study the woman. Her face glows with the dancing light of the candles hopeful parishioners have placed beside the altar. She looks peaceful. As if she has found some sort of comfort at the altar.

Maybe I'll find some comfort, too.

"Good evening." A priest approaches me. "I'm Father John." He holds out his hand.

I don't take it.

"I used to ride a Honda." Father John nods at my helmet. "What about you?"

"What?" I did not see that coming. "No God bless you?" I ask the priest. "No welcome to my church? Would you like to join us for Bible study?"

"Rather predictable, wouldn't you say?"

"Definitely." I squeeze my wrist. The band burns my palm. I close my eyes for a second, take a deep breath, and then say, "Do you still ride that Honda?"

"Would if I could." Father John glances at my shackle. Goosebumps pop up on his arms, but he stays focused on what he wants to say to me. "A broken hip and three fractured ribs have kept me off it for going on twenty years now."

"Sorry . . ." I turn and head for the door. "I shouldn't be here." My wrist feels as if it's going to melt.

"How about that Bible study?" Father John calls out after me.

"Sounds boring." I rub my wrist. Memories of Malakiy's mind-numbing Daily Reflections propel me toward the door.

"I'm sure you can make it more interesting."

I stop, my hand on the doorknob. "No, I don't think so." Father John has no idea what he has let into his church. Or maybe, he does. And is simply not afraid.

"Come on," Father John says. "Join us."

I know I shouldn't but somehow, I can't resist. I follow Father John into a back room where a group of young people has gathered.

"Good evening." Father John says. "How's everyone tonight?" The young people murmur uninspired responses. Father John pulls out a chair and extends his hand. "Please, sit down," he says to me.

"That's okay. I'll stand." I lean back against the wall and cross my arms. The minute this gets boring, I'm out the door.

"Let us pray." Father John bows his head. "Father God, we ask you to bless this night. May it be Your voice we hear. Your words that reach our hearts."

A cold shiver slithers down my spine. The mere mention of His name forces me to take two steps back. I'm about to head for the door when Father John says, "Thank you, Father God, for our new friend." He looks up at me. "What's your name, son?"

I hesitate. Introducing myself seems too committed. But I like that he called me *son*.

"Jadiel," I say.

"Thank you for Jadiel," Father John says. "In Jesus's name we pray, Amen."

I recoil. Something dark inside me stirs. I suppress what I feel and stand my ground.

As much as Equus wants me to believe it, I am not evil.

"As you all know," Father John says, "Jomar's mother is battling cancer. This is a tough time for Jomar and his family." All eyes turn and focus on a scrawny boy sitting on a tattered floral couch. He stares at the floor. "But Jesus is the same compassionate physician now that He was during His earthly ministry. In faith we must pray for Jomar's mother. For as the Bible says, the prayer of faith shall save the sick."

Such simplistic faith. The darkness inside comes closer to the surface. "Jesus did not heal everyone who came to him." My spirit is rebelling. I'm stealing hope. I know it, but I can't stop myself from saying, "He cured many of their infirmities and plagues, but many is not all."

Attacking faith is the last thing I wanted to do when I entered this sanctuary. But what else could I have expected? I'm not with God anymore.

Father John studies me, and then says, "Yes, you are right. Jesus did not heal everyone that came to Him. But the word *many* is not a restricted quantity. In Romans five, verse nineteen the Bible says, '*For as by one man's disobedience many were made sinners, so by the obedience of one shall many be made righteous.* In this verse, and throughout the Bible, the word *many* is used to refer to all of mankind, for all have sinned and need healing."

"Oh yeah?" I'm about to say something horrid, and that something is not of God.

"Have you sinned, father?" I'm being used to disrupt this Bible study. I know it, but I can't stop it. I hope Father John counterargues. Lucius can have no victory here.

"We are all sinners in the eyes of the Lord," Father John says.

"Indeed, we are." I stare at the priest. "So, tell me, Father, what's your sin?"

Eight days living under the shadow of Abaddon have made me a first-class jerk.

"Failing to reach you," Father John says.

"I'm out of here." *No one can reach me now.* Every day I spend in Lucius's school is one less day I can be saved. I stumble for the door.

"God bless you, Jadiel," Father John says. "You are always welcome here."

I stop. And then slowly, I turn back to face the priest. He's struck a nerve. And I strike back. "God will never bless those he has condemned." This is all me, without the manipulation.

"God never condemns his children."

"No, you're right. He punishes them. Cruelly and without mercy."

"I used to think that way too, once."

"You would be wise to think it again."

My phone vibrates. I dig it from my pocket and read the incoming text. I can almost hear Equus, screaming out his message. *A Bible Study Group? You insolent fool! You stole my bike to go to a BIBLE STUDY GROUP?*

My heart thuds. The band is not only a deterrent, it's a tracking device.

I sprint to the door. I have to get away from Father John and his youth group. Just to spite me, Equus will make them my next target.

The phone vibrates in my hand. I read the next text. *Interaction with this group was not authorized.* I feel the menace in the tone of the text. *You are fraternizing with the ENEMY.*

I shove open the door. Another message comes in. *There are consequences to acting outside of my instruction.*

I fall back against the outside wall. Equus's final message freezes my blood.

You have been called back to Abaddon.

16. JADIEL

White Cell White

Called back to Abaddon doesn't mean what I thought it would. I thought I would be shoved back onto my slab in the communal dorm room. Maybe deprived of food or water. I did not think I would be deprived of the one thing that makes me feel alive. Color.

I'm alone in a white cell, naked — except for a piece of white cloth around my middle. The walls of my prison are made of white stone. The floor of white pebbles. White. In Abaddon. *How is that even possible?*

A white grate slides open, but there is no sound. Any sound that would have been there is muffled. Through the narrow opening, someone slides in a white tray. On the tray is a white plate with half a cup of white rice. Next to the plate is a white glass, half-filled with milk. I take the tray. And then with a white plastic fork, I shovel the food in. My philosophy hasn't changed. Food is food. Even if it's white.

My hand stops midway to my mouth. A white fly frees its wings from the rice. My stomach turns over. I gag on the rice I've only half swallowed. Then I backhand the bowl. "Get me out of here!" I leap to my feet and punch the wall. "Please! Get me out of here!"

No one answers, but someone is listening. I can feel a presence on the other side of the wall. "Where are you?" I walk around the wall, feeling for whoever is there. "Who are you?"

When I get no answer, I become more agitated. "Get me out of here!" I claw at the wall. "I know you're there." The scar on my chest throbs. It's him. Lucius is watching me. "Come out of the shadows. Coward!" I hit the wall. "Lucius! Come in here and meet me face to face!"

A whishing sound starts, and then, a cloud of white smoke envelopes the room. I feel faint. And then, I collapse, unconscious, to the floor.

Sometime later, I wake up. My eyes flicker, but I can't open them. It feels like they're weighted down with lead. When I finally manage to half open one eye, I see another white tray, with another bowl of white rice and another glass of milk. Under the glass is a piece of white paper. I slide it out and read what is written. *Escaping from the mansion was bold, I'll give you that, but you disobeyed a direct order.*

"What order?" My brain is too foggy to focus.

I read on, hoping the words will sort themselves out. *You compelled Pedro to leave the mansion instead of getting him to enlist.*

Pedro. Compulsion. It's coming back to me. "No." I shake my head. "I wasn't the one who did something wrong." My heart beats faster. "Equus ... that girl ... she didn't deserve ..."

I'm talking to the walls. No one cares. No one's listening. Except maybe, he is. "Hey! Lucius! What's the matter? You afraid of me? You think you can break me?" A bead of sweat pops out on my forehead. "Think again! Not happening!"

A cold silence meets my outburst. The grated window opens. Another tray. Another bowl. Mashed potatoes this time. More white. White. WHITE.

I'm going to go insane before I ever get out of here.

17. DANTE

Trapped

I'm trapped in the hallway. It's the second day of school, and the principal has finally caught up with me. I try to untangle myself from Gia's embrace, but she holds on tighter. That annoys me, just a little.

"Come with me," Mr. Martínez says.

I glance up at the principal. This weird expression has come over the man's face, like the one parents get when they think they've come up with a new way to deal with an old problem.

I move to go but Gia does not unwrap her arms.

"Now," Mr. Martínez says. He glares at Gia until she finally lets go. The corner of her mouth lifts. She's playing him. I sigh and shake my head. Then I follow Mr. Martínez to the office.

"Have a seat," Mr. Martínez says.

I sit on the chair in front of the principal's desk.

"I didn't know you were composer as well as a musician." Mr. Martínez sets down my composition book while assuming his official position behind the desk.

"There's a lot you don't know about me," I say, acting tougher than I feel.

"I'm sure that's true." Mr. Martínez relaxes into his black vinyl executive chair.

I zone out. Like I usually do in the principal's office. And then for whatever reason, I start thinking about that new girl, feeling only slightly guilty. I mean, I have a girlfriend —although I wonder how seriously Gia takes our relationship. She stood me up the last two times we were supposed to go out.

My mind drifts back to the new girl. I wonder where she's from. Definitely not from around here. She's naturally blonde. And her skin is white. Not pasty pale, like the kids who came to the island from New York. But porcelain white, like the alabaster statues in the Museum of Fine Art. Not even the fairest-skinned Puerto Ricans are that white. The Caribbean sun will not allow it.

"Dante?" Mr. Martínez's voice calls me out of my thoughts.

"Yeah?" I look out the window. C.J. is in the courtyard with his girlfriend, Cristina.

"Are you listening to me?"

"Uh huh." I continue to stare out the window. Cristina takes C.J.'s cane from him and props it against the flamboyan tree. C.J.'s right leg is two inches shorter than the left. He stumbles when he walks. But it doesn't matter to Cristina. She loves him anyway.

A muscle tightens in my gut. I wonder if Gia would love me if I tripped when I walked. I shift in the chair. The truth, I know, is in the wondering.

"Dante ..." Mr. Martínez drags me back into the conversation he still wants to have with me. "There's something I'd like to talk to you about."

I watch C.J. lean on Cristina as he moves toward a stone bench. She holds onto him until he is safely seated. Sweet.

"Would you please look at me?" Mr. Martínez's voice is impatient now.

I roll my head back and stare at Mr. Martínez.

"Look, you're a smart young man, with a lot of potential. But I'm afraid you might throw it all away" — he clears his throat and pretends to search through the papers on his desk — "by not making wise decisions."

"Meaning?" Too much parent talk. I need specifics.

"I would like you to start thinking about some of the choices you have made. Some of the ... friends you have chosen to be with."

"MEANING?" The principal is starting to get on my nerves. "Just tell me what you're trying to say, Mr. Martínez. I can handle it."

Mr. Martínez crooks his finger over his mouth. For a while he just sits there, staring at me. Then finally he says, "Gia comes from a troubled family."

"And?" I lift up my hands, emphasizing the question. "What's your point?" Part of why Gia and I connected was *because* of our troubled families. My story is her story when it comes to absentee dads.

"I want to encourage you to think about the relationship you have with her."

I press my lips together. And keep them together until I can control what I say next.

"I don't mean to be rude," I say, "but how is it any of your business who my friends are or what I do with my life?"

Mr. Martínez picks up a pencil and circles spirals onto the nearest piece of paper. "It may be none of my business, as a principal, but as a man who is also a father, I —"

I spring from the chair, knocking it to the ground. "You are not my father. You have no right to —"

Mr. Martínez stands up. "Pick up that chair." He points at the chair toppled backward on the floor. "And sit down. *Now*."

I want to kick that chair. Hard. But instead, I pick it up and sit back down.

I do *not* need a father. Never have. And never will. Martínez has crossed the line.

"Look ..." Mr. Martínez speaks quietly. "All I'm trying to say is that maybe you should think about making some new friends, meeting new people." He fiddles with a paper clip. "Mr. Claudio says you're a pretty good guitar player."

I twist the silver band on my thumb, wondering how, and when, my music teacher had come to tell Mr. Martínez that.

"Why don't you think about auditioning for the music school in Monte Grande? Many of our students go there. They offer after school classes in almost every instrument, as well as *rondallas*, choirs, and other group activities."

I stare at him, not comprehending. "I'm not getting it, Martínez," I finally say. "You mean they go to *another* school after they get out of here?"

"Exactly."

"Why?" I cannot wrap my brain around it. "Why would anyone want to do that?"

"Because they're serious about their music." Mr. Martínez is looking at me as if he is trying to make a point.

"I'll think about it." I stand up. "Is there anything else?"

Mr. Martínez looks down at the papers on his desk.

"The new girl ..." Five seconds pass before he says, "Her name is Kiriela." Five more seconds. "She has an impressive background in classical music."

"So?"

"So, you might find her ... interesting."

"Can I go now?"

Mr. Martínez stares at me over his glasses.

I hate when adults do that.

"Go." Mr. Martínez tries not to smile. He hands back my composition book.

I grab it. Then jump up from the chair.

"Oh, and Dante."

I drop back my head. "Yes?"

"Please, do me a favor. Stay away from Armando."

"All right. All right. I'll avoid the dude."

I leave the principal's office nervous and uneasy. Mr. Martínez is okay, but he talks too much. Like it's any of his business who I go out with. Gia has her problems. Okay, I get that. But she loves me. My heart skips a beat. *Shit*, now Martínez has me doubting her.

No one ever doubts that Cristina loves C.J. It's so damn obvious.

I dig out my phone and text Gia: *I've officially had enough of school. Meet me in the parking lot. Let's go to the beach.*

18. KIRIELA

Sandals in the Sand

I slip my phone out of my pocket and glance at it when the teacher's not looking. The cell phone is an incredible human invention. If Jadiel and I had one of these in Maion, it would have made life a whole lot easier for us. Along with all the other *ifs*. If we hadn't lived in lock down. If we had freedom. If so many other things the humans take for granted.

Spanish class is almost as boring as The History of Puerto Rico, but that's not why I took out my phone. I left Malakiy twenty text messages about Dante. Twenty more about Armando. He hasn't answered a single one. Why did he give me his number if he never answers his phone?

Come on Malakiy. Come on. Check your phone.

I look one more time. Still no answer. I'm starting to get worried.

I glance out the window. A forced distraction. Most of the students are suffering inside, but the boy with the cane is still outside — with a girl that seems in love with him.

I sit up. Dante is walking across the courtyard toward the parking lot. Two seconds later, a girl with black hair joins him. My hand shoots up. The girl must be Gia, but why are they leaving school? I wave my hand, like the students do when they have an urgent request.

"Yes?" the teacher says. She sounds irritated.

"May I go to the bathroom, please?" I squirm, just to make my fake request appear authentic. I'm learning how to be a human teen.

"Can't it wait?" Mrs. Aponte says.

"No, it really can't." I need to follow Dante. Something's not right. I can feel it. He's in danger. I don't know from whom or why. All I know is that I have to go after him.

"Here." Mrs. Aponte hands me a pass.

"Thank you." I snatch my bag off the floor and stumble past her.

I dash into the bathroom, unzip my bag, and pull out my new sandals. As soon as the sandals touch my feet, a tingling sensation on my heels grows into a huge shiver. I release the wings. And then — just like my father said they would — the wings on my sandals give flight to my feet. In a flash, I'm out the door and running behind Dante's Cavalier.

I have no reason to feel guilty. I struggle to convince myself. I'm actively going against my father's orders. *"Under no circumstance are you to leave the school yard."* I hear his voice, echoing in my head.

I also hear Marius's voice, reading aloud the terms of my exile. *The defendant will be exiled to Earth for a mandatory six-months, after which her case will be re-evaluated. Restoration to Heaven is possible, given full obedience to the terms of her exile, which include submission to her father's absolute authority.*

But then, I listen to my own voice. The boy has been targeted by Lucius. Malakiy has mysteriously disappeared. I am the only one who can protect him. What is the higher moral choice? Obeying my father or saving a human life?

There's a pain in the pit of my stomach as I follow Dante to the beach. Disobedience is never guilt free.

Dante and Gia sit down under a coconut palm. She kicks off her flip flops and leans against him. He puts his arm around her. I sit a few feet away, hidden behind the trunk of an uprooted tree. I don't think they can see me. Humans can't see angels when we're serving as guardians or warriors. At least that's what we were taught, what seems like forever ago.

I draw my legs to my chest and put my arms around them. For the first time, I get a good look at Gia. She's petite. Fragile. Her eyes are heavily lined. Her hair is midnight black. What strikes me most about her, though, is her face. She's sad — even though she's laughing.

My hand drops off my leg and slips onto the sand. It's warm. So warm. I drag the tip of my finger over the coarse sand. It feels like roasted mustard seeds. My fingers trace patterns in the sand. I pick up a small handful and let the sand slide through my fingers. I scoop up another handful. This time, I let the warm sand drizzle over the openings in my leather-bound feet.

A soft, breathless sound escapes my lips.

Lethargically, I look back at Dante. He's burying Gia's feet in the sand. Her *bare* feet. Every time Dante piles sand over her feet, she smiles and closes her eyes.

I continue sprinkling sand over my well-protected feet. A small voice whispers, in the back of my head, *take off your sandals, you know you want to*. I do, I really do. I *so* want to take them off, but my father … his instructions were clear. *"Unless you are in your school shoes, do not, for whatever reason, remove these sandals when you are outside our home. Is that clear?"*

The message is clear, but the reasoning, not so much. I wear my school shoes when I'm away from home. They are not designed to protect me, like the sandals are. And yet, nothing bad has ever happened. Then I think, *did my father really say not to take them off? Or just that I should wear them when I'm away from him?*

My father *can be* overprotective.

These thoughts startle and confuse me. It's as if there's this small, dark voice, whispering in my head. *Take them off. There's no danger here.*

It's true. I look around me. The sea is calm. The sun is soothing. A gentle breeze stirs the branches on the palm trees. I feel no sense of danger here. Both Gia and Dante have taken off their flip flops. Nothing bad has happened to them. What harm can come from taking off my sandals? For a little while. A few minutes. That's all. Just so I can feel what it's like to have sand on my feet. In between my toes. That feels natural, on a beach. Wearing sandals in the sand does not.

The more I try not to think about burying my bare feet in the sand, the more I want to. Is this what temptation feels like? A nagging, insistent suggestion to do what you know you shouldn't, but so desperately want to do?

I resist. I cannot disobey my father two times in one day. That would be foolish.

How's he ever going to know? The dark voice slithers back inside my head.

He won't. I'll only have the sandals off for a few minutes. He'll never know.

I hesitate. And then, I untie the laces. My sandals slip off. I throw back my head. And then once again, I sigh.

It is only in a dark, hidden recess of my mind that I hear my father say, with that stern but loving, fatherly voice, *Remember, Kiriela, you're not in Heaven anymore.*

19. JADIEL

White not Black

Living without color is a special kind of hell. I have no idea how long I've been locked in here. Could be days. Maybe only hours. It feels like an eternity. The lack of color is a cruel form of punishment. It makes me anxious. I do a bunch of sit ups. That doesn't help, so I pace the room, looking for a spot of color. There has to be one, somewhere. The floor is hot. That means there's probably a geothermal pool, underneath my feet. All that time studying the geology of God's creation finally means something to me.

I stand over the hot spot, close my eyes and imagine the colors. The water in the pool is azure blue. There's steam rising off the water. A light-stone mist. I'm painting the picture in my mind. Around the pool there are volcanic rocks. Black rocks. And somewhere, there must be a heat source. Lava, maybe. I see the boiling river sliding down an active volcano. Lava is red, but there's also some orange. And yellow. I see the vibrant colors. And the colors comfort me. Calm me. Until …

The grate slides open and another note comes to me under another white meal. *Take responsibility for your error in judgment and you'll be out of here. Free to join the rest of the comrades.* I put my hands on my head and squeeze hard. "There was no error!" I feel like I'm losing control. Losing my mind.

Which is exactly what Lucius wants. A broken, compliant comrade.

The pressure is building. Building. BUILDING. My head feels like it's about to explode.

"Help me! Someone. Please! Help me!"

I bang my head against the wall. Again. And again. And AGAIN. A drop of blood falls to the floor. I freeze. Red. A spot of color. My mind accelerates. More blood means more red. More color. Less white. I'm about to do serious damage to my head when I hear movement above me. I look up. There's a small opening where the ceiling meets the wall. Sticking out of that opening is a pink nose. There's a scraping sound — stone against stone. A few pieces of gravel fall from the hole. Some dust. And then there are two eyes staring down at me. "Nube," I whisper.

A soft bleat answers me. I have no idea how she found me, but I do know that her presence isn't random. Slowly, the pressure in my head eases up. I calm down.

A wave of emotion sends me to my knees. And there, on my knees, I quiet my mind and find my strength. I eat my food. Not white rice and milk but fig and almond yogurt. That's what I'm eating. *That's what I'm eating.* I tell myself two more times, until finally, I believe it.

Calm now, in control, I push away the plate and fall back on the floor. Seconds later, I drift into a much needed, and until now, elusive sleep.

"Get dressed." Equus barges into the cell and jolts me out of sleep. "Lord Lucius wants you out of here." He throws a shirt and a pair of pants at me.

What? I must be dreaming. Lucius wants me out of here. *Why would he want that?*

"You are rebellious and impulsive." Equus spits out his descriptors with an extra dose of venom. "I can barely stand you. But Lord Lucius wants you out of here. Somehow, you've managed to impress him."

I'm half-awake now, at least I think I am. But I'm still not processing. Impressing Lucius is not on my agenda. My eyes blur, and then focus on the clothes Equus threw at me. My heart starts racing.

"No, it's the wrong color!" My voice rises. "These clothes are black. I wear white." My brain is flipping. *Why did he give me black clothes?*

"Get a grip." Equus tosses a pair of black boots at me.

I pick them up and hand them back. "I'm not wearing these. They're the wrong color."

White. *White.* That's the only color I can wear.

"Control yourself." Equus grabs my shoulders and forces me to look at him. "Forget about the color white."

"I can't." A bead of sweat trickles down my face. "It's all I see."

"Rethink what you see." He snatches the shirt off the floor. "What color is this?"

"Black. It's black, but —" I'm an angel. Angels wear white. *White.*

"What color do you wear?" Equus's voice is intense. "Control your mind. You did it before, managing to impress Lord Lucius. So, do it AGAIN."

"White, I wear —"

Equus slaps me. "Bind your mind. Bend it to your will."

I close my eyes. At first, all I see is myself dressed in white. I'm in Maion, ready to receive the morning blessing. I shake my head. No. I re-paint the picture. Black seeps in and takes over the white. I'm in Abaddon, working my way into the Inner Circle. Slowly, I open my eyes. And then, I wear my black clothes. "Now what?" I'm back in the game.

"You're going to go to class —" Equus breathes out a puff of pent-up air —"and you are going to pay attention to your next lesson." He hands me a bottle of water. "Here. Drink this."

I drain the bottle, and then follow Equus out of the white prison cell.

Class has already started when I enter the War Room. I look up at the chess board on the ceiling. My eyes gravitate toward the white pieces, but I force them to focus on the black ones. I keep my gaze fixed there until black is all I see.

I shift my attention downward. The students are staring at me. I don't look at them. I focus on the screen. There's a list of student rankings projected there. At the top of the list is an angel named Azazel. He's scored two contracts to my one. There's no doubt in my mind who that angel is. Comrade Brawn has one-upped me.

I stare straight ahead. By the next class, my name is going to be on the top of that list.

"Our lesson today focuses on the principle of mass." Professor Mendax nods at Professor Bellator, who flips to the next slide. A black and white image appears on the screen. "What do you see in this old photograph?"

"War ships," one of the students says.

"Army tanks," says another.

"Aircraft," someone else adds.

"A massive, unified attack plan." Azazel speaks with an arrogance that comes from being on top. His tone projects boredom and superiority. A lethal combination.

"Precisely." Professor Mendax shifts his sightless eyes to Azazel. "The principle of mass means exactly that. A coordinated attack that concentrates all of its power in a specific place at a specific time."

Azazel crosses his arms over his chest and sits back, clearly pleased with himself.

"An iconic example of "Mass" is the Normandy Invasion during wonderful World War II." Professor Mendax fists his right hand and points the ruby ring on his index finger at the screen. "This classic photograph is the perfect visual." He thumbs the side of his ring. A laser beam pointer hits the fleet of ships. "Forces by sea." The beam shifts to the aircraft. "By air." And then to the tanks. "By ground." A beautiful, organized attack appropriately named "Operation Overload."

"Awesome," one of the students says. "Look at all that military power."

Power which led to the liberation of Paris. I studied this in World History. The principle of Mass can liberate as well as it can destroy.

"The military power amassed here is impressive." Professor Mendax clicks off his pointer. "But it was the specificity of the attack that secured an Ally victory. There was a specific time and date for the invasion. Anybody know it?"

"6:30 a.m. on June 6, 1944," I say. I don't cross my arms. Or sit back in my chair. I'm not pleased with myself nor proud of what I know. I'm just glad my head is still able to think.

"Yes, Jadiel, that's correct. At this specific time, in a specific stretch of beach in Normandy, France, 5,000 battle ships, 50,000 armored tanks, 11,000 fighter jets and 156,000 troops attacked in mass. By June 11, the beach was secured. So" — Professor Mendax shifts his egg-white eyes around the room — "how do we apply this strategy to human beings?"

"We gain the tactical advantage by combining and increasing combat power." Azazel comes out with the answer first. No surprise there. He's on top.

"Yes." Professor Mendax nods, and then says, "We will mount an offensive assault in a specific area at a specific time. A coordinated effort with combined power for a devastating defeat. Your S.T.s have been given the specifics. Go now and enter into battle."

20. JADIEL
The Battle Begins

Fifteen minutes later, I'm out of Abaddon, on the Vista Linda lookout — a hill overlooking the marina. Rows of white boats are anchored in the water. *White.* The color triggers me. White is the color of punishment. *Will I be locked in one of those boats if I fail this mission?*

No. I refuse to allow my mind to focus on the boats. *Look at the houses,* I tell myself. The houses lining the shore are colorful. Red. Yellow. Pink. Many have blue tarps covering the roofs.

"Enjoying the view?" Equus comes up beside me. His tone taunts me.

A gull flies over the water. I focus on the bird's grey wings, and not on its white belly.

"Specific place," Equus says. "The Vista Linda lookout. Specific Time, 1500 hours." He stares out over the marina. "So far, you've had it easy. A signature for money and alcohol. Not challenging." His tone turns dark. "That changes today, with Operation Overload."

I match his gaze, staring with him out over the sparkling sea. Operation Overload is a coordinated attack against Dante Vega. I've been given the battle plan. Attack in mass. Multiple forces, one smooth, efficient, coordinated offensive. I am no more interested in attacking Dante than I was in signing on Armando. But it's a means to an end.

I focus on the colors in front of me. The Caribbean Sea is a painter's paradise. There is not just one color or one mood. Today, the sea is turquoise blue. Once, long ago, I would have wanted to paint the sea. Now, I find painting impossible.

I watch the waves. They curl higher, and then crash onto the shore. White foam rides on top of them. I stare at the black granite rock, far out at sea. *Black* is the color of victory. The color of my clothes. I finger the cuff of my shirt and ground my thoughts on the color black. Black is power. Black is one step closer to the Inner Circle. One step closer to Lucius.

"What's the strategy?" I say. The principle of mass is good in theory, but the victory is in the details.

"Start the offensive with the less important, expendable part of your troop. The foot soldiers. They serve only to instigate an altercation. When they have provoked your target and inflamed his emotions, send in Armando. These are your ground troops."

"And where is my air force? My navy?"

"Where they are most effective. In the air and on the water. Leave those forces to me. I will deploy them at the precise time they are needed."

I nod. "And what am I to offer our target in exchange for his signature?"

"What he values most," Equus says.

"Let me guess, protection for his little sister."

"No. Lord Lucius has something else in mind."

That rattles me. Not using Elena goes against all that Equus taught me about Dante's vulnerability. "So, what's the offer?" I speak calmly. Even though I'm far from it.

"A signed contract, in exchange for his life."

I force my eyes not to blink. That was not the answer I was expecting.

"I'm not killing him," I say flatly. "Should the bargaining not go according to plan."

Equus inhales, like he's annoyed with me. "Lord Lucius does not want him dead. That would be pointless. He wants him to sign a contract."

"Yeah, I *get* that. What I *don't* get is why you feel the need to threaten his life."

"Let's get the hierarchy straight, shall we?" Equus turns to face me. "*Lord Lucius* wants to threaten his life." His eyes bore into me. "Do you have a problem with that?"

"Yes, actually I do. It's inconsistent with the Lobster Principle. "How is a direct attack on the enemy's life a slow and measured, gradually-kill-the-lobster strategy?"

Equus glares at me. "Understand this, *comrade*. Your job is not to question why —"

"But to do or die. Yep, I get it."

It may not be my job to question Lucius's decisions. But by questioning them, I see the nature of my commander. He's capricious and inconsistent. I can use that information to my advantage when I get to the Inner Circle. Dutifully falling into line, I ask, "How, exactly, does" — I remember to add the title — "Lord Lucius want this attack to play out?"

"However you can make it happen." Equus's eyes turn a darker shade of black. "You're smart. I'm sure you can figure it out. But let me give you a hint." A slow smile pulls up the corner of his mouth. "Your well-trained brain isn't what you need for this particular assignment. Your well-trained body, however, is." He makes his point with a finger to my chest. "That and the help of Dante Vega's ex-friend and current enemy, Armando Ayala."

"I don't need Armando's help."

"No, you don't. But you do need the pain and humiliation that Armando adds to the equation." When he sees that I'm not following, he says, "One of our most effective forms of attack among humans is setting up conflict. Dante and Armando used to be inseparable, until

131

our forces provoked them into fighting over a useless girl. Now, these two are arch enemies. They hate each other. The emotional intensity that emotion brings is exciting to see. Use Armando. Give Lord Lucius a good show. But if Armando becomes too self-serving and threatens the mission, step in quickly. When human emotions are involved, shifts in power often follow."

"I'll handle it." I pull out my phone and text Armando. *Meet me at the Vista Linda lookout. Bring Pedro, Julián, and a couple of girls.* If it's a show Lucius wants, it's a show he'll get. And then I'll sign on Dante. With that signature, I will be two souls down and two steps closer to gaining Lucius's trust. And more importantly, physical assess to him.

"Dante Vega is down the hill to your right." Equus nods at a distant palm grove at the bottom of the hill. "He's with his fake girlfriend."

With that announcement, Equus turns and leaves without another word.

I look down and to the right. I see him. He's sitting with a girl that looks different from the ones who party at the mansion. She's not wearing bling. Instead of a gold chain around her neck, she has a silver one hanging from her skirt. Like Dante, she's dressed in black. Everything about her is dark. Her hair. Her makeup. The sandals she kicked off and tossed into the sand. Nothing about her gives any indication that she will oppose my advance on Dante. She's more interested in the texts coming in on her phone than in the boy who is sitting beside her.

My skin prickles. I scan the shoreline, from the coconut grove on my left to the mangrove channels on my right. I sense the presence of another divine being.

I rub my wrist. It's red and inflamed. I continue to survey my surroundings. Nothing. Maybe whoever was there fled from me. That would be the smart thing to do.

There's a rustle to my right. A gull squawks and takes off in flight. I search the area. Something has frightened it.

My heart kicks. And then races out of control. Through the palm trees, I see Kiriela.

Mixed emotions run through me. I can barely breathe. Most of what I feel is not good. Kiriela's presence, so close to the battleground, feels like a trap. *Why now? Why here?* Equus is taunting me. Threatening me. Messing with my head.

My heart pounds. She'll hate me if she sees me now. Lucius's soldier-in-training. For a fraction of a second, I think of hiding. But the thought of seeing her again grounds me. I suck air into my lungs, and then sprint down the hill and through the palm trees.

"Kiriela." I wish I wasn't panting. But at least I've kept my tone controlled. Muted excitement is safer than open emotion — just in case she's not as excited about seeing me as I am about standing here in front of her.

"Jadiel?" The way she says my name, with equal amounts of surprise and excitement, opens a fragile crack in my heart. She runs into my arms. "Are you all right?" Her wings envelop me. My blood pumps. "Tell me you're all right."

"I'm —" My words melt into her mouth. Her kiss is sweet. Mine long because I never want it to end.

Straining against every energized nerve in my body, I pull back. I don't have much time, and I need to know everything that happened to her.

"I see you still have your wings." My voice comes out strangled. I trail the tip of my finger down the edge of her feathers. "That's good."

I cheer inside. That she still has her wings means that she was not stripped of her status. I wonder if she notices, though. The tips of her wings have turned black.

She caresses my shoulders. "Release your wings," she whispers. "I want to feel them around me." She moves her hands to the back of my shoulders.

"No, don't." I cringe.

Her fingers press into my back. "Jadiel, your wings." Her eyes widen. "What —"

"Don't worry about it." My gut twists. I take my hand off her wings. A single white feather flutters to the ground. I pick it up. This one feather is more precious than all of mine combined. I pocket it. A slow warmth spreads over my thigh.

I push a hand through my hair. I have no idea what I'm supposed to say next. She tries to speak, but I hold up my hand. I stare at her bare feet while she makes circles in the sand with the tip of her toe. A pair of white leather sandals lie in the sand beside her.

For a moment, I can't breathe. I've never seen her without shoes. Her feet are slim and delicately arched. The tips of her toes are painted pink.

Forcing myself to look away, I say. "Did you stand trial?"

"Yes." The circles stop.

"What was the charge?"

"Unlawful gathering in a public place outside of specified hours."

I nod. A minor crime. Good. "And the punishment?"

"Exile to Earth."

"What?" A severe judgment for a minor crime. "Why? What happened?"

She looks up at me. "The Council wasn't as forgiving as Marius, who supported a six-month suspension from the school. The Council overruled him. They voted for exile."

The twist in my stomach just keeps getting tighter. "What are the terms of your exile? Is there a chance you can return to Heaven?"

She looks away. "Maybe. My case will be re-evaluated in six months. Restoration is possible. As long as I obey the rules."

"Which are?"

"Submitting to my father, having no contact with you." She manages a weak smile. "Simple things, like that."

I close my eyes. Our meeting like this is not a coincidence. "What about your father?" I press on. "What happened to him?"

"The Council found him guilty of breaking the law of peaceful co-existence among the inhabitants of Heaven." She relates the facts but there's an edge to her voice. "He was exiled to Earth, along with me."

"That doesn't make any sense." Adriel is Marius's most trusted military official. You'd think the Holy Warden would have had more influence over the Council.

"Jadiel, why …" Kiriela's tone shifts. She's not narrating anymore. "Why did you have to confront my father?" She's accusing. "You could have walked away."

Her accusation unleashes my defense. "And gone back to what? More secrets and lies?"

"Yes! At least with lies we weren't hurting anyone."

"No, no one." I look away. "Not even each other."

I rub my manacled wrist — an unconscious move. An unconscious, stupid move.

"What is that?" She stares in horror at the bracelet.

"Nothing." I feel the color drain from my face.

She grabs my arm, and with her finger, lifts up the chain. "Nothing?" she repeats.

I pull back my arm.

"Wait a minute." She takes back my arm and inspects the burn mark. "You're hurt."

"No big deal." The warmth of her hand on my arm makes the pain worth it.

"What's happened to you?" she whispers.

"Nothing. I can handle it."

"Jadiel, look at me." Raw fear rides under her voice. "Where, exactly, did the Council send you?"

"Didn't your father tell you?"

"He said you were sentenced to Abaddon." Her voice takes on a new intensity. "But where, *exactly*, is the school? We have to get you out of there."

"Not possible." I show her the bracelet. "I'm chained to it."

The horror on her face is painful to see. "Then we break the chain!"

My phone vibrates. I glance at the incoming text. "I have to go." I turn to leave, but the sound of a guitar holds me back. I follow the sound until my eyes land on Dante.

"That's Dante Vega," Kiriela says, shocking me.

"So it is." My throat tightens. "How do you know him?" The fact that she does sets off a warning bell. Nothing is random in Lucius's realm.

"He's Malakiy's charge."

Of course he is. Malakiy is assigned to all the humans with prices on their heads. Dark thoughts seep into my brain. Malakiy's presence is an obstacle for me. I will have a harder time getting at Dante with Malakiy protecting him. Unless ... I look around. Malakiy doesn't seem to be anywhere nearby. I can't sense his presence.

"Where's Dante's guardian?" I say, as casually as I can.

Her eyes shift away from me. "I'm not sure," she says, and then quickly corrects herself. "Around." She always was a bad liar. "It's not like he hovers over Dante all the time." She's talking fast now, uncomfortably fast. "He only stays close by when Dante is in danger."

"And the presence of a fallen angel so close to his charge doesn't call Malakiy's attention?"

"I don't see any fallen —"

I stare at her, forcing her to see what she does not want to. "Look a little closer, Kiriela."

She shakes her head. "No matter what you are trying to project, you're not going to hurt him." She speaks more confidently than she should. "Malakiy knows that. I know that. But if you try, I will protect Dante — from you and from anyone else who tries to hurt him."

I did not see that coming. But I should have. A vein throbs in my forehead. Kiriela always wanted to be a guardian angel. It's in her blood — her mother's DNA.

"Stay away from Dante," I say. "There's a price on his head. Malakiy was an idiot for leaving him unguarded. If you act on your impulse and try to protect that boy, your battle is going to be with me."

Her eyes open wide, as if she cannot believe what she is hearing.

I can barely believe it either. My new enemy may be the only true friend I have ever had.

Out of the corner of my eye I see Armando, Pedro, Julián, and a couple of girls. I take out my phone. In Armando's message box I write: *We need to move. Now.* Like a general commanding an army, I give my new recruit explicit instructions: *Weaken Dante. Throw a few punches. Insult him if you want to. But do not hurt him. I will do the rest.*

In Equus's message box I write: *Malakiy is AWOL. All the players are in place. I'm starting the attack.* And then with no identifiable emotion, I say to Kiriela, "Meet me back here in an hour. We need to talk."

"So, let's talk," she says. "Now."

"I can't." I shift my eyes to Dante. Now is the time to strike. I turn and walk away. With Malakiy out of the picture, Dante will be an easy target.

21. KIRIELA

Black Sand Beach

Jadiel walks away and I'm left picking up the pieces of my heart. The severance of all contact with Jadiel is the second term of my conditional exile. I watch him climb the hill above the marina. He's as strong as I remember him. Confident and self-assured. But there's a new vulnerability to him. He's been wounded. In ways I can't even imagine. He lost his wings. And even though he pretended he didn't care, he does. Angels cherish their wings. Our wings are our identity. Our connection with God. Our power. A wound as deep as the loss of his wings will drive Jadiel further into himself — and farther away from me.

Jadiel is at the top of the hill now. He's talking with someone there. *Wait a minute, that boy looks familiar.* I snap into high alert. The boy talking with Jadiel is Armando Ayala.

The warmth drains from me, and my mind goes into horror film freeze frame. Dante's enemy is not Armando, not directly, anyway. It's Armando, working under Jadiel's orders.

"You snake!" I reach for my sandals, pushing away panic. Jadiel may be strong, and he may have Armando's allegiance, but I have power, too. With the sandals my father gave me, I will be quick. Untouchable. I can save Dante from whatever evil Jadiel has planned before he has a chance to mobilize Armando.

My heart spikes. The sandals aren't there.

I collapse onto the beach and dig into the sand like a ravenous dog clawing for a buried bone. Sand flies from my hands. Black sand. I look up and over the beach. White waves crash over lava black sand. Someone with dark powers has taken over the beach.

I dig more furiously now. *How could I have been so stupid?* Those thoughts I allowed into my head about my father "just being over-protective," that was the enemy — messing with my head.

I keep searching, but my frantic effort does not uncover the missing sandals. I scan the horizon. Mind manipulation is one of the enemy's signature tricks. How could I have fallen for it? My heart thuds. Or was it Jadiel who implanted those thoughts? Who is the real enemy here?

I start to hyperventilate when I see my sandals, floating out to sea. I run to retrieve them. When I reach the shore, I splash into the water. Something sharp stings my ankle. I cry out. And then I panic. I don't know how to swim.

Terrified, I force myself to go forward. The waves grow stronger. They push me back. I fight their force and move forward. But then the wind picks up. A brutally unnatural wind that knocks me down and blows me onto the beach. The sand sucks me down and slimy strands of seaweed tangle around my legs, binding my ankles. I see my sandals, bobbing in the distance, but I can't reach them. They float further and further from my grasp.

For one sinful moment of pleasure, I lost the only gift my father ever gave me.

Winged sandals that would have given me the power to save Dante.

22. DANTE

Enemy Attack

"Gia, get up." I reach for my flip flops. Someone is in the trees behind us. I glance over my shoulder. An iguana scurries, startled, around a nearby palm tree.

"What the...?" Gia sits up. Her eyes flit over the beach. "The sand ... it's —"

"I know." My heart pounds like a tightened snare drum. The sand is black.

I scan the shore. It's gotten dark. Something bad is about to happen. Behind me there's shouting. Laughter. I look over my shoulder. Two girls and their pumped-up partners stumble out from the trees. My blood chills. It's Pedro and Julián, together with their latest sidekicks.

My heart goes into overdrive and for a moment, I stop breathing. I try to ignore the group behind me, but I know they will never ignore me.

"¡Oye, maricón!" Julián shouts.

I react, but only internally. A bead of sweat pops out on my brow.

Female giggles join with male laughter. A stone hits its mark on the back of my head.

Seriously? I spring to my feet. Another rock follows, landing in the middle of my chest.

"What the hell's your problem?" I shout.

"Yo, dude, you're our problem." Julián spits out a few expletives and the usual gay rocker slurs.

I tolerate his idiocy for two slow beats before I shout, "Go to hell!"

I pull Gia to her feet. "Come on, let's get out of here."

"If anyone knows how to get to hell," Julián's sidekick says, "I'm sure it'd be you!"

I try not to say what I know will be ugly but resist the temptation for all of two seconds. "Why don't you descend into The Darkness with me," I shout at the girl, using the standard satanic rocker trash to return her insult. "Looks like you'll go anywhere with anybody."

I flatten my hand on Gia's back. "Start walking," I say. Then I freeze in my tracks. Armando is standing on the top of the hill, like a general, observing his mobilized army. Beside him stands a dark-looking dude dressed in black.

Slowly, the dark dude raises his arm. And then, chaos.

Julián charges after me. Two seconds later, Pedro joins him. Pedro pins my arms to the ground with his knees and sits on my chest. Julián holds down my legs. I fight to get loose, but they have the advantage, easily aborting my struggle and rendering me defenseless.

Julián continues throwing out his tediously unoriginal insults, but Pedro is more specific in his attack. "Armando says you came on to that new girl."

Get up. On your feet, is all I can think. I push Pedro off, but Julián takes his place. I don't see the punch that leaves my ears ringing.

Julián shifts on top of me and reaches into his pocket. I hear a sharp click. And then I see the knife. Julián switches open a blade and slides it under the silver dragon hanging from a chain around my neck.

"Nice necklace." Pedro lifts the chain with the tip of his knife.

The blade slices the underside of my chin on the uptake.

"What're you doing?" One of the girls grabs Julián by the arm and distances the knife from me. "You crazy?"

I gag and roll over on my side.

"*¡Suéltame!*" Julián jerks his arm away. "Let go of me!" He retracts the blade and shoves the girl back. Then he takes two steps forward and grabs her by the upper arms. He shakes her roughly. "Stay out of it, Yari." He shakes her again and she flops like a rag doll in his hands. My eyes land on Gia. She looks petrified. Painfully, I dig the car keys from my pocket.

"*Toma.*" I toss the keys at her. "Go. Get out of here."

She takes off and I brace myself for the next attack.

"Leave, all of you." Armando saunters into the scene and takes charge of his minions. There's a chilling, confident look in his eyes, the eyes of a sociopath calculating his next move. "Go" He dismisses his soldiers. The metal end of a broken fishing pole gleams in his hand.

Like good soldiers, his army obeys.

"*Vámonos.*" Pedro jerks his head toward the parking lot. "Let's go."

"*Pendejo.*" Julián sends me to hell with a swift kick to the gut.

I groan and fold my body into a fetal position.

"Get up." Armando grabs me and in one swift, powerful move, yanks me to my feet. "This is between you and me now." He raises the rod.

The first blow hits hard. I stagger back. The beach washes out to white. The next hit strikes me to the ground. But I don't go down alone. As I fall, I snag Armando's shirt and drag him to the sand with me. He drops the rod. I roll over, straddling him. "Hit me again, asshole, and it's the last thing you'll ever do." With Armando immobilized, I pummel his face. And for one fleeting, insane moment, I feel like the boxer Miguel Cotto — knocked to the tarp but ready to get up and KO my opponent. Seconds later, Armando slams me back to reality.

"You think you can take me down?" Armando grips my wrist and holds back my fist. "Think again, *cabrón.*" His voice takes on the tone of Heath Ledger's joker — slow, methodical. Psychotic.

I struggle to my feet.

Armando is already standing. His steel-toed boot knocks the life out of my stomach.

Steel-toed boots? This is not the Armando I know.

I clutch my gut and gasp for air. Then I grab a handful of sand and fling it into Armando's eyes, thwarting the next attack.

I stagger back, and then trip over a fallen coconut. My ankle twists out from under me. A sharp pain shoots up my leg. I collapse into the sand.

Armando goes for the rod. The maniac doesn't say anything. He just roars — like a freaking psycho in a B-rated horror flick. He pulls back his arm. "You fucking piece of shit!" Then he takes another crack at my bleeding head.

As the world spins around me, I hear voices, but they sound vague and distant. A girl cries out from somewhere far away. Armando shouts something about killing me, but I can't register the threat. Rage, or maybe too much rum, has distorted his voice.

Armando pulls back his arm. But before he can split open my skull, I grab the coconut and hurl it. The hard shell draws blood when it hits his face.

23. JADIEL

Enemy Offense

I flex my fist. *Enough*. Armando is losing control. Tedious predictability. I want this to be over. In a few long strides, I'm down the hill and on the beach.

"I'll take it from here." I toss Armando aside. He lands on his back several feet away.

I stand in front of Dante. "This fight is going nowhere." I grab the neck of Dante's shirt and pull him to his knees. "So, let's get to the important part." My hand shoots behind Dante's head and catches the silver chain around his neck. "I'm going to make you a deal." I wrap the chain around my hand, forming a noose around his neck. Deliberately, I find the sweet spot between twisting tight enough to choke him without strangling him.

Dante digs his fingers underneath the chain, desperate to lift the coiled dragon pendant off his windpipe.

"Here's how it works." I pull tighter on the chain. "I let you live." I give a sharp twist. "And you pledge your life to me."

Dante punches my arm in a frantic attempt to pop my elbow and break the hold on my throat. I hiss but do not fold.

"You're making this more difficult than it needs to be." I twist the chain tighter. "Do you want to live?" I reach for the discarded rod. "Or die?"

The rod is a prop I don't plan on using. But the decision to reach for it costs me whatever control I had. In the fraction of a second it takes for me to pick up the pole, the chain slackens, offering Dante a small window of advantage.

Dante slaps his hands against my chest and pushes me back. "If I die," he chokes out, "I'll drag you down with me." The chain snaps and breaks off his neck.

The power reversal leaves me stunned. A low growl explodes from my mouth. I raise my arm. The fishing pole gleams red in the sun. "You can't take me down," I snarl. "I'm already there." The pole raised over my head lengthens as the sun outlines its shadow on the sand. *What am I doing?* The shadow jolts me. I lower the rod. I swore I was not going to harm this boy.

I back away from Dante. But then Armando, unhinged and homicidal, grabs the rod from me. The pole comes down and Dante crumples to the sand.

"No!" I rush forward.

There's a flash of light. Movement on my right side. A wave of warmth envelopes me. And then the beach, and everything on it, fades into white light.

I shield my eyes and back away from the light. My legs shake, and I trip over the discarded pole. A figure forms inside the light.

"Malakiy." I hiss the word like a snake about to strike.

The light grows dimmer. Waves break against the shore. The last thing I see before the light finally fades is the dragon pendant, partially buried in the sand. And then there is nothing but a cold and terrifying darkness.

Something evil is near.

24. JADIEL

Darkness Descending

There is no moon. No stars. No light of any kind. Loose planks creak on the dock. The air smells of sulfur and salt. The beach and everything on it is cloaked by the descending darkness.

"Malakiy?"

A cold chill runs through me. I was expecting to hear Equus's voice. Or maybe even Lucius's. Not Kiriela's.

"Where are you?" she says.

"I'm here, Kiriela." Malakiy's voice sounds far away.

"Where?"

"Beside Dante."

"Is he okay?"

Somewhere at the pier a shutter bangs. Over and over again. Boats knock together, and the scary sounds of the night grow louder and more intense.

"He's unconscious but alive," Malakiy says.

Good. I dig out my phone. The boy does not deserve to die.

"Where were you?" Kiriela says. "You left Dante unprotected."

"He was ambushed. I came as fast as I could."

A dog barks. Something rustles in the branches of a nearby tree.

"Malakiy?"

"Follow my voice, Kiriela."

"Keep talking," she says.

"Here, take my hand."

"What happened to our light?"

"God is angry," Malakiy says.

"It's all my fault." Kiriela's voice sounds sad. "I wasn't smart enough to stop him."

I cringe. The sadness in her voice. Her inability to say my name. She must hate me now. Maybe almost as much as I despise myself. She should never have taken off her sandals. She made it too easy for Equus to toss them into the sea. Too easy for me to allow it. Had she interfered with Lucius's plan, she would have set herself up to become his next target. At least this way, Malakiy will become Lucius's new interest.

"No, Kiriela," Malakiy says. "It's my fault. When I received a supposed order to go to Haiti, I should have questioned it. Something didn't seem right."

Wait, *what?* I take two seconds to process what I heard. Equus probably already knew, before I texted him, that Malakiy was out of the way. It was probably him who sent the fake work order. Why, I wonder, did he not tell me?

"Where's Dante?" Kiriela's concern for this human boy is unmistakable. It was only a matter of time before she would become who she was meant to be. A protector.

"Here. On my other side. He's safe."

The air turns cold. A light bobs in the distance. And then Equus and his pet creep up behind me.

"Does he really believe that?" Equus talks over my shoulder. "Does he really think that Dante is safe?"

I don't answer, but yes, he does. As long as Malakiy is around, everyone is safe.

"Lord Lucius is not happy." Equus steps into the beam from Chupa's head lamp. His face looks distorted in the fragile light. "Do you know what he is saying?"

"Do you think I care?"

"You will." Equus pauses while Chupa snorts out a laugh. "When you understand what this failure will cost you."

Chupa is snickering so hard that his light bobs schizophrenically over the sand.

"What's wrong with you?" I shout at the beast. And then I turn to Equus and finally ask what I have been wondering ever since I first met Chupacabra. "Why is he wearing a lamp strapped to his head?"

Chupa stops laughing. He's growling now. And then suddenly, the light from his lamp grows dim. His eyes widen. His head thrashes from side to side. The light goes out. And then Chupa lunges for his master.

"It's okay, Chupa. I have another bulb." Chupa quivers beside his master while Equus digs into his pocket and produces a replacement light bulb. He screws it into Chupa's headlamp. The light comes back and Chupa returns to his pre-crisis, obnoxious self. He bares his teeth, as if that will make him look fearful.

Finally, I get it. Chupacabra is afraid of the dark. Who knew? Even demon pets have their insecurities.

"You want to tell me why you didn't inform me that Malakiy is Dante's special protector?" I force Equus back to the more important issue at hand. "That's the kind of information you might have wanted to share."

Equus ignores me. He's staring at Kiriela. "An interesting hybrid, that one. A friend of yours?"

My heart stops. The way he says *friend* sends up warning bells. "Just someone I used to know." I start to walk away, hoping Equus will follow. I have to get him away from Kiriela.

"Chupa." Equus sends his guard dog after me. The brute blocks my path.

"Get out of my way." I move around Chupa, but then Equus grabs my arm.

"Leaving so soon?" He grips my arm tighter. "Don't you want to hear what your friend has to say? She's talking to God."

"So?" I shake off his arm. "That's her business, not mine."

"Is it now? You might change your opinion when you hear who she is praying about."

My spiritual trainer's smooth set-up leaves me cold but hanging on Kiriela's not-so-private prayer.

"You're not going to leave him here to die, are you God?" Kiriela's voice drops to a whisper. "Please, please help him."

"What a faithful angel," Equus says. "Just the type Lord Lucius likes to attack."

"Leave her out of this."

It is pure torture, standing here, listening to her pray over the same boy I am supposed to sign over to Lucius. But even more excruciating is hearing Equus Centurion's mocking tone that tells me I am being set-up.

"Interesting." Equus stares at me. "Looks like someone has a rather passionate concern for an angel he *only used to know*." He shifts his gaze from me to Kiriela. "She seems quite attached to our target. Quite dedicated to protecting him from — *who?*" He pretends to think. "Oh yes, *you*." A slow smile lifts the corner of his mouth. "That makes the pursuit of Dante Vega even more challenging, wouldn't you say? Considering she's still bound to the rules and laws of Heaven."

There's no denying it. Kiriela still answers to Heaven's laws. The fact that she has her wings makes that clear. But she is not a guardian angel. So, what is going on between her and the boy who is now my target? She does seem to have an overly intense interest in his well-being. Negative thoughts, but I can't shake them. The mind is Abaddon's greatest battlefield.

"Quite unexpectedly," Equus Centurion continues, "your friend has handed me the perfect opportunity for your next lesson: how to break down the spiritual stronghold of prayer." He snaps his fingers and Chupacabra leaps to his side. "I want you to listen too," he says to his pet. Chupa wags his tail. "Today you are going to learn how to take control of a human mind."

"She's not human," I have to say.

"You'd be surprised how human an angel can be. Wait and watch."

Equus closes his eyes. "Mind control is all about taking dominion over the air, which is Lord Lucius's true power here on Earth. All you need to do is concentrate on the power that is inside of you. A power you already used without knowing it."

Power I like. Using it against Kiriela, not so much. I don't even attempt what Equus is doing — some kind of swirly evil-wizard-type of motion with his hands.

"Now imagine your power being released from your head and seeping into your victim's mind. With that transfer of energy, you whisper what it is you want her to hear."

The wind blows and onto it he whispers to Kiriela, "God is not listening." And then he says to me, "The intention of prayer manipulation is to keep the victim from the serious pursuit of praying altogether. This detestable activity makes both humans and angels momentarily immune to demonic influence. But with the right strategy, you can break through the barrier she has erected." He stares at Kiriela. "In this case, I implanted doubt, the purpose of which is to turn the subject's focus away from God and toward herself. Watch what happens."

"Where are you, God?" Kiriela's voice wavers. "Why aren't you answering me?"

"Excellent." Equus smiles. And then he points a warning finger at me. "But don't get too comfortable, the Enemy will not be idle. Whenever there is prayer, there is the danger that God will intervene."

God being synonymous with *The Enemy* has still not sunk into my psyche.

A siren wails. Secretly, I'm relieved. The sound of the siren grows closer and then an ambulance stops a few feet away. Equus's face grows hard. And then he turns on me. "You weren't working with me." As if it was my fault that his lesson failed.

He digs into his pocket and pulls out his phone. "Prayer interruption strategy unsuccessful," he says as he writes. And then he is silent but continues to thumb out his text.

There is no doubt in my mind who he is texting. And what information he is providing that can be used against me.

Equus pockets his phone. "You are resisting your training." He watches as the paramedics load Dante into the ambulance. "Go to the hospital and sign on Dante."

"He's not conscious."

"I know what that girl means to you." Equus stares straight ahead. "She is not safe if you are unsuccessful. Deliver Dante to me ... or she will pay the price of your stupidity."

25. DANTE

Gumby Legs

The sound of a siren swirls over my head. Red streaks circle the sky.

Runnnn! The voice in my head sounds like a nightmare version of my own, echoing and stretching like a psychedelic zombie. *It's the cops.*

I try to run, but the effort gets me nowhere. I'm stuck inside my own head.

"Splint his right leg." A muffled voice speaks from a parallel universe.

Go! I command my legs to move, but my mind has gone into freeze frame. *Run, damn it!* I curse my Gumby legs — for they feel that wide and flat and soft. My rubber legs move up and down, but I'm only going through the mechanics of motion, not the action of it.

My heart hammers a blow to my chest. The siren screams. And then I feel myself being lifted in the air. I struggle to break free, but I'm immobilized.

I cry out. First in fear. And then in pain.

"Start a morphine drip."

The air around me thickens and I fight to breathe.

"Hook him up to oxygen."

My chest heaves as it claws for air.

And then suddenly, my mind expands. Swirling red flashes morph into flames. The sky darkens and the sea smolders. *"You're going down with me."* An evil voice hisses over the blackened sky.

No! I fight against the voice.

A black, shifting shape passes over my body.

"Stay away from him!" A glittering trail of light parts the darkness and an angel, with flowing hair and shining armor, materializes against the smoking sky.

Evil laughter echoes back from the abyss. *"It is I who rule here, Malakiy."*

I pass out, evil voices echoing in my head.

"Dante. Can you hear me?" A soft voice seeps through the horror, calling out my name.

My eyes twitch, but I can't open them. Something soft brushes over my forehead and then I hear the female voice again.

"Everything's okay now," the voice says, gently. "You're safe."

I nod. And with what little strength I can find, crack open my eyes.

Shapes and colors swim before me, silver, red, and white. I hear the rustle of movement and a low beep that sounds like my alarm clock. I reach to hit the snooze bar but can't lift my arm. A fuzzy white shape fades in and out of sight.

I blink, try to focus, and then blink again. The shape morphs into a beautiful girl dressed in white. "Where am I?" The words come out slowly in a voice that sounds drugged.

"You're in the hospital." The girl's voice is sweet. I want to tell her that but can't get my mouth to move. It's then I notice that I'm lying flat on a bed enclosed by silver rails.

"I'm *where*?" I stare at the girl, unable to look away. It's as if all the love in the universe has pooled in the sapphire blue of her eyes. "Who are you?" She looks otherworldly, but at the same time, familiar. My mind battles through the fog. I know this girl, but I can't place her.

"I'm" — her voice wavers — "your nurse." She moves closer to the bed. I'm enveloped by a warm, white light. "I need to ask you a few questions." She hesitates, as if wondering what to do next. "For the neurological record," she adds. Her eyes land on a metal holder at the end of the bed. She slides out my chart, and then pulls a pen from her pocket. She snaps at the pen's four-colored tabs before finally pushing down on the black one and releasing the point. "Can you tell me your name?" She fumbles with the pen.

I continue to stare at her. She's beautiful. Her skin sparkles, as if brushed with silver glitter. "Are you an angel?" I say. Because what other explanation could there be?

Her eyes get huge, and her thumb slips as she clicks and releases the tabs on her pen.

I scrunch my brow, grimace, and eventually become aware of the dull pressure in my head. It feels as if my brain is being squeezed between two sides of a tightening vice. Even if she is an angel, I am definitely not in Heaven.

"Dante," I finally say, answering her question.

"And your last name?" Her voice trembles slightly and she clicks the pen again.

I swallow and look past her to the monitor beside the bed. Blankly, I stare at the red line that peaks and falls, peaks, and falls.

"Please," she says, sounding slightly desperate. "I need to know if you're all right."

My eyes slide back, meet, and hold onto hers. "Excuse me," I say. "But are you for real?"

This time, she drops the pen.

I'm sorry I can't pick it up for her. When she bends down to get it, I look away.

"Vega," I eventually say.

"What?" She clutches the pen to her chest.

"Vega," I say again. "My last name." I want to add an apology for the rudeness I hear in my voice, but gasp against a spike of pain instead.

"Oh, right." Her hand shakes as she scribbles on the chart.

I stare at the clipboard. And then look harder. The page is blank. Weird, I think. And then I cringe. It's too painful to think.

She moves closer and places her hand on my head. Slowly, the dull ache subsides. The pain is still there, but I feel sheltered — as if she has folded me into the soft underside of an angel's wing.

"Do you know what month it is?" she says.

"May." My lids droop over my eyes.

The pen snaps.

My eyes roll open and my bandaged hand tightens over the bed rail.

"Are you sure?" She sounds worried. "Are you sure it's May?"

My mind groans.

"No," I finally say, after processing her question. "It's only August."

Even now and only half conscious, I want it to be May — the first month of summer, the last of school. This time the groan that comes from my mouth is audible and loud.

"Are you okay?" She moves forward, and then stumbles back.

The space she vacates feels large, and lonely, and empty. I stare past her toward the far wall. There are cracks in the concrete and the blue paint has started to fade. "Do I look okay?" I close my eyes. "Sorry." I feel like a first-class jerk. "It's not your fault I'm here."

I hear a sharp intake of breath, and then feel the bed shake — as if she has staggered against it. The movement makes my head throb. I clutch the top sheet. A sharp stab of pain pierces my fisted hand. My eyes fly open. And then I see the needle taped against my skin.

"No!" I rip out the needle. Blood spurts. A machine sounds an alarm.

My mind flashes back to when I was five years old. I'm trying to get my father's attention, arms stretched out like airplane wings. "Look at me, Papi. I'm J.J. the Jet Plane." I trip. Fall forward, hit my face on the floor. And then there's blood. So much blood. *"Stop crying."* Papi's voice is harsh. My two front teeth dangle from the gums. The pain is bad, my fear, worse. I scream all the way to the hospital. *"Shut the fuck up."* My father grabs hold of my face so that the doctor can do his job. The needle draws blood when it pierces my gum.

The door swings open and once again I am seventeen. A man wearing a white lab coat enters the room, followed by a uniformed policeman.

"What happened?" The man in the white coat rushes forward.

There is no one there to answer his question.

The man snatches a gauze compress off the bedside table and presses it over my hand. He applies pressure, but I fight against him.

"Take it easy," the man says evenly. He speaks urgently but his voice is calm.

Blood rushes from my head and I feel faint. But then I notice that the needle, and the tube attached to it, is gone. Slowly, I stop fighting.

"Where's the nurse?" the man says, scanning the room.

"I'm here," says a flustered, middle-aged woman with gray streaks in her hair. She's still panting from the effort of having run into the room.

I blink. That is *not* my nurse.

"Don't restart the I.V.," the man says to the woman-who-is-not-my-nurse. "Give him oral liquids to keep him hydrated." Pressing two fingers against my wrist, he clocks my pulse.

"But doctor, what about the pain?" says the impostor nurse.

"I'll take care of it," the doctor says.

I stare at the man the nurse called *doctor*. He looks vaguely familiar. He has blonde hair and powerful shoulders. More Hulk Hogan than Patch Adams.

"God must have special plans for you." The doctor releases my wrist. "Just a few centimeters lower and that blow would have killed you." He points to a spot on my neck, the tips of his fingers hovering over but not touching the skin. He draws back his hand and stares at me. His expression doesn't waver. Not even when I scowl.

My eyes droop and my head rolls to the side. I'm almost out when I hear …

"Excuse me, young man." The voice that speaks now is rough and tired and does not belong to the doctor. "I need to ask you a few questions." Someone places a hand on my shoulder. It isn't a soft hand, like the girl's. Or a gentle one, like the doctor's. It is a thick hand. I want to shrug it off but find I don't have the strength to move.

"Dante." It's a kinder voice now, the doctor's voice. "I know this is not the best time, but Officer Collado has a few questions he'd like to ask you."

My eyes flutter. "I don't feel like talking." I hear the creaking of leather, a holster being re-adjusted, and then feel a heavy presence over the bed.

"Do you know the boys who did this to you?" A rough, impatient voice forces me awake.

My eyes crawl open and land on Officer Collado. He looks like a cross between an aging Harley biker and Porky Pig. Chest hair sticks out through the open buttonhole on his official blue uniform.

"I said I don't feel like talking." I let escape a low, irritated sigh. "Didn't you hear me?" Why do adults think they have the right to ask a question and ignore the response?

"Yes, we heard you." The doctor holds the cop back with his hand. "I apologize." His eyes penetrate my defiant stare. "I know you're hurting, but the sooner Officer Collado can file his report, the better for his investigation."

I hold the doctor's gaze. "Fine." I shift my eyes to Officer Collado. *To serve and protect* reads the man's badge, *la policía de Puerto Rico*.

The lines around the cop's mouth tighten as he flips open a small spiral-bound notebook. His bushy brows meet and crease as he brings the point of his pencil to the empty page.

"Do you know the boys who attacked you?" There is barely concealed anger under his clipped professional tone.

"No," I say, in a bored, tough voice reserved especially for Officer Collado. "I don't."

The cop looks up from his notepad. "You sure about that?"

I turn my eyes to the ceiling. There's a large brown water stain above my head.

"Their names, son, what're their names?"

My eyes shoot back down, landing on Officer Collado's bloated face. "I am not your son." A muscle tightens in my jaw. "Don't call me that." It hurts to frown.

Officer Collado shifts his eyes to the doctor, who is writing on a prescription pad. The doctor communicates restraint with nothing more than the power of his eyes. The cop brings his fist to his mouth, coughs harshly, and looks away.

"I can't make an arrest," he says, his voice tightly controlled, "unless you identify your attackers."

I watch the doctor rip off the top sheet of his pad and hand the paper to the impostor nurse. Does Collado really think I am going to name my attackers? With the kind of power Armando has? I may be stupid, but I'm not insane.

"They weren't from around here," I finally say, more for the doctor's sake than the cop's. I never met a man before who could command that kind of authority without abusing it. "I've never seen them before."

I cringe at the half truth, but it's not totally a lie. I have no idea who that dark dude was.

The door swings open, and the imposter returns, saving me from further interrogation. She has a small plastic cup in her hand.

The doctor takes the cup from her. "Thank you, that will be all." He turns to Officer Collado, "The boy needs to rest. I'll contact you as soon as I know anything."

"Fine." Collado can barely keep the aggression from his voice. He presses his lips together, and then swaggers out the door.

After he leaves, the doctor turns his back to me. Seconds later, he places the cup in my hand. "Here, take this." There's a small white pill in the bottom of the cup. He pours a glass of water from the pitcher on the nightstand.

I take the water and swallow the pill. My head sinks like lead onto the pillow. Whatever's in this pill is welcome. I'm drifting off to a pain free place.

26. KIRIELA

Dante's Angel

After Malakiy leaves the room, I return to Dante. He'll soon fall into a peaceful, angelically altered sleep. Malakiy added a little supernatural to the synthetic pill he offered Dante as his "doctor." In about two seconds, Dante will have no conscious awareness of his surroundings and will be pain free.

My stomach twists. The seriousness of what I did weighs heavily on me. My insides have tied themselves into a gigantic knot and I feel as if I'm strapped to a medieval stretching rack — with boulders piled on top of my collapsing chest. Not only did I fail to protect Dante, but I failed to tell Malakiy the truth about me and Jadiel. If Malakiy knew that Jadiel had approached me, he would have been the avenging angel I hope Jadiel never sees. Part of me still wants to believe that Jadiel does not deserve to be cut down with all the force of Heaven. But if he does, that vengeance will come from me.

With a heavy heart, I return to Dante's side. Despite what happened, I will not fail to comfort the boy I could not protect.

"You're back." Dante's eyes are closed, his speech lethargic.

How does he know I'm here?

"I can feel your presence." He groans and that triggers me.

No. No. No. I feel my body changing. There's a tingling on the back of my shoulders. My skin is hot. I fight to suppress my wings but they're straining to be released. Helpless against a force I can't control, I silently plead, *Don't open your eyes. Please. Please. Don't —*

Dante opens his eyes. And even though he's half out of it, he's completely focused.

On my wings.

"You are an ..." He can't continue. His mind is floating. Sleep weighs down his eyes. He tries to fight it, but his body is crashing.

I breathe out a sigh of relief. With him at peace, my wings will retract. I place my hand on his cheek and keep it there. His eyes flutter. The corners of his mouth lift. And then he's out. Deep into a drug-induced, angel-softened sleep.

"What are you doing?" Malakiy's voice startles me. "Your wings are out!"

"I know. I'm sorry." The heaviness in the pit of my stomach weighs down my voice. "I couldn't control them." My face asks the question my mouth cannot. *Why?*

Malakiy breathes out an exasperated sigh. "Your protective instinct is stronger than your resolve. It's triggering the release of your wings." He presses his hand over Dante's forehead. The tension lines around Dante's mouth relax. Malakiy can't heal Dante. But he can block the pain. "He's out now." Malakiy looks at me. "Stay with him. I have to talk to the nurse." He turns to leave.

"Malakiy ..." My voice falters.

"Yes?" Malakiy looks at me impatiently.

"How did you work directly beside that nurse without her suspecting anything?"

"I know how to control my powers," he says. "She wasn't seeing me. She was seeing Dante's doctor." He hesitates, and then adds, "It's called transfiguration, a skill they teach in senior year."

I brave another question. "What is Dante seeing when he looks at me?"

"You are not real to him, Kiriela. Except in his dreams."

Malakiy turns from me and heads for the door, but I can't let him go without asking one final question. "Have you had any communication with my father?"

Malakiy stares at me. A muscle jumps in his jaw. "He's furious, Kiriela."

My throat tightens. "If he would just let me explain." My wings droop, and then retract.

Malakiy shakes his head. "He won't hear you now."

"I know." I study the floor. There is nothing to explain. I lost his precious gift.

"Let some time pass. He'll calm down. But be careful. He's watching you."

I nod. My father may not be omniscient, but with all the surveillance equipment he has at his disposal, I don't doubt that he is monitoring my every move.

"Stay here," Malakiy says. "I'll be back."

Malakiy slips out the door and I sink into the chair beside Dante's bed. My father may calm down, but I will never stop feeling like what I lost is more than a pair of sandals. I swallow against the wedge that has formed in my throat. The one happy memory I have of my father will be erased by the sadder memory of his fury. He will never care for me in the same way again.

The door swings open. "Is he okay?" Jadiel bursts into the room.

"Get out of here." I jump out of the chair. My wings unfurl. I spread them over Dante.

"I'm not going to hurt him."

"You already have."

"No, I haven't." Jadiel talks fast, like he always does when he's trying to prove his innocence. "He was not supposed to get hurt. Armando went rogue, he disobeyed my order —"

"Your order?" My wings tremble in fury. "What are you now, Lucius's Lieutenant?"

"No, that's not what I meant." Jadiel trips over his words. "The plan was to intimidate him. Not to harm him."

I don't buy the defense.

"Let me put it to you this way," I say. "Since you seem to have developed a new fondness for military lingo, tell me, who is responsible for a failed offensive? The foot soldiers or the commanding officer?" Let no one ever doubt that I am the daughter of the highest-ranking military official in Heaven. Least of all, Jadiel.

"All right, point taken. But I am not the enemy here, Kiriela."

"*Really?*" I shut my mouth and hold my breath. Cutting oxygen to my brain should stop the angry thoughts that are forming in my head. "You're working for Lucius. What part of that tells me you are not the enemy?"

My body drains of warmth. The voiced truth pierces me like a stab to the heart.

"And my sandals did not end up in the sea by themselves. They were thrown there, by someone who was working against me." The intensity of my heightened emotions compels me to add, "Or maybe it was *you* who tossed them into the sea."

"No, it wasn't me." His hands are trembling. "But I did allow it." Despite his shaking hands, his voice is firm. "It was the only way to stop you from getting involved."

"That was not your choice to make."

"Maybe not. But it was my choice to keep you off Lucius's radar."

A glimpse of the Jadiel I once knew surfaces. Hope tempers my anger. He is not completely lost to me.

"If you had not stopped me," I say, "Malakiy and I would have stopped you. And Lucius would have gotten the message. Dante is protected by a force far greater than him. Lucius would have run away like a wounded pup who lost the fight."

"Maybe." The tension in his face relaxes. "Or maybe he would have only made you believe that. Lucius is more cunning than you give him credit for."

"I'm not afraid of him. Are you?"

Jadiel's eyes soften when he looks at me and says, "I'm not afraid of him. I'm afraid for you." His eyes shift to the door. "Someone's coming." He scribbles a phone number on a pad he snatches off the bedside table. "If anything feels not right, call me." He rips off the top sheet and shoves it at me. "Nothing is at it seems anymore." He turns and walks out the door. Even before it has swung completely closed, a young girl rushes into the room.

"Dante!" The young girl's black school shoes clatter over the tiles as she charges across the floor. "Are you all right?" She grabs a handful of sheets and pulls herself onto the bed.

I snap back my wings and pray I have the power to disappear. Unlike Jadiel, I can't walk out the door. There's a woman standing there, blocking the exit. I vanish behind the curtain of the unoccupied bed on the other side of the room.

"Elena!" The woman rushes in after the girl. "Get down from the bed!"

I peek through a crack in the curtain. Dante's eyes move under the lids, but he doesn't open them. He cringes as Elena throws herself on top of him, but he doesn't push her away.

"It's okay, Ma." His voice is slow. "She can stay."

His mother sighs. She takes his hand and squeezes it between hers. "Your sister raced me here." She speaks softly. "She was so worried." Eyes closed, she kisses his bandaged hand. Over and over again. "Thank God you're all right."

"*Ya*, Mom. Enough." Dante slides his hand out from under hers. He's waking up.

"What happened to your hand?" Elena grabs his bandaged hand. She cups it between hers. "It looks hurt."

Dante cringes. And then, in a voice barely audible he says, "You only think it looks hurt, and that's good, because I was trying to make it look like a boxer's hand." With a slight grimace, he slides Elena to his side. "I was thinking about dressing as Felix Trinidad for Halloween," he whispers. "What do you think? Should I go trick-or-treating with you dressed like a boxer?"

Elena giggles. "You would look funny."

"I suppose I would." His mouth lifts into a weak smile. "How was school today?"

The giggles end. "It was terrible." She snuggles into his side.

He nods slowly, opens his eyes, and looks up at his mother. "Mario?" he asks.

His mother gives a slight nod. "The kids were teasing her at school today," she whispers. "Mario hid her lunch box in the bushes."

Dante stiffens. "As soon as I'm out of here," he says, "I'm going to her school." His voice is low but intense. "I'll catch that bully Mario by the throat and —"

"*Ya.*" Dante's mother squeezes his hand. "That's enough."

"All right, all right." Dante holds up his hands in mock surrender.

Elena giggles. He smiles. And as suddenly as it came on, her distress is forgotten.

"Dante, your father ..." Dante's mother traces her finger over the top sheet. "He ..." She drops her gaze, not meeting his eyes when she says, "He's worried about you, but ..." Her voice wavers. "He's in the Dominican Republic, with his new wife."

Dante's lips tighten, and his eyes turn hard. He pretends like he's listening, but his mind is on another planet. His mother doesn't catch the "I-don't-want-to-talk-about-it" nonverbal.

"He said he'll call you," she says. "Sometime tonight."

"He doesn't have my number." Dante's voice is tight.

"I ... I gave it to him this morning."

Dante shakes his head. And then closes his eyes. From that moment on, he doesn't say another word.

When his family finally leaves, I come out of hiding and sit next to him. His eyes are closed and he's very still. I wait for him to say something, no longer wondering — or caring — if he thinks I'm real. His life is more painful than my hurt feelings.

"Do you have a mom and dad?" he finally says.

"Yes, both. An awesome mother and a powerful father." My voice trails off. "Who is incredibly angry with me right now."

Dante opens his eyes. "I can't imagine anyone being angry with you."

"Angry may even be too mild a word." My eyes flutter, but I push away the sadness and force myself to smile.

"You don't have to pretend to be okay around me," he says. "That way I won't have to pretend, either."

"I don't even know how to pretend."

He smiles faintly. "I don't believe you."

"I'm not sure I know how to answer that."

"Then answer this." He struggles to keep awake. "Are you still going to be here tomorrow?"

"Yes," I say softly. "But only in your dreams."

27. JADIEL

Mind Binder

"Two signatures. Within the next twenty-four hours. That's what it will take to get Lord Lucius to stop fuming about your failed mission." Equus sits down beside me in the hospital lobby.

"Not happening." Signing on souls is the last thing I want to do right now.

Equus lets out an irritated sigh. "Let's be clear, shall we? Because of *your* failure, Malakiy aborted the mission. Lord Lucius is irate, but fortunately for you, Malakiy is the source of his rage. However, that focus can change in an instant. I can make sure of it."

"What is that supposed to mean?" Warning bells go off in my head. "Are you threatening me?" My heart short circuits.

"Giving you a choice," Equus says.

"A choice?" I curl my chained hand and shove it in his face. "Is this a choice?"

"*That* is a consequence of a stupid decision *you* made in Maion." He throws back my fist. "Don't make the same mistake twice. Rebellion is an admirable quality, but only when it is intellectually conceived and mentally controlled." He pauses, and then delivers the punchline, "Secure two souls and I keep quiet. Lucius need not be reminded about your ... *friend*." He looks away when he says, "Make the right choice, Jadiel, or that girl you claim means nothing to you will pay the price." He fixes his gaze on me. "That's not a threat. It's a fact."

I detest the manipulation, but I get the message. Kiriela will suffer if I don't cooperate.

"What do you want me to do?" Tension lines form around my clenched mouth.

"Now that's the spirit." Equus sounds more sinister than happy. "I have a new skill for you to learn, and a hospital is the perfect place to teach it. See that boy over there?" He nods at a boy sitting in front of us, close to the chapel door. His name is Adrián."

"And poor Adrián's mother has cancer," I say. Bile creeps up my throat when I anticipate what will come next. The promise of a cure for Adrián's mother will be hard to resist. I'll get the boy's signature and Equus will switch his mother's records for someone else's in the hospital. Adrián's mother will be "cured,"and Lucius will have one more soldier. I read all about this bait-and-trap in Equus's journal, conveniently left on his desk in the library.

"No, his mother is fine." Equus switches the narrative. "It's his girlfriend he's worried about. She has a rare blood disorder called Paroxysmal Nocturnal Hemoglobinuria."

"Never heard of it."

"Most people haven't."

"And your point is?"

"Rare medical conditions are fertile ground for us. Hard to treat. Ripe with despair. An excellent set-up for treachery."

"Fine. I get it. So, what's the lesson you expect me to learn?"

"So eager to learn your lesson." Equus can barely suppress the smile that creeps across his face. "Interesting. So, let's get on with it." He shifts into his teacher-with-hands-behind-the-back mode. "This disorder can be treated with a blood transfusion but, as luck would have it, this particular girl is AB-negative, *the most* uncommon blood type. Only .6 percent of humans have it. But here comes the good part. We can get the blood for her from one of our operatives in Aguas Calientes, one of our outposts on the outskirts of San Juan."

"Okay, good, so it's an easy deal. AB-Negative blood for Adrián's signature."

Equus shakes his head. "You still have much to learn. The thrill of the hunt is not in acquiring a signature, it is in the destruction and corruption that takes place around it." He begins to pace, part of the teacher/student dynamic. "Adrián is a believer. One of our Adversary's loyalist. He has prayed about his girlfriend's condition for several months now."

"So, your prayer manipulation is not going to work on him," I surmise.

"It will, but that's not the lesson I want you to learn tonight. In this case, Adrián's prayer was answered. Six months ago, The Adversary promised that the appropriate donor would be found, from an undisclosed blood bank."

"Okay, so what's the problem then?"

"The problem is that Adrián, like most humans, is impatient. He does not like to wait. Six months is an eternity to a sixteen-year-old who has a lot of living to do, right now, in present time. So, while this young man waits on God, he begins to ask, *did God really promise that the correct blood would be found? And if he did, then why hasn't Tasha received it yet?* The longer the wait, the more confused the boy becomes. Eventually, with our help, he will start to question God. *Did you really mean what you said? Did you even say anything? Or did I just hear what I wanted to hear?* The more he thinks like this, the more unstable his belief becomes. Doubts begin to creep in. It's flawless. This trusted technique is what we proudly call *mind binding.*"

"*Mind binding is an iron band that the enemy tightens around his victim's head.*" Marius's voice rises above Equus's noise. "*It steals hope, obliterates joy, and destroys faith.*"

"Mind binding is one of our most powerful weapons," Equus says. "But a weapon is only as formidable as he who wields it. So, sharpen your weapon and bind that boy's mind.

"Sounds like you've already done that. What do you need me for?"

"To personalize the binding. Until now, the technique has been applied anonymously, through mind binding spirits that work unseen." He stares at the boy with cold derision. "Lord Lucius requires that the final bind be dealt in person, so that the victim can look our operative in the eye and realize — but only when the deception is done — that they have been deceived by someone who pretended to be a" — he air-quotes the word — *"friend."*

Pretending to be a friend is exactly what Lucius does — what he did to my parents. Smile as he inserts, and then twists, the knife. I will never forget my father's face when, at the end of his life, he realized that Lucius was loyal to no one. Not even to the woman he killed my father for. Still smiling after the fatal thrust, Lucius claimed my mother like a trophy. Still smiling, he dragged her away, his arm around her waist, her arms stretched out, reaching for my father. Reaching. Reaching. Until her arms grew tired, and she slumped into Lucius's arms.

My jaw clenches. This trophy is not going to come as easily. "There will be no signature from this boy until his girlfriend gets her blood." At least one life will be saved as I steal another.

"You are not in a bargaining position." Equus stares coldly at me.

My eyes lock onto his. "Get the girl her blood and I will get your signature." One thing I have learned about my Spiritual Trainer is that Equus does not get his hands dirty. No face-to-face attacks ever come from him. He needs me, and I know it. "Call your contact."

"Have you forgotten so soon what you are fighting to protect?" Equus takes back the upper hand. "Your assignment can change with the snap of my finger."

Kiriela is safe, for now — if she stays close to Malakiy. "I'll take my chances." I can't back down now. I can only trust that Malakiy will be smart and keep her away from me. "Just give the girl her blood. What difference does it make to you?"

"Fine. I will give you this one concession." Equus takes out his phone and makes the call. When he hangs up, he says, "The blood will be in the hospital's bank tonight."

"Good. When it is there, I will have it tested. If it is the correct blood type, I will be your mind binder. When it is transfused into the girl's body, without any adverse reactions, I will be your notary. You will have a signed contract within one hour of her successful transfusion."

"You strike a hard bargain." Equus seems too easily resigned. As if, somehow, he is still in control. "While we wait for the blood to arrive, go and befriend that miserable boy."

"Fine." Wanting to get this exercise over with, I walk over to the boy and say, "Hey, are you all right?"

The boy shakes his head.

"You mind if I sit down?"

He shrugs.

"Is someone you know in the hospital?"

"My girlfriend. She's sick again."

"Sorry to hear that. Is she sick a lot?"

"Yeah. She's got some kind of rare blood disease." Adrián speaks in a monotone, as if he's said these words too many times before.

I feel his pain, in a way I never could through my textbook lessons on human suffering.

"Is there anything the doctors can do for her?" I find myself hoping there is.

"Not until they get the right blood for a transfusion."

"I'm sure they will." A pang of guilt shoots through me.

Adrián nods, but he looks far from convinced.

"I saw you coming out of the chapel, are you a believer?"

"Yeah." He rests his elbows on his knees and clasps his hands together. He bows his head, completely defeated.

And I, because of the scum I've become, am going to capitalize on his misery.

"Let me ask you something." I pretend to search for the guts to say, "Has praying helped any? I mean, I don't know, I have a friend who got beat up. I don't know what else to do. The doctors are doing all they can, but —" I leave it there, hoping Adrián takes the bait.

"I don't think praying's the answer, dude. It's like you're just talking to yourself. Once, I thought God said that the doctor would find the blood Tasha needs, but that was six months and five hospitalizations ago."

"Yeah, it's like God just tells us what we want to hear." My stomach cramps. Mind binding comes too easily to me. "That is, if we are even talking to Him. Sometimes it feels like I'm talking to myself."

Not everything I'm saying is a lie.

"I know what you mean." Adrián stares at the floor. "I feel like that a lot. Like I'm talking to myself."

"Why is it so difficult to get blood for Tasha?" I steer the conversation away from the thought I so easily implanted. The boy repeated, almost verbatim, what I said to him.

"She's AB-negative," Adrián says. "It's hard to find."

Time to go in for the kill. "I can get you that blood." My heart sinks.

Adrián looks up, for the first time since I sat beside him. "How?"

"My friend's father owns a blood bank. And from what I've heard, he's got contacts all over the world. He should be able to find AB-negative blood."

"You really think you can get that blood for me?" Adrián sits up.

"I know I can." And now the final blow. "For a price."

Adrián looks at me suspiciously. "I don't have any money." His voice trails off. "Forget it." He looks down. "God will do what he said he would. She'll get the blood, eventually."

"Really? You really believe that? Six months is a long time to wait."

"What choice do I have?"

"Take my offer. I didn't ask you for money."

Adrián looks at me, cautiously optimistic. "So, what are you asking for?"

"A signature."

"Sounds too simple."

"One signature, and you'll have the blood your girlfriend needs."

I've seen the desperation unanswered prayer can bring. What I have not seen is the joy a lie brings to a desperate face. What I have not felt, ever before, is the utter betrayal of trust that brings on such a smile. Adrián agrees to sign the contract after I secure the blood.

Score one for Lucius. Two down and four more to go.

Maybe with Dante, the reaping will be easier. Maybe it won't feel like it's my own soul that has been bought and sold for the advancement of "The Kingdom."

28. DANTE

Only in My Dreams

If I am dreaming, I never want to wake up. The girl sitting beside me is so sweet, and so beautiful, she can only be real in my dreams.

Maybe it's the pain pill I just swallowed. Or the fragile deception of my mind. But as I float into oblivion, I see wings unfold behind the girl's glowing body. Soft feathers cover me, and I drift into a dream. The perfect teenage fantasy. Where the girl beside me is an angel and I a superhero.

Five days later, I wake up from my fantasy and face reality. I'm still in the hospital. Physically, I'm healing. But mentally, I'm all messed up. My father is back from the D.R., but the new wife must need him more. He has not yet found the time to visit.

Gia has. After five days of unanswered text and phone messages, she has finally come to see me. She's spent the last two hours silent, huddled in a corner of the room.

I can't look at her, so I keep my eyes focused on the only thing that comes close to comfort — my guitar. The paramedics found my black Gibson on the beach and put it in the ambulance with me. My mother wanted to take it home, saying I needed to rest, that the guitar would still be there when I got better. I argued with her. Being without my guitar is like cutting off a leg and expecting the rest of my body not to feel the loss. She sighed a lot, and rolled her eyes, but eventually she let me keep the guitar.

My fingers fly over the strings, energized by my electric thoughts. *I get beat up by a gang of psychopaths and Gia is the one pouting in a corner.* I slide my fingers down the fret board, finding a new chord along with another tormented thought. *And it took her five days to finally get here.* My mind runs laps inside my head. And then it trips and falls on the memory of The Night That Should Not Have Been. The night I got hooked on Gia.

When she called me crying that night Armando used her as a human punching bag, I should have just kept her on the phone and let her sob into the receiver. But no, I had to invite her over and allow her to soak my shirt with her fricking tears.

The next thing I knew, I was holding her in my arms. And yeah, the sympathy I offered benefited me. After the tears stopped, we talked. She had a new stepfather. My mom had a new boyfriend. The misery of poverty and family dysfunction sucked us into each other. Friendship grew into romance. She left Armando and started going out with me. And I fell for her ... hard. Wouldn't listen to anyone that tried to tell me what I didn't want to hear. Carlos tried to warn me. *"She's playing you,"* he said. *"She doesn't love you,"* C.J. added. So why, after all that happened and all that I knew, did I allow her back into my life?

Too many blows to the head must have made me an idiot.

I look up from my guitar and stare at Gia. I need to see what I once loved so much about her. And in some way, I want to believe that she felt something for me, too. It disturbs me to see her now. Her painted black hair covers both eyes. I think of all the times I brushed that hair back so she wouldn't look — and feel — so scared. Today, she won't allow me to touch her. She started her silent vigil with only one eye hidden, but the darker her mood became, the longer she stayed glued to the shadows, the more hair she pulled across her face. After two hours sitting without moving, there is little of her face still left to see.

I flatten my hand across the soundboard, stopping the music. I know the drama well. It always starts this way — with punishing silence, a black curtain over her emotions, and me going berserk, wondering why I can't stop loving her.

I lower my guitar to the bed, hesitate for a fraction of a second, and then say, "Gia, what's wrong? Why won't you talk to me?"

Gia doesn't move from her position on the floor, knees drawn tightly to her chest.

"Will you just say something? Please!"

"They cut your hair." Her voice is flat, void of any compassion.

"*Seriously?*" I do not know how to respond to that. I need a few seconds to process before I say, "Anything else you'd like to say?"

"It's your fault they attacked you."

"What?" I can't believe what I'm hearing.

"I heard about you and the new girl."

"What are you talking about?" A nerve jumps in my jaw. "There's nothing between me and the —"

"Whatever." She unfolds herself off the floor.

I clench my teeth, press my fingers into my thighs to keep myself from squeezing them into her neck, and look away as she heads for the door.

Her phone rings.

Even before she answers it, I know. She's found someone else.

The night nurse comes in and gives me another pill. I wash it down with a gulp of water, craving its effect. Intravenous Morphine is a more powerful narcotic, but the neurosurgeon who stitched up my head no longer orders I.V. drips. I know what the doctor must have written on my chart. *Suspend all intravenous interventions. Possibly belonephobic.*

Belonephobic means a person with a fear of needles. Doctors have been writing that word on my chart for as long as I can remember. From as early as the first grade.

The pill begins to have its effect. The pain dulls, and I float into another world.

"Rest now," my angel says.

Or so I think. Or wish. Or imagine. Or dream.

I so want my angel to be real.

My mind eases into a Percocet fog. I slide into semi-sleep. And then I see her.

The angel of my dreams.

29. KIRIELA

Fallen Daughter

"Rest now," I whisper to Dante as he drifts off to sleep. I pull up his blanket and sit beside him. His eyes draw open.

"You are real, aren't you?" He fights against the fog.

"Shhh," I say. "You must be dreaming." As real as our conversations seems to him, once he sleeps, I am nothing more than a pleasant dream. Malakiy's pills make me a fantasy.

Dante reaches for a glass of water. I take the glass from the bedside table and bring it to his mouth. My fingers brush his lips when I tip the glass. I shiver, just a little.

"Are you cold?" His voice is heavy with pending sleep.

"No, not cold. I feel ..."

"Scared?"

I gaze into his sleepy eyes. They're dark green today, like sea glass. I have never seen green eyes before. Jadiel's are blue. Mine are blue. My mother's and father's, too. I have to look away from his eyes. If I look one second longer, they'll pull me into their depths and drown me. I never thought I could feel something special for anyone other than Jadiel.

"Yes," I finally admit. "I'm scared."

"Me too."

We stare at each other, and for a moment, I stop breathing. Any minute now, Dante will be asleep, and I will be a dream. I'm not sure how I feel about that.

For the last three years, Jadiel has been my world. It wasn't a perfect world, but it was ours. I never looked at anyone else. Never wanted to. But now, my world is broken. The boy I thought I loved is capable of harming a human. And I am capable of caring for that same human in a way which seems more than simple protection. Knowing that both excites and terrifies me.

Dante clutches the railing, fighting sleep. Hand gripped on the metal bar, he struggles to sit up.

"No!" My heart pounds. "What're you doing?" I try to ease him back, but he resists.

My breathing turns shallow, and my head feels light. Somehow, I know that everything I understand about myself is about to change.

"Please, don't be frightened." He touches my cheek. "I have to know if you are real."

I shudder at his touch. The tips of his fingers are calloused, like warm, coarse sand. He runs his fingers over my eyes, my nose, my mouth, my hair. I pull back. My senses are too heightened. But then, he takes my face into his hands, and where his fingers are rough, his palms are smooth. I close my eyes. And then I feel his lips, on top of mine. Lips that slowly part, and then, with the slightest brush of his tongue, form into the softest kiss I have ever known.

"Kiriela!" The room shudders with the power of my father's voice. Light streams through the room. And then suddenly, my father stands in front of me. "Get away from that boy!" He flings me aside and places his gigantic hand over Dante's eyes.

Dante tosses his head back and forth, and then his arm goes limp. When my father removes his hand, Dante's eyes are closed in supernatural sleep.

"What were you doing with him?" My father turns to face me. "Haven't you caused enough problems?" His eyes blaze with anger.

"It wasn't what you think." I steady my voice against his anger. "I was —"

"Sinful child." A warm spot grows where my father's hand strikes my face. Dark humiliation rises from deep inside of me. I am so angry, so hurt I can't form a coherent thought.

"It wasn't enough that you ruined our family by defying me with Jadiel. Now you completely dishonor me with your obsession over this human boy." The room fills with my father's presence. "That boy." He points a finger at Dante. "Will be your demise."

Or maybe ... my salvation. A coherent thought forms. I straighten my back and stand taller. For the first time in my life, I am ready to defy my father. "There is no dishonor in what I did." I lift my chin. My legs feel wobbly, like they are going to fold under me, but my voice is firm. "Caring for someone is not a crime."

My father's chest heaves. "No, the crime is not in the caring. It is in the *disobedience*. You lost the sandals I told you never to take off."

I flinch. Suddenly, my lost sandals have taken on more weight than a human kiss.

"I'm sorry, father." My heart pounds. "You have a right to be angry. I was wrong to disobey you. But I did not lose them, Jadiel ..." The warmth drains from my face when I realize my mistake. Until now, my father did not know that Jadiel was anywhere near.

"Ahhhhh!" The window rattles with the hurricane force of my father's voice. "You met with Jadiel?" A bolt of lightning electrifies the sky.

"Yes, I did. And it was a mistake." I have never trembled so violently in my entire life.

"A mistake?" My father is over-the-top furious. "Reuniting with Jadiel was not only a mistake, it was a trap."

I refuse to believe that. "Jadiel can be impulsive," I say. "But he would never harm me."

"Enough!" Gale winds churn. "You are a foolish child. It's time for you to come home."

Something snaps then. My pride. My pain. My need to please my father. It doesn't matter anymore. I am tired of being weak.

"No. I will not go home." Every fiber in my being trembles with the weight of these words.

"What?" A crack of thunder rolls over the room.

"I can't leave now." My heart crashes. I glance over at Dante. My throat is so tight I can barely speak. I hesitate for a moment. And then I say the words that will lock me out of my father's house. "I caused this." My voice quivers for I know that what I am about to say next will secure my father's wrath. "Dante is wounded because of me." I stare at the bloody bandage wrapped around his forehead. "And with or without your permission, I am going to stay here, with him, until he is completely healed." These are the saddest words I have ever spoken.

For I know the consequences they will bring.

"Kiriela, my child." My father's voice is a pained whisper. "My beloved daughter. Why do you force my hand against you?" The room trembles. The water glass tumbles off the bedside table and shatters to the floor. "You were once careful in your ways, but now your heart has grown rebellious. You have given me no choice." A heavy wind swirls over the last words he says to me. "So be it."

A thunderous explosion blasts me from the room. A crack of lightning follows, and then rain pours from the angry sky. God's tears, I know. For now, I am a fallen daughter.

I fall in the middle of a burnt sugarcane field. The pouring rain sinks black ash into the scorched ground. The smell of rain-drenched smoke hovers over the air.

For a long time, I can't move. It hurts too much. Every bone in my body, every nerve, feels the shame of my descent.

Finally, I find the courage to lift my head and survey my surroundings. The land is desolate. White feathers litter the ground.

My feathers. My stomach flips. The feathers have black tips. I touch my wings. They're tattered but have survived the fall.

My shoulders tighten. I feel a sharp pain. Chains link around my wings. And then, with a jerk, my bound wings retract — locked inside my body.

I cover my mouth and choke back a sob. A single tear trails down my face as I lift myself to a half sitting position. It's as far as I can move. A turkey vulture flies overhead, searching for dead prey. But amongst the ruins of the landscape, bright orange flowers drift down from the flaming *flamboyan*. By these flowers I know. I am still in Puerto Rico.

Which is exactly where I need to be.

I wobble to a stand. And then I cry out. Something sharp has pierced my foot.

I look down. For the second time since I arrived on the island, my feet are bare. Only this time, the choice was not mine. I stare at my soaked clothes and steel my mind. I understand why I have no shoes.

I swallow against the thickness in my throat and gaze out over the lonely landscape. In the distance, I see a small wooden house — set back amongst a grove of mango trees. I take one step forward. My legs shake like a new-born lamb's, but I force myself to move. Malakiy will be waiting for me inside that house. He has to be. I can't do this without him.

When I reach the house, I call out, "Malakiy! It's me. Are you there?"

Thunder rolls behind a distant hill.

"Malakiy?" I try again. But again, my voice is met with silence.

A cold shiver passes over me. I feel a dark, sinister presence. It's as if someone is watching me, hidden in the shadows that surround the house. I hesitate before climbing onto the porch. A loose board has lifted. I step around it. And then I absorb the details of the farmhouse. There's a wooden rocker on the balcony. A canvas hammock sags between two weathered support beams. I take a step forward, but then

I stop. I look back over my shoulder. The hammock sways — as if someone is lying on it, rocking the ropes. My skin prickles, but I choose to ignore the possibility that I am not alone.

Without a backward glance, I push open the door. Immediately as I enter, I sense that the house is empty, but not abandoned. The worn floor-boards creak as I cross the room. The banister wobbles. The old house feels unstable. And maybe a little unsafe. I hobble past the living room and into a narrow hallway. Three wooden doors close off what must be bedrooms. One of the doors is decorated with foam flowers. That's the door I choose to open.

I take a deep breath and enter the room. The springs squeak as I sit on top of a simple wooden bed. I scoop a stuffed cat off a purple pillow and hug it to my chest. The animal is soft, with a few rough spots where the black and white fuzz has worn away. I look around me. It's a simple room. There are only four pieces of furniture: the bed, a travel chest, a wooden desk, and a chair. I squint. There's a note on the desk, underneath the lamp. I prop the cat on the pillow, slide off the bed, and read the note from Marius to me.

My dear Kiriela:

My heart is saddened by this latest turn of events. But considering that you have made your choice, I am forced to make mine. From this day forward, you are banished from your father's house. You will live here, in this humble farmhouse, for a period of no less than six months and no greater than one year, for the purpose of repentance and restoration.

During this period of reconciliation, you will be confined to your human form and will have no access to your supernatural powers. You will live as an ordinary, unremarkable sixteen-year-old girl, with all the weaknesses and frailties that come with being human.

My fingers shake as I clutch the note and continue reading.

Following are the rules that will govern your new spiritual status.

Rule number 1: From this day forward, you must give up all claims to the status of the daughter of Alexa and Adriel, and all powers associated with said status. You will no longer be allowed to guard, protect, watch over, or engage in any other activity associated with your former family. Additionally, you will surrender all claims to the title of holy muse. You are no longer allowed to sing celestial songs.

My stomach heaves. Marius is stripping away the very essence of me.

Rule number 2: It is your parents' wish that you continue with your education. Considering this, you will return to La Colina High. To cover living and educational costs, your parents have provided a bank card to a shared account. The card is in the top desk drawer.

There are more rules, but I can't read anymore. The note slips from my hand, and I fall back onto the bed. I am now officially an orphan. Stripped of my status and forbidden from doing the very thing that makes me *me*. Sing. That is the worst punishment of all.

I think about calling Jadiel. But I don't. I can't. He is no longer the Jadiel I once knew.

My spirit deflates. Losing him is like giving up a piece of myself.

I limp over and stand in front of the mirror on the closet door. I touch my hair. It has darkened to amber, with blonde highlights. My cheeks are smudged. My clothes are dirty. I bring my face closer to the mirror. *What?* The color of my eyes has changed. They look darker. There's a rim of green around the once pure blue of my irises.

A cold draft creeps under the windowsill and wraps itself around me. I shiver. Again, I feel as though I am not alone. I search the corners of the room. There's no one there. That I can see, anyway.

A flash of fear darts over me. *What's happening to me?* I feel like me. I think like me. But I look like a Snap Chat altered version of me.

Then the thought comes, unbidden, to my mind. I am not Kiriela the holy muse anymore. I am Kiriela the fallen daughter. Good words, uplifting thoughts, protective behavior will no longer come naturally to me. Bad words, disturbing thoughts, destructive behavior will. Because now, I am a damaged angel living in a fallen world.

30. JADIEL

Dante's Kiss

The lights go off and chaos reigns. An alarm sounds. My heart snaps. For a moment, I think I've been double crossed. I'm in Tasha's room, monitoring the transfusion—making sure she gets the AB-Negative blood that I had tested. Seconds later, the hospital generator kicks in and restores power. I breathe a sigh of relief. The blood I brought continues to flow into Tasha's arm. Slowly but surely, color returns to her face.

An hour later, I get not only Adrián's signature, but also his brother's. Adrián wanted blood. Iván an unlimited supply of sleeping pills. I supplied him with over-the-counter Benadryl re-labeled in the prescription pill bottles provided by the same broker who delivered Tasha's blood. But as successful as I was with Adrián and Iván, I cannot get near Dante.

Between Malakiy and Kiriela, they have formed an impenetrable shield. For five excruciating days, I have tried to break through their protective barrier. But it has proven impossible. After five days of intensive angel care, Dante is soon to be discharged, but I am no closer to signing him than I was when I first met him on the beach. Malakiy, I get. He's the ultimate guardian. But Kiriela? She has proven to be even more overprotective than her father.

My phone pings. I read the incoming text. *Abort mission.* Equus's cryptic message leaves me cold. *Go to the cave entrance to Abaddon. I will meet you there.*

It's pouring rain when I leave the hospital. The wind is gusting. It's like a funneling tornado disguised as a tropical storm. The way the wind blows the rain horizontally is unsettling. It makes me feel like there's something more to come.

When I arrive at the cave, Equus is waiting for me. Slowly, he circles me, and then stands behind me. "You got what you wanted. Tasha will heal from her once incurable illness, according to my sources at the hospital. But" — he whispers in my ear — "you made one very stupid mistake when you dealt that hand."

I stare at the wall in front of me. The stones are red today.

Equus continues to circle, and then stops in front of me. "You failed to hide your only vulnerability."

My stomach clenches. I focus on a grey goat cowering in a corner of the cave. Chupa is leering over it, looking hungry.

"Not smart." Equus leans in closer, and then says, "She's a liability."

"I told you" — I keep my eyes steady on my opponent — "I barely know the girl."

A corner of his mouth lifts as Equus takes two steps back. "Rumor has it that this girl you barely know has developed ... *feelings* for the boy she is protecting." He turns and starts walking. "But I'm sure that means nothing to you."

My heart throbs. That's not possible. He's playing with me.

"But don't worry." Equus stops and looks back at me. "Those feelings won't last. Eight days ago, she was in love with you."

He turns and says to Chupa, "Don't touch that goat."

Like a cat caught with a canary, Chupa shuts his mouth and backs away from the trembling animal.

"Why was I summoned here?" I steel my mind against Equus's insult. I refuse to allow him to get inside my head.

"Not so fast. All in good time. I'm not finished filling you in on the latest news."

"What news?" My heart beats faster. It's obvious this "news" has to do with Kiriela.

"Not only has this girl-you-barely-know developed some deliciously decadent feelings for our target, she has also defied her father's order to stop protecting him."

Equus nods for Chupa to join him as he starts to pace. "Lord Lucius is loving it. I believe Adriel's exact words were, 'It wasn't enough that you ruined our family by defying me with Jadiel. Now you completely dishonor me with your obsession over this human boy.' Lord Lucius is so pleased by Adriel's humiliation that he has forgiven your delay in delivering Dante. In fact, he wants to build you up. You and her. She has potential."

My stomach thuds. "No, believe me, she does not." Kiriela may be more rebellious now, but she in no way has what Lucius is looking for. What Adriel calls her "obsession" is what I call her compassion. I am not surprised by her behavior. But I am a little hurt. Why couldn't it have been me that inspired the defiance against her father?

"Adriel has banished her from his home." Equus delivers his bombshell report without any emotion. "She's living alone, in an abandoned farmhouse on the edge of a sugarcane field."

"I don't believe it." Adriel may indeed be furious, but he would never send her away, alone and unsupervised. That would give her too much freedom — and him too little control.

"Believe whatever you like." Equus stops short, and then turns to face me. "Adriel didn't have a choice. It is written in Marius's boring Book of Laws. Because of her rebellion, Adriel had to banish her."

I take a minute to process. "What exactly did she do?" I'm not getting the full story.

"How do I put it … delicately?" Equus looks like he wants to be anything but delicate. "Adriel caught her in a … compromising position with your human target."

"What is that supposed to mean?" What feels like a lead ball drops inside my stomach.

"You're a smart boy. Figure it out." Equus smiles in that cruel way I have come to despise. "I'll give you a hint. Demon Twitter is going viral with the hashtag #Dante'sKiss."

I process what I heard. And then I get angry. At whom or for what, I'm not sure. All I know is that I need to take back the control that Equus stole from me.

"Teach me how to draw out my full powers." I turn toward Equus, the full fury of my rage clenched in my fisted hand. The only way to deal with the anger that I feel is to get stronger.

Over Equus's shoulder, I see Nube, half-hidden behind a boulder.

I turn away from her. "So, are you going to teach me or not?"

"Why do you think you were summoned here?" Equus pushes me into a hidden room. Chupa follows with the goat clutched in his claws. "It's time for you to get strong. Lord Lucius believes that you can be an asset. With the appropriate motivation. And the right training."

"Get on with it, then." My motivation was artfully manipulated. Now all I need is the training.

"Hold out your hand. Like this." Equus extends his arm, palm down, fingers spread. "From this position, you will call forth your power." I copy his position and he continues, "Now with your mind, draw forth the power that is inside of you." He moves his hand toward the goat Chupa dropped on the ground. "You are going to use that power to pin that goat to the wall." With a twist of his hand, he pins the goat against the wall. "Now you."

The goat thuds to the ground when Equus releases it from his clutch.

I try to do what Equus did, but nothing happens.

"Try again."

I grit my teeth. This time, I am determined to summon the power Equus says I have.

"Focus." Equus stands in front of me. "The power is all here." He touches his index and middle fingers to my head.

I focus on the goat. This time, when I hold out my hand, I feel some strength in it. Chupa circles me as I prepare to trap the goat. The circling distracts me and my attention shifts.

"You're not concentrating." Equus snaps his fingers in my face. "Focus."

I glare at him. "Back off. I know what I need to do."

I stare at the goat, cowering in the corner. Somehow, I can't bring myself to exert my control over a helpless animal. That must be why I can't conjure the power.

Chupa snorts at me. Then he marches over to his master. He's mocking me. The smug grin on his face is saying, *I knew you couldn't do it. You're weak. A LOSER.*

Something primal surges inside of me. Anger. Rage. Powerlessness. Determination. And strength. Conflicting emotions rise, all at the same time. I shift my hand so that it falls in line with Chupa's face. I close my eyes. *Concentrate.* I think about how much I hate this beast. About how much I hate being weak. About a kiss that should have been mine.

The full-on negative energy is what I have been lacking because suddenly, a surge of power flies from the tips of my fingers and blows Chupa back.

I've trapped him. For the first time since entering Abaddon, I am in control.

"Nicely done." Slow applause echoes over the walls of the cave. "A clever move."

The mark on my chest throbs. I can't breathe. Lucius is lurking in the shadows, watching ... talking to me.

"I knew I wasn't wrong about you." His voice is smooth. Chilling. Unnaturally calm.

My eyes dart from one dark corner to another. "Where are you? Show yourself."

A hot coal hisses. "Nor am I wrong about that girl-you-barely know." Lucius's voice wraps around the shadows. "She'll convert to our way of seeing the world. That's a guarantee."

"Leave her out of it!" The air I've held in comes out choked. "She's of no use to you."

A slow, evil laugh slithers off the walls. "There's something especially exciting about one fully committed fallen angel and his slower to convert former *friend* working together to trap/protect one pesky human boy. But alas, we need to show her who is in charge."

Chupa struggles back to his feet, and then goes for me. Equus grabs his collar and holds him back. "No, Chupa, he's communicating with Lord Lucius."

Chupa snarls but doesn't fight his master. The perfectly trained pet.

"While your mission remains the same," Lucius says, "there will be one slight modification to the plan." I brace myself against what's to come. "You will still secure Dante for me, but here's the fun part — you will do so by either working against your former friend or converting her to our side. Conversion is the recommended choice. I have faith in you, Jadiel. Accomplish this double deal and you will join me in the Inner Circle. Fail any part of it, and she becomes collateral damage."

I stare straight ahead. My fist clenches. Lucius knows exactly what he is doing. Purposefully and painfully, he is upping my suffering.

31. DANTE

Things Change

A Category 1 Hurricane lashes the island the day I'm discharged from the hospital. The electricity blows. Boarded windows strain against violent winds. And then in the calm that follows, things change.

"Don't mess with me, dude." I slam the door to my bedroom and switch the phone to my other ear, not wanting to hear what I already know. As Carlos poisons me with the truth about my ex-girlfriend, I sink to the bed. Gia dumped me for Manuel. It hasn't even been two weeks.

"I'll talk to you later." I disconnect the call. Screw it. I'm done with girls like her.

I toss the phone to the bed and fall beside it. Gia is a shallow, emotionally challenged mental case with too much gothic angst and too few cells in her nutrient-starved brain.

Ouch. It hurts to hear myself think. I know it's only the anger talking, but Gia's betrayal feels like the end of the world to me. I cared about her. A lot. Why couldn't she have cared a little more about me?

I unlock my computer and go to my chat group. There are hundreds of messages, sent directly to me. *Where are you, dude? Missing you. Tell me how to stop hurting through the hate.*

Two weeks ago, before my brains got bashed in, I might have been able to reply to that message with something halfway meaningful. Now, all I can write is, *I have no fricking idea.* I click out of the chat. I'm in no condition to be the motivator. Not anymore. Hatred can be defeating, sometimes.

I dig my iPod from my pocket and shove the buds in my ear. I scroll through the playlist, searching for a song that matches my mood. "Waking the Demon," by Bullet for my Valentine, feels about right.

I find my crutches and hobble outside. Then like an idiot, I climb the ladder to the roof. Pain shoots through my ankle every time I step onto a higher rung, but I continue to climb. I need to get to the one place that offers some semblance of peace.

When I reach the top, I swing my good leg over the ledge and lower my body to the flat cement roof over the house. I lock my hands under my head and stare up at the night sky.

The last two weeks were the nightmare version of "Welcome to your Reality." Gia's gone. Armando officially psychotic. I have a demon on my ass. And very little memory of what actually happened. It's like someone pushed the off button on my brain. The last thing I remember was Gia huddled in a corner, looking miserable. And something about my hair.

I reach out and touch my head. I feel like Shawn the Sheep — after a shearing.

I haven't totally wrapped my brain around the demon — not being a hundred percent convinced that the supernatural isn't more than just good TV. But one more person walking out of my life, *definitely* part of my new reality.

I gaze up at the stars, contemplating how insignificant I feel before the vastness of the universe. Ironically, "Wish I Had an Angel," by Nightwish, is playing from my song list.

I lie back on the roof, clench my hand into a fist, and cover my eyes. The pain pills I swallowed are starting to have their desired effect. I begin to drift away.

Sometimes in my dreams I see angels.

I hope I see one again tonight.

32. KIRIELA

Unremarkable

I am no longer an angel. How can that be? How can my identity change because of my behavior? I'm not even a fallen angel, like Jadiel. I'm what the Council calls a "Fallen Daughter." Marius's directive rolls around in my head. *During this period of reconciliation, you will be confined to your human form and will have no access to your supernatural powers. You will live as an ordinary, unremarkable sixteen-year-old girl, with all the weaknesses and frailties that come with being human.*

Is one of those frailties, desperation? Because I feel desperate. I hold my breath and scrunch up my shoulders. Once again, I try to shiver out my wings. But like all the other times I tried, nothing happens. My wings are worse than clipped — they're chained inside of me.

I arch my back to relieve the pressure. My shoulders feel raw. Punished. Unlovable.

Is another one of those frailties self-pity? Because I feel sorry for myself. I'm lonely. No one has come to see me. Not Malakiy. Not Marius. Not even Jadiel — whose company I crave more than anyone else's. We once thought we could fight the world together. Now, all we are fighting is each other.

I'm angry and confused. I need to talk to someone, but Malakiy doesn't answer his phone, and Jadiel is not an option. I'd probably punch him in the face if I saw him right now.

"Where are you, Malakiy?" I yank on my school uniform. *"Call me whenever you need me."* I repeat what Malakiy said when he etched his phone number into the sand. "I need you, Malakiy. Do you hear me? I NEED YOU." As usual, the walls give no reply.

I grab my book bag and head out to the main road to catch the bus. It's a long ride into town. A long, lonely ride. I don't talk to anyone. And they don't talk to me. Sadness sends out its own special signal: *Stay away. Toxic teen ahead.*

An hour later, I'm sitting at my desk in the Spanish classroom. A few minutes later, Dante arrives. It's his first day back after a nearly two-week absence. My heart accelerates, racing from adagio to allegro in two swift beats. I wonder if he'll recognize me. If he remembers anything before my father forced shut his eyes. The human part of me hopes he will. We shared a moment. A moment I will never be able to explain — or justify — to Jadiel.

I steal a glance at Dante. There are bruises on his face. He's wearing a black cap. Will he remember who I am? In the hospital, he broke through Malakiy's synthetic barrier, saw that I was real. But does he remember what he saw? Or was that moment in the hospital only a blurred memory? Another dream?

There's no way of knowing because he doesn't look at me or anyone else. He walks to the nearest desk, dumps his backpack on the floor, and takes out his phone.

My heart thuds. *He's forgotten about me.* My pulse accelerates. *I mean nothing to him.*

Is this what it feels like to be an "ordinary, unremarkable sixteen-year-old human girl?" If so, I hate the feeling.

I observe the other students. From what I see, Dante is a much more interesting subject to most of our classmates than 19th century Spanish literature. With his eyes glued to his phone, Dante doesn't see his classmates turn around in their chairs, but I see them. He probably can't hear their hushed whispers, but I do.

"Do you think he's dressed in black because he's depressed?" That question comes from one of the smart girls.

"What do you think his head looks like under the beanie?" That girl is more curious than smart. "I bet it's all messed up. Blood and stitches and shit like that."

I feel a sharp pang. My gut instinct is to say something protective. But I say nothing at all. I feel empty. A hollow shell of my former self. Maybe somewhere, I'm still me. But right now, I'm not sure who I am. Guarding and protecting no longer feel natural to me.

Maybe that instinct was locked away with my wings.

I lower my head to the desk, like I've seen other students do. I get why they do that. Life on Earth becomes unbearable, sometimes.

33. DANTE

Multi-colored Click Pen

I can feel their eyes on me. Definitely no angels here. Only overly-curious girls who cannot stop wondering — or confirming — how messed up I am.

I know exactly what those clucking chickens are thinking. The smart girls are wondering if the blows to my cranium have made me a moron. The rich kids are sneering, hoping I'll transfer to El Valle — with all the other juvenile delinquents.

Little do they know that I literally begged my mother to transfer me to the neighboring school, but she refused. El Valle, she says, is a juvenile delinquents' playground. La Colina, I informed her, is the convicted delinquent's jail. The pseudo-strict dress code is supposed to "even out the playing field," but even dressed in identical school uniforms, there is no doubt who the "predators" are and who the "prey." Carlos, C.J. and I belong to the latter group. Fallout from my failed friendship with Armando. When I explained that to my mother, she sighed, put her hand on her hip and told me to suck it up and get my butt back in school.

So here I am. Counting down the days.

249 left until I'm finally free.

A pen drops to the floor. I look up. A pack of girls is staring at me while whispering to each other. Girls are good at multitasking.

I'm about to look away when my eyes land on the pen. I do a double take. It's a multi-colored click pen. I stare at it. Something about that pen seems freakishly familiar.

"What are you staring at?" Susana picks up the pen and hands it to the new girl.

"Nothing." *Bitch.* I stare at the new girl. This weird, déjà vu feeling crawls over me. I've seen that girl somewhere else. Somewhere outside of school.

"Do you have a problem?" Susana snarls at me like an angry cat.

"Get spayed," I answer back.

I hear a few scattered words from Susana's Girl Club. *Shut up. Loser. Weirdo. Freak.*

I turn around in my chair. I can't just sit here, like a deaf mute. So, I say something stupid, just because I can.

"Time to scurry back to the hen house, ladies. It must be almost feeding time."

Their mouths drop open. I'm about to say more when I decide it's better to just shut up. No point being the lone wolf snarling at the hens. Mean girl roost mentality is something I'll never understand.

That's one thing I liked about Gia. She never cared about being the same as anyone else, not even like the other Goth girls. The latest Hot Topic fad never interested her. She had no trouble buying her Goth garb off the clearance rack. I liked that about her.

Shit. I slap down my pencil. Why can't I get that girl out of my head? I really want to be over her, to puke her out of my system, but I guess the mind defends itself as long as it possibly can. I cannot accept, will not accept, that I made a mistake in loving Gia.

Dante Vega, please report to the principal's office. The announcement crackles over the intercom.

I pocket my phone, grab my crutches, and head for the principal's office.

"Good morning, Dante," the principal says. "Have a seat."

I slouch into the familiar chair in front of Mr. Martínez's desk.

"I'm glad to see you back." Mr. Martínez assumes his official position behind the desk. "I tried to call your house, but a message came up saying your number was no longer in service."

I say nothing. The telephone company cut off our phone months ago. I'm still trying to help Mom pay off the past-due bill.

Mr. Martínez crunches his brow together. He hesitates before speaking, but finally says, "I wanted to tell both you and your mother that strict measures are now in place to ensure that you, as well as the other students, are safe. I'm sorry you had to be the reason the school board finally decided to approve the hiring of two additional security guards."

I squeeze my eyes shut to process the ridiculousness of that statement. The attack did not take place on school property. But instead of responding to the principal, I simply say, "Is there something you want, Mr. Martínez?"

"Hold on." Mr. Martínez takes an old cell phone out of his desk drawer and scrolls through the pictures. He looks perplexed. "My son's," he says. He looks up, gives a half smile, and then turns the device toward me. "You know this guy?' He shows me a picture.

"Yeah, that's Chester Bennington."

"He was a hell of a singer, but he was misunderstood." Mr. Martínez pauses for half a beat. "As many creative people are."

First *yeah,* and then *what*? How does Mr. Martínez know about the ex (now dead) lead singer of Linkin Park?

I stare at the principal as if he just landed his spaceship in the courtyard and is waiting for me to get in.

"Come on, Dante." Mr. Martínez offers an awkward smile. "I'm the father of two teenage boys. I know a thing or two." He turns off the phone and stuffs it back into the drawer. "Believe it or not."

"Huh." A burst of air accompanies my surprise.

"Did you know that Mr. Bennington was knocked around and bullied at school for being skinny and looking different?" Mr. Martínez presses a finger to his lips. I feel a lecture coming on. "But, joining a band, where his voice mattered, made him matter, too."

"That's really interesting, Mr. M. Is that all?" I'm about to add that the dude also killed himself, but figure, what's the point? I edge forward in the chair, ready to stand up.

Mr. Martínez rocks back in his chair. The springs groan as he reclines. "Your clothes are against school regulation." He folds his arms across his chest. "I'm sure you know what I'm talking about."

"No, sir, actually I don't." I know exactly what Mr. Martínez is referring to, but I'm in a bad-ass kind of mood and Mr. Martínez is on the receiving end of my less than welcome back to school.

"I'll overlook the studded belt and the leather wrist band. I'll even ignore the fact that you're not in uniform — for today — but" — he waves at my black beanie — "*that* has to go."

"Why?" I sit up straight, looking forward to the debate. "Am I hurting anyone? Do you think I'm making a subversive statement, or that I belong to some kind of cult?" I nail my eyes on the principal, all tough like. "It's him, isn't it?" I point to the grinning head of Jack Skellington on the front of my beanie. "Demonic, right?"

"That's not it, and you know it." Mr. Martínez sits up in his chair. "Rules are meant to be followed." He opens the top drawer of his desk and pulls out a terry cloth headband. "You may wear this, if you like." He tosses the headband at me. "To cover up the ... the wound." He brings his fist up to his mouth, coughs, and looks away.

I stretch the band between my fingers. There's a penguin embroidered into the material. "Yours?" I say.

"My wife's." Mr. Martínez smiles lightly, and then draws his brows together.

I stuff the headband in my pocket, mumble a garbled thank you, and then sprint for the door before Mr. Martínez can formulate the thought brewing behind the brows.

"Dante." Mr. Martínez calls me back.

"Yes?" I huff the word out on a sigh.

"The cap. Please remove it before leaving this office."

My heart flips. While the shorn sheep analogy was funny when I was alone on the roof, there is nothing funny about teen cruelty. I rip off the hat. Fear is never too far from my heart.

34. JADIEL

Bottled Brains

"What does your enemy fear?" Professor Mendax begins his lecture with a question. "Do you know?" His empty eyes scan the rows of black benches where the students are seated. We've moved from the war room into the research laboratory. Abaddon's science lab is a sinister place lined with endless rows of bottled brains.

"To defeat your enemy," Professor Mendax continues, "you must know him. What is he afraid of? What drives him? What are his strengths? What are his weaknesses?"

Not a single student is paying attention to the professor. We are all morbidly focused on the brains in lidded bottles shelved around the room.

"Disturbing," Jophiel says.

"Awesome," says another.

I look closer at the jars. Each one is labeled with a name, a weakness, and a strength.

"Lord Lucius's neuroscientists have spent years studying the intricacies of the human brain," the professor says. "And they have worked diligently, over many years, perfecting the art of human brain reconstruction." Professor Mendax gestures at the bottled brains behind him. "While the field agents are out observing and recording human behavior, our lab scientists are taking that collected data and reconstructing individual brains — for study purposes."

"Neuroscience at its most disturbing," I say.

"Found within each human brain is a unique alteration in structure that makes each individual distinct from the other. The challenge is to read the differences in the tucks and folds of these replicated human brains." He turns to Professor Bellator. "The first slide, please."

Professor Bellator turns on the projector and an image appears on the screen. It's a picture of twenty brain scans, each one showing different patterns of color. Some have bright blue borders. Others have large areas of fluorescent green. Most have splotches of red and orange. I'm fascinated. The colors can't be random. Colors are never random on a canvas. Each one represents something different to the artist.

"In front of you is a chart of our scientists' neuro mapping protocol." Professor Mendax gestures toward the screen. "As you can see, each scanned brain lights up with different colors. From these colored areas, we can study our subject. We can determine his strengths. And his weaknesses." He nods at Professor Bellator. "The next slide, please."

A second image replaces the first one. It's a chart, or table, with a summary of standardized coordinates. Complicated words, like *ventral striatum, subgenual cingulate, thallmus* are written under *target regions* — followed by a whole bunch of numeric formulas.

"I hope we don't have to memorize all that," Zadkiel says.

"You will have access to these materials on your trainer's computer," Professor Mendax says. "But because of the complicated nature of this lesson, you will continue to study this subject alone with your S.T's, who have all mastered the dark and curious art of brain mapping. Before we break off into individual study, however, I will remind you that you have all been assigned one specific target. Others you can choose randomly. It is these *specific* targets that are of interest to Lord Lucius. These targets will challenge you. Or they will defeat you." His eyes shift down to a black ledger open in front of him. "There was a total of five signed contracts this week. Two by Jadiel, and one each by Zadkiel, Jophiel and Azazel." He looks up. "That ties Jadiel and Azazel for the most signatures to date."

I glance over at Azazel. He's staring straight ahead, arms crossed.

"But despite those numbers, there have been no contracts secured from assigned targets. Meaning, none of you are up to standard yet."

I stare straight ahead, with my arms crossed, too. I need to work harder. Lucius is watching me. I need to impress him if I'm going to make it to the Inner Circle.

"You will now separate and study individually with your S.T's." Professor Mendax shifts his head to the back of the room. I didn't notice before, but all the trainers are there, with their computers. In one synchronized move, they get up, and then go with their laptops to pre-assigned tables. I, along with the other trainees, follow them to the designated workspace.

Equus flips open his computer. He types in a passcode. A set of brain scans and a tabulation chart appear on the screen. "These are simulated images of the pertinent people surrounding your target victim." He minimizes the scan and brings up the tabulation chart. "This chart interprets the scans." He slides a bottled brain in front of me. "Watch as I identify the name, weakness, and strength of the first case study, Dante's mother."

In a little under forty-eight hours, I have learned how to interpret the twists and turns of a human brain. Equus and I are still in the laboratory. Everybody else left hours ago.

"Name, weakness, and strength." Equus shoves a bottled brain at me.

I consult the chart. There's a blue ring around this specimen, with a large area of florescent green. On top of the green are bright spots of orange.

"Well? Get on with it."

My Spiritual Trainer makes me feel that if I slack up for even a minute, I will either fall from favor, be cast out, or even killed. Fear drives me, but it is sheer determination that pushes me to be an obsessive-compulsive-over-achiever. I have been training for forty-eight hours. Every twelve hours, Equus gives me two hours of sleep. I'm exhausted, but I have nailed every test he has hit me with. For two equally compelling reasons: 1) if I fall out of favor, I won't reach the Inner Circle, and 2) if I give up now, I give up on Kiriela.

I snatch the unlabeled bottle off the stone slab in the middle of the lab and study the replica brain inside. According to my spiritual trainer, I shouldn't care about what happens to Kiriela. *"She doesn't care about you."* Equus has tried to brainwash that point into my head from the moment he first informed me of her "betrayal." She sided with someone else, he likes to remind me. She worked against me. Even after I warned her of the consequences of that choice. And now I am compromised. Or maybe, I already was.

Equus knows exactly how to attack me. He has been watching me, observing me from the moment he first met me. He knows my imperfections and my weaknesses. And now, with the skill of a high-ranking military tactician, Equus is training me to look for the perfect point of entry to implant destructive thoughts. And I've gotten good at it.

"Name: C.J." I force my mind back to the task at hand. Slowly, I rotate the model brain, looking for the strengths and weaknesses hidden in the colors and cracks. "Weakness: Lack of Discernment. Strength: Capacity for Love."

"Excellent." The corner of Equus's mouth snakes up into a smile. "Star potential, my friend. Star potential. You keep going like this and you are going to be one of our top students."

Name: Jadiel. Weakness: Fear of Failure. Strength: Obsessive Compulsive Perseverance.

"Next one." Equus pulls another jar from the unlabeled ones on the bottom shelf.

I look closer at the shelf. Nube is hidden between the bottles. I glance at Equus. He's busy checking his phone. He either doesn't see what I do, or he doesn't care.

In between glances at the lamb, I study the folds of the brain in front of me. Carefully, I look for the small cracks that will be our entry points. This model has several fissures. Several points of weakness. But one is dominant. I consult the chart. By combining a series of equations, the answer comes to me. "Name: Carlos. Weakness: Money. Strength: Gift of Persuasion."

"What a sharp student you are." Equus does not look up from his phone. "And now for today's final test." He slides one more unlabeled jar in front of me.

I study the brain, as I did with all the others. I look at the color patterns, and then compare them to the chart. I show no emotion when I finally say, "Name: Dante. Weakness: Fear of Needles. Strength: Loyalty."

"Yes, loyalty." Equus smiles. "The very strength we are going to use against him."

He stares at me, probably to drive home the point he has already made a hundred times: Lucius preys not only on human weaknesses but on human strengths as well. Whichever one will give the greatest margin of profit.

"So, now what?" I return the brain to the bottle, label the jar, and place it on the shelf with the others. "I know my enemies' strengths and weaknesses. What comes next?"

"Like any good scholar, we will use the data we've collected to design our strategy."

Like a professor teaching a lab no one is interested in, Equus continues with his lecture. "We will use our subjects' strengths and weaknesses to wreak havoc and chaos in their lives. At 0700 hours, you are going back up to Earth, where you will approach Carlos before he goes to school. You will offer him money — his predominant weakness. In exchange for that money, you will have him commit to provoking a low-level conflict with his friend, Dante. You will implant seeds of discord — subtle seeds that will grow into more stubborn weeds."

Why does this strategy seem so familiar to me? Oh yeah, I know, because my Spiritual Trainer is using the same strategy against me.

Hopefully, Dante will resist my advances in the same way that I am fighting off Equus's insidious insinuations: by reminding myself who I am, and what I choose to believe — regardless of my trainer's negative energies.

"So, we're back to slow-boiled lobster," I say.

"Will you forget about the lobster." Equus does not like to be reminded of military inconsistencies.

"As he does every day," Equus continues, "Carlos will eat lunch with Dante, C.J. and Cristina. Today, that lunch is going to take an unexpected turn — thanks to your interference."

My interference. That's rich. When have I ever been interested in interfering in other people's lives? Never. And I never will be. Someday, I'll make up for all the bad things I've done. For now, I'll follow the path I've been thrown onto.

"What about Malakiy?" I don't need any more surprises from Dante's guardian.

"He won't be a problem."

"You sure about that?"

"He's been taken care of." Equus stares at me, like a mob boss communicating a message he does not want challenged.

"After offering Carlos the money" — Equus continues with his strategy—"you are going to encourage him to believe that his friend, Dante, is starting to spoil the fun. That thought is going to tumble around inside his head for several hours, until Carlos finally sees that Dante should be brought down a notch or two."

"What is the point to all this?" My question is irrelevant. I'm only asking it to keep myself from saying what I'm really thinking. *What have they done to Malakiy?*

Equus stares at me. "So many hours of training, and for what? If you don't know what the point is, you are even more stupid than I thought." If his eyes could throw daggers, they would be doing it right now. "The *point* is, we need to make Dante as miserable as possible. For as long as possible. By using his strength this time, and not his weakness."

Equus mocks me with a smile. "What was that strength?" he says. "Refer to your notes, if you need to."

When I don't answer, Equus says, "What was that?" He cups his ear. "I don't think I heard you."

Intentionally ignoring his attempt to knock me down, I give him the answer he asked for. "Loyalty," I say.

The word sounds oddly inappropriate here. It resonates with me. The word sounds strong. Noble. I hold onto the positive energy coming from it.

"Yes," Equus says. "Loyalty is Dante's strength. Find a way to use that strength against him." He draws a black curtain across the jar-filled shelves. "There's no need to sign him. Not yet. The Master is enjoying the chase. Carlos, on the other hand, is an easy conquest. Take him if you want to. He's insignificant."

As insignificant as I am. I and every other soldier in Lucius's army.

"Shut down the computer and take two hours rest." Equus barks out his order and leaves the lab.

I power off the computer and glance over my shoulder. There's no one around. I grab a petri dish from the supply cabinet. Then I dig into the bottom pocket of my pants and tug out a bottle of water. "Here,

Nube." I stoop down and pour the water into the dish. "Drink." I push the dishes in between the jars.

First, I see her eyes. And then her pink tongue, lapping up the water. I nod. Chupa should not be the only pet to drink from Equus' unlimited supply of water at the mansion. I drink from the bottle, and then lay down beside the shelf.

Two hours later, I'm awake and eating my morning gruel — in the lab like a true scientist. Also like a scientist, I've learned how to investigate. When Equus leaves for a meeting of the Inner Council, I hack into his computer. Capturing his password was as easy as looking over his shoulder. What's not so easy is figuring out what happened to Malakiy.

I scan through the folders on the home screen. Training Protocols. Recruitment Statistics. The Shadow Game. I continue scanning until I land on a folder labeled Enemy Agents. There are hundreds of files. I scroll through them until I find the one labeled *Malakiy*.

I skim through the file. Name. Position. Strengths. Weaknesses. Not important. My gaze stops on what is: Current Status: captured. Current Location: cell 113 S, Abaddon.

I'm both relieved and worried. Malakiy is no longer a threat. He can't protect Dante from his cell in the dungeon. But, nor can he watch out for Kiriela.

I'm about to shut down the computer when I see a folder that attracts my attention. Wing Progression. I open the folder. There are dozens of files, listed alphabetically by name. I find my file. There's a graph with a jagged line that's spiking upward. On the bottom of the graph are the days since "The Fall." On the left side are percentages. Despite a few ups and downs, my wings are charted at fifty percent blackened. I'm halfway to fully evil.

I shut down the computer. The chart worries me. The corruption of my wings has happened fast. But then I start to think. If there's a chart, with spikes both up and down, that means the corruption is variable. It can be advanced. And reversed.

I release a burst of pent-up air. Hope is not lost, not yet anyway.

35. JADIEL

Entry Point

An hour later, I catch up with Carlos. He's in his car, smoking a hand rolled cigarette. I rap on the window.

"What up, dude?" Carlos rolls down the window.

"You interested?" I hold up a hundred-dollar bill.

Carlos tilts his head to the side and stares at me through his scratched sunglasses. He'd like a new pair, according to our Intel. But he has no money and his father — the only working member of the family — just lost his job.

"Well, are you interested or not?" I struggle to appear likable. If I manage to come across as pleasant in appearance and personality, I can set up a false reality. And then sell this boy almost anything. One more useful piece of information gleaned from Equus Centurion's journal.

"Shit yeah." Carlos gets out of the car.

"Follow me." I lead Carlos to the far end of the parking lot.

"So, what, you want me to score you some weed?" Carlos looks back over his shoulder.

"No." I wait for him to look at me. "What I need you to do is much simpler than that."

"I'm liking you already, dude." Carlos grins, and then makes an odd gesture with his hand.

I squeeze his shoulder, in that too-familiar, used-car-salesman kind of way. "Your friend, Dante" — I modulate my tone to a slower, quieter pace — "always looking for attention. Wanting everyone to notice how bad his life is."

"I know, right? Crutches? Give me a fuckin' break. I saw him climbing up to the roof of his house. *Climbing*, you know what I'm saying?"

"That's what I'm talking about." I lean back on a nearby car and cross my arms. Carlos is standing the same way against his car. Salesmanship is all about focusing on what the buyer is doing. What makes him feel comfortable. So that he can feel comfortable with you. "I want someone to mess with Dante." I slide the hundred-dollar bill into Carlos's hand. "Can you do that?"

"I can do that." Carlos pockets the money.

"Good."

"But dude, like, what do you want me to do? Start a fight or something?"

I go rigid. "No." *No more violence.* This is not where I wanted the conversation to go, but maybe, I can use it to my advantage. I regain my composure, and then calmly I say, "You're his friend. Will a fight with you be believable?"

"Maybe. We do fight, sometimes."

"About what?" Treachery among friends never starts without a negative impetus. An impulse that is manufactured by one of Lucius's very own field agents. Like me. Unknowingly, Carlos has opened a crack in the door, and I'm going to walk right through it. "What makes him lose his cool?" The answer to this will determine my next move.

"Drugs. He always blows a gasket when C.J. and I start talking about drugs."

"C.J." I act like I'm not sure, but I know who C.J. is. "He's the boy with the cane, right?"

"Yeah, Dante's faithful friend." Carlos smirks. "Dante would do anything for C.J."

"And for you?"

"Not so much."

I nod. There's an entry point here, just as the model brain suggested.

"Don't worry about it," I say. "You don't need him." I re-adjust my tone again, this time to suggest a shared understanding of unequal friendship. "Just do this." I lower my voice. "Set up a situation involving drugs, with a touch of criminal activity. Make C.J. an accomplice. Let's see how Dante reacts. But stay clean. Work your game from a distance. Hide the hand that throws the stone."

"Cool." Carlos grins. "What'd you say your name was?"

"I didn't." I turn and walk away. My way of pretending that I don't care that Dante is going to get hurt again.

36. DANTE

Loyalty

I got through the last two days because of my friends. If it hadn't been for them, I would have been a statistic: one more frustrated high school dropout. I stand in line at the cafeteria. While waiting, I search for Armando, figuring it's smart to keep tabs on my enemy. I don't see him anywhere. Maybe the rumors are true. Maybe he isn't coming back.

I would accept that, had I believed it. Nothing in my life is ever that easy. I hold both crutches in my left hand, my tray in the right, and then head for my usual table in the corner to wait for Carlos and C.J.

Not fully understanding why, I start thinking about that pen again. I feel like I'm missing something. Like there's something I should be remembering. Something important. But as hard as I strain my brain, I can't remember anything.

"Hey, Dante!" C.J. holds up his fist in our customary gesture of friendship.

"Hey, what's up?" I knock fists with him.

"Dude!" Carlos plunks down his tray, throws his arm around my shoulders, and rubs his knuckles into my head. "Nice crop."

"Drop it, Carlos." Even as I say it, I'm thinking, *something seems off about Carlos today.* His knuckle rub hurt. Any idiot would have known that. Even more so, a friend.

"You know I'm just messing with you." Carlos laughs as he steps away.

I shovel a forkful of rice and beans into my mouth. My brows draw together, like they always do when I stress think. Carlos is messing with me, and I don't like it.

"Dude, what's going on up there?" Carlos pushes at my head and then sits down beside me.

C.J. flops on the opposite side of the table. Seconds later, Cristina joins him.

I stuff a chunk of leathery meat into my mouth. "Not much," I say. "Just thinking." I shove in another huge slice of beef. The fuller my mouth is, the less I need to say.

"Let me guess." Carlos grins like a drunken ass. "You're thinking how you'd like to screw Gia by hooking up with" — his eyes shift to a random table — "*that* girl."

I shake my head. "Shut up, dude. That's not what I'm thinking."

Carlos laughs. "Damn, that girl looks like she came straight out of a porn video."

"Bouncing boobs the size of soft balls," C.J. says. "I mean ..." He glances over at Cristina and quickly adds, "Not that I like softballs, or anything."

Cristina rolls her eyes.

"Can we change the subject?" I say.

"What's wrong with you?" Carlos punches my shoulder. A friendly gesture, I suppose.

"Show a little compassion," Cristina says. "He's sad and hurt and trying not to show it."

Carlos puts his arm around my shoulders and briefly hugs me against him. "I'm sorry for your pain, bro. I feel for you. Really, I do. You gonna eat those *tostones*?"

I wave them away and Carlos stuffs the plastered plantains into his grinning mouth.

The four of us sit there for a while, and under Cristina's gentle questioning, I spill out some of what I feel. There's a lot more I don't share. Partly because I'm a guy, and we don't tend to gush, but mostly because I'm embarrassed by the depth of my emotional distress. I don't want them to know how messed up I really am.

Cristina puts her hand over mine. "I don't know who the next girl's going to be, Dante, only that meeting you will be her lucky day."

"Hear-hear." C.J. raises his plastic milk bag in a toast.

I don't think any of them realize how fundamentally the ground under my feet has shifted. How lost I feel. I don't want them to know. It's embarrassing. So, I make myself smile, raise my milk, and pray for someone to change the subject.

"Take a look at this." Carlos pulls a black spiral notebook out of his backpack.

"What is it?" I say, more relieved than interested.

"Just a little something I came up with." Carlos brings his face closer, grins, and lowers his voice. "For a dare I gave to C.J."

I grab the notebook from Carlos's hand and study the drawing.

"A dare?" I say, mildly intrigued. "What's he supposed to do?"

Carlos looks over his shoulder before answering. "He has to spray paint this on the front wall of the school tonight." He engages my eyes. "You with us?"

"Idiots." Cristina snatches the notebook from me, scowls, and then turns to C.J. "You're not going to do this, are you?"

Before C.J. can answer, I say, "What's in it for C.J.?"

As usual, I feel like I need to ask on C.J.'s behalf. Carlos often takes advantage of C.J.'s trust.

"He gets twenty," Carlos says.

"Bucks?"

"No, dude, ounces ... you know ... a stash."

"Seriously?" Cristina tosses the notebook. "Your payoff is in drugs?"

I look away. My mouth stretches tight. Carlos and C.J. started messing with drugs only after Armando showed up in school — and that after swearing they'd "never start doing that shit." Yet one more of Armando's amazing talents. He is a skilled salesman.

"Stay out of it, Cristina," Carlos says.

Cristina picks up her tray and walks away. C.J. hobbles along behind her.

"So, what, Dante ..." Carlos's voice holds an unspoken challenge. "You wimping out?"

I push back the chair and stand up. "I don't wimp out." Annoyed, I stare at Carlos. "I protect my friends. I'll be there for C.J."

"Whatever, dude. Ten p.m. At the front gate." Carlos looks oddly triumphant. Once again, the feeling comes over me that something is not right with him.

Meeting up with Carlos and C.J. to carry out some stupid prank is totally not what I want to be doing tonight. But if I don't go, C.J. may get screwed. Carlos can be an ass, sometimes.

At 9:45 pm, I jump into my Cavalier and head down the street to pick up Carlos.

Carlos is standing at the curb, clutching a paper sack. There's a duffle bag on the street beside him. He grabs the bag and opens the passenger side door.

"Hey man," he says, "everything cool?"

I twist up the volume on the CD player. Disturbed's "Perfect Insanity" blasts from the speakers. I glance over at Carlos. "Yeah," I lie.

Carlos hands me a Coors Light from the paper bag. I snap back the tab and swallow half the can.

C.J. is already at the school, standing in front of his faded red Lancer. He holds a rolled-up joint pinched between his thumb and index finger.

"Yo dude, take a toke and pass the joint." Carlos jumps out of the car.

C.J. smiles, lifts the weed-stuffed cigarette to his mouth, drags, and then passes it on to Carlos.

Carlos inhales, holding the smoke in a few seconds before exhaling. Then he offers me the joint.

"You know I don't do that shit." I fit my crutches under my arms. I already regret my decision to come out tonight.

"Dante, you're my *pana*, you know, my brother." Carlos wraps his arm over my shoulder. "But when you start getting all pussy on me, I just LOSE IT!"

I shrug off his arm.

"You ready for this, dude?" Carlos turns toward C.J. His question offers no indication of concern.

I glance over at C.J. The boy is trying hard to project a level of confidence I know he doesn't feel. He looks like a lost puppy trying to find his way home.

"You don't have to do this," I say.

"No problem." C.J. grabs the sketch Carlos holds out to him. "I'm good." He scans the drawing quickly and then shoves the paper back at Carlos. "Let's do this." He hobbles to the fence, hands me his cane, and secures his stronger leg in the hand brace Carlos offers. Then Carlos passes him the duffle bag containing the spray paint.

I look down at the ground. I hope C.J. will do what he has to do quickly.

Once over the fence, C.J. paints Carlos's drawing — two bare butt cheeks — on the side of the school wall. He's now working on the acrostic. SCHOOL. S.hitty C.rap H.ole O.f O.btrusive L.osers.

I have to admit, Carlos's graphics are crude, but his creative writing is dead on.

C.J. is just starting to add color to his artwork when a siren wails in the distance. My heart crashes. A flashing blue light cuts into the darkness.

"Run!" Carlos bolts.

I look back at C.J., who's struggling to clear the fence. He almost makes it when his pant leg catches on one of the rails. I drop my crutches, free C.J.'s leg, and pull him over. My eyes flash back to the road. I catch a fleeting glimpse of Carlos just before he turns the corner and disappears.

"Go!" I shove C.J.'s cane at him. "Get in your car!" I grab my crutches and try to keep up, but my weakened ankle suddenly gives out. I gasp and double over, hands on my knees. C.J. is at the driver's side door when he turns and looks back. "Don't just stand there!" I shout. When C.J. doesn't move, I scream. "Get the hell out of here!"

"Come on, man, hurry," C.J. says. "I'm not leaving without you."

"Just go!" I shout. "I'll be all right."

The police cruiser screeches to a stop as C.J. jumps into his car and speeds away.

Two angry cops tackle me to the ground. One of them steps on an empty beer can, crushing it with the heel of his boot before cuffing my hands behind me. The other spits expletives as he grabs my shackled arms and shoves me into the squad car.

I feel like the loser they accuse me of being.

37. JADIEL

More Good Times

"That felt good." Carlos runs up beside me. It takes him a few seconds to catch his breath before he pants out, "I'm sticking with you, dude."

I watch the scene unfold in front of me. A burly cop pushes Dante's head down before shoving him into the squad car. Nothing about what just happened feels good to me.

"Sign here." I hold out the pre-filled parchment. "If you really want to stick with me."

"Wait, what am I signing on to?" Carlos glances at the contract. "Explain it to me again."

"Even more good times."

"You know it!" Carlos doesn't hesitate before inking his signature to the contract.

I roll up the parchment. Loyalty has come at a high price to Dante. It costs him a friend he never had.

"Decisive. Ruthless. That's how to get a contract signed. "Here" Equus holds out a key.

I assume the key belongs to his Harley. "Thanks, but I don't feel like riding your bike." I feel like curling up in a corner and pretending none of this ever happened.

"It's not my bike you'll be riding."

"What?" I take a closer look at the key. It's attached to an unfamiliar fob. "What is this?"

"A gift. For a job well done." He extends his hand and I follow it to — my breathing stops. Parked on the side of the road is a brand-new, shiny-black, Harley Davidson.

"Here." Equus presses the fob in my hand.

I close my hand over it. Ownership is an exhilarating feeling.

I finally understand how easy it is to be bought.

"Keep this in your storage bin." Equus hands me a black box. "Tools of the trade."

I take the box. My mind is somewhere between shock and elation. No one, not even Marius, has ever given me a gift. The feeling of being appreciated, maybe even — to some extent — *liked* is intoxicating.

I open the box, curious about its contents. There's a portable battery charger, surveillance equipment, and a rope.

"What's the rope for?" I ask.

"To restrain uncooperative or combative enemy operatives." He stares at me, as if he really wants me to get the message that follows. "The fibers are supernaturally strong. No one, not even a holy angel, can break free of those cords."

"Got it." I store the box and straddle my bike. The rope is insignificant. I don't care what it's for or who it can restrain. I insert the key and set the run switch to its on position. My heart rate accelerates. The rush of ownership is a natural high.

Only for a fraction of a second do I wonder how much black this bike has cost my wings.

38. DANTE

Faith

"Destruction of public property. Intoxication by an illegal substance." Principal Martínez throws the police report across his desk.

"I only had one beer," I say, with only a mild interest in defending myself. "It takes a little more than that to become ..." I raise my fingers and air quotation marks around the word *intoxicated*.

"Watch the attitude." Mr. Martínez rips the glasses off his nose. "Drinking alcohol is against the law for any minor under the age of eighteen." He regards me coldly. "The last I looked at your file, you were still only seventeen."

I shake my head and look down at my feet. There's a rip in the side of my Converse high tops.

Mr. Martínez sits back in his chair. "The police said you refused to give them the names of your accomplices."

I don't look up.

"So, you're going to take the fall?" Mr. Martínez presses through my disinterest in this conversation.

"Yeah, sure, why not? It gets me out of school, doesn't it?" Tough talk. The truth is, I am terrified. But it's better that I take the hit than get my friends in trouble. C.J.'s mother is one Xanax away from a mental breakdown; Carlos's father is an amateur boxer.

"Not exactly," Mr. Martínez says.

I look up.

"As of today, you have been officially suspended from school for the next two weeks. But you are not going to be sleeping in late or spending your days surfing the internet. All of your assignments will be sent home to you, and —"

"What?" I lean forward in the chair. My heart jackknifes in my chest.

"If you want to take the hit for your friends, Dante, that's your choice. It is my decision, however, how your punishment will play out."

"No, it's not." I jump out of the chair. "The court will decide that."

"It already has." Mr. Martínez returns his glasses to his nose and pretends to look through my file. "Your probation officer granted me the authority to oversee the mandatory eighty hours of community service you were assigned instead of jail time." He rests both elbows on the desk, weaves his fingers together, and places them under his chin. "Defiling public property is a crime the courts take seriously."

"But ...?" I stammer. "How ...?" I shake my head. "What are you talking about? Things don't work that fast in Puerto Rico."

"Sometimes ..." Mr. Martínez pushes his glasses down to the tip of his nose and stares at me over the black plastic frame. "The right connections are all you need to speed things up." He continues to stare over his glasses. "My brother-in-law is the chief of police. He knows how to get things done."

"Great. That's just great." I look up at the ceiling. Martínez just made it perfectly clear. He is the one in control right now. I form a fist and punch the air by the side of my chair.

"As you seem to have developed a new interest in painting and the ... creative arts ..." Mr. Martínez pauses and I lower my gaze, meeting the principal's eyes without blinking. "Besides buying the paint and providing the labor required to cover over your friend's graffiti, you will spend the next two weeks at the music school in Monte Grande, helping the maintenance staff repair and paint the classrooms."

"Whatever." I drum my fingers on the side of the chair. The muscles around my mouth are so tight they hurt.

"And when it's convenient to Professor Cabrera ..." Mr. Martínez removes his glasses. "You'll audition for the school."

"What?" I scramble to a stand. "That's insane!" You can't make me audition —"

"Sit down." Mr. Martínez speaks with such quiet dignity that there is nothing for me to do except sit down.

"Your teachers have told me that you are constantly drumming the desks. That you nod off, but that you're not sleeping because your head is moving."

"Fantastic." I return my eyes to the ceiling.

"Look at me when I speak to you." Mr. Martínez calls my eyes back down with the sternness of his voice. "Many well-known composers have created entire songs in their heads ... because they hear rhythms and sounds that no one else hears."

I press my fingers into the chair to stop them from moving.

"The music school has already been in session for over four weeks." Mr. Martínez continues talking as if he has not just said something that completely blew me away. "But Professor Cabrera has agreed to give you a late audition."

I don't have a single word to come back with.

"My reputation is on the line." Mr. Martínez nails me with his eyes. "You screw up this opportunity, and you screw me as well."

"Oh, that's just great! No pressure there."

Mr. Martínez stands behind his desk, his fingers sorting through the pile of paperwork in front of him. "I know you won't disappoint me," he says, picking up the police report and placing it in my file.

"Don't be so sure." I slouch into the chair, trying — unsuccessfully — to uphold the assumed tough guy attitude. Inside I don't feel so tough. I feel humbled. Faith is a funny thing. The mere expression of it makes a person want to live up to someone else's belief.

39. JADIEL

Lower than a Goatsucker

"Well, that was an unexpected twist." Equus comes up beside me. I'm about to head out to the mansion's garage and hop on my bike — but Equus wants to talk.

"I don't want to talk about it." I'd heard about the silver lining to Dante's suspension. The boy may get a shot at a happy life, despite my interference.

I take two steps forward, planning to walk away. But then I stop. When someone gives a gift to a person who has never received a gift before, it builds an unexpected loyalty. I temper my resistance and listen to Equus.

"That's why you always have to have a back-up plan," Equus says. "Scene projection will be your next lesson."

I'm okay with that, for the most part. But not now. "Can we talk about it later?" I head for my bike. I'm almost there when my senses are assaulted. The smell of wet dog makes my stomach turn. Chupa, his arm in a sling, is standing beside my Harley. His arm is broken — because of me. I pinned him to a wall, and he's angry about it.

I break into a run. "Get away from my bike!"

Chupa grins at me. Then he lifts his leg, bends it, and karate kicks my brand-new Harley.

"What're you doing?" I shout.

While I'm shouting, he's swirling into another kick. His paw sends the Harley skidding along the floor.

"Are you crazy?"

Chupa strolls over to my toppled bike. And then as if to say, *screw you*, he cradles the arm confined by the sling and flops down. "NO!" I let out an agonized cry. My Harley is a heap of scrap metal, crushed under three hundred pounds plus of demon weight.

I raise my hand. "You're dead!" One bolt. That's all it will take to—

"The powers I taught you are not meant to be used against my pet." Equus clamps my wrist with an iron grip. "Raise your hand against Chupa again, and I will unleash all the fury of hell on you." He flings down my arm.

Had I been unsure before, I am now clear. I'm lower than a goat sucker in Equus's life.

Equus turns to his pet. "Chupa, that was uncalled for." He orders his pet to his side with a finger pointed to the ground. Chupa heaves himself off the bike, snorts at me, and hops over to his master.

"And you need to learn how to channel your anger." Equus stares at me. "Lord Lucius's comrades DO NOT lose their tempers. Striking out in anger is a flaw that we exploit. If you haven't figured it out yet, learn one thing now. We cannot hear what humans say in whispers. We can, however, use what they shout out loud against them. Without even knowing it, they play right into our hands when they are angry." He scratches Chupa's head. Chupa lifts his chin and waits to be scratched on the neck. I gag back the bile that has crept into my throat. "Don't give *your* enemy the opportunity to walk through a door that you opened with your anger."

"Thanks for the warning," I say, fully aware that *my* enemy is standing in front of me.

Equus glares at me. "Given this morning's unfortunate outcome, we need to proceed with our next lesson." He looks like he'd rather be doing anything else than teaching me my next lesson. "Scene projection is like thought projection. The only difference is that instead of planting negative thoughts, you will now create a sinister scene in your victim's mind."

"I can do that. Let me practice on your pet." My voice is even, nowhere near reflecting the rage I feel. Fury has made me confident.

Chupa's eyes grow wide. He shifts his gaze from me to Equus. He's practically begging his master to dismiss my request.

Equus considers my proposal. "You have enough dark energy now to make good on your claim." He looks down at this pet. "Fine." He takes two steps back. "Place your hands around Chupa's head and create your scene." Chupa edges back. I grab him by the collar, but despite the bravado, I'm not sure how to proceed. "Create the scene in your mind first," Equus says. "And then project that scene into Chupa's mind the same way you did before with negative thoughts."

I nod. Scene projection is only a more sophisticated form of mind binding. Chupa snarls but he's been trained to obey. I clamp my hands over his head and focus on the scene I want to project. I imagine the chess pieces on the War Room's ceiling, coming to life. The King unsheathes a sword. He advances. The Queen brandishes a bayonet. The pawns produce daggers. Without a word, they follow the King forward. Chupa shivers, and then begins to shake as I transfer the scene to him. Next, I insert a large steel trap. And then I imagine Chupa caught in the trap, the advancing King nearly upon him. I'm not sure exactly how I'm creating the illusion he is seeing, but it's working. Chupa shakes his left paw — the same one I imagine ensnared in the trap. Steel teeth snap down. Chupa howls. And then he starts to wail.

"Okay, that's enough." Equus pushes me back.

The scene dissolves and the connection breaks. Chupa stops his screaming.

"Good. You got it." Equus grabs Chupa's collar to keep him from attacking me. "That's what you're going to use on that girl-you-barely-know-but-seem-to-care-a-lot-about." He studies me for a reaction. "She needs to see what will happen to her if she does not convert."

I recoil, but only internally. I will *never* use this dark skill against her.

"My in-school agent informs me that Dante is having sensory flashbacks," Equus says, ignoring my restraint. "Brief moments of connection with his one-time guardian angel. That cannot happen. If he believes that a holy angel is on his side, he will think himself immune to our advances. Faith in God's warriors makes our work more difficult. You need to get her to sign on with us. If she's not holy, she's not harmful. She still thinks she can be a sacred angel living in a fallen world. You need to show her otherwise. Your friend is in dire need of a Spiritual Savior."

Yeah right. Kiriela is the last person who needs saving, and she is never going dark. It isn't in her nature to be unholy. There is no malice or harm in her heart.

Inside me, there is a bad button waiting to be activated. A predetermined genetic code inherited from my parents. Kiriela was not cursed with flawed DNA. She will fight harder than I to hold onto herself.

"What about Dante?" I change the subject.

"Dante is now enjoying a momentary high as he basks in his principal's misplaced faith, but the seed of the conflict you implanted is germinating." Equus snaps at Chupa. "Come Chupa," he says to his pet. To the air he says, his back turned to me as he walks away, "Wait and watch. Soon you will see how the destruction you planted grows with our tender care and persistent attention. Dante is in the school yard now, cleaning up the mess you started."

40. DANTE

Hearing the Music

"Loser!" Pedro throws a rotten mango at me. I'm up on a wooden scaffold, in the school courtyard, painting over the graffiti C.J. sprayed onto the wall. The mango sails past me and splatters on the wall above my head. Pedro misses his mark. Again. Why, I wonder, is Pedro now considered the substitute leader of the pack?

And together with that question I have to ask, *where is Armando?* He should have returned to school by now. His suspension was over two days ago. Not that I care. Armando's presence or absence are insignificant to me. I have bigger things to think about right now ... like how Carlos threw me under the bus. He took off before I even had a chance to process what had happened. It was like he knew those cops were coming.

Maybe he was the one who called them.

Whatever. I have no proof. All I can go on is a gut feeling that he betrayed me.

I dip my brush and paint a few more strokes. C.J. left at least a dozen desperate calls the night I got arrested. I couldn't answer them. My phone was in a police locker at the local precinct. Carlos never called. Never offered to help clean up his mess. C.J. wanted to help, but Mr. Martínez wouldn't let him. *"No one else was involved,"* the principal said, *"so no one but you will paint the wall."*

I wipe the sweat from my face and go for more paint when the courtyard suddenly turns silent. The blood drains from my face.

Armando is standing in the middle of the courtyard, thumbs hooked into his belt loops. His Ray Bans shade his eyes, but they don't cover the smirk on his face. He knows I see who is behind him. Gia — hanging on Manuel's arm.

"Looks like your ex-girlfriend finally got smart." Armando's words sting. "She's moved on, dude."

A burst of laughter breaks out. And then Pedro and his fellow foot soldiers band around Armando. They don't say anything. They just stand there, sunglasses on, faces super serious. Like infantile members of the Secret Service.

I put down my brush. I'm done. I climb down the scaffold and walk out of the courtyard. I choose not to fight today.

I shove my shoulder against the door and fall into the bathroom. I jerk open the tap and splash cold water on my face. By the time I turn off the faucet, I've already decided that I'm getting into my car and driving as far away from school — from Armando, from Carlos, from Gia — as I can possibly get. It hurts to see Gia with Manuel — partly because I thought love meant something, but mostly because I'm insanely jealous. What does Manuel have that I don't? Hair, maybe, and a few more tattoos. The jealousy is bad, but it isn't the worst of it. The worst is the horrifying realization that I have been really and truly rejected. She's through with me. That hurts.

I rip off a paper towel and dry my face. I'm hot and sweaty and irritated. Pedro got under my skin. Armando's dramatic entrance shook me. But it was Gia's surprise appearance that put a wrench in my fragile peace. I shove open the door and head for my car. Standing in front of it, arms folded across his chest, is Mr. Martínez.

"Hello Dante," Mr. Martínez says. "Do you need something from your car?"

I punch my arm to the side, throw back my head, and sigh.

"Do you get off on harassing me?" My anger at the Universe comes out as an unintended insult. I drop my head and meet Mr. Martínez's eyes. "Sorry ... I didn't mean that the way it sounded." I shake my head. "Couldn't you have just suspended me?"

"I could have. But then I would not have given you the chance to become the young man I know you can be."

I groan. "That sounds like a line written for Life-time TV." I drop my bag to the ground. "Have you ever thought that maybe you're in the wrong profession?" I feel my anger lighten. "Why do you insist on torturing me? What have I ever done to you?"

Mr. Martínez relaxes against the car, right foot crossed over the left, arms still folded. He stands there, watching me.

"Stop staring at me, Martínez." I can't hold back a smile. "It's creeping me out." I look away, still smiling. "Someone might think you're gay or something."

"It wouldn't be the first time someone was wrong about me." Mr. Martínez keeps his eyes focused on my face. "People make mistakes in judgment all the time." He unfolds himself from the car. "Good luck tomorrow." He strides back to the school.

I watch Mr. Martínez disappear inside. *I've got this*, I tell him. *I've got this*, I tell myself.

The next day, I'm the only person in the music school not carrying an instrument. My guitar remains in the car while I walk around all day with a bucket of paint, a roller, and two brushes. I spent the morning painting the group practice room, and maybe took a little longer than necessary to finish it. I wasn't trying to screw off. I just kept hearing all this music in my head. I stack the cleaned brushes and rollers in the maintenance closet and straddle the rusted metal chair left out in the hallway.

I close my eyes. Sounds form into a rudimentary composition. It starts with the guitar. A strong, flamenco lick. I finger the chord progression on my imaginary guitar. And then I add other instruments to my mental composition. A bass holds the agitated rhythm, and then a drumbeat starts with the kick and snare, followed by the conga. The lead guitar picks up the melody. It's a wild mix of Spanish romance, Latin movement, and Afro-Caribbean angst. I smile. I haven't felt this creative, this — *alive* — in a long time.

"Did you bring your guitar?"

My eyes pop open. "What?" The school's director, Professor Cabrera, is standing in front of me. "I mean, sorry." Blood rushes to my face. "Yes, sir, I did."

"Go get it. Let's hear what you can do."

My heart jumps. I swallow, look away, and then swallow again.

"Meet me back in my office," Professor Cabrera says.

I nod, and then walk out the building to my car. All sorts of doubts and insecurities flood my brain. Everything I know about music I've learned on my own. I can probably fake my way through a sight reading but I don't know the first thing about an audition.

I open the trunk and pull out my guitar. My hand slips on the handle. I put down the case and wipe my sweaty palms on the back of my pants. Then I grab my guitar and walk back up the steps. I'm about to enter the building when I see the new girl. She's sitting on the wall next to Salena — who's talking to a guy who looks about as much her type as ... as I do. The dude has an earring and wears a leather band around his right wrist. He has a guitar on his lap, which he is strumming with a ringed thumb.

Seeing Salena here stumps me for a moment. The new girl, I get. Mr. Martínez told me that she's into music. But *Salena?* Who would have thought? Salena. Here. In the music school. Hanging out with a rocker. It takes a few seconds for me to process that. Maybe Salena isn't as "Armando-owned," or as "plastic," as I thought she was.

And maybe, I'm not the screwed-up "loser" she thought I was.

I yank open the door and head for the director's office. I'm not totally ready to accept that Martínez was right in sending me here. But I'm getting there.

41. KIRIELA

Dark Shadows

I'm sitting in the hall outside Professor Cabrera's office when Dante comes out of the room. Like him, I just sweated through an audition — in my case for the music school's Concert Choir. I got here not because I was chasing after Dante — not this time. This time, my own sadness brought me to the same place where Dante was sent.

I couldn't stand watching the spectacle in the courtyard, so I left when Gia arrived. I went to a wooded area behind the school and hid from the ugliness. Mr. Martínez was in the area, so I knew Dante would be safe. I, on the other hand, was in danger of falling apart. I felt sad. Confused by humanity. How can people be so cruel? To make myself feel better, I reverted to the only thing that brings me comfort — singing.

I struggled for only a moment when choosing what to sing. Marius had no reason to fear or further punish me. By decree, I was banned from singing celestial songs. By emotion, I had no interest in doing so. "Broken Hallelujah" was the song that came into my head.

I thought I was alone when I sang my sad rendition, but Salena was nearby. She told me I had a beautiful voice. I told her I always sing when I'm stressed. She knew what I was talking about because she sings, too. Before the day was over, she talked me into auditioning for the choir, where she goes after school. I couldn't say no. Music still lives inside of me.

My stomach cramps. I feel nauseous. Something horrible is happening inside of me. I pick myself up off the floor and head toward the auditorium. Choir practice is about to start, and I've been offered a place among the sopranos. I may no longer sing celestial songs. But I will sing. No one — not even Marius — can stop me from being me.

The rehearsal goes smoothly through the first few songs — mostly all local ballads — but then the choir director, Mrs. Carmona, flips through her music and decides she wants us to learn Handel's Hallelujah chorus, for the Christmas concert.

A rush of sudden heat runs through me as the pianist starts playing those painfully familiar chords. My mouth freezes shut. I can't sing this song. Marius has forbidden it.

But then, I glance around me. Fifty-plus human teens are harmonizing my favorite song. Would a parent's — or guardian's — order stop them from singing? Somehow, I don't think so. I've observed enough human teenage behavior to know that disobedience is the norm. In a fraction of a second, I decide to become a human teen.

I can't even begin to explain how wonderful it feels to hit the high notes of one of Handel's most glorious songs. For one fleeting moment, I'm in Heaven.

"For the Lord God Omnipotent reigneth." I sing with the others. "Hallelujah! Hallelujah! Hallelu …" Oh, no. Something strange just happened. I'm not singing soprano anymore.

"Kiriela!" Mrs. Carmona puts down her baton. "What is going on?"

Fifty teenagers turn and stare at me. One girl stifles a laugh. Another nudges the girl to her side and mouths the words, *Did you hear that?*

"Weird," the other girl says.

A cold chill shivers over the back of my neck and up around my throat. Icy fingers clamp around my neck. "Nothing." I drop my gaze. "I'm sorry." I look up when a tenor in the back row laughs. And then quickly return my eyes to the floor. I know what happened. Someone

— or some*thing* — altered my voice. Black shadows slither across the speckled tiles.

Mrs. Carmona balls her hand on her hip and sighs. "Then why are you singing out of your register?"

More muffled laughter.

I shrug, not wanting to hear that deep, alto voice that isn't mine.

"Are you in the alto section, Kiriela, or the soprano?"

"The soprano," I manage to say. The shadows pass over my feet and circle my legs.

"Then would you please remember that when it comes time to sing?"

The shadows swim around my neck and tighten over my throat. I choke against them. Evil is present and palpable. I have to get out of the room. I swallow hard, barely able to speak.

"May I get a drink of water?" I finally choke out. "My throat hurts."

Much to my relief, Mrs. Carmona lets me go.

I dash from the room. An explosion of laughter chases me out the door.

I punch the button on the fountain and gulp a long swallow of water. As I drink it comes to me. The pressure in my throat began when we started singing the Hallelujah chorus. The darkness inside of me is rebelling.

Fight back.

I force myself to focus on the music, rising up and out through the practice room door. I concentrate on the soprano voices soaring above the choir. *Sing with them.* I have to saturate my mind with my voice, with my spirit. It's the only way to control the evil that wants to overtake me. I absorb the tone and pitch. I sing with the sopranos, horribly at first, but after several repetitions, I'm able to force the change in register.

Relieved, I'm ready to go back. But then I see Dante, sitting on the outside steps.

A frightening premonition takes hold of me. I freeze in place. *Dante's in danger.*

I snap out of freeze frame and run toward him. The darkness I feel is coming from either Armando or Jadiel, back to finish what they started. I have to warn Dante.

"Hello, Kiriela."

Jadiel. I come to a full stop. My heart weakens. It feels as if someone has smothered it with a pillow. The darkness I feel is coming from him.

"Leave, Dante," I say flatly. *"Now."* Dark clouds edge out the sun. "You're in danger." Every fiber of my being trembles at those words. My best friend is now my enemy.

"I'm sorry, Kiriela." Jadiel raises his hand. A second later, Dante crumples to the ground, unconscious.

"What have you done to him?" I start for Dante, but Jadiel holds me back.

"He's all right." Jadiel's hand is shaking, but other than that, he's in control. "He'll wake up." Jadiel grabs my hand and leads me away from Dante. "I need to talk to you, it's important."

"Wake him up first." I stop in front of him.

"I promise, he'll be all right." Jadiel's voice is low but intense. "Trust me, Kiriela."

42. JADIEL

Welcome to My World

"Trust you?" Kiriela glares at me. "You're trying to destroy Dante!"

"I'm trying to ..." A rush of adrenaline pumps through me, stopping me saying save you. Overpowering a human in no way compares to trapping a baby goat. I'm literally shaking now.

"Dante's all right," I finally repeat. "I didn't hurt him."

"Yes, you did. But I'm going to make sure that never happens again."

Seeing her concern for this boy who cost her so much sucks to the surface all the negative thoughts I have tried to suppress. *I could have shown you the world, Kiriela. But you chose to see it without me.* I glance back at Dante, and then look away. "You lost everything because of him. I hope it was worth it." Jealousy always sounds ugly; mine sounds worse. It's pathetic.

"It's not what you think," she says quietly. "I was only trying to protect Dante when things got ... complicated."

"Complicated? That's the best you can come up with? I heard you kissed him."

"Then you heard wrong." She looks up at me. "He kissed me."

"Oh, thank you for the clarification." The sarcasm comes out painfully strong.

"Now clarify something for me." Her voice is even stronger. "Have you joined up with Lucius? Your sworn enemy? Those powers you just displayed are not from God."

"No, they're not. And ..." *No, I have not aligned with Lucius.* That's what I want to say. But Equus may be listening. I feel his oppression in the dark shadows around me. "And right now," I say instead, "I have more power than I have ever known before. And I *like* it."

For the first time, I admit that truth aloud. I like the power.

"Clearly." She stares at me with a look I know well. "So, let me get this straight. You would rather be a slave to Lucius than a vessel of God?"

"God's vessels are his slaves. When will you understand that?"

"That will never be part of my understanding." She looks shocked. "You've changed, Jadiel. I barely recognize you."

"Demon. Remember? Or have you forgotten where I was sent?"

My heart collides. I swallow against her scorn. The truth is hard to hear. I have not — until now — taken ownership of my new spiritual status. Kiriela always did have a way of making me see what I did not want to about myself.

And to make me feel even worse, I see Dante, lying on the ground, unconscious. "I almost had him." I turn away from her. "Until you showed up with Malakiy."

"How could you hurt him like that?" She grabs my arm and forces me to face her.

"Things got *complicated.*" A muscle tightens in my jaw. "He was my assignment, nothing more. I would have delivered him to Lucius and moved on. But because you interfered, things have gotten a whole lot more *challenging* for me."

I immediately regret saying what I did. She won't let a word of it slip past her.

"In what way?" She speaks quickly, the way she always does when she's afraid for me.

She has no idea how much I want — need — to talk to her about all that has happened, in both our lives. But I can't. I can only be loyal to one side — openly, at least.

"You and I need to be working on the same side," is all I manage to say.

"I will never be on the same side as you." Her voice slows down. "Not as long as you continue to side with Lucius." A crease appears between her eyes. She clamps her hand low over her stomach and gasps out a groan.

"Are you all right?" I reach for her, but she steps back.

"I'm fine," she says.

She must have convinced herself. Her forehead is smooth now, pain free.

"I am not siding with Lucius," I say carefully. "I'm surviving."

I swallow against the knot that has formed in my throat. Any thought that we might have a civil discussion about a change in her spiritual status is not going to happen right now. All I can do is speak the truth as I know it. "Dante Vega has been marked by Lucius. And there is nothing you or I can do to stop that."

"There's one thing you're forgetting." The crease is back. "Dante has also been marked by God."

I nod. "And who do you think is going to be more powerful, here on Earth? God? Or Lucius?"

"I'm surprised you even need to ask." Pain seeps through her words. "God is not only more powerful. He is just."

"Look at me, Kiriela." I throw open my arms. "God's *unjust* law has made me what I am. All I was trying to do was to love you. Where is the crime in that?" Once again, I loop back to the thought that has been haunting me since my expulsion. I can't get it out of my head. It's like a slow-working poison that torments before it kills. "Why was I punished for loving you?" This is *not* the conversation I should be having with her. Every word I say takes me farther away from what I am supposed to accomplish.

"I don't have all the answers," she says. Her voice comes out like gravel, as if it's been put through a stone grinder.

I squeeze the bridge of my nose. "There is no redemption for the fallen, Kiriela. The sooner you accept that, the easier it will be for you to accept me. The way I am now — not the way you once knew me." My voice sinks further with every word.

"You are not as different as you think." Hope smooths out her tone. "You may want to believe that you are lost, but I'm not buying it. Redemption is what God wants for all of us." She stares at me. "You just have to want it, too."

"And I don't." A lie I couldn't stop from spewing from my mouth.

"Why? Because God wants it and so you don't? Is that what you believe is free will?"

"No. Free will is an illusion. I have no more capacity to change the way I think or behave than you do. God made me who I am. The Great Creator chose my passions and my path. He made some people good, like you. And others bad, like me. So, if anyone is to blame for my wicked ways, it is He."

"No, that's all on you. God not only made you wicked, if that is what you believe, he also made you smart. Use the brain He gave you, Jadiel. You don't need to turn dark. Evil is a choice."

"You're right. I don't *need* to turn dark, Kiriela. I just did." I head towards Dante. "I obviously can't convince you that working with me is better than working against me, but I can show you my new reality. If you get in my way again" — I snap my fingers and wake Dante from the trance I sent him into — "your friend will be worse than damaged. He will be dead." I stand and turn toward her. "Lucius will make sure that happens, and I won't be able to stop him."

I turn and walk away. "Welcome to my world, Kiriela."

"That went well." Equus comes up beside me. "Except ..." He watches Kiriela rush toward Dante. "She's still not with us."

"It's going to take some time." Which I'm glad about. The moment Kiriela loses her convictions, she loses herself. I head for my recently refurbished bike. Body shop technicians are also on Equus's extensive payroll.

Equus stands in my way, blocking access to my bike. "I don't care what happened between you and your-ex-whatever-she-is. Your arguments are tedious and unproductive. And they are distracting you from your assignment. But hopefully, you have learned something useful from that last boring encounter." His nostrils flare as he stares at me.

I learned what I needed to. As Equus himself once told me, one of the most effective forms of attack among humans is setting up conflict between friends. Divide and conquer. One of Lucius's favorite strategies. "I get the point," I say tersely. "Move on."

Equus looks at me with obvious derision. "Lord Lucius is growing impatient. And when he gets impatient, he becomes ... unpredictable." Equus drags out the adjective. "So, here's what's going to happen. You're handing over Dante. Within the next forty-eight hours. And" — his eyes bore into mine — "make sure that your-whatever-she-is does not interfere."

"She has a name," I say. "Respect her enough to use it."

"Respect is earned, my friend. Remember that the next time you fail to please me." Equus stares at me with a look that reminds me who holds the power in this relationship.

He steps away from the bike. While walking away he says, "Oh, and by the way, that girl is pre-menstrual."

"Pre-*what*?"

"Take care of your *Kiriela* problem." Equus over emphasizes the use of her name. "Or I will take care of it for you."

43. KIRIELA

The Pain of Being Human

Dante is conscious but confused. I'm confused, too. Why do I care so much about this boy? I can't hide the way I feel. Jadiel was right. I've lost a lot because of this human boy-I-can't-stop protecting. So why do I keep doing it? Why can't I stop worrying about him? If I look deep inside myself, will I find something more than my protective instinct? I glance over at Dante. His gaze meets mine. My face flushes.

Confirmed. There's something more than my protective instinct hovering between us.

I may be unpracticed in human behavior, but I've seen how human girls act around boys they find attractive. Their cheeks turn pink. They stare at the ground when a boy meets their eye. They notice things about the boy that they may not have before — like the way the side of his mouth dimples when he smiles. Or how one strand of hair falls over his right eye.

Dante pushes back the loose strand.

My heart tip taps. Guilt sets in. *What's wrong with me? I'm in love with Jadiel. Not Dante. Jadiel.* My fingers tremble. *Where is Malakiy?* If he were here, I wouldn't be so focused on Dante.

"Where am I?" Dante's question forces me to face my reality. Malakiy has disappeared. Jadiel has become stronger. I am the only who can stand between this boy and the evil planned against him.

"At the music school." I drop down beside him.

"What happened to me?" His voice sounds muffled.

"You passed out." A lie, but less traumatic than the truth. "Do you remember anything?"

"No, not really." He struggles to sit up.

Good. I suck in some air.

"Dante, come back inside." Professor Cabrera is standing at the school door. He's framed in the light streaming from the hallway. The darkness lifts. As if it had never been there at all.

I return to the choir room.

Two hours later, I reconnect with Dante.

He's in the study room, with his head on the desk. I slide into the desk beside him. "I need to talk to you." I take in a gulp of air. Approaching Dante like this is a major violation of Marius's decree. But I don't care anymore. Protecting Dante is the only right thing to do. "Please, I don't have a lot of time. Armando is—"

"Leave me alone," he says, groggy and half asleep. "I don't want to talk about—"

I crunch my brow and squeeze it between my fingers. A vein throbs above my temple. I massage my forehead, and then breathe out a long, low *owwww.*

His eyes pop open. "I'm sorry, I didn't mean ..." He sits up. "Are you okay?"

"I'm fine," I lie. A sharp cramp pulls, from deep inside me. I force myself to recover my composure. "I've been getting a lot of headaches lately."

That's as much as I'll share about the pain I'm in. This conversation is not supposed to be about me.

I breathe against the agony. Another sharp pain cramps below my stomach. It hurts so much it makes me nauseous. I groan and close my eyes. I have never felt this kind of pain before. It's a twisting, tightening wrench that comes on strong, and then is gone. But while it lasts, it's intense.

Another cramp rips through me. I stumble to a stand.

"Sorry, I need to ..." I pick up my bag and stumble for the door.

Dante follows behind me. "Is there anything I can do?"

"No, I'll be okay." I stagger down the hallway and push through the bathroom door.

I swing open the stall door, lock myself in, and double over. There is only one person I feel like talking to right now. And that person is not Dante. It's Jadiel.

Am I dying? That's what I would ask him, if he were here. Because that's how scared I am. He would grab my shoulders, look me in the eye, and say, *No, you're not. Take a deep breath. I'm here, with you.* And those words would be enough.

I breathe in, and then out, leaning on Jadiel in my mind. I do this several times. Until finally, the pain subsides.

I drag myself out of the stall and rummage through my bag, looking for loose change. There's a white canister on the wall labeled with the words *tampon* and *napkin*. And the price, 25¢. I have no idea what those words mean. All I know is that when the other girls feel as horrible as I do now, they go to the bathroom and buy whatever is inside that box.

My frantic search comes up empty. I have no change.

Holding back the tears that lurk behind my eyes, I walk out of the bathroom, return to the study room, plop my head over my arms, and let out a low moan. I feel sick.

"Hey, what's wrong?" Dante edges closer. "Let me help you."

"I'm okay." Somewhere in the back of my mind, I suspect that I'm not sick. But I don't want to talk about it. "Please, can we stop talking about me?"

"If that's what you want." Dante raises his hands in mock surrender.

None of this is what I want. I fight back. "Do you have twenty-five cents?"

Dante sticks his hand into his pocket and fishes out a few coins. He slides a quarter across the table.

"Thanks." I take the coin and go back to the bathroom. I put the quarter into the box on the wall and select *tampon*. That sounds like a word I heard in the hospital. *Oxycodone*. A pill prescribed for pain. A small box falls out of the machine. I stare at it, and then open the top flap. No pain pills. Only something white and cylindrical. With a string attached.

I let out a long sigh. Then I dig my phone from my bag and dial Jadiel's number.

He doesn't pick up. Hope deflates. I stuff the phone back into my bag, walk out of the bathroom, and find Dante.

"Do you have any Motrin?" Somehow, the word *Motrin* seeps into my mind. The girls in school say this word a lot, especially when they walk cramped over, like I'm doing now.

"No, but I can drive you to Walgreens."

"Can you take me home, instead?"

"Yeah, sure. Where do you live?"

"Off Route 114."

"Can you be a little more specific?"

"Past the sugar cane fields."

"A little more?"

"I'll direct you." I sigh. There are no street names where I live.

When we arrive at the farmhouse, I hesitate before getting out. I hate the thought of being alone tonight. If only I could hide under Jadiel's wings, I'd be okay.

"It looks like no one's home," Dante says. "Are you going to be all right?"

My eyes blink. The trees blur wet in front of me. "I'll be fine." I get out of the car. Jadiel will answer his phone. Eventually.

"Wait." Dante scribbles on a loose paper. "Call me if you need anything."

I nod, and then I climb up the porch and into the house, not bothering to turn on the light.

44. JADIEL

Female Things

Six hours after my encounter with Kiriela, I'm in front of the farmhouse where she lives. I've avoided coming here before, but now see no other option. She tried to call me, at least ten times. I couldn't answer her. I was holed up with Equus, strategizing our next attack. I cut the engine and swing off my bike.

"Kiriela!" The wind blows through the dry stalks of sugar cane surrounding the farmhouse. "Are you there?" Red eyes watch me. Demons crawl around the property.

A cold shiver passes over me. Where's Malakiy when you need him? The house is dark, but I sense her presence. Every nerve in my body activates. Something is wrong. I climb up onto the porch. "Kiriela?" I look in a dusty window. No sign of her. I try the door. It opens, and I step into the farmhouse.

The door slams shut behind me. "Kiriela?" I walk past the living room and into a narrow hallway leading toward the bedrooms. The only open door is decorated with foam flowers. I take a deep breath and peer into what must be her room. There's not much in it. A school uniform hanging in the closet. A tattered book on a scratched desk. Besides that, the room is empty.

"Kiriela?" No answer. "Kiriela? Where are you?" I stride down the hallway. The bathroom door is closed. I hesitate, and then knock on the door. "What's wrong, Kiriela? Please, answer me."

"I'm bleeding." Her voice is so soft I can barely hear it.

"What?" My tone notches down several decibels. "Open the door, Kiriela."

She opens the door, and then crumples back against the wall.

I rush in to support her. "What happened? Did someone hurt you?" Equus and his threats are forefront in my mind.

She shakes her head from side to side.

I scan her body, petrified. "I don't see any blood, Kiriela. What —"

She doubles over. "It hurts so much, down there."

At once I am relieved and terrified. She's not physically hurt. Equus hasn't touched her. But somehow, he knew she was premenstrual. Did he have something to do with that?

"Breathe, just breathe." I sit down with her on the floor. I finally figured out what "pre-menstrual" means. The term is a scientific way to say the same thing we learned about in Human Physiology, *monthly flow.*

"Get up." She pushes me away. "You can't be near me."

"Why not?" I stagger to my feet.

"I'm unclean." She's in full-blown panic mode. At first, I don't understand, but then I get it. She's filtering what we learned in Human Physiology through the Bible verse taught alongside it. Leviticus 15:19. *"When a woman has her regular flow of blood, the impurity of her monthly period will last seven days, and anyone who touches her will be unclean."*

"Forget about what the Bible says." I'm the one panicking now. "And let me help you."

"Why is this happening to me?" She avoids looking at me. "I'm not human."

"You're more human than angel right now. With human girl problems." I release a breath of pent-up air, and then dig my key fob out of my pocket. "I'll go to the store and buy" — what, I have no idea, but I know she needs things she probably doesn't have in the house.

"Is this what you're going to buy?" She digs a box out from her bag. The word *tampon* is written across it in bold blue letters.

My face feels hot. "I don't know. Uh ... maybe." It is the first time I have ever heard myself stutter.

"What ... what do I do with it?"

I freeze in place. "You're asking me?"

"Who else do you see around that I can ask?"

I cannot imagine this conversation happening with anyone else. What human teen — male or female — would ever understand how clueless I — we — both are?

"Can I get you something?" Asking how to help makes it feel less awkward. "I mean, before I go."

"A cup of tea?" The creases around her mouth ease out.

"Chamomile, right?"

She nods *yes*. Her shoulders relax. "I need to take a shower."

"Yeah, of course. I'll be in the kitchen."

She smiles. "Thanks, Jadiel. I'm glad you're here."

I smile, too. Because today, I see hope for a future, with Kiriela in it.

I prepare her tea. Demon eyes watch me through the window. I leave the tea seeping on the counter and go outside. I raise my hand and shout, "Leave, all of you!" With the power that's growing inside of me, I blow back the demons. When the last one scampers away, I hop on my bike and speed toward the nearest store.

Once inside, I grab a basket and head for the female hygiene aisle. "You have *got* to be kidding me." I stare at the unfamiliar products. Kotex. Sanitary pads. Tampons. Overnight protection. Light days. What am I supposed to buy?

A young woman stands beside me, scanning the shelves. I move away. Heat rises up my face. I pretend to look at the soaps on the opposite aisle while watching the woman closely. She has put a pack of Always Regular with Wings in her basket. Then a pack of Always Overnight.

I stroll to the end of the aisle, look over my shoulder, and then walk back. The woman passes by me, her basket full of what I also probably need. I snatch a pack of Always Regular with Wings and Always Overnight and toss them in my basket. A young man not much older than me walks up beside me. He glances down at a crumpled piece of paper, takes a pack of the light day pads, and adds them to his basket. I glance at the light day pads, and then grab a pack and toss it in the basket. Just in case.

I stare at the contents of my basket. The two humans who inspired this selection have chosen different things. And ... I glance back at the shelf. There are still other products to choose from. There is the box labeled tampons, and the Always Regular *without* wings.

Am I making the right choice?

"Excuse me, I don't mean to intrude, but can I help you?" A middle-aged woman comes and stands beside me.

My first reaction is knee-jerk, *No, go away. It's embarrassing enough already.* But the woman seems kind, maternal, approachable. So, when I finally speak, I say, "There's so much to choose from, I don't know..."

"It's not really all that complicated." The woman smiles. "Is this the young lady's first time?" The way she talks to me, her voice low and her words discreet, invites me to trust her.

"Yeah, so I don't know if I should get ..."

"What you have selected is good. She will use these during the day" — the woman points to the Always Regular with Wings — "and these at night." She moves her finger over to the Always Overnight. "And these when the flow gets lighter." She points to the light day pads.

I absorb that, and then ask, "But what about these?" I point at the box of tampons.

"Not necessary. She'll be fine with what you have in your basket." She smiles. "Your girlfriend's lucky to have you."

"Oh, no, she's not my —"

Before I can correct her, the woman collects what she has come for, a bar of scented soap, and wishes me a good day.

My girlfriend. The words sound good. Maybe without all of Maion's restrictions, and without interference from Abaddon, Kiriela and I could be together that way. I've already made a step in the right direction. I've shopped for female products.

You're funny, Equus. I'm sure he's behind this, somehow. The last humiliation, right?

Wrong. Taking care of Kiriela in this way is a new experience. She's hurting. I'm here to help. In all the years we spent together in Maion, there was never an opportunity to care for her the way I'm doing right now. She needs me.

That feels fantastic.

I stop at the food section and look through the boxed teas. I almost throw a box of Chamomile into the basket when I see something called Lavender Chamomile. And Vanilla Honey Chamomile. And Honey Sleepy Time Chamomile. That might work. I grab a box of the Honey Sleepy Time. She'll probably have trouble sleeping, with all that pain. Maybe this tea will help. That reminds me, I should buy a box of Motrin, too.

As an afterthought, I add a box of the Lavender Chamomile to my basket. I once heard her say that lavender is a soothing scent. Like that meant anything to me, then.

What else has she said to me that should have meant something? Maybe I should try listening, just a little bit more.

My phone rings. I dig it from my pocket and glance at the number on the screen. It's Kiriela. My heart trips. "Are you all right?"

"I'm fine, physically, but ... will you be back soon?"

"Yes. I'm paying now. I'll be there soon."

"Good." She releases a long sigh.

"Kiriela, are you okay?"

I hear her catch her breath.

"What's wrong?" I say.

"I don't know." Her voice sounds small and vulnerable. "I'm confused. And sad. And tired. And right now, probably incoherent. You must think I'm weak."

"Not possible. You want to tell me what's going on?"

She hesitates a moment before answering. "I have never felt this way before, as if I could walk straight into the ocean and drown without anyone even noticing."

"Where are you now?" I say.

"In my bedroom."

"Go to the window." I shift the phone to my other ear and pull out my wallet.

"What?"

"Go to the window and look outside." I pay for my purchase and head for my bike. I know what's happening. She's scared and she's alone. As bad as things might have been in Maion, none of us were ever alone during the hardest moments of our lives.

The floorboards creak as she heads toward the window.

"Do you see anything" — I choose my words carefully — "*unusual* outside?"

"I see the moon. And the stars. It's a beautiful night."

Good. I nod. The demons are gone. "Go outside," I say.

"Jadiel, what —?"

"Just do it," I say, gently.

The springs on the door squeal. She's outside.

"Is there someplace you can sit down?" I store what I bought and lean against the bike.

"There's a hammock on the porch." She breathes in. "It smells nice." The hooks holding up the hammock scrape the wall when she sits down. "It's the *Ylang Ylang.* The tree's in full bloom tonight."

I capture the scent in my mind — stronger than jasmine but equally as sweet.

"Look up," I say. "What do you see?"

"Stars, lots of stars."

I look up, too. "I see the same stars," I say. "So, if I'm seeing what you're seeing, neither one of us is alone right now."

"How did you know that's what I was feeling?"

"A lucky guess."

"Do you see how some of the stars are brighter than others?"

"And if you look closely," I say, "you'll see they have different colors. Some look yellow, others orange. Some are even blue."

"I wonder why that is?"

"For no other reason than to make you wonder."

I think maybe there's a smile in her sigh.

I close my eyes and smile along with her.

When we hang up, I thank the stars for this perfect night.

45. KIRIELA

Fig and Almond Yogurt

After hanging up with Jadiel, I feel better. Now all I have to do is de-program Maion's teaching about a woman's monthly flow. *Anything she lies on will be unclean. Anything she sits on will be unclean. Anyone who touches her bed will be unclean.* Random verses from Leviticus 15 flash in and out of my head. I work with each verse as it comes. *This hammock is not unclean. My bed is not unclean. And Jadiel will not become unclean if he touches me.* Those were old beliefs bound to a specific time and a specific culture. I keep talking to myself. Until finally, I believe what I'm saying.

When Jadiel returns to the farmhouse, I'm sitting on the porch, staring at the stars. He climbs up the steps, peels off his jacket, and drapes it around my shoulders.

"It's cold out here," he says. "Come inside with me."

I hug my arms across my chest. The night is chilly, but I don't want to go inside. Looking up at Heaven, at the stars, focuses me on something bigger than myself.

"You'll catch cold." He offers his hand. "Come on."

I hesitate. De-programing doesn't happen automatically. Timidly, I take his hand.

"Here." Once inside, he hands me a paper bag. "There's a lot of stuff but start with" — he pulls out a pack of Always Overnight with Wings — "this." His cheeks turn pink.

I nod. Words are not necessary. I trust what he says. I head to the bathroom with my bag.

A few minutes later, I return to the kitchen. Jadiel is boiling water. There's a tea bag hanging inside a cup. It's not awkward anymore. We're just learning about life, together.

"I brought you something to eat." Jadiel nods at a sack on the kitchen table.

"Thanks." I almost forgot how hungry I am. I open the bag and take out a container of Greek yogurt, a pack of figs, and a bag of split almonds. My heart flutters. "It's what we used to eat in ..." I can't bring myself to voice aloud the name of our former home. A dull ache pulses around my heart.

The bump in his throat bobs up and down. "I know." He looks away, turns from me, and grabs two bowls from the cabinet. With his back still turned, he cuts a few figs into bite-size pieces, and then divides them equally between the bowls.

I open the yogurt and add it to the figs. Heat swells behind my eyes as I think about what used to be.

"I miss it sometimes," I say. "Our old life." It's the first time I've talked to Jadiel about what used to be.

He takes the almonds, rips open the bag, and adds them to the yogurt.

"What do you miss the most?" His voice is steady, but he doesn't look at me. He knows that if he does, I'll see the longing in his eyes.

"Stolen moments. Seeing you each morning." My heart leaps at the memory. "Our sign."

A light smile lifts the corners of his mouth.

He puts two fingers to his heart. "Stolen moments. Our sign. Not everything is lost."

I smile with him. What seemed so long ago is now within our reach. "Jadiel, maybe —"

His phone dings. The sound interrupts, and then cancels, what I would have said next. Probably better that way. What's the point of talking about a past we will never live again?

Or a future we can't have.

Jadiel's brows draw together as he reads the incoming message. He deletes the message, and then pockets his phone.

"I can't return all that we have lost," he says, setting a kettle of water to boil on the stove. "I can, however, offer you a safe future."

"What?" My skin turns cold. "What are you talking about?"

The word *safe* raises a red flag.

"Nothing." He puts a tea bag in a mug. "We'll talk later." He offers me a bowl of fig and almond yogurt. "Eat. You must be hungry." He hands me a spoon.

I take the bowl and scoop up a spoonful of yogurt. The first bite tastes like Heaven.

"Try this." Jadiel brings me a cup of tea.

I wrap my hands around it. A soft, floral aroma floats upward. I smile. "Lavender."

"Lavender Chamomile," he says.

"Even better." I close my eyes. With Jadiel beside me, life no longer seems so scary.

"Will you stay with me?" Slowly, I open my eyes.

He sighs and closes his. "For a few more minutes. That's all the time I have."

It's enough. Dante feels far away now. Which is exactly how it should be.

Jadiel still has my heart.

46. JADIEL

A Happier Place

A few more minutes. That's not nearly enough. But soon, I'll be called back. To the mansion if I'm lucky. To Abaddon if I'm not.

"I need to lie down." Kiriela lets out a small breath of air.

I wish I could take the pain away, but I don't have that kind of power. All I can do is help her to the bedroom.

"Lie with me," she says.

I inhale sharply. *That's the last thing I should do and the first of many things I want to do.* I struggle with how to respond. My brain tells me to make sure she's comfortable, and then to *leave* the farmhouse. The more time I spend with her, the more I put her at risk. I haven't forgotten about the demons lurking around the house.

My body tells me something different. It aches to be with her. How can I comfort her if I can't touch her? Hold her? Put my wings — I swallow — my arms — around her. I tuck her under the sheet and lie beside her. She rests her head against my shoulder.

I sigh and close my eyes.

"Tell me what to do," I say. One moment like this is worth all the bleak hours to come.

"Make the pain go away," she whispers. "All of it." The pain she's talking about now is no longer physical.

"Close your eyes." I can't take away her pain, but I can alter her reality. I place my hands on her head. Her hair is damp — still half wet from the shower. It feels like the soft strands of the weeping willow in Maion's garden, just after a summer rain.

I rub her hair. She smiles. She loves when I caress her hair.

But then suddenly, her body tenses. She grips the sheet and bunches it in her hand.

"It's okay," I whisper. "I'm going to take you far away from here, to a more peaceful place." I superimpose my mind over hers, creating a mental image that should make her happy. "Follow me into the room your mind is seeing."

"Jadiel, it's beautiful." She relaxes against me. "How did you —?"

"Shh, it doesn't matter." I've created an elaborate music room using a skill I once practiced on a goat sucker.

Through her mind, Kiriela enters the imaginary room with me. She runs her fingers over the grand piano, feathers them down the golden harp, across the polished violin and over the antique cello. She circles the room, gliding from the gold-framed mirrors to the music-themed wall frescoes. I paint the scene I want her to imagine in her mind. She stops in front of a mirror, where I help her see herself dressed in a sapphire blue gown. I insert myself behind her.

"Imagine singing here," I say. "In this gown, in this room. Where there's no one else but you and me."

"How did you do that?" Her eyelids flutter. "I can see myself in a music room, dressed in a blue gown. And I can see you, standing behind me."

I nod. Scene projection is a type of mind manipulation, but it doesn't have to be for an evil end. Happy thoughts can be implanted, too.

In the fantasy I'm creating, I put my hands on her shoulders. "You look beautiful," I say.

Her face softens as she imagines the scene I'm projecting.

"Now imagine me, standing beside you, dressed in a tux."

She smiles. "You would never wear a tux."

"I'd wear one for you."

In front of her eyes, my black pants and button-down shirt transform into a black tuxedo.

"You look handsome," she says.

This time, I'm the one who smiles.

"Kiss me," she whispers.

I raise her chin and gaze into her eyes. They are as blue and deep as the Caribbean Sea. I no longer need to paint an illusion to calm her fears. She's at peace, with both herself and me.

She meets my lips halfway. I start the kiss with slow, gentle pressure. Her lips part on a sigh. The air between us fills with the scent of almonds and lavender.

She responds with a sweet caress. The tip of her tongue sends shivers down my spine.

I place my hand behind her neck and draw her closer. "Tell me this moment will last forever," I whisper against her lips.

"It will." Her lips lift into a smile. "It will live on in your memory, as it will in mine."

I seal her words with another kiss, and then quietly, she falls asleep in my arms.

I turn off my phone.

Tonight belongs to us.

47. DANTE

The Magic Stone

For the first time in weeks, I don't feel that dark oppression that seems to follow me everywhere. I feel lighter, happier. Maybe because my two-week suspension is finally over; or maybe because I'm no longer thinking about Gia.

I close up Tito's garage. I've been here since three in the afternoon, but my mind's not been on the work. All day — all frickin' day — I've been thinking about that new girl, Kiriela. She didn't come to school today. I want to call her, but I never got her number. A shiver passes over me. Again, there is the trace of a memory, a sense of something familiar, but I can't connect that feeling to any specific time or place. That's why it's probably nothing. And I need to re-focus. It's the end of the month. Never a good time for my family.

It's past eight when I finally leave Tito's body shop. I'm exhausted, but hopefully, the extra money will ease some of the stress on my mom. End of the month means that bills are due.

I arrive home and find my mother seated at the kitchen table. Her hands cover her face, fingers pressed into her temples. A stack of bills is on the table, a calculator and checkbook beside it. The bill from the electric company is stamped with a second notice. The one from ATT wireless is marked past due. She quickly removes her hands, relaxes her brow, and scoops up the bills. And as she does, she instantly replaces the frown on her face with a beautiful smile. Mom would protect me from the world if she could.

I bend down and kiss her cheek. "Is everything all right?"

"Everything's fine *hijo*." The crease returns between her eyes. "You're home late tonight." She stands from the table and stuffs the bills into a drawer near the refrigerator. "Can I get you something to eat?"

"I'm not hungry, Ma. I had a late lunch." I throw my jacket over the chair. But then it occurs to me. Maybe she is hungry. Sometimes Mom will get so busy, or so tired, or so worried that she'll forget to eat. "On second thought, I wouldn't mind a sandwich. Do we have *mezcla*?"

She smiles and kisses my forehead. "You know we always do."

She opens the refrigerator door and pulls out a loaf of bread and the covered plastic container where she keeps the blended spread of cheese whiz, spam, red peppers, and pickles. *Mezcla* isn't about hunger. Mom and I always share a *mezcla* sandwich whenever we sit down to talk. It's one of the few things she never refuses.

"*Toma,* Ma." I dig a wad of money from my back pocket and offer it to her.

She turns her back to me and places one plate with two sandwiches on the center of the table. I grab the two glasses of *parcha* juice she poured and follow behind.

"Just take it, Ma. Please." I leave the money on the counter.

"*Hijo*, we're fine." Her voice is firm. "Use the money to buy yourself some new clothes. Your jeans are ripped, and you have exactly one pair of sneakers."

"I don't need more than one pair of sneakers." My voice is equally as firm. "And I like wearing ripped jeans."

She begins to protest but I cut her off. "Take. The. Money." I grab her by the shoulders and stare her down. "I'll buy what I need, when I need it."

She is the first to look away. "*Está bién, hijo,*" she says. "We'll talk about it later." She smiles and reaches for a sandwich.

I smile with her. Any strength I have, I inherited from my mother.

A few minutes pass as we both concentrate on our sandwiches. Mom finishes hers in less time than it takes me to eat half.

"Where's Elena?" I miss my sister's presence. She's always wherever Mom is and usually the first to greet me.

"In her room. She's not feeling well." My mother looks down at the table. "Dante" — she slides her finger around the edge of the plate — "I was talking to your father today."

I drop the last of my sandwich to the plate and push my chair back from the table. "I'm tired," I say. "I'm going to bed."

"He wants to see you play." She hesitates before continuing. "At the music school," she finally says, not looking up from the finger that now lies still upon the plate.

I snatch the plate from underneath her hand and throw the scraps into the garbage.

"No. I don't want him there." I open the faucet and dribble detergent on the plate. I scrub the dish as if it were dripping oil rather than crumbs.

"He's really proud that you're pursuing music."

I make a fist with my right hand and punch down on the faucet to shut off the water.

"What does he know about my music?" I set the plate on the dish stand and swipe my hands across the back of my jeans. "He doesn't know anything about me." My voice rises with my anger. "Or my music."

She's quiet for a moment. "Maybe you should give him the opportunity to find out." She raises her gaze to meet mine. "Your father's a great musician."

"So I've been told." I press my fingers against my temples. "Except it wasn't him that taught me how to play the guitar, or the keyboard, or ..." My chest heaves and I silence my mouth, finishing the thought in my mind. *Or how to shave. Or talk to girls. Or anything else a father is supposed to teach his son.* If it weren't for Mr. Martínez, I'd know nothing about what it means to be a man. I squeeze my eyes shut as she puts her arms around me.

"*Hijo,* he may not have been there for you"—she strokes my hair—"but try to understand"—she takes my face between her hands—"he was sick."

I pull away from her. "He was drunk, Ma. There's a difference."

"But he's still your father."

"Shooting sperm into a woman's body does not make a man a father."

I probably deserve the slap that follows.

"Don't you ever speak to me that way again." Mom turns from me and walks away.

My face burns under the mark of her hand. I slam my fist into the table. And then I slam it again. I slam it until my skin is bruised and raw.

And through the pain, I convince myself that I have never needed a father, and never will. I'm going to make it on my own.

"Dante?" Elena calls out in a sleepy voice when I crack open her bedroom door. "Is that you?" Her bedside light is still on.

"*Si, mi amor.*" I take a deep breath, push open the door, and enter her room. "It's me."

Elena sits up. Bubbi, her stuffed monkey, is under her arm. Her eyelids flutter. She rubs the sleep from her eyes and smiles as I sit next to her on the bed.

"I was waiting for you to come home," she says, "so we could sing our song."

"I'm here now." I ignore the sharp pang in my chest. I'm not going to be able to give her what she wants: her goodnight lullaby — with the guitar. "You ready to sing?" Tonight will have to be *a cappella.* My hand hurts too much to strum.

"Where's your guitar?" she says.

"Why don't we sing without the guitar tonight?"

"Noooo! We always sing "*La Nanita Nana*" with the guitar!"

"I know, but let's do something different tonight." And then without thinking, I reach out and stroke her hair. Mistake. She sees my hand.

"What happened to your hand?" Her eyes stretch wide.

"Nothing." I hide my hand. "Why did you go to bed so early tonight?"

Her face goes blank.

"I don't feel good," she says.

"I see." I move my hand to her forehead. "Oh yes, you feel terribly warm."

Her skin is smooth and cool.

"Guess I can't go to school tomorrow."

"I guess not." I brush her hair back behind her ears. "Don't you like school?"

"I hate it."

"Is Mario bothering you again?"

She nods, her eyes large and sad.

"He said I was ugly." She batters her eyes to fight the tears. "It made me feel bad."

"That's because you didn't evaporate Mario's words with the magic stone."

"The what?" She sits up in the bed.

"Wait here." I rise from the bed and head for my room. When I come back, I place a smooth turquoise stone in her hand.

She looks up at me, her eyes bright.

"This stone has magic powers," I say, sitting next to her. "It can wipe away any painful words faster than you can blink your eyes."

She giggles and blinks her eyes. The corners of her nose crinkle as she smiles.

"Keep this stone in the pocket of your school uniform, and the next time Mario says something ugly to you, reach into your pocket ... slowly ... you can't let him know you're reaching ... and say ... to yourself, because if he hears you, the magic will be broken ... I am a beautiful girl, and your words don't hurt me. Those are the magic words. And while you're saying the magic words, rub the stone between your fingers, like this ..."

I take the stone from her hand and hold it against my thumb, passing my forefinger over the glassy surface. "The warmth from your fingers will heat up the stone and release the magic. But never show Mario the stone. If he knows you have it, he'll want it, and the magic will be gone."

She looks up at the ceiling and lets out an amused laugh.

"What, you don't believe me?"

She shakes her head no.

"Go ahead, try it." I place the stone in her hand.

She rubs the stone vigorously between the palms of her hands, as if she's preparing to throw a die onto a gaming table.

"No, no, no." I hold her hands still, then lower them to her lap. "You can't let anyone know you have the stone. It's your secret weapon. You have to rub it gently. And, it has to stay in your pocket." I bring her hand to the pocket of her gown and help her release the stone. "Now go on, touch the stone like I showed you ... then say the magic words."

"I am a ..."

"*Shhh.*" I lift my finger to my lips. "Remember, you can't say the words out loud."

Her eyes open wider.

"I am a beautiful girl," she mouths, her hand moving slowly, invisibly inside her pocket.

"And your words don't hurt me," I whisper.

"And your words don't hurt me." Silently, she forms the words with her mouth.

"Good." I kiss her hair.

"Dante, your father is on the phone." Mom appears at the door, phone in her hand. "He wants to talk to you."

"I told you ..." I press my lips together, containing my frustration. "I don't want to talk to him."

"Please, for me." She holds out the phone.

I blow out an irritated sigh.

"Fine." I grab the phone from her hand. Then I prepare myself to speak to the man I once idolized, but now barely know.

"What is it?" I say, more curtly than I intended.

Silence.

I'm about to hang up when I hear my father say, "How are you, son?"

How am I? Let me think. Hurt, angry, and so not ready to be having this conversation.

"Your mother tells me you're studying at the music school." More silence. "Your grandpa studied there."

"I did not know that." Anger oozes off my clipped words. How much more do I not know about my father's family?

"I knew you had it in you," my father says. "My son, the musician."

I grip the phone. "I've been playing the guitar since I was five. Music is not new to my life." When I say that, it trips Omar Vega up for a minute.

"Oh, really," he says. "I didn't know."

"What do you want, Dad?"

He breathes in, and then says, "To make things right."

I don't know what that means or how our family can ever be right again. The conversation continues awkwardly until finally I say, "I can't do this right now." I *cannot* have this conversation. A lifetime of pain cannot be healed over a simple phone call.

"I understand." Omar Vega swallows into the phone. "We can talk some other time."

Or not. I shut off the connection and hand the phone back to my mother. After slamming the door to my room, I flop down on the bed.

After twelve years of indifference, now all of a sudden I matter to him? My father first walked out on us when I turned five. He walked back in four years later and fathered Elena. Six months later he was gone again. Why does he think he has any right to stroll back now?

Mom is angry at me for not hearing him out.

I'm angry at her for not understanding.

Without even being in the room, Omar Vega has successfully shoved a wedge between me and my mother. Again.

Oppression is never too far from my messed-up life.

48. JADIEL

Lesson Learned

"Parents can be ... oppressive, don't you agree?" Equus clicks off the radio receiver, which for the last twenty minutes has been receiving audio information from Dante's house. "They walk out on their families, follow their own agendas, and then expect their children to be happy and well-adjusted." He returns the receiver to its case, and then puts the case in the Harley's storage bin. "If parents only knew how tragically their selfish decisions affected their innocent children" — he shakes his head in mock concern — "they would never stray outside their precious homes."

I know I'm being baited. And I take the bait. My father walked out on me, too. Maybe he didn't find another wife, or turn to the bottle, but he abandoned me none-the-less. He left me for a cause. For Lucius's rebellion. There were very few nights when he was at home. Lucius was more interesting than me or my mother. So interesting that he successfully persuaded my mother to join him. Funny, though, unlike Dante, I would give anything to see my father again.

"Moving on," Equus says. "Tomorrow I want you at La Colina High. Dante has completed his two-week suspension and returns to school tomorrow. Let's see how the seeds you planted in the fertile ground of Carlos's head have germinated."

And just like that, any good feelings I had from caring for Kiriela have been blown away. It's back to business as usual. Me against Dante.

Me against Kiriela. Divide and conquer.

Except, Equus did not divide us yesterday when I was at the farmhouse. There were no threatening texts. No condescending phone calls. No mention at all that I had left the mansion and spent the night at the farmhouse. There's something suspiciously wrong about that.

"Why didn't you challenge me about being with Kiriela last night?" I'm not worried that I'm revealing anything Equus doesn't already know. He tracks my every move.

Equus stares off into the distance. "One more lesson you need to learn."

"Lesson? What lesson? Anything I learned last night had nothing to do with you."

Equus shifts his gaze back to me. "*Need* to learn is what I said." His tone is condescending. "Today's lesson will illuminate what you did not learn last night."

"What? How to wiretap a house? Is that your important lesson of the day?"

"Any idiot can learn how to plant a bug. Not all idiots can see a spiritual attack" — his eyes narrow as he focuses on me — "not even when it is played out right in front of them."

The next day, I rumble into the school parking lot and cut the engine. I'm early. Dante won't be here yet, but I'm hoping to see Kiriela. I scan the parking lot. The buses are starting to pull in. She should be on one of them. A primer-patched Cavalier drives into the parking lot, dragging me back to the task on hand. I lean back on my bike. Carlos is parked a few feet away. I wonder what will happen when Dante meets up with Carlos after having a bad night.

"Dante, my man!" Carlos swaggers toward Dante's car. "La Colina's very own music nerd." He smirks. "I did not see that coming."

Dante shoves the keys into his pocket and gets out of the car. Frowning, he pushes past Carlos, slings his backpack over one shoulder, and walks away.

"Don't get me wrong dude!" Carlos runs two steps ahead and blocks his path. "I admire you. School in the morning. School in the afternoon. You are one ... *dedicated* student."

"Get out of my way." Dante pushes past Carlos.

Carlos holds him back. "What? I can't tell my number one friend how proud I am of him? That hurts, dude."

"Shut up, Carlos." Dante hikes up his backpack. Then he blurts out what he's probably wanted to say to Carlos for the last two weeks, "You could have at least called me. That's what *friends* do. They stick together. Oh, but I forgot, you're NOT A FRIEND."

I can see where this is going. Dante is angry at his father. But, since Dad is not here to take the heat, Carlos will get a full swing of deflected anger.

Talking to an absentee father stirs up all kinds of internal drama.

"I was gonna call you, dude. But my battery" — he lowers his shades and looks over them — "it just keeps dying on me." Smirking, he pushes back his glasses.

"You're full of shit!" Dante shoves Carlos back.

Is this the lesson I'm supposed to learn? That a bad night at home leads to a worse day at school? If so, that lesson is uninspiring.

Carlos throws down his bag. "Come on, man, you wanna fight me?"

And so it begins. Another boring, predictable fight. Equus's "next lesson" is becoming clearer by the minute. Uncontrolled anger is an easy bait and trap.

A crowd begins to form, shouting for blood. This schoolyard fight could get Dante permanently suspended. I can work with that. It would be a major blow for him. That should gain me some momentum. Finally, I feel like we're closing in on Dante.

The two go at each other, punch for punch. Dante almost takes down Carlos. But then, Kiriela pushes her way through the human circle and changes the dynamic.

"No, Dante!" she cries out. "Stop!"

Dante turns toward her voice and Carlos takes advantage of the distraction. He drives a punch to Dante's stomach. With the wind knocked out of him, Dante can't fight back.

Dammit, Kiriela. I unfold my arms and take two steps forward.

"All right break it up!" The school guard runs into the circle and plants himself between Carlos and Dante — arms stretched out. To Carlos he says, "Go to the principal's office. Now!"

"This isn't over fucker!" Carlos points a finger at Dante. Then he turns and walks away.

My chest tightens as it absorbs the truth. Kiriela's intervention saved Dante's butt. In two long strides, I reach her. "Why did you have to interfere?" I'm almost as angry as Dante now. The only difference, I'm not deflecting.

"Why wouldn't I have? Dante was in danger." She's angry, too.

Lesson learned. No positive moment can last. Not when you are under attack by Lucius and his legions. "Here." I hand her my helmet. Fifteen minutes later, we're at the farmhouse.

I stare at a tattered book on the desk in front of me. There's a piece of paper sticking out of it. I slide it out. And then I read what Marius wrote to Kiriela after she was banished from her father's house.

My dear Kiriela, the letter begins. It continues with words of regret and sadness, and then spells out the terms of her new life. *Rule number one: From this day forward, you must give up all claims to the status of the daughter of Alexa and Adriel, and all powers associated with said status. You will no longer be allowed to guard, protect, watch over, or engage in any other activity associated with your former family.*

"Looks like I'm not the only one disobeying the rules." I'm calmer now. More frustrated than angry.

"The rules are unfair." She's reflective. Her way of tempering heightened emotion.

"Yes, they are," I say carefully. Unlike before, when anger meant power, now it only means division.

She takes a deep breath. And then she says, "I don't understand how the fallen are expected to obey yet another set of rules when we fought so hard to be free of God's."

I squeeze my temples. "There are bigger issues here than the theology of the fallen." My voice is tight. Despite my best effort, negative emotions are resurfacing. "If you hadn't interfered, Dante would've been suspended. That would have given me the chance to breathe."

"What do you mean, *breathe*?" Her voice amps up. "Are they hurting you?"

I turn from her. She doesn't need to know how much Equus is breathing down my neck.

My phone pings. I read Equus's message. *Have you learned your lesson yet?* The chilling precision of his words makes my blood turn cold. *If so, move on. Lucius wants the soul he assigned to you. You have twenty-four hours to either get Dante's signature, or hand KIRIELA over for proper spiritual instruction. She's obviously learned nothing from you.*

My stomach plunges. Fingers trembling, I pocket my phone and turn to Kiriela. "I need you to listen to me." My words better count, or I won't have any words left to share with her. "I need six humans to sign a contract for Lucius. Dante has been pre-selected as one of those six." I purposefully neglect to mention the other part of the *Grand Commission*. "If he doesn't sign, I will be punished. There's a dungeon with my name on it, waiting for me to fail."

"No, that's not happening." Kiriela is back. Strong and determined. "There has to be a way out. We can —"

"There is no way out. It's either pledging my way into the Underworld or being chained out of it." I stare at her. "My choice is clear. I'm pledging in." I take the opportunity to add, "And so will you." I turn from her. "I'm not leaving you unprotected."

"Eternity chained to Lucius is your way of protecting me?"

I sigh and shut my eyes. "Do you think this is what I want for you? I don't have a choice. I need Dante. He's been marked. And I need you, on my side. Not working against me."

"No." She shakes her head. "I refuse to join forces with you. Not if it will hurt Dante."

"And I refuse to leave you vulnerable."

"I can take care of myself."

"I know you can." I decide to say it like it is. "But if you don't agree to work with me, my trainer will destroy you. Collateral damage, he calls it. The cost of war."

"The cost of war?" She spits my words back at me. "You don't even sound like yourself anymore!"

"Because I'm not!" The words come out strong. "And neither are you."

"All right, Jadiel, I get it." She softens her tone to temper me. "We've both changed."

I stare at her. "No, you don't get it. You don't get even the half of it." It takes me two seconds to decide whether I want to elaborate. Decided, I say, "It's time you start acting like the fallen angel you are rather than the holy one you still think you can be." I take her hand. "Let me show you something." I lead her to the closet door mirror. "Release your wings."

She hesitates, as if knowing that doing so will change everything she thinks she knows about herself. She folds out her wings. Half of the feathers have black tips.

"Get the picture?" I stare at her through the glass.

I don't break the connection, until her eyes turn wet.

"Now, back to business." I turn from her. I can't bear to see the pain in her eyes. "You violated rule number one of the fallen angel code." I snatch the note from the desk and hold it out in front of me. "What part of this do you not understand?"

"I understand all of it. Completely. What I don't understand is you, and why you're giving up so easily."

"You're making this *really* difficult for me." I toss the note back on the desk. "Your obsession with Dante is going to screw things up, for both of us."

"What're you talking about?"

"The same thing we've been talking about what seems like *forever*. You need to stay away from Dante."

"Why are you so obsessed with him?"

"Because you are!"

I focus on the floor, because I can't look at her when I say, "I asked you this once, and I'm going to ask you again." The lines around my mouth tighten. "You gave up everything for that boy. Has it been worth it?"

Her gaze drops, like mine, to the floor.

"Answer me, please."

"No," she says, and that's all she's giving me.

Enough. My words will not convince her. There's no point talking anymore. I can't force her to go against herself. I need something that only Malakiy can get. If he does what I ask him to do, Kiriela will be untouchable.

But first, I have to find him. Then, I'll need to set him free.

49. JADIEL

Angel Sword

I find cell 113 S with the help of one of the prison guards. All I had to do to get him to cooperate was to offer the key to my Harley.

"Hurry up." He's taking too long to unlock the cell. I shoot a glance at Malakiy. His eyes drag open and focus on me. He's sitting on the floor, his knees clutched to his chest. He looks drugged but he's not. Dehydration is the mind-numbing agent of choice in Abaddon.

"Give me that." I snatch the key from the guard and open the lock. Malakiy wobbles to a stand. I grab him. He's about to fall. Dizzy, I imagine. Extreme thirst has predictable symptoms. I shove a bottle of water at him. "Just a few sips," I say. "Slowly." Unlike me, he shows constraint. He drinks discreetly, caps the bottle, and steadies his breathing. I push him down the corridor. "Don't even think about doing something heroic," I growl at him. "Kiriela needs you."

"Here." I shove my key fob into the guard's hand. He takes off running. Unlike me, he doesn't wear a tracking device. My Harley is his ticket out of Abaddon.

I look at my right wrist. By googling *how to jam a tracking device*, I was able to tamper with the band's GPS. All I needed to do to interfere with the signal was to cover the transmitting device with an electrically conductive metal. I found some copper wire in the science lab. By wrapping the wire around my wrist band, I successfully disrupted the signal. I think. For now, it's enough that we're underground. GPS signals don't work in Abaddon.

When Malakiy and I are outside, I use the dagger I stole from the jailer and slice off the rope binding Malakiy's wrists.

"Go to Maion," I say. "As fast as you can. And get my sword out of the armory."

"Are you insane?" Malakiy rubs his rope-burned wrists. "No one gets near the armory without Adriel's permission."

I stare at him. "You mean to tell me that you — Adriel's favorite son — are incapable of convincing him that you need access to the armory?"

"Access he will grant me." Malakiy stares back at me. "What he will not authorize is the removal of a weapon."

"Then maybe" — my tone hardens — "you will have to steal it. I need my sword. And you are going to get it for me." I bring it home with, "For Kiriela."

"Why your sword?" Malakiy speaks slowly now. He looks confused.

"Drink." I nod at the water bottle. I don't have time for dehydration disorientation.

Malakiy screws off the cap and takes a long drink. "Why *your* sword?" he repeats. "And why does Kiriela need it?" Amazing what a little water will do.

"Because *my* sword has a history." I'm annoyed with the undertone to Malakiy's newly found lucidity. "Lucius's blood is on it." I stare hard at him. "You know what that means. A holy weapon that has been defiled by unholy blood is more powerful than any other. It is the only weapon that can kill a demon. Do I have to say more? Kiriela is in danger. Equus has made her a target. Without my sword, she is defenseless."

"Fine." Malakiy's wings snap open. A brilliant trail of light flashes across the sky as he disappears over the horizon.

I sprint back inside. There's one more thing I have to do. I head for the dorms. Nube is there, hidden underneath my bed. It's time to get her out.

"Come on, Nube." I fall to the floor and reach under the bed. She touches my hand with her paw. I pull her out. She smiles — unless I'm just imagining it — and curls into my arms.

Twelve hours later, I have both Nube and my sword and I'm back at the farmhouse. Malakiy wanted to come with me, but I talked him out of it. He can't be seen with me. Word of his escape is all over Abaddon. I jump off Equus's bike. Yeah, my trainer will soon put two and two together. But until he does, I'll do what I have to do.

I yank open the door and stride into the kitchen. Kiriela is sitting at the table, reading.

"Jadiel! What's wrong?" She pushes out the chair and leaps to her feet.

"Here." I hand Nube over to her. "Take care of her for me."

Nube cranes her neck to look at me. "It's ok, Nube. You've safe here."

Kiriela glances down at the lamb, and then up at me. "How did you … is she yours? What is going on?"

"I don't have time to explain. Her name is Nube. She's been with me since—" It doesn't matter. I quickly get to what does. I unbuckle my sword. "Take this." I hold out the sword. "Hide it where no one will find it. Use it when you are threatened. And kill with it if you must."

She gasps, and then sets Nube down.

"Your angel sword," she says softly. "How did you get it?"

The lump in my throat jumps up and down. I avert my eyes. "I convinced Malakiy to take it from the armory."

"You did what?"

I don't get into the whole rescue story. She'll ask too many questions and I'm running out of time. "Like I said, he stole the sword for me." That's all I'm giving up.

"No, that's not possible." She looks up at me, eyes wide. "Malakiy would never steal the only weapon that can kill Lucius. That can kill *you*."

I nod. "We have to talk, Kiriela."

"Yes, we do." She sets down the sword.

I drop the bag I've been carrying.

"Malakiy did not raid the armory for me. He did it for you."

Kiriela nods. "That sounds like him."

"There's a reason he risked everything to bring back my sword."

"I know." She studies the floor. "I am Equus Centurion's bargaining chip. He's using me to manipulate you. To threaten you. And if I don't do what he wants me to do, he'll hurt me. Own me." She looks up. "I know, Jadiel."

"Then you also know that by hurting you, he will destroy me. So please, I'm begging you, stop interfering with my assignment. You're attracting too much attention."

"I would have no need to interfere, if your assignment didn't threaten Dante." Her sigh sounds as defeated as the words that ride on it. "We are both caught in an impossible situation."

I look away. "Yes, we are. That's the way things work, in Abaddon. Lucius wins, no matter what we do."

"No," she says quickly. "Lucius will *not* have that victory. We can fight him. Together." She lets out a small gasp. Her face twists into pain. She grips the edge of the table.

"Are you all right?" I'm thinking it's more female pain, but then I see a dull red glow, spreading down her shoulders. "What's going on?" I rush to her. "What's happened to your wings?" The burning glow originates at her shoulder blades, where her wings should be.

The color drains from her face. "They're chained inside of me."

"What?" My stomach heaves. "Who would do such a cruel thing?"

"It doesn't matter. I'm okay." She regains her composure and the red glow fades. "It happens, sometimes, when I start feeling overly ... protective."

I shake my head. "This is so messed up." I take a bowl from the cabinet and fill it with water. I put the water in front of Nube, and then force myself back on task. "There is no redemption for me. Not anymore. But for you —"

"No." Kiriela speaks with the authority that comes from conviction. "Have you forgotten all that we once learned? Every soul deserves a second chance."

Nube stops drinking and looks up at her.

"Stop being naïve." I look away. How can she still think the way she does, even after being mutilated? I say what she won't accept, "The fallen never get a second chance. If you really want to help me, do what I'm asking you to do. Then maybe we can alter our realities."

The expression on her face changes. The muscles around her mouth relax and her eyes soften. "What do you want me to do?" She recognizes the words I used to say when trying to offer hope, *maybe we can alter our realities.*

"Prove to me that you're on my side."

"You know I —"

"Prove to me that you no longer have the need to protect Dante." I turn and stare at her.

She looks away. "How am I supposed to prove that to you?"

"First, by not interfering. And second, by allowing me to do what I need to do."

Nube wobbles to a stand. A drop of water slides off her nose.

"If you don't interfere, I'll do what I need to do, and Dante will sign the contract when I offer him an out. He'll be miserable, for a while, but he won't be dead. That will pacify Lucius and get Equus off my back." I allow myself a sliver of hope. "So, do we have a deal?"

She looks straight at me and says, "I don't make deals with Lucius or any of his demons."

"You're not making a deal with Lucius you're making it with me."

The damning look, and the silence that follows, puncture my heart.

"So, are you with me or not?" I already know the answer, but I need to hear her say it. A dull ache throbs in the middle of my chest. I need her words to justify what I plan to do next.

"No, Jadiel, I'm not." Her gaze doesn't waver when she adds, "I never will be, if your mission is to destroy Dante."

My battered heart takes one more hit. "Even if that means destroying me?"

Her eyes flicker. "I will do what I think is right, and then work really hard to protect you from the consequences of my decision."

I nod. She's made her decision. Now I will make mine. I reach into my bag and pull out the rope that used to be stored in my Harley. And then, knowing that she will never forgive me for what I am about to do, I draw out the speed and power that are inside of me and before she can fight me, I use the rope to bind her to the kitchen chair.

"Forgive me, Kiriela." With an aching heart, I take the sword and head for her bedroom. "I'm putting this under your mattress."

Nube scurries behind me. She's bleating. A sad, unhappy sound.

"Why are you doing this?" Surprise and fury mix equally in her voice.

"You left me no choice." The muscles in my jaw tighten.

I stride into the bedroom and hide the sword. When I return to the kitchen, she's struggling to break free. The cords hold tight. They would. They were strengthened by the power of evil weavers.

My heart jumps up into my throat.

"You cannot keep getting in my way." My voice sounds like gravel. I can barely speak. Every word I say hitches in my throat. "This time, there will be nothing you can do to stop me."

I tighten the rope that binds her to the chair. I know only one way to save Kiriela from herself. I have to immobilize her while I go after Dante. She's not going to stop protecting him and I've run out of time. I'll snag my fifth soul without her. And then hope that Lucius moves on to torment someone else.

"If you hurt him, I will never forgive you!" Her words come out pained as she struggles to get free.

My mouth tightens. I mark Armando's number. "Meet me at the corner of Dante's street. Bring Pedro with you. Dante needs to be taken care of." I end the call. "I'm sorry, Kiriela. But I will not allow you to be a pawn in my chess game."

Nube races in front of me and blocks the door. I scoop her up and set her aside. "I'll be back for you, I promise." I yank open the door. "For both of you."

Heat sears my face as I step outside. Soon, this nightmare will be over.

50. DANTE

Papi

I feel heat on my face and wake up with a start. Sunlight pours into my room. I look at the clock beside my bed. It's almost noon. I groan and knock off the covers.

"Wake up, Dante." Elena bursts into the room. "I have a surprise for you." She sing-songs her message.

"Not now, Elena. Please —" I start to pull the sheet over my head, but then freeze in place. My father has entered the room, pulled forward by my sister. Omar Vega has not stepped inside our house for almost seven years. And he does not, in any way, share any kind of affection with Elena. *So why the hell is he holding her hand?*

"Look Dante, it's *Papi*." Elena uses the affectionate term for father. Not *padre*. Not father. *Papi*.

I nearly choke on the word.

"He came to see you." Elena jumps on the bed. She takes my face in her hands and says, "You're *still* in your school clothes? That's not how you're supposed to sleep."

I have no idea how she can do that. Skip from our father to my clothes. As if the weight of them is equal. I'm about to ask her where our mother is when Omar Vega cuts me off.

"A long night?" my father says, as if he lives here. As if he has any right to ask.

"Why are you here?" I rise from the bed and push past my father.

Omar Vega hesitates. He looks away, swallows, and then says, "May I ... sit down?"

"Why?" I grab a towel off the chair and head for the bathroom.

My father follows me.

"I thought maybe we could ... talk."

I crank open the faucet and splash water on my face. My legs feel unsteady, but I forbid them from buckling.

"I'm proud of you. And I" — he coughs — "I miss you, son."

I increase the volume of water pouring from the faucet.

Elena appears at the door. "I'm hungry."

I force a smile and say to my sister, "Go wait for me in your room. I'll get ready, and then take you for an ice cream."

"But I haven't had lunch yet."

"Perfect," Omar Vega says. "Why don't I take you both out to lunch?"

I stiffen, wipe my face, and then turn toward Elena. "Go, I'll take you to McDonald's." My mother must have left early for work, expecting me to handle lunch.

"*Yahhh!*" Elena spins around and runs to her room.

Omar Vega is still there, blocking the bathroom door.

"Your mother says you're thinking about applying to the Conservatory of Music in San Juan."

I reach for my toothbrush.

"I'd like to ... sit down with you sometime. Maybe teach you a few things."

I spit into the sink. "I have to take a shower. Excuse me."

I slam the door. *This cannot be happening.* I strip off my shirt and fling it to the floor. The rest of my clothes soon follow. I punch on the water and step into the shower. Cold water spills over my head and trickles off the tips of my hair. I feel nervous, out of control — as if the master chip in my brain is being re-programmed. It's as if someone ... or some*thing* is inside of me — either trying to heal ... or to destroy me.

I pour shampoo into the palm of my hand and lather it over my head. Then I scrub my scalp so hard it aches. *Why is he here?* I press the heels of my hands against my throbbing temples. *And how am I supposed to respond to him?* I dump my head back and allow the water to wash the suds down my back and onto the floor. *Am I supposed to just pretend that everything's normal? That I don't resent all the years he wasn't here?* I take the bar of soap and rub it over my body. *Forget it. I can't even think straight right now let alone tax my brain with analysis.* I crank off the shower, wrap the towel around myself, and return to my room.

My father is still there.

"Maybe this isn't the best time." My father's voice trails off.

Shit. My heart twists. Omar Vega looks disappointed.

Struggling with myself I say, "Sorry, I can't talk right now." My feet leave soggy prints on the floor as I head for the dresser and pull out a set of clean clothes. "I have to go somewhere, but ..." The *but* stops me. *But* means that maybe I'll consider not being a jerk.

"Look ..." My father's voice trembles. "I know what I did was —"

"No, we're not going there. Not now. I can't ..." I can't talk with my father about how his infidelity hurt my mother. About how his drinking and self-absorption destroyed our family. "I can't do this right now."

"Okay, maybe later."

Or *not.* I pull a T shirt over my head and bolt for the door.

My father smiles weakly as he follows me out of the room.

Ten minutes later, I'm out of the house and headed for McDonald's with my sister. She is non-stop chatter and I mostly silent. When she finally finishes with her Happy Meal — leaving most of it on the tray — I scoop up the only thing she is interested in (the toy) and stuff it in my pocket. "Come on, let's go play in the plaza."

"Can we go to Papi's house?" She jumps up and down like a manic cheerleader.

"No." I take her hand. I don't even know where his house is.

"I want to go to Papi's house!" She stomps her foot.

"We're going to the plaza." The muscles in my jaw tighten. As an afterthought I add, "I'll bring my guitar."

"It's a deal!"

If only it were so easy to convince girls over the age of seven to bend to my will.

The damaged road leading into town is full of loose stones and potholes. Progress is slow, but we finally make it through the traffic and reach the plaza in front of the Catholic Church. I park the car and get out. Elena is already ten feet ahead, chasing pigeons around the fountain. I grab my guitar from the back seat and sprint to catch up.

When I reach the fountain, I sit on the ledge and pull out my guitar. I strum a few chords as I watch Elena play. She's picked up a dry seed pod that looks like a small machete and is swiping it in the air like a Taino princess. I wonder who she's pretending to be, wishing I could pretend to be someone else, too.

Nothing makes sense to me anymore. I can't identify with my past or my present. My father is back in my life — after an almost seven-year absence. I don't know how to respond to that. Whether I should be happy. Or cautious. Defensive. Or angry. In some way, it's what I always wanted. In another, it's an emotional mind blow I don't want to deal with.

I take in a deep breath. And then like any tormented soul struggling to control his mind, I push away the voices clawing at my head. There is no way I'm going to let those voices — or my idiocy — defeat me.

51. JADIEL

The Final Attack

Dante is sitting in the plaza. Just as Equus told me he would be. I'm in Armando's Corvette, watching him. He seems pensive. Like someone's gotten into his head.

"Elena!" Dante yells at his sister. "Leave the birds alone." She's provoking them with a seed pod, brandishing it in front of her like a miniature machete.

"Always with his little sister." Armando's eyes are fixed on Dante, his nemesis since the seventh grade. "As Equus says, know your enemy's weakness."

As Equus says? He's quoting a demon trainer now? I wait for two beats. And then say, "Know his strengths, too. And be careful he doesn't use them against you."

"As if," Armando says. "Dante Vega is a loser. A waste of time. Why are we going after him? Remind me, 'cause I'm not getting it."

I stare at him. "You don't need to *get it*. You just need to obey." The shift in power is an uncomfortable dynamic. Soon it will be I who will *just need to obey.*

"Whatever, dude." Armando's nostrils flare. He doesn't like not being in control.

"Go," I snap at Pedro and Armando. "Grab them both and bring them back to me. But do *not* hurt the girl, you hear me? She is not our target and cannot be harmed."

On my command, they get out of the car and move towards the plaza.

"Wait." I dig a sedative-filled syringe out of the lower pocket of my cargo pants. Equus made sure I had it before heading out. I hand the syringe to Pedro. "If he fights too much, use this." According to Equus's Intel, Dante is afraid of needles. The sight of it alone will stop the fight in him. If it doesn't, there's always the sedative inside the syringe.

I have only sixteen hours before my time runs out. If I've strategized correctly, neither Malakiy nor Kiriela will be a problem. She's tied up and he will be distracted trying to free her. I sent him a text, *Go to Kiriela. She needs you.* That should help him forget all about Dante.

My heart thuds. I *hate* what I did to her. Exerting dominance over someone you love is *not* what I believe. I never wanted to treat her with anything but kindness. I'm no better than Armando. The only difference between him and me is, I don't enjoy my power over people. It does not make me strong; it only serves to highlight my weakness.

"Well, well, well, what have we here?" Armando plants himself in front of Dante. "Dante and his little sister."

Dante's eyes shoot from Armando to Pedro, and then back to Armando. "What the hell's going on?"

"We're going for a ride." Armando grabs Dante while Pedro goes for Elena.

"Let go of her!" Dante shouts.

"Let me think about that for a minute." Armando blocks Dante from reaching her. "No, I don't think so." He sinks his fist into Dante's gut.

Elena screams. "Don't hurt him!"

Dante coughs, and then forces himself to stand straight. He lurches to the side. And then he sinks a solid right hook into Armando's jaw.

"Asshole!" Armando shouts. "You're gonna pay for that!" He nods at Pedro. "Do it," he says. Pedro stabs the syringe into Dante's arm.

52. DANTE

Definitely a Demon

The last thing I remember is being stabbed in the arm. Sometime later, I wake up in the back seat of Armando's car. Elena and Pedro are in the back seat with me. And sitting in the suicide seat is the maybe-a-demon from the beach. Immediately, I react. I go for Armando. And then I collapse back on the seat. My hands are tied, and my head feels as if someone stuck a plastic bag over it and sucked out all the air.

"Dante?" Elena's frightened voice calls out to me. "Are you okay?"

"I'm okay," I tell her. "Don't worry. We're going to be fine."

My cell phone rings.

"Get that," the maybe-a-demon says.

Pedro snatches my phone and gives it to the maybe-a-demon — who throws it on the dash.

"Give me back my phone!" I lurch forward but Pedro pulls me back. From the corner of my eye, I see the maybe-a-demon raise his hand. And then, a sharp bolt of energy throws me back onto the seat. My heart beats like a tightened snare drum. I couldn't move if my life depended on it — which apparently, it does.

"Settle down," the definitely-a-demon says.

Whoa. I'm frozen to my seat — not physically, but psychologically, hell yeah. Power like that is dark-shit supernatural.

"It's an interesting thing," the demon says, "how easy it is to bring down a tough guy."

"Stop the car and give me a fair fight and I'll show you how easy it is." A bead of sweat drips down the side of my face and my hands feel slippery. I'm trying not to freak out. Pedro is twirling a needle between his fingers, making sure I notice it.

Don't look at it, I tell myself. *Keep your eyes off the needle. That's all you have to do. Keep your eyes off the needle.* I start to hyperventilate.

"Don't be scared, Dante, I won't let him hurt you." Elena's eyes are huge, but her hand is steady when she weaves her fingers into mine.

"It's okay, Elena." I take in a deep breath, and then slowly let it out. "Nothing's going to happen to us. This is a game. And to win it, you have to brave. Do you understand?"

She nods.

"Your brother is right, Elena." The demon looks at Elena through the rearview mirror. "Don't be frightened." His voice is softer now, more human. "This is only a game."

"Did you know," Pedro says, ignoring what the demon was trying to do for Elena, "that after winning the title of Heavyweight Champion, Sonny Liston, one of the most feared boxers in Heavyweight history, refused to go on an exhibition tour of Europe when he was told he would have to get shots before he traveled overseas?"

"And that matters to me ... *why*?" I try not to watch him twirl the needle between his fingers. But as much as I try, I can't focus on anything else. Exactly as Pedro intended.

"The champion died of a supposed overdose of the injected drug heroin," Armando says, studying me through the rear-view mirror. "How could that be?" His face twists into mock surprise. "Why would a man who was deathly afraid of needles die from a self-injected dose of drugs?" His eyes shift to Pedro. "Does that make any sense to you, Pedro?"

"Uh, not really, Armando. But look at this." He grabs a book off the floor: *The Devil and Sonny Liston* by Nick Tosches. "Maybe it wasn't a suicide. It says here that the dude was murdered by the mob." He's reading the back-cover copy.

"Sounds like something the devil would do," Armando says.

"Enough!" The demon shoots a glance at Armando. "Your story is irrelevant." He shifts his eyes to Elena. "Don't pay any attention to him."

Elena meets his gaze. "He's scaring me," she says. "Why is he talking about" — she lowers her voice and whispers — "the devil?"

"Because he's an idiot," the demon says.

At least on this point, I'm siding with the demon.

Hours must have passed as I lay hurting on the cement floor of an abandoned warehouse. But time no longer has any meaning. Every conscious hour I have I spend thinking my way around Armando's unspoken but very real threat: the execution of a slow and agonizing death through an injected poison — heroin maybe? He seems well-read on mob murder strategies.

I've been thinking about a lot about my own death. About how and when and where I will die. But now that death is near, what I imagined has no meaning. The how is murder. The where, an abandoned building. The when? Who knows? A few hours. A few days. A week if I'm incredibly unlucky. The hour is uncertain, but one thing is sure. I am going to die fighting.

53. KIRIELA

Demon Ropes

Dante is going to die. I struggle against the rope that binds me. If I don't free myself, his life is over. I can feel it, an ominous premonition. *How could you do this to me, Jadiel?* I struggle harder, fueled by fear and confusion. I have never seen Jadiel more distraught than when he knotted the final cord that restrains me. But yet, he still did it. He overpowered me.

I fight against the rope, but I can't move. The cords that confine me are stronger than iron bands. Nube nibbles on the hemp, but her baby teeth are useless. Only a miracle will set me free.

"Kiriela!" Malakiy swoops into the farmhouse. "What's wrong? Are you ..." His words cut off when he sees me "Who did this to you?"

"Who do you think?" I yank my body against the rope.

Malakiy pulls out his dagger and slices at the cords. His blade slides over the rope without making the smallest scratch. "Who did this to you?" His voice rises with his rage.

Nube backs away. She looks frightened.

"Jadiel." I can't keep the anger out of my voice.

Malakiy's hand tightens on the dagger. Furious, he hacks harder on the rope.

"I can't cut these cords." He stabs his dagger into the tabletop. The point slivers the wood, leaving cracks along the surface.

"Try again." His anxiety rubs off on me. I can barely breathe.

He inserts the dagger under the rope and tries to cut upward. He can't. His blade is like a butter knife trying to cut through stone.

"Demon ropes." His voice turns hard. "No holy weapon can cut through them."

"Forget it." Hot blood runs through me. "Just go to Dante. He's in danger."

"I'm not leaving you like this." Malakiy's eyes flick from one corner of the room to another. His gaze lands on Nube. He looks like he wants to ask about her, but instead he says, "Where's Jadiel's sword? Did he give it to you?"

Of course. Jadiel made sure I knew where it was. "It's under my mattress."

"Use it when you are threatened. Kill with it if you must." Jadiel's words tumble around my head. If I weren't tied to my chair, I might think what he said was meant to protect me.

Malakiy returns with the sword. He unsheathes it. And then in one swift cut, he slices through the rope.

"Give me the sword." I free myself from the severed rope.

Malakiy hesitates, but then sheathes the sword and hands it to me.

"That's a powerful weapon," he says.

"Yes, it is." My voice is controlled. My gaze, steady.

"To be used only against an enemy agent." Malakiy sounds like he's warning me.

"Do you know where Dante is?" I cinch the sword around my waist.

"I can find out."

"Good. There's an enemy agent out there, thinking I won't find him."

54. JADIEL

Dante's Choice

Dante grabs onto a rusted rod cemented into the wall and pulls himself to his feet. He takes a few steps forward, and then collapses back onto the floor. I watch the scene unfold from the small window in the door. Heavy footsteps cross the room. A boot sinks into his stomach. A kick hurls him to the wall. Armando goes after him and grabs his upper arm.

"Looks like the game is about to end." Armando wields a needle and syringe as if it is the ultimate weapon. "And guess what ... YOU LOSE."

I snap into high alert. The plan was to intimidate Dante with the needle, threaten him with the possibility of an intravenous injection of a placebo drug, and then get him to sign the contract in exchange for his life. There was nothing dangerous in the needle I gave Pedro. But that is not the needle Armando is flashing in front of Dante.

I grip the handle, open the door, and stride into the room. "Leave him to me." My heart races. Armando was too interested in Sonny Liston's story. Fearing he might act out his fascination with illegal intravenous injections, I sped to the pharmacy and bought a bottle of Narcan nasal spray, available over the counter in most states to block the effects of heroin.

I approach Dante, and then yank him to his feet. "You have a choice to make." I push up his sleeve. I have the original needle, emptied of its sedative, and refilled with water.

Dante starts to thrash. Sweat pours down his face, but he fights back his fear and holds me off.

I stare at him. "Impressive," I say.

Dante's eyes shoot to the needle and he starts to hyperventilate.

"Humans." I shake my head in mock reproach. "They're just so weak." I grab Dante's arm and twist a rubber tourniquet around it. When a vein pops, I press the needle to it, my thumb on the plunger. "And now that we all know that here's the question." I look him directly in the eye and say, "Are you going to join me and live?" A drop of blood forms around the tip of the needle. "Or fight me and die?" I hope Lucius is listening. My words are a lie, but he won't know that. My truth lies inside of me.

The drop of blood pools into a red circle around the needle. Dante looks like he's going to puke. But then he takes his free hand, fists it, and aims a punch at my jaw. The blow misses its mark. Not surprising. Between controlling his buckling knees and coordinating a left-handed punch, the odds of a strike were severely against him.

"Did you not hear me?" I shove Dante up against the wall, for no other reason than to exert the authority I fear I'm losing. An exposed nail digs into his back. He grits his teeth to hold in the scream. I push him back and hold him on the nail. I'm being watched. I can feel it. I can't afford to be merciful or weak. Dante cries out. I press harder. "I asked you a question."

"Go to hell." Dante shoves me back. Then he collapses to the floor.

I crouch beside him, the syringe still in my hand. I grab Dante's chin and twist his face so that our eyes are forced to meet. "You don't want to send me there." I stare hard. "I might come back with an even more ... *diabolical* plan." As if there is anything more diabolical than trying to destroy another human being.

I release my grip on him. "Here's how *this* plan is going to work." I jerk Dante to his feet. "You either sign on with me, or I give you enough of what's in this syringe to cause you a very painful, very violent death." I hold up the needle. "You decide."

The door creaks open. My heart plunges. Elena is standing at the door between Pedro and Armando.

No. I panic. For a moment. Then I use Elena's presence to my advantage. Dante doesn't care about himself. This fight is futile. But like Equus once taught me, he has a weakness. What he won't do for himself, he will do for his little sister.

"Bring her to me," I say.

Armando grips her arm and drags her over to me.

I can't look at her, at the finger marks that have left red impressions on her skin. So, I look at Dante instead and say, "Join me, and we don't touch her."

To make the threat look real, I grab Elena and pull her close to me. And then, discreetly, I squeeze her hand, hoping to communicate that I won't harm her.

She gets my message. "I'm okay, Dante," she says. "He won't hurt me."

Dante doesn't believe it. Willing all the strength in his body to his arms, he shoves me back. "You need to find someone else to torment. I have no interest in what you're selling, and my sister is OUT OF BOUNDS."

He rushes toward her. I block him. Then I lift him in the air and blow him across the room. A display of power seems appropriate now — for all those who are watching. He crashes into a window and lands on the ground among the shards of broken glass.

Elena screams. I grab her arm. And then I fight to hold her back.

Dante can barely breathe, but he calls out to his sister. "It's okay, Elena." He gathers what is left of his breath and says, "Look out the window." He can't get up. He can't touch her. But he can reach her.

The terror in her eyes breaks and she stops screaming.

"Shut up!" Armando charges after Dante, and then socks him in the face. The force of the blow snaps back Dante's head, but it does not silence him.

"Look out the window," he repeats. This time, his voice is stronger. He unglues his eyes from Elena's and leads her gaze to the window. A feeble ray of moonlight enters from outside. "Do you see that light?"

"Yes," she says. The fear has left her voice.

"It's a sign. You're going to be safe. Bad people run away from the light." He keeps his eyes fixed on Elena. "Don't be afraid. Remember, we'll playing a game. Be brave."

My boots crunch glass as I go for Dante. I need to silence him. He's rebuking me.

"Jadiel, no!" Kiriela's voice stops me in my tracks.

"Kiriela?" I whip my head around. *How is she here?* And with Malakiy — who looks like he wants to kill me.

She unsheathes my sword. "Stay away from him."

What? She's pointing the sword at me. Elena is behind her, shielded and safe.

"Put down the sword, Kiriela." My heart is in my throat. I was just about to put the truth card on the table for Dante. Subtly, without anyone hearing, I was going to get him to trust me. But, Kiriela's surprise appearance has taken that strategy away from me.

Desperately, I turn to Dante. "Join me." I'm talking so fast that I'm barely coherent. "Pledge your life to Lucius and you will know more pleasure than you can possibly imagine." I say what I have to, hating every word I utter. Knowing that Dante won't go for it. Knowing that he has no idea who Lucius is. Knowing that if I could have whispered my plan to him, I could have saved him.

"Be careful what you pledge." Kiriela has the sword trained on me. "Jadiel's promises are even more destructive than his lies."

No, Kiriela, please. You have no idea what you're doing. Before I can tell her that, Dante comes after me. Immediately, I turn on him. A crashing blow to the gut knocks the air out of him. Dante grips his stomach. His voice is weak, his strength almost gone, but through a ragged breath of air, he manages to say, "You are nothing more than Satan's scum."

His insult inspires my aggression. I go for his throat. He claws at my hands. I tighten them like a vice around his neck. I feel like the scum he accuses me of being.

"Jadiel, stop!" Malakiy unsheathes his sword.

Kiriela steps out in front of him. "Leave him to me," she says. Her tone is angry. Defiant.

"He's all yours." Malakiy backs away.

"Stay out of it, Kiriela." My eyes shift wildly from her to Dante. "You need to get out of here." When she doesn't respond, I add, "Now!"

"Take me!" she says. "My life for his."

No. I loosen the pressure on Dante's throat. He slumps to the floor. My voice is urgent when I lower it to just above a whisper and say, "Trust me. Please, Kiriela."

55. KIRIELA

The Sacrifice

Something fundamental shifts inside of me. Jadiel never planned to let Dante die. Not because he's good or bad or made by God in any particular way. But because he's still an angel. Still walking in the light. I touch my fingers to my heart to show him I understand.

But then out of the corner of my eye, I see Armando, rising to a stand.

"Finish it," he says, staring at Jadiel. "Or I will." A knife gleams in his hand.

I glance at Dante, half dead on the floor. There is no way I will allow Jadiel to compromise what he started. Calling Armando's attention away I say, "Leave him. He's weak. A human. Where's the challenge in that? Lucius doesn't care about Dante. Take me instead. If I go with you now and sign the contract, he will be satisfied and lose all interest in Dante."

"He will never be satisfied." Jadiel grabs me by the arm and pulls me behind him. "But this time, he is not getting what he wants."

Armando takes two steps forward. "The hell with what Lucius wants." He raises the knife. "*I* want Dante *dead!*"

He lunges for Dante's chest.

"No!" Jadiel and I scream together.

Jadiel raises his hand and blows Armando back. Armando lands hard into a pile of wooden crates. Blood drips from the knife he holds in his hand.

I run to Dante and lay my hand on the wound bleeding out from his chest, sure that I can heal it. Screaming, Elena follows behind me.

Blood seeps through my fingers but no healing energy comes through me. Seconds pass. More seconds. But Dante remains unresponsive. "Malakiy!"

Malakiy is already beside me. "Let me try." He pushes me away.

"You have to hold on." I take Dante's hand. "Do you hear me?"

"Wake up, Dante! *Please*, wake up!" Elena is crying, sobbing. Shaking him.

Jadiel scoops her up and holds her close, her head against his chest. "Don't worry." He cradles the back of her head. "My friends are helping your brother. They have special powers."

"Superpowers?" She looks up at him. Tears stream down her face.

"Yes, love, superpowers." He wipes her tears, and then eases her head back to his chest.

I breathe out, and then glance over at Malakiy. He has his hand over Dante's wound, but no healing light is coming from it.

"What's happening?" I force my voice down. "Can't you heal him?"

"I'm trying, but ..."

But only God can heal. I know. I *know*. I rub Dante's hand, desperate to warm it. *Father in Heaven, please help this boy.* I rub more vigorously but his skin remains cold.

"Please, Dante. *Please* wake up." Elena's words come out choked between her sobs.

"Elena?" Dante's voice is a faint whisper.

Elena stops sobbing. "Dante?" She lifts her head off Jadiel's chest. "Are you all better?"

The air is heavy with that thin metallic odor that often accompanies death. A smell I will always associate with the hospital. And humanity. Pain and suffering. No, Dante is not better.

Malakiy lowers his hand. "There's nothing more I can do."

I plead with God to heal Dante, but as I do, his hand falls — lifeless — to the floor.

"Dante?" Elena squiggles away from Jadiel, runs to her brother, and grabs his hand. "Dante!" She shouts out his name between sobs.

Jadiel rushes over and kneels beside her. "I know you're scared right now, but you need to come with me." His voice is steady, but he sounds terrified.

"No!" Elena beats down the hand he offers her. Then she throws herself over Dante's body and lets out a long, excruciating cry.

Warm tears slide down my cheeks, down the sides of my face and into the corners of my mouth. Darkness overtakes my heart.

"Take the child and come with me, Kiriela." Jadiel speaks calmly, but underneath the calm is an avalanche of panic. "There's nothing more you can do." He goes to help me up.

I push his hand away. "I will give you anything and everything you want, if you find a way to save Dante."

"The only power that can save him now is the one that will condemn you."

"Then call on that power."

A lifetime of belief, of faith and trust crumbles when I ask, *where were you God? And why did you not answer my prayer?*

"You're not thinking this through." There's a desperate insistency to Jadiel's voice now. "Come on, we need to leave."

I know what's coming. Lucius's minions will be here soon to assess the damage. Jadiel is right, Elena needs to leave. Gently, I pull her away from Dante. I take her hands in mine. "Go with Jadiel," I say. "And don't worry, Dante will be fine. I'll take care of him." I nod at Jadiel. "Take her," I whisper under my breath. "I'll leave with Malakiy." He helps Elena to her feet, takes her in his arms, and carries her away.

"Let's go." Malakiy releases his wings.

"In a minute."

I march over to Armando and crouch beside him.

"I know why you are here and what you want." I stare into his dilated eyes. "Riches. Glory. Lives chained to Lucius. But what are you going to offer Lucius now? Dante is dead. By your hand." I control the surge of pain that threatens to explode from me. "Lucius is going to be livid. But, if you take me, you won't need Dante." I lower my voice to almost a whisper. "With only one good angel turned bad, you can have it all. Right now. No more hunting. No more waiting. Take out the contract. I'm ready to sign."

Armando stares at me, his expression somewhere between greed and disbelief. He wobbles to a stand, takes out his phone, and starts texting.

"No, Kiriela." Malakiy pulls me back. "You don't know what you're doing."

I struggle free from him. "I know *exactly* what I'm doing." My voice is hard. "Dante did not deserve to die. He got dragged into a lethal game. I tried to do what was right, to honor God. But where was God when I needed him? Where is He now? Dante is dead."

"Dante's death is not God's fault." Jadiel sets down Elena and runs up beside me. "It's *mine*." His eyes turn an intense shade of blue. "Please, for once in your life, please listen to me."

"You were right, Jadiel. God is cruel. And I no longer wish to serve him."

"Why are you listening to me now?" Jadiel throws out his arms. "God may be cruel, but He doesn't want this for you. Lucius's contract is irrevocable."

"None of your business, dude." Armando jabs a needle into Jadiel's neck. And then does the same to Malakiy. "You're right." He turns to me. "If I secure you, I secure my position." He holds the phone up to me and shows me a text from Equus Centurion. Then he produces a rolled sheet of paper and a black ink pen and says, "Sign the contract."

"What have you done to them?" I rush toward Jadiel and Malakiy, who lie crumpled on the ground. Before I can reach them, Armando stops me.

"Don't worry, they're not dead." Armando holds me back. "I had to stop them from interfering." He thrusts the contract at me. "Sign it."

I glance at Jadiel and Malakiy. And then I look back at Armando. "I will sign your contract when I know that everyone in this room is both alive and safe." I look over my shoulder. Elena is standing at the door, frozen into place.

"One signature will buy all that." Armando holds out the pen.

"Fine." I scratch my signature across the parchment. Then I run over and crouch down beside Jadiel. I feel his neck for a pulse. His heart's still beating. Malakiy's too. Relieved, I move over to Dante. He gasps, and then breathes again.

"Is he all right?" Elena runs up beside me.

"Yes," I whisper. "He's alive."

I reach for Jadiel's sword, which is lying a few feet from me.

"Go to your brother." I nudge Elena closer to Dante. When they're together, I hold the sword out over them.

"I love you," I tell Dante, "and will always watch over you. But I have to let you go."

I lift up the blade. There's a blast of light. And then there is darkness. A darkness so complete, it's as if light no longer exists.

56. JADIEL

Loving Kiriela

From a distance, I watch the tragic conclusion to my foiled plan. Dante is lying on the beach. Elena is beside him. The power Kiriela conjured from my sword sent them to the same beach where I first landed, after my expulsion from Maion.

A wave crashes and inches forward along the shore. It touches Dante's toe, and then disappears into the sand. Another wave follows. And another after that. Each one is stronger and more violent than the last. A black shadow slithers across the beach. Equus will not leave this job undone. I have failed him. Furious, he will now take matters into his own hands.

"What's happening?" Kiriela did not leave with Malakiy when she had the chance. Now, she stands with me. On the dark side of the spiritual divide.

"Equus has come for Dante."

"No!" Her voice accelerates. "I signed a contract. Armando promised they'd be safe." She takes two steps forward.

I hold her back. "It's over. There's nothing more you can do." Sickness slides up my throat. As much as she still wants to, Kiriela can no longer guard and protect.

The shadow passes over Elena first. It circles her legs. Drags her closer to the water. Darker and larger the shadow grows. Stronger and higher the waves. The darkness sucks the girl in. And then, she's gone. Covered completely by a churning, white-capped wave.

"Elena!" Dante cries out for his sister. But he's too weak to move. The shadow is over him now.

"Let me go!" Kiriela struggles to pull free but I hold on tighter. "I can save her."

"No, you can't. Neither you nor I can stop what's been set in motion." I hope she hears the urgency in my voice. Black shapes, with red eyes, fly through the sky. "Don't fight me on this one, Kiriela, please. Trust me, she's not dead."

Her arm slackens under my hand. "Not being able to stop evil goes against everything I have ever believed in."

"I know." I don't let go of her. My eyes harden, but I keep them focused forward. If I look at her now, I will lose my resolve and allow her to run for Dante. Equus would be only too pleased to have her show up. Gloating over promises broken is his favorite intoxicant.

"This isn't how it's supposed to end." Kiriela's voice slows down to a whisper.

"Not in any way." I release the grip on her arm and take her hand. She weaves her fingers through mine. Together, we watch Equus pull out a contract.

"Can't you blow him away?" Kiriela's fingers twitch against mine. "I've seen what your powers can do."

"I can, but he's surrounded by a legion of soldiers." Red eyes burn on top of the waves. On the shore. In the trees. "I don't have the power I would need to destroy them all."

"Then the choice is clear." Kiriela holds my hand tighter. "We stay here, for now. Later, we will fight them. Together."

A half smile lifts the corner of my mouth. I'm not sure who she intends to fight. Her faith has been shaken. But I'd be willing to bet we have a common enemy now. As much as we both may be angry at God, our fight will ultimately be with Lucius.

I kiss her hand. "Together, we are strong."

She rests her head against my arm. "Together, we are whole."

I watch the scene before me. Words are exchanged. There's a desperate look. An extended hand. And then, the signature.

"He won," I say. "Equus got Dante's signature. Lucius has won."

"The battle," Kiriela says. "He won the battle. Not the war."

I nod. And then I see Elena, washed up on shore, gasping for breath. She's alive, for now. Equus will keep her barely breathing so that he can keep Dante completely loyal. That's how it works. In Abaddon.

White wings glow, cutting through the darkness. "Malakiy's here." My tone is flat. He's come for Kiriela.

I ease her off my arm and go for my sword. I'm not giving her up without a fight.

"No, Jadiel." She stops my hand. Her eyes are wide but there's no fear in them. "This is not our fight."

Her words silence me. And in that silence, I hear shrieks. Low, throaty growls. Hell's hounds. Come to escort me back to Abaddon.

Malakiy stops in front of us. "By order of the Corrections Council …" His voice trails off. Adam's apple bobbing, he says, "I'm so sorry, Kiriela … I have to …"

Wrist and ankle cuffs dangle from his hand.

The cuffs set me off. I push Malakiy back. "The cuffs are not necessary. Does it look like she's resisting?"

"Stop, Jadiel. Please. You'll only make it worse."

I stand down. What else can I do?

Kiriela — now cuffed and shackled — leaves with Malakiy for the makeshift interrogation pit on the edge of the dark woods. The Council has come down to Earth. They had to. Kiriela and I are not allowed back in Maion.

Nube skitters over and stands beside me. I scoop her up and follow behind them.

My wrist begins to burn. I didn't jam the tracking device before leaving for the plaza. I didn't think I needed to. I was on an overt mission. Soon, Equus will find me.

Marius takes his place behind a bench made out of fallen logs. His golden robe billows in the breeze. The fire before him crackles. The Holy Warden studies the scroll in front of him. He raises his hand. "Bring forth the accused," he says.

Malakiy, now cloaked under a heavy hood, ushers Kiriela forward. She stumbles over her shackles. I go to help her but Malakiy holds me back. "No," he says. He catches Kiriela by the arm and steadies her. "Take courage, Kiriela." His voice is low and cautious. The words float out from under his canvas hood and give her strength.

She lifts her head, and then stands firm before the fire.

I wish it had been me who gave her that confidence, but it was neither I nor Malakiy who gave her strength. She found it within herself.

The gold-robed jurors regard her in silence. And then Marius speaks the same words he once said to me, "State your name and the crime for which you stand accused."

Without hesitation or fear, she says, "My name is Kiriela and I am accused of the act of treason against God."

A flame crackles and spits out sparks. Waves crash against the shore. But not a sound escapes from the jurors' tightly drawn lips.

"Go on," Marius says. His long white beard ripples on the night breeze.

Kiriela's eyes flicker but she stares straight ahead.

I take two steps forward. I'm not going to stand by and allow this circle of hypocrites to judge her. I take another step, but she shakes her head, stopping me.

Quietly she says, "I signed a contract with God's enemy. I succumbed to the dark powers of the air and ..." She stares at the sand, as if there she will find the courage to go on.

"Proceed." Marius's voice is stern, uncompromising.

A smoldering ember jumps from the fire and lands on her foot. Kiriela winces, and then closes her eyes.

"Your testimony will be judged fairly," Marius says.

No, it won't. How can it be? Her confession confirms her guilt. Nube squirms in my arms. I shift her away from my burning wrist. Her wool is warm where it lay against the band.

Kiriela opens her eyes and looks up at Marius. Without flinching she says, "I signed Lucius's contract. Not because I wanted to change allegiance or rebel against God. I signed it to save a human boy who was in danger." She stares into the fire. "And as a result of that decision, I became God's enemy."

A glittering piece of driftwood crumbles to ash, sizzling into the fire.

"Indeed, you did." Marius speaks above the hissing of the fire.

Kiriela glances over at her father, who is staring at the ground. She falters, but then finds her composure and says, "I was deceived, but I accept the consequences of my choice."

Somewhere in the distance, a dog barks.

Is this the same girl I fell in love with what seems like forever ago? The one who hesitated to stand before Marius and take ownership of her sin of loving me? She is strong now, sure of herself. And I am in awe of her.

Apparently, the Council shares my astonishment. I can sense them waiting for Marius's response in the captive silence that follows.

"You *were* deceived, as all are who trust in the enemy." Marius's voice is as soft as it is cold. "I cannot undo what has been done." He blinks, and then lowers his gaze. His white brows draw together and then quietly, he says, "I am afraid I must stand by the sentence recommended by the Council. For the crime of treason against God, you are hereby sentenced to Abaddon."

"No!" I rush forward. "Let me take her punishment upon myself."

I'm restrained by a guard, who holds me back.

Marius shifts his gaze to me. "You do not yet have the capacity to love God the way you should, yet you love this girl more than you do yourself. There is honor in that. But what Kiriela signed for Lucius cannot be undone. Only she can break the chains that bind that contract."

His eyes shift back to Kiriela. "You will journey to a dark place. Abaddon is a wasteland, a place of sorrow and despair." His voice cracks with the strain of age and harsh responsibility. "But if you remember what you've been taught, if you stay strong, you will conquer Abaddon." He motions for Malakiy to come forward. "Unchain, and then remove her wings."

Malakiy hesitates. *What cruel punishment is this?*

"It is better this way," Marius says. What he doesn't say is, *better than to leave the task to the vicious guards of Abaddon.* Hidden pain surfaces in his eyes. "Malakiy, please —"

"Your Honor" — Adriel steps forward — "would you grant me a moment alone with my daughter?"

Marius stares at Adriel, considering his response.

"One minute is all I ask." Adriel stands tall before Marius. "Then it will be I who does as you command."

"Very well." Marius nods. Then he turns to Kiriela. "May God's mercy be with you, child."

Deep dark loathing churns inside of me. Where is God's mercy now?

There is no compassion for the damned.

A low laugh echoes over the air. Abaddon's guards are getting closer.

Helpless I watch Adriel place his hands on both sides of his daughter's head. He kisses her hair, and then he whispers something that only she can hear. His eyes grow wet as he unsheathes his sword. Fingers shaking, he triggers the release of her wings. They squeeze out behind her. She stifles a scream. Her wings, her beautiful white wings, are chained together.

Shock shuts down my body. I can't speak, much less scream. When Adriel unlocks the chains and frees her wings, I gasp. Half of her feathers are black.

There is a heavy thud as Kiriela's wings hit the ground. For a moment, I stop breathing.

"Step forward." Marius summons me to the interrogation pit. I can't move. Kiriela's agonized scream is brutal to hear. When I finally gather back my strength, I move forward on auto pilot. Only for a second do I allow myself to wonder why I am being summoned. Marius has no authority over me, not anymore.

When I reach the pit, Marius studies me. "You are no longer under my jurisdiction, Jadiel, but I cannot help but wonder, what exactly happened in that warehouse? Was there possibly a plan that might have been … interrupted?"

My heart flips. "No, there was no plan," I speak too fast, too desperately. If Abaddon's guards overhear, no punishment will be horrible enough. "The only plan I had was to threaten Dante, so that he'd sign the contract."

Beads of sweat pop out on my brow. I never was very good at lying.

"Is that so?" Marius squints.

My eyes shift wildly over the beach. Lucius's henchmen will now be gathering in for the kill. I'm dead. Worse than dead. Tortured for all eternity.

My wrist is so hot it feels like it's on fire.

I swipe at the sweat dripping down my face. "I have to go." I hand Nube over to Marius. "Take care of her, please. For me." I turn to leave but Marius's next question holds me back.

"You did it for her, didn't you?" He cradles Nube in his arms.

I look around me. A line of armed guards has formed at the edge of the forest. The hell hounds stand beside them. Equus is at the front of the line. Chupa is beside him, wearing a white army helmet. The guards stand with their legs apart, hands fisted at their sides. With their white uniforms and black chest plates, they look like any other dystopian army. Unlike most soldiers, though, they don't carry weapons or shields. Only chains.

"I did it for myself." I glance over at the army. They are advancing, chains held out in front of them. White plastic masks hide their faces. "I couldn't let the boy die. It would have destroyed Kiriela. And that would have killed me. So, like I said, I did it for myself."

"Uh huh." Marius studies me. He could always tell when I was lying. "You almost destroyed an innocent young man," he continues, "in the process of acting only for yourself."

"I had it under control!" My blurted-out response reveals the truth I had refused to speak. "I never planned for him to die! The plan fell apart when other people got involved."

I shoot a glance at the army. Equus calls someone to his side. I swallow. It's Comrade Brawn. Stone faced, his chain rattles as he stretches it out in front of him. Chupa grins, salivating like a hyena who has finally trapped its prey.

"That is unfortunate," Marius says, drawing my attention back. "But it is done." He signals to Malakiy. "Put out the fire."

With a bucket of water, Malakiy extinguishes the flames. Grey smoke billows into the air. The night grows darker. Trees, before unseen, begin to take shape behind the Council table. And then, a twisted path becomes visible through the trees.

"You will return to Abaddon," Marius says, "in accordance with the rules established there." He waits until my gaze is fully upon him and then says, "Stay strong, Jadiel. Do not give up the light that lives within you and never forget what you already know. The strongest weapon in your arsenal is the one you used today. Love. Stronger than steel and more resilient. Love will bring you home."

Marius's words reach me. I will never step into the Inner Circle, but that no longer seems important. What matters to me now is what always mattered: loving Kiriela.

ACKNOWLEDGEMENTS

If ever I believed in the crippling power of darkness, it would be during the writing of this book. Through personal attacks to a devastating hurricane, earthquakes, and a world-wide pandemic, the enemy tried as hard as he could to keep me from completing this book. But despite unprecedented setbacks, I got to the finish line by God's grace and a lot of people helping along the way. My thanks and gratitude go to the following people, who made this book possible.

To Principal Carlos R. Molina Rivera, thanks for opening the doors to your school (La Escuela Superior Leonides Morales Rodriguez in Lajas, Puerto Rico) and allowing me access to the students and classrooms. My knowledge and understanding of Puerto Rican public school culture was greatly enhanced by your generosity and cooperation.

To Cynthia B. Delgado, thanks for welcoming me into your classroom, for allowing me to meet and get to know the beautiful students who helped to shape this book. Being with you, and sharing books, writing, and film production with the students, was one of the most memorable, most creative experiences of my life!

To the awesome students of Leonides Morales Rodriguez High, thanks for sharing your youth and your culture with me. To the following students I give special thanks for their help in either beta reading early versions of the manuscript, brainstorming ideas, or forming part of our creative team: Adriana Victoria Acosta, Sara Liah Acosta, Tashalyn Astraid Alix, Zurisadai Ayala, Albert Louis Cruz, Aluisca Naomi Irizarry, Nathalia Irizarry, Eva Elisa Morales, José Ramírez, Joshua Rodríguez, Ricardo Jacob Rodríguez, Luis David Torres, Esteban Urayoán.

To Edwin Arroyo and Freddy Zapata, thanks for your musical and video graphic expertise during the filming of the trailer, "Conquering Abaddon." We got through filming one month before Hurricane María changed life as we knew it on the island. Thanks for making that happen!

To Dra. Melissa Rodríguez, thanks for pushing me to "go deeper." You were a constant source of inspiration and a fantastic spiritual/psychological mentor. You were one of the first to believe in this book. Even though I hated to hear another "go deeper," it was exactly what I needed to make this book what it is today!

To Laura Ownbey, Brooke Whaley, and Suzanne Claudina, thanks for all the time you spent strengthening, re-shaping, editing, and beta reading this book. Initial drafts were all over the place, but your sharp eyes and incredible attention to detail whipped the manuscript into shape.

To my very talented and creative cover designer, Danial, thanks for working with me, over many mock-up drafts, on what became the perfect cover. Your patience, professionalism, and unique sense of design are much appreciated!

To my daughter, Sita, thanks for sharing this journey with me. I love our discussions on story and character and value your professional insight on human behavior. Thanks for sharing life with me, in all its beautiful stages.

And finally, to my husband, Govind, thanks for your unconditional love and support. Thanks for putting up with all the craziness, drama, and self-doubt that goes with living with a writer. You're my hero for taking care of our home when I was away, seeking solace to write and inspiration to keep me going.

ABOUT THE AUTHOR

Susan Nadathur is a widely traveled writer, teacher, and self-proclaimed "outsider" from Connecticut who now resides in the small town of Lajas, Puerto Rico. She loves teen drama and is a fan of the supernatural. After the writing is done, you'll find her relaxing with a good book, which will definitely have something to do with ordinary young people involved in extraordinary (and certainly supernatural) experiences. Connect with her at SusanNadathur.com, Twitter.com @SusanNadathur or Facebook.com/susan.nadathur.